SKULLY

PERDITION GAMES

By L.E. Fraser

In loving memory of my grandmothers,
Estelle Leadbeater and Gladys Fraser.

What do you see my daughter, when you gaze across the water?
The carnage on the whitecaps is your empathy's collapse.
Inner wars halt salvation with destruction and damnation,
because your cacodemon's bait twists around eternal hate.

Everything that you have done and all the things you have become,
you camouflaged with etiquette, seldom seen as counterfeit.
So lie about your monster and let the poison fester
but fallen angels lie in wait, as hope rots and dreams mutate.
L.E. Fraser

PART 1: Vacation from Hell

CHAPTER ONE

July 1980: Batchawana Bay, Ontario

Nina

AFTER NINA AND Gabriella had hiked through the forest for half an hour, the woods grew dark and ominous. It was tough to tell if the weather was turning nasty or if a single cloud hid the sun, because the branches of the towering trees created a canopy that hid the sky. Nina knew she should turn back but wanted to go a bit farther. She picked her way across jagged rocks and exposed roots along a narrow path winding through dense shrubs and large evergreens. Without a care in the world, her five-year-old daughter,

Gabriella, skipped along beside her. She was dropping pinecones, wildflowers, and pretty stones into a small wicker basket.

Thunder rumbled in the distance and Nina stopped. Raindrops hit her face when she gazed up at the sky. She hoped it was a brief summer shower, but within moments, it was pouring rain. Gabriella cringed by her side with her face hidden in Nina's skirt. Torrents of water soaked them, and the sound of the wind whipping through the trees mimicked children screaming.

There was a fork in the road, and she didn't know which way to go. Confused, she turned around in circles. They were lost. How could she have gotten lost? Her daughter was crying, and Nina took her hand. She tried to speak but heard her grandmother's voice. "Life is a path with forks and corners. You don't know what's around the corner, or down either path. Life is blind faith."

Gabriella tried to pull her hand free. Tears stained her pale cheeks, and her eyes widened with fear. "Mama?"

"Someday you'll find the path that leads home."

Nina let go of her daughter's hand and ran away, leaving her child lost in the forest and abandoned in the storm.

WITH A YELP, Nina jerked awake. Her child's screams of terror were ringing in her ears.

"No! I'd never do that." Crying, Nina fumbled in the pockets of her shorts for a tissue.

"Hush now, you were dreaming." Quentin patted her leg. "I hope you didn't wake Gabriella."

She twisted in her seat to glance into the backseat at her daughter. Gabriella's wet thumb pressed against her chin, and she clutched a stuffed puppy to her chest with her other hand.

"She's sleeping," Nina told her husband.

"Was it the same dream?"

She nodded.

"Do you remember anything?"

For just a moment, the time it takes to exhale, she remembered a white dog. Just as fast as it materialized, the image disappeared and her mind fogged over. "It's the same as always. All I remember is abandoning Gabriella alone in the woods in a storm."

"Babe, it's nothing to worry about. Lots of pregnant women have vivid dreams."

"But Quentin it's always the same. Grandma would call it *An Da Shealladh*, the 'two sights'."

He pushed away the hair in his eyes. "I loved your grandma, but she was wacky. Remember your sixteenth birthday party when she told everyone you'd inherited the 'Scot Highlander's prophetic vision'?" He shook his head and chuckled. "You're the one who insisted it was impossible because you aren't a Highlander."

She gazed at the book on her lap. "Grandma was a Highlander and said *An Da Shealladh* stays in the blood, passing from mother to daughter."

"That's ridiculous. You'd never abandon Gabriella. You're the best mom in the world."

She rummaged in the bag from the gift store where she'd bought the book and took out a small pair of moccasins, turning them over in her hand to admire the beadwork. "The storm, the woods, Gabriella crying — it must mean *something*."

"It's just a bad dream. Come on, babe. I've looked forward to this vacation for months. Shake it off and enjoy the fantastic scenery."

Outside the car window, the view was spectacular, but Nina didn't care. She wasn't feeling well, and the flashes of sunlight peeking from between the boughs of the evergreens made her head ache.

Quentin was coaxing the Volkswagen Rabbit along a dirt road lined with towering pines. As he concentrated on navigating the twisting turns, the tip of his tongue poked out from the corner of his lips, a gesture she loved. At over six feet tall, he hunched over the steering wheel, although he had sufficient headroom to sit upright. They hadn't seen another car in over an hour, yet his dark eyes roamed across the mirrors. Another cute habit. His long black hair hung across one eye and stubble shadowed his square jaw. Sexy.

"I can feel you staring at me," he said.

She put the book into the empty bag and jammed it into the narrow space beside her seat. It slithered down and disappeared into the dark wedge between the gearshift and the bottom of the passenger seat. "Have you ever had the same dream over and over again?"

"No, but I don't dream."

Tears welled up in her eyes again. "Why would a mother dream about abandoning her child?"

He sighed. "I get you're upset, and I'm sorry. Babe, it's a dream. We saved all year for this vacation, and I want you to have a good time."

She put the moccasins in her purse and stared out the window. "I have to pee. Are we nearly there?"

Quentin hated to stop, driving from point A to point B, period. She was surprised he hadn't made her pee in a cup.

"Yeah, around the next bend."

She tried to arch her back in the uncomfortable seat and the seatbelt strangled her belly. Her panties felt wet. She hoped she wasn't bleeding again. The spotting had started ten weeks ago, along with a pulsing abdomen pain.

This pregnancy wasn't the same as last time. She was seven and a half months and felt awful. Her doctor told her she was fine, but she didn't feel well. She worried about something happening to the baby all the time.

A year ago, their neighbours' baby had died of sudden infant death syndrome. Nina didn't know how Grace McNamara was coping. The marriage wasn't doing well, even though Grace was pregnant again. Everyone in the neighbourhood suspected Detective McNamara was sleeping with Megan Shannon. Nina would die if Quentin cheated. She wouldn't want to live if he left her.

"We'd have cut time driving through Michigan instead of taking the Trans-Canada Highway. Will you consider going home that way, worrywart?" Quentin grinned.

She shrugged, feeling a little foolish but refusing to commit. What if they drove through the States and she went into early labour or Gabriella had an accident? There wasn't any government health care in the US. How were they supposed to pay? Did hospitals take credit cards?

"Well, look at that," Quentin said.

Tucked into a clearing was a cute brown cabin with dark green shutters and white gingerbread trim. Dense evergreens shielded the back and sides, and the scent of pine perfumed the air. It was pretty but Nina couldn't see any other buildings. The cabin was sitting alone in the woods.

"It's isolated," she said.

"Sure, that's the point. There are two other cabins, but they're not renting them out this summer. The owners are getting ready to sell. It's busy during the day. Local fishermen rent dock space." He undid his seatbelt and scrambled from the driver's seat. "Hey, look who's awake."

Nina looked into the backseat. "How long have you been awake, sweetie?"

"You woke me up. You screamed. You were being mean to Papa, too."

"No, I wasn't," Nina said. "You should have said something so we knew you were awake." She hoped her daughter hadn't overheard them talking. It would be horrible to find out your mother was dreaming of leaving you.

Gabriella studied her solemnly and Nina smiled. Her daughter's eyes were the colour of violets. Shiny, dark ringlets stuck to her pale, chubby cheeks and she was the most beautiful child in the world. Nina couldn't believe she was lucky enough to be the mother of such a gorgeous little girl.

Quentin opened the back door to the car. "Get out here and explore with your papa." When he was too slow in undoing the seatbelt, Gabriella's forehead wrinkled and her lip lowered to a pout.

"I want out," her daughter whined in the pre-tantrum tone Nina dreaded.

Quentin unlatched the belt. "As my princess requests." He stepped back to bow before scooping Gabriella into his arms.

"I want to see the water," was the next demand.

Quentin complied, as usual, leaving Nina alone to waddle after them. "Quentin, wait," she said. "Where's the key to the cabin? I have to go to the bathroom."

They were running toward the water, and Gabriella's squeals of delight drowned out Nina's words. She trotted around the car and shaded her eyes. Gabriella was on Quentin's shoulders, and he was leaping in and out of tiny waves hitting the shore. In the late afternoon sun, the dark blue lake was still and smooth. The lapping water made her desperate for a bathroom. Frustrated, she scurried to the trees.

While squatting in the bushes, she looked to her right at the ridge circling the lake and saw a buck poised on the top of the escarpment. His head was high with large antlers reaching to the sky. He was all alone in a clearing of land jutting thirty metres above the lake. Nina pulled up her shorts and stood to see the animal from a better angle. The stag was so still that the scene reminded her of a Robert Bateman painting. He was staring at her.

She walked to the beach, and the buck's head shifted to follow. As a child, her Gaelic grandmother had told stories about how a stag — *damh* in Gaelic — was a protector. Raised with Scot Highlander superstitions, Nina often needed to remind herself not to place too much stock in the old myths. It wasn't working today. She was experiencing a creepy premonition that the animal was warning her to stay away from the beach.

"What are you looking at?" Quentin asked.

"Nothing." She turned to him. "For a minute, I thought..." She glanced at the ridge, but the buck was gone. "Never mind, I had to pee in the bushes. You have the key."

"Oops, sorry."

"Where's Gabriella?" she asked.

He gestured over his shoulder. "She's fine. Stop being such a worrywart. She's old enough to play on the beach with us a couple of metres away. Speaking of which, how do you like it here?"

She scanned the ridge. No buck. *Get a hold of yourself,* she thought. Wrapping her arm around Quentin's waist, she snuggled her cheek against his chest, breathing in the familiar scent of his cologne. "It's wonderful."

"My God, look at how beautiful she is," Quentin said.

The beach was empty and Gabriella was skipping across the sand toward the long dock. Her arms swung at her sides with a touching lack of inhibition.

"Did you talk to her about going into the water?" Nina asked.

"Yes, she knows to have one of us with her." Quentin tugged her around. "How do you like the cabin?"

"You checked to make sure there's a phone?"

"Yes, babe, stop worrying. It's a twenty-minute drive to town for groceries and less than an hour to Sault Ste. Marie."

Nina swatted at a horsefly. "Sorry. It's a great location." A sudden muscle spasm gripped her hamstring, and the ache in her stomach turned to a stabbing pain. "Let's go in, I need to sit down."

Gabriella was at the end of the dock, balancing on the tips of her toes while bending over to peer into the water. She leaned a little too far forward. Her arms rotated while she struggled to keep her balance. Nina sucked in her breath, tightening her grip on her husband's arm.

"Easy does it." He held her hand on his arm, never moving his eyes from their daughter. "Don't yell for her. Wait a minute until she has her balance."

Gabriella's arms propelled wildly. She tipped backwards to gain her balance and took a step behind her. Nina let her breath out in one long sigh.

"Ella!" Quentin hollered. "Come on back, princess."

She skipped down the long dock and ran into her father's arms.

"I saw a fishy," she said. "A big fishy, and I heard a doggy, too. Does a doggy live here? I want a puppy, Papa."

Quentin rolled his eyes before reaching down to pick up their daughter.

"Let's go see our castle. How does that sound?" He balanced Gabriella on his hip and rummaged in his pocket for the key. He caught Nina's eye and frowned. "You okay? You look pasty."

She took a compact from her pocket and checked her reflection. He was right. Her complexion was white with spots of high colour across her cheekbones that made her face appear gaunt. She'd always been thin, but it was unhealthy for a five-foot-five woman to weigh one hundred twenty-eight pounds this far along in her pregnancy. Her nose was too long and sharp, but her large brown eyes compensated. Quentin called them 'bedroom eyes'. Today, they were bloodshot and lined with tiny wrinkles, and her shoulder-length black hair was greasy.

"I'm okay, just tired." She closed the compact and avoided his eyes.

She wasn't okay but didn't want to spoil everyone's fun. The more she studied the dense forest surrounding the cabin, the more anxious she felt. She didn't want to be here and longed for home so much it was a physical ache.

Quentin flung open the door to the two-bedroom cabin. "Wow, it's nicer than the pictures."

Inside was a large space with rooms off the centre. A kitchen and bath ran along the back with bedrooms on either side of the living area, built as additions to the original structure.

The cabin was hot and stuffy and smelled of fresh cut wood, plaster and a hint of paint. The furniture was shabby but clean, and there was a television. Hopefully, colour. There would be complaining if Gabriella had to watch *Sesame Street* in black and white.

Nina inspected the kitchen while her husband opened the cooler and grabbed a beer. He finished it in four long sips, belched, and opened a second.

Together, they checked out the bedroom Gabriella would use. It was nice and had a small closet, a chest of drawers, and twin beds. The room had a large window facing the forest. Nina's prickle of dread returned. The window didn't have any drapes or shades. She felt watched again.

Get a grip, she scolded herself. Was she going to be spooked every time a squirrel peered at her from a tree branch?

Quentin stood behind her and wrapped his arms around her huge stomach, kissing the back of her neck. "I'm sorry. It was too long a drive to do in one day. It was thoughtless."

"It's okay," she repeated, for what felt like the tenth time since they had left the house at four-thirty in the morning.

Leaving Gabriella to organize her stuffed menagerie, they went to find their bedroom.

Standing inside the room, they gaped at the stained glass covering the lake-facing window.

"Wow," Quentin said, "how did we miss that from outside?"

Dark red, dirty orange, and mucky brown panes of glass painted dismal ribbons of colour on the white bedspread. It looked like streaks of dried blood.

Nina crinkled her nose. "It's awful."

"What's that going to look like during sunset?" Quentin ran his fingertip across the lead outline.

"Gross. Why would someone do that?"

"Maybe the owner's an amateur artist." He sat on the bed. "Comfy." He wiggled his eyebrows at her. "Not too close to Gabriella's room."

She laughed and sat beside him. "Do you ever think about anything but that?"

"Sure, lots of things, when you aren't around." He kissed her before getting to his feet and stretching. "You stay here and rest. Gabriella and I will unpack the car."

She kicked off her flip-flops. "Make sure the lasagna goes into the oven at 350 degrees. It'll need about an hour."

Nina lay on the bed, feeling stressed and uncomfortable. "Too long a day," she mumbled. "Everything will be better after a nap."

She dreamed of a storm, a fork in the road and a white dog.

CHAPTER TWO

Nina

QUENTIN LEFT THE lasagna in the oven too long. The edges were overcooked, and the cheese top was hard and brown.

Gabriella whined and refused to eat it. Nina was strict about eating what was served or doing without. Quentin, on the other hand, bustled to the kitchen and made their daughter her favourite. She wouldn't eat the peanut butter and jelly sandwich either.

Gabriella had her elbow on the table, another no-no, and her chin was perched in the cup of her open hand. With the other hand, she poked the tip of her index finger into the sandwich. "What are we going to do now?"

The smell of peanut butter was upsetting Nina's stomach. Saliva filled her mouth, and she closed her eyes and breathed through her mouth to keep from vomiting.

"What are we going to do?" Gabriella repeated in a shrill voice. The five-year-old was cranky, tired, and probably hungry. An explosive mix.

Quentin grinned. "Now, we do the dishes." He picked up their daughter's plate and rubbed the top of her head. She swatted away his hand, crossed her arms on the table, and threw her head on top.

Gabriella was old enough to clear her own dishes. She certainly shouldn't be slapping at her father.

"Sit up, please," Nina said, "and take your arms off the table. Why don't you help Papa clear the dishes?"

Her daughter ignored her. "Why can't Mama do the dishes and we play? It's boring here." She didn't lift her head from the table.

"After the dishes," Quentin continued, as if she hadn't spoken, "we'll play a game. Hey, I know, maybe Mama could give you your treat."

Nina glared at him. She was saving the gift as a distraction when boredom turned Gabriella into a troll.

Gabriella sat up straight. "I want a treat. Give it to me"

"Ask nicely," Nina told her.

"Can I *please* have it?"

"May I," Nina automatically corrected.

Quentin leaned down to whisper in her ear. "Pick your battles. Don't poke the bear cub. It was a long drive."

She studied her child from the corner of her eye and decided he was right. It had been a long drive and everyone was tired. If Gabriella saw the craft material, maybe she'd be excited about the project.

"If I give it to you tonight, you have to promise to go to bed when Papa tells you. No shenanigans."

Gabriella frowned and there was a belligerent expression on her face, but she nodded.

Nina went into the bedroom to fetch the box. When she returned, she'd barely managed to let go before her daughter pounced on it.

"We're going to make a memory book for the baby," Nina explained. "We'll collect things from the woods and shells from the beach and add the items to the book. Every day, we'll write about what we did. After the film is developed, we'll add photos."

Gabriella crossed her arms and said in a haughty voice, "We did crafts in kindergarten. They don't do that in grade one. It's for babies."

"This is a big girl craft. You didn't write on your crafts in kindergarten."

Her daughter gave her a steely glance. Other than displeasure, Gabriella's eyes rarely showed any expression. They were violet spheres devoid of emotion.

"We'll put it away for now. Tomorrow morning, while Papa's fishing, we can gather things you'd like to add."

Gabriella studied the stickers and coloured pens. "I wanna play with them now."

"We'll start tomorrow," Nina repeated.

"How about I clean up, and you guys start?" Quentin suggested.

Nina shook her head. "No, we'll start tomorrow. We can take a nice hike in the forest to find neat things."

Bits of her nightmare flashed before her eyes. She carried the box to the bedroom and shoved it under the bed.

When she returned to the living room, Gabriella announced, "We're gonna play skully."

Nina raised an eyebrow at her husband. "May as well since we have lots of beer caps."

He laughed. "Lighten up, I'm on vacation. Besides, I grew up with skully."

She pulled her daughter onto the sofa. "Papa was born in New York City. We played a similar game called caps, but Papa brought skully from the streets of New York to little old London, Ontario."

Quentin bounced eight beer caps in his hand. "We have extra, in case we lose one or two. Did you bring candles?"

Deciding to ignore the amount of beer he'd consumed, she nodded. "Emergency candles. They were in the box with the dry goods."

"Why do we need candles?" Gabriella asked.

"We melt wax into the bottle cap to make it slide faster," Quentin said. "You slide your cap so it lands on a number." He demonstrated by flicking one across the coffee table.

Gabriella caught it and flicked it back. Quentin grabbed it before it flew off the table.

"What numbers?" she asked.

"We use chalk to mark off a big box on the cement patio. Inside the box, we draw smaller ones with the numbers one to twelve. In the centre is a box for thirteen, with four rectangles around it, like a skull and crossbones," Quentin said. "We can pretend we're pirates, *arr.*"

　　　　　　　　　　　　　　　　　　L.E. Fraser

Nina grinned. "When you're sliding your cap, don't get stuck in the skull. I spent most of the game in the skull when I played."

"No way, I always hit your cap to set you free and protected you from the killer." Quentin winked.

"What's a killer?" Gabriella asked.

"After you've landed on all the outside numbers, you go to each box around the number thirteen. When you land on one, you say a word until you complete the phrase 'I am a killer'. Once you're a killer, you knock players' caps off the board until you're the last one and win the game."

"I want to play now." Gabriella scrambled out of her seat and raced to the door. "I want to be a killer and I want to use the chalk."

The cement patio was at the front of the cabin, facing the lake. Together, they watched the sunset colours bleed across the horizon. They'd built a small campfire in the pit, and Nina was enjoying the sweet smell of burning wood and the crickets' evening serenade. Quentin was taking her turns. Lounging in a wicker patio chair — cocooned in a woolly blanket and sipping tea — was much more her speed.

Quentin was letting Gabriella win the game. She'd completed the twelve board numbers and was flicking her cap around the skull. She lay on her stomach, her eyes wide, and her face pale, while she focused.

"I," she hollered, "am..." her lips tightened in concentration and her eyes narrowed when she flicked the cap, "a... killer."

She jumped to her feet and turned a flushed face toward Nina, beaming. "I am a killer," she said. "I won. You and Papa lost. You're losers!"

Quentin crouched so he was eye level with her. "Princess, that's not nice. Besides, you haven't won yet. You still have to hit me to take me off the board, remember?"

She slapped him hard across his face and shoved him in the chest. He rocked on his heels and fell backwards.

"Gabriella!" Nina pushed on the chair arms so she could stand.

Looking dazed, Quentin sat up and waved his hand. "It's okay. I didn't explain it properly." He rubbed his elbow, which he'd skinned on the patio.

"It's not okay. Gabriella, we do not hit. We do not push people," Nina said.

Gabriella's lip lowered to a pout, her forehead wrinkled, and her eyes blazed. "I am a killer. I won."

"Say you're sorry this instant." Nina struggled to keep her voice calm. "You're sorry for hitting, for being a poor sport, and for talking back."

"Chill out, it's not a big deal." Quentin climbed to his feet and brushed chalk off the back of his shorts. "It's late and we're all tired."

Nina ignored him. "We're waiting for you to apologize."

"Sorry." She studied the skully board. "I did win. Papa's cap isn't on the board."

Quentin laughed. "Guess my big bum knocked it off." He leaned down and lifted her up. "Mama's right. It was naughty of you to hit your old papa."

She touched his cheek, and for an awful moment, Nina expected her to hit him again. Instead, she giggled. "Your face is scratchy, Papa."

"Papa bear, *grr*. Time to get Goldilocks to bed." He carried her into the cabin.

Nina wrapped the blanket around her shoulders and poured a bucket of water on the campfire, staring at the red-hot centre.

"She's just high-spirited, it's nothing to worry about," she murmured to the dying embers.

After the last wisp of smoke drifted from the dead campfire, she trudged inside to tuck her daughter into bed.

IT WAS AFTER eleven by the time they settled Gabriella. It was two-thirty when her screams woke them.

Quentin put his hand on Nina's shoulder. "It's another nightmare. Stay here."

"Bring her in with us," she suggested.

A moment later, he tucked a moist, sleepy Gabriella between them on the bed.

"It was a dream," Quentin said to the sobbing child.

"Mama, you left me," she said. "It was raining and the woods were scary."

Nina's blood ran cold and a shiver raced up her spine. She looked at her daughter's tear-streaked face in the dim light, unable to speak.

"Why, Mama?"

Quentin sat up. "Has Mama been telling you silly ghost stories, princess?"

Ignoring him, their daughter said, "I want a doggy."

He smiled and hugged her. "It wasn't such a scary dream after all. Want some of Papa's water?" He held the glass to her lips.

"A big white doggy." She shoved the glass aside.

Quentin tucked her against his side. "Sorry, kiddo. No doggy, Papa's allergic." He squeezed Nina's hand a little too hard. "Too bad Mama can't shake off her bad dreams as fast as you can."

Gabriella must have heard them talking in the car. Nina was positive she'd never said anything about her dream in front of their daughter. Laying silent and uncomfortable in the dark, she felt anxious and out of sorts. Something was tickling the back of her mind. When she peeked at Gabriella, her daughter was fast asleep between them.

"Quentin, are you sleeping?" she whispered.

"No," he mumbled.

"Why does she want a big white dog?"

He rolled over with a sigh. "I don't know. Didn't we see a picture of a dog sled team at the Ojibway store we stopped at on the way up?"

She relaxed. "Right. That's probably where Ella saw the dog from her dream."

He studied her in the distorted moonlight from the ugly stained-glass window. "She didn't say anything about a dog being in her dream. She said she wanted one, and she's been asking for months." He paused. "That dream you've been having, is there a dog in it?"

She slowly shook her head. "No, I don't think so." *Was there?* "Let's go to sleep."

He yawned. "Have pleasant dreams for a change."

Watching the moon through the ugly window and feeling the baby kick, Nina listened to her husband's breathing even out and waited for sleep.

They'd saved all year for this vacation. Nina wished they'd stayed home and camped in the backyard.

CHAPTER THREE

Nina

"GET UP! GET UP! Get up!"

She locked eyes with her daughter, who was leaping up and down on the bed. Gabriella was already dressed in an embroidered peasant top and a cute pair of denim shorts.

Groaning, Nina rolled over and glanced at the travel clock. It was five-thirty in the morning. When she tried to sit up, a wave of dizziness knocked her back to the pillow. Her mouth was dry and a headache throbbed in her temples. Worse, she was having cramps. The contractions had started a few weeks ago. The first time it happened, they'd raced to the hospital to have an ER nurse inform them — condescendingly — that Braxton Hicks contractions were 'normal and nothing to worry about'.

"Where's Papa?"

Bounce, bounce. "Getting ready." *Bounce.*

He was going fishing. Nina moaned and tried pulling Gabriella down to a seated position.

She could sense the tumbling movement of the baby. While she lay still and waited, the baby kicked, so she didn't think her illness had anything to do with her pregnancy. But her body felt sluggish and achy. It was probably a twenty-four-hour bug. Gabriella had had it the week before.

"Sweetie, go get Papa for me please."

Gabriella leaped off the bed and hollered for her dad.

A moment later, he glanced through the bedroom doorway. "What's up?"

He looked so relaxed and happy in his fishing kit. Quentin was an eternal optimist and seldom complained about the extra hours he put in at the office. Fishing was the only activity that separated him from the family, and he needed the solitude to unwind. She wasn't stealing his fun because of a flu bug that would be gone by evening.

"Just wanted to wish you happy fishing." She smiled. "Don't forget your hat. The afternoon sun will be hot."

He grinned and placed a crimson hat decorated with colourful lures on his head. "Pretty spiffy, eh?"

"You bet. Can you help me up?"

He lifted her out of bed and put his lips on her forehead. "You're warm."

"No worries, it's just sleep sweat." Another stabbing cramp assaulted her stomach.

"Babe, you're pale."

"I'm fine."

"Gabriella can come with me, we have the life jacket," he suggested. "She said it's yucky and doesn't want to go, but she'll enjoy herself once she's on the boat."

She'd be cranky if they forced her and would pout. Quentin would have to bring her back. There wasn't any point. Instead, Nina would relax her TV rule and nap on the sofa while Gabriella watched cartoons as a treat. "No, it's okay."

"Did you have that nightmare again?" he asked.

She nodded.

"You know, you've always had wild dreams."

He was right, but usually she remembered the details and could figure out the dream's origins. This time was different.

Because An Da Shealladh is a vision of what's to come, not a memory of what has been, Grandma's voice warned.

Gaelic nonsense. Her subconscious was dragging out the dream every night because of guilt, a mother's best friend.

"Do you think Gabriella is excited to be a big sister?" she asked.

"Sure, what little girl wouldn't want a baby to play with?"

"I suppose." Nina reached for her housecoat. "She's spoiled. Maybe she's worried the baby will take attention away from her."

He crossed his arms over his chest. "She is not spoiled. Kids need to feel loved and safe."

She sighed and wrestled with her housecoat.

He helped her navigate her arms through the sleeves. "Babe, you're warm."

"I'm fine. It's an oven in here."

She wasn't fine. Now she was standing, the room was lurching. Her legs felt rubbery and her bowels felt loose.

"It's cooler in the front room, but it's going to be a hot one today. Maybe I'll wait until a little later to go out. I don't want to leave if you're sick."

She'd rather have a quiet day watching TV and laying on the beach with Gabriella than a wild, rambunctious day filled with high-octane Quentin fun. "Seriously, I'm fine. It's supposed to rain for the next two days, and we'll be stuck inside. Go."

"Want me to come ashore at noon to check-in?"

"If you want, but you don't have to."

For a moment, he seemed torn. Then they heard the calls of the anglers from the dock.

"I better get going or all the good spots will be taken." He winked.

In spite of how awful she felt, Nina laughed. Lake Superior was over eighty thousand square kilometres of clear blue water. There would always be good spots.

"How about a trout or northern pike dinner?" he asked.

"Probably bass," she said. "Whatever the catch of the day is, it better be cleaned and filleted before it hits my kitchen."

She waddled to the front room and watched him close his tackle box and kiss Gabriella.

The second Quentin was out the door Gabriella pouted and said, "I'm hungry."

"How about cereal? There's Count Chocula." Nina rubbed her hand across her sweaty face.

"I want bacon."

The idea of bacon frying made her stomach flip. "Not this morning. Maybe we can do bacon and Cheese Whiz sandwiches for lunch."

Gabriella grabbed a bowl and the cereal box from the cupboard and sat at the scratched wooden table. She looked at Nina. "I can get juice," she said.

It was rare for her to be helpful. If Nina was honest, her daughter could be a brat. Gabriella's teacher had described her as 'precocious', but the judgment in her eyes had suggested it wasn't a compliment. The teacher had also used the words 'submissively non-compliant' and 'impertinent'.

"Thank you, juice would be great."

Her daughter took the carton from the fridge, put it on the table, and sat down.

Nina sipped the orange juice. The acid churned in her upset stomach, and she felt chills. Gabriella nibbled on her cereal, and they sat in silence.

"What are we going to do?" Gabriella spun a feather from an abandoned lure between her fingers.

"Well, we could make a sand castle."

Her daughter frowned.

"I think *Sesame Street* is on television."

The frown deepened.

"We could make cookies later." A bubble of bile rose in Nina's throat, and she grasped the table edge and closed her eyes.

"I want to go with Papa," her daughter said.

If she slept a little longer, she'd feel better. Quentin could bring Gabriella back for lunch and have the afternoon on the lake alone.

"Okay," Nina agreed. "I'll get dressed, and we'll go down to meet him before he leaves." She struggled to her feet.

"No! He'll leave without me. You're too slow." Gabriella's pug nose crinkled and the crimson bow of her lip jutted out to a pout.

Part of the dock was visible from outside the cabin, and it was a short walk down the beach. She thought about the last parent-teacher meeting, when Gabriella's teacher implied Nina was overprotective.

"Well, if he's not there, come straight back. I'll watch from the patio."

Her daughter bolted through the door and raced to the beach. Nina spotted Quentin in his red hat standing with the other fishermen. She waved and pointed at the running child. He raised his hand.

When Nina walked across the patio to get a better look at the dock, the orange juice shifted in her stomach and her mouth filled with saliva. She clamped a hand over her mouth and shuffled to the bathroom as fast as she could, just making it. Sitting on the cool linoleum, she took shallow breaths. Just when the nausea was passing, her bowels churned. She scrambled for the toilet seat and sat panting and sweating through the awful cramps. Yes, it was the flu. The best solution was to go back to bed.

On her way to the bedroom, she stepped out the screen door and looked toward the dock. Gabriella was gone. A scattering of boats was heading to the deeper waters of the lake, and the dock was empty. Relieved, Nina plodded inside, returned to the bedroom, and fell asleep.

CHAPTER FOUR

Quentin

WHEN QUENTIN STEERED his boat to the dock, he had to hunt for a spot to tie it off. It was seven-thirty, and the sun was low on the western horizon. Everyone else had left hours ago, and the beach was deserted.

It was late because he'd lost several hours of fishing. Anglers had invited him to a fish fry at a secluded beach up the coast. Lunch was fantastic and the spot was stunning. The sandy beach hugged the rocky base of high escarpments that rose thirty metres above the water to crests dotted with rolling evergreens. The scenery was simultaneously wild and elegant, and the tiny beach was a luxurious oasis. Perfect for his girls. He'd take them for a boat ride and a picnic tomorrow to make up for being so late.

Quentin pulled his cooler from the boat, tossed his empty beer cans into a plastic bag, and removed his copious catch. His prize was a salmon, and Nina would be thrilled. The cold, deep waters of Lake Superior were ideal for salmon, but tackling the aggressive fish was difficult.

He set to work cleaning his fish and decided to polish off the last two beers before going up to the cabin. He brushed a fly away from his nose and winced. He'd been on his way back to shore to retrieve the forgotten zinc cream when he caught the salmon. All thoughts of sunburn had evaporated under the euphoria of the catch.

Quentin glanced at his watch. It was after eight. He put the fish in the cooler, rinsed the table, and headed to the cabin.

When he arrived, the closed door surprised him. He wondered why Gabriella and Nina weren't enjoying the fine weather. He moved his fishing hat to a rakish angle, pulled open the door and strutted into the cabin, imitating Jimmie Walker from *Good Times*.

"*Dyn-o-mite!* The fisherman king returns." He waved his catch over his head and swayed his hips, waiting for their giggles.

The cabin was musty and quiet.

"Hello?"

No answer. He looked around the living room on his way to the kitchen. No sign of them. They must have gone for a walk. Quentin put the fish into the fridge and rinsed out the cooler.

An acid and unpleasant odour hung in the stale air. Rentals often had odours from the ghosts of past tenants hanging around, but this smell was downright funky. Maybe fish guts had spilled on his shorts.

Nina wouldn't take Gabriella on a long hike this late. He'd change clothes and set up the campfire so it was ready when they returned.

At the doorway to the bedroom, Quentin stopped abruptly. Nina was asleep in the bed. The room reeked of vomit and diarrhea.

He stumbled to the side of the bed and pawed at his wife's body. "Nina? Nina, wake up. What's wrong, what's going on?" He knelt by the bed and shook her. Her flesh was burning beneath his fingers and dried vomit soiled the bodice of her nightgown.

He put his hand beneath her nose and felt her breath on his fingers. He shook her harder. "Nina, please! Wake up, babe."

Slowly, she swam up to consciousness. She blinked at him and mumbled something incoherent. Her breath was rancid and her eyes were dull. He was ashamed but had an overwhelming urge to drop her hot, stinking body back onto the bed. He put his hands under her armpits to lift her into a sitting position. Holding her with one arm, he stuffed pillows behind her back and tried to pull away the blankets. He loosened the neckline of her nightgown and saw clammy sweat rolling down between her large breasts.

"Nina," he shook her gently, "where's Gabriella?"

No response.

He ran to his daughter's room. Empty. He checked the bathroom and sprinted back to Nina.

A wave of cold white panic took hold. "Babe, what's wrong? Where's Gabriella?"

No answer. He wiped strands of hair from her face, tapping her cheek with the tips of his fingers.

"Where is she, where's Gabriella?"

Quentin's throat was dry and there was a ringing in his ears. His stomach flopped and adrenaline rushed through his body, making his legs rubbery and his heart race.

"So hot," Nina whimpered, and he didn't recognize the weak, willowy voice. Her tongue poked from between dry lips.

He grabbed water from the side table.

Suddenly, her eyes opened wide. She gasped in pain and curled inward. Water sloshed across her chest, accentuating the stench. Beneath the smell of vomit was something else, something metallic and nasty, like spoiled fish.

She must be in early labour. Where was their daughter? He hadn't seen Gabriella outside. She must have gone for help when Nina started having contractions. But where did she go and how long ago?

Quentin took a deep breath. "Babe, you're in labour. Is that what's going on?"

Her left hand snaked down to her abdomen. She feebly kicked at the tangled blankets.

"Nina, where's Ella? Did you send her for help? Why didn't you call the police or the ambulance?"

Through the ugly stained glass, the setting sun painted wide red stripes across her fingers. His mind was sluggish when he gazed at her hand. He held up his own fingers, and the diffused light cloaked them in a red shadow.

Just a trick of the light, he thought, but he felt the sticky, congealing blood and smelled the thick coppery odour.

His heart careened into his stomach. "Hold on, I'm calling help."

He ran to the living room before remembering the phone was on the kitchen wall. He slipped and grappled for the doorframe. The middle finger on his right hand smashed into the wood. His finger bent to the back of his hand. With a roar of pain, he scrambled to his feet and grunted when he seized the phone. Emergency numbers were on the wall. His fingers trembled while he dialled.

His mind was blank. He couldn't remember the name of the cabins or the road they took.

"Sir, give me the number you're calling from and describe the cabin," the calm dispatcher requested.

"It's white. No! It's brown with white trim and green shutters. It's on the lake. There's a dock and a cleaning table and—"

"Break the window," Nina yelled from the bedroom. Her voice was full of pain and terror.

"Sir, stay with me. I need your help. Where did you exit off the Trans-Canada Highway?"

Conversations from their drive raced through his mind, all mangled together. *Okay girls, watch for Havilland Shores Drive.*

"Havilland Shores Drive," he shouted.

"Please stay calm. Try to remember the name of the rental. Who did you make the deposit out to?"

"Run," Nina screamed.

Quentin sobbed. "Redington, I think. Something Pines. Please, my wife is bleeding and my daughter is gone. The baby—"

"Sir, I know where you are. I've dispatched paramedics. Stay on the line with me, and—"

Nina screamed again. He dropped the phone and sprinted to the bedroom. She was squirming against her tangled, blood-soaked sheets.

"Run," she mumbled.

Quentin tried to loosen the sheets, bending his dislocated finger in the struggle. With a yelp, he switched hands, fumbling with the sheets while his wife twisted and turned, rolling against his efforts.

"Skully, killer."

The hair on Quentin's arms stood on end. His balls crawled up and were tight against his groin. There was a ringing in his ears. His vision distorted and the sunset colours bled together. Through the stained glass, the dying sun bathed the bed covers in a macabre spiral of red and orange, resembling Dante's rings of hell.

QUENTIN DIDN'T KNOW how long he sat in the stinking room holding his unconscious wife before he realized people were in the cabin.

"We need you to step out, sir," said a calm voice, the owner of which was tugging at his arm. "What's her name?"

Quentin climbed to his feet. When he stumbled, the man supported him.

"Sir, what's your wife's name?"

"Nina." Quentin cried harder. "My daughter, I can't find my daughter. She's only five."

"The police officers will help you find your daughter. Let us take care of Nina."

Quentin staggered through the doorway, listening to the emergency medical team speaking to Nina in quiet tones. When they released her body from the nest of linen, blood dripped from the sheets and pooled on the plank floor.

"*Ganawenim*," she screamed at the top of her lungs and swatted at the paramedic's hands.

"Yes," the man assured her, "we'll protect you."

"*Nishiwe.*"

The Aboriginal paramedic frowned and followed Nina's eyes to Quentin. She reached a hand that dripped with blood toward her husband and pointed her index finger at him. "*Nishiwe*," she repeated. "*Nishiwe. Nishiwe.*" Each time she said the word, her voice grew louder and more hysterical.

Quentin lurched through the bedroom door, reaching for his wife. A cop clamped a hand on his shoulder, roughly pulling him away and shoving him into the other room.

The officer asked the medic, "Did I hear that right?"

　　　　　　　　　　　　　　　　　　　

"Yes," came the clipped reply.

The paramedic and cop stared at him with hard expressions. Quentin struggled in the officer's steely grip. "Let go of me. Why aren't you helping my wife?"

"*Ganawenim Nishiwe.*" The colour ebbed from the medic's face. His eyes blazed with fury. "I can't believe you. You sick fuck." The man spit and the gob of phlegm hit the side of Quentin's face.

For a moment, he was too stunned to move. When he raised his hand to wipe the spit from his cheek, the officer grabbed his wrist, twisted his arms behind his back and threw him into the wall with such force that two pictures fell off the wall.

Glass smashed against the floor. Jangling handcuffs forced his wrists together. The officer shoved aside his dislocated finger and tightened the manacles until they pinched skin. White-hot pain flooded down his finger and bathed his hand.

"What's wrong with you? Why are you doing this?" Quentin thrashed against the restraints. "We have to find my daughter."

The officer squished his face into the wall. The man's breath was hot and moist in Quentin's ear. "What did you do with your daughter? Where is she?"

Quentin sobbed in frustration, pain, and fear. "I don't know. That's what I'm trying to tell you. Why are you doing this?"

"Your wife," the officer snarled, "asked us to protect her from the killer — to protect her from you."

CHAPTER FIVE

One month later: Sault Ste. Marie, Ontario

Nina

NINA WOKE WITH a gasp. Again with crazy dreams all mixed up in her head. "*An Da Shealladh*," she whispered. Her dream was telling her Gabriella was alive. She could feel this was true, deep in her bones.

Something heavy lay across her chest, and she tried to throw away the blanket to dislodge it. An infant cried and she gazed with indifference at the baby. It nestled against her chest, searching for her breast, and she felt an overwhelming urge to slap it away.

She heard a sharp *tsk* to her right. "It's important for you to cuddle her, Mommy."

Over the past month, Nina had grown to hate the sound of the nurse's condescending voice. Lethargically, she shoved the baby off her body. Capable hands scooped up the tiny infant before it toppled off the bed, and the baby's indignant wails heightened to ear-shattering tones.

"You're very lucky," the nurse said. "Little girl is five pounds two ounces now, amazing for a preemie after one month."

Nina didn't respond.

"Your husband is in the hall, speaking with the... ah... speaking with a doctor."

Speaking to the psychiatrist, Nina silently amended. She had never been a fan of mental health professionals, and now she despised them. If they couldn't find scientific evidence something existed, they refused to consider it as an explanation. You were crazy as a feral cat, simple as that, and Nina swore she'd never deal with another one. Strangers didn't have the right to decide how she should feel.

Staring sightlessly out the window, she felt the nurse's eyes drilling into the back of her head, judging and persecuting her for being a bad mother. A door opened. Over the paging system, a woman's voice requested a doctor to report to the ICU nurses' station. Nina didn't turn, continuing to stare at the window blinds.

"Have you picked a name for this little darling?" the nurse asked.

"Isabella." There was no expression in Quentin's voice. "Can you please take the baby? I need to speak with my wife privately."

He walked over and stood in her line of sight. His right hand was still in a cast from his accident at the cottage, and his expression was cold. What was it going to be today? More accusations and anger, or pity tainted with disgust. It wasn't possible for a marriage to survive so much pain.

'Placenta previa', they'd learned, caused her to hemorrhage. Paramedics had saved the baby but the hospital surgeon had had to perform a hysterectomy. Her dreams of a large family were gone. Her daughter was gone. All that remained was pain and crippling guilt.

The door opened and closed before Quentin said, "They haven't found her body."

"She isn't dead."

"It rained for three days, and there was nothing for them to track when they realized I hadn't done something to her." He ran his fingers through his hair. "Gabriella's gone. We have to face it."

She said nothing. Her daughter wasn't dead, but she was tired of trying to convince Quentin of what she knew in her heart.

"We have to go home. Nina, we can't carry more debt, and I'm a heartbeat from losing my job. If I do, we'll lose the house."

Quentin's company had given him an emergency leave of absence, but it was without pay. The psychiatrist had recommended transferring her to London Psychiatric Hospital, but Quentin had arranged to co-pay the Sault Ste. Marie hospital so she could stay. It was expensive but Quentin wanted to help the Search and Rescue teams. She knew her husband well. Now they weren't searching for a live child, he wanted to try to move forward. His willingness to give up infuriated her.

"She couldn't survive alone in the woods. Gabriella's dead." His voice was flat.

"Gabriella's not dead," she replied. "*He* has her."

Quentin flapped his hands at his side. "Again with this shit about a mysterious abductor. No one has her, Nina." He sunk into the chair beside her bed. "Why didn't you take her to the dock? Why did you let her go alone?"

"I told you. There was a man with a red hat at the dock, I thought it was you."

"I'm not the only person who owns a red hat."

"I told her to come straight back if you weren't there." She let her tears come. "I don't know why she went into the woods. Why didn't those men stop her?"

Fishermen had told the police that Gabriella went to the dock. She didn't speak to them and walked into the woods. Why would they let a little girl go into the woods all alone?

"A man has her," Nina said. "I'm her mother. I know. She's not dead. He took her from the woods. He believes he's a *Wendigo*, a demonic spirit. You have to believe me."

"Stop with this shit. The staff psychiatrist is not going to discharge you to my care if you don't cut it out." He slipped his hand into hers and squeezed hard. "Take care of our baby, Nina. Isabella needs you, and you won't hold her or feed her. You're her mother."

"I'm Gabriella's mother," she yelled. "Why won't you listen to me? He took her. He has her." She pulled her hand free and wiped her fingers against the crisp sheet. "Grandma was right, I inherited *An Da Shealladh*. From mother to daughter," she said. "Gabriella has the 'two sights', too. She's sending me the dream. We have to find her."

"We have to go home," he said. "The question is whether you're going to be at home or transferred to London Psychiatric Hospital. Do you understand what I'm telling you?"

"*Ganawenim*, it means to take care of or to protect. *Nishiwe* means killer. The dog protects the killer. *An Da Shealladh* comes in dreams. *Wendigo* can possess in dreams. That's the connection."

Quentin stood and knocked a book off the bedside table. "What dog? What man? Don't you get how crazy you sound?"

"*Nishiwe* took her from the woods. He was the storm in the dream."

"It was a fucking dream. You weren't even in the woods when Gabriella got lost." He picked the book up from the floor and threw it against the door.

Nina cringed against the headboard of the bed. She'd never seen her husband violent before.

"Stop reading these damn books on Aboriginal myths," he yelled. "You have fucking nightmares, Nina. That's all they are. They aren't prophecies."

It took all of her courage, but she held his eyes. He rubbed the heel of his hand across his forehead, turned away, and stared out the window.

"I don't speak Ojibway. How do I know those words?" she asked.

"Nina," he said with a sigh, "we stopped at the Ojibway store on our way to the cabin. Remember? You and Gabriella looked at the picture of the dog sled. Please try to remember the picture."

She did recall the picture. She didn't understand what that had to do with anything.

"Beneath the picture," Quentin said, "was a list of the dogs' names. One was 'Ganawenim'. I went back to the store and looked at the picture."

Frustrated, she shook her head. "There wasn't anything written on the picture we looked at. They must have put up a new one."

With a heavy sigh, he continued. "We bought Gabriella a pair of beaded moccasins and you bought a book."

"I didn't buy a book. We bought the moccasins, they were in my purse."

"You did buy a book." He stomped to the door and grabbed the book he'd thrown, turning the cover so it faced her. "This book, actually."

She'd asked the nurse to bring her a book on Ojibway myths, and the nurse gave her the book Quentin was holding. Feeling confused and angry, Nina tried to think back to the day they were in the store. She was certain she'd never seen the book before the nurse gave it to her. "We bought the moccasins. I remember helping Gabriella try them on."

"And you bought this book." He slapped it against the side of his leg.

Was his intent to confuse her? Her anger mounted. If she had bought a book, it would be in the cabin. "Where is this book you're telling me I bought?"

"I can't find it."

"Because it never happened. I never bought it at all. I don't know why you're lying to everyone," she screamed.

He walked to the bed and placed the book on the table. "Nina, you're paranoid. Why would I lie? These dreams of a demonic spirit possessing a man who abducted our daughter are your subconscious. Don't you see? You've manifested this fantasy. The doctors can help you, if you let them."

She stared at him. His cheeks were hollow, and purple rings circled his eyes. She didn't recognize him at all. She felt frightened and vulnerable, trapped in the hospital with everyone disbelieving her. "Why are you doing this?" she sobbed. "I'm not crazy. Why can't you believe a mother could have a link to her child?"

Quentin leaned over and brushed hair from her forehead. "Gabriella is dead. She couldn't survive in the wilderness for over a month."

"She's not dead."

"Please, babe, you have to accept the truth. Let the doctors help you. Let me help you." He held out his arms.

She refused to lean into his embrace. Her pain and suspicion was too deep to offer him support. She needed to hoard her strength to keep the link to Gabriella open. She couldn't understand why he was trying to confuse her.

He dropped his arms. "We have to go home." He walked to the door. "We are going home."

CHAPTER SIX

Five months later: London, Ontario

Nina

NINA WASN'T SURE if she was dreaming. A bell kept ringing and ringing. The pills she took every night usually stopped her from dreaming. Confused, she realized she heard pounding. The medication made it hard to focus. Was someone at the front door? She peered at the clock, wondering who would be at their door at three o'clock in the morning.

"Quentin?" She rolled over but her husband wasn't in bed. Nina strained to see through the shadows and blinked when the bedroom light turned on.

"Stay here," Quentin said, tugging his jeans over his hips.

"What is it? What's going on?" She sat up, throwing back the covers and grabbing her housecoat from the foot of the bed.

"Nina, stay here. Someone's at the door."

Right, as if she was going to stay in the bedroom alone. From across the hall, Isabella was crying, wailing really.

Nina reached the hallway and saw Quentin jog down the stairs two at a time. The person outside their house was leaning against the doorbell while pounding on the door.

She ran into the baby's room, scooped the terrified child into her arms, and dashed down the stairs to peek around the corner. Detective McNamara, their neighbour, was speaking rapidly to Quentin. Something must have happened.

"I can take you," Colin said. "Get Nina and—"

She ran to the door. "Colin? What's going on, what's wrong?" Isabella's wails were reducing to small hiccups against her shoulder.

"They found her," Quentin said. His hair was sticking up at the back of his head and all the colour had leached from his face. "They found Gabriella."

She swayed against the wall, and Colin grabbed her arm and led her to a chair. "You remember I was the London detective assigned to the case when you came home last summer. The FBI identified her yesterday and contacted the RCMP. Gabriella's at the Children's Hospital in Detroit. I just got the call."

"Is she okay? I don't understand. She's in the US. What happened? Please, Colin, is she okay?"

He crouched so they were eye level. "She's alive and in stable condition. Ice fishermen found her walking alone on the Michigan side of Lake Superior. I don't have any more details."

Nina watched Quentin stuffing a diaper bag with bottles from the fridge and jars of baby food from the pantry. She couldn't move. *Get up. Get moving,* she screamed to herself, but her legs felt like jelly. She was afraid she'd drop Isabella if she tried to stand.

"Quentin, take a minute, please," Colin said. "Let's figure out the best way to get you to Detroit. I can drive you myself, or I can ask an officer to take you in a cruiser."

Now she could move. Her legs were quivering with the need to move. She leaped to her feet, ran upstairs, and placed Isabella on the changing table. Her fingers trembled while she changed the diaper and bundled the baby into a snowsuit. She couldn't think. She just did. Her daughter was alive. Gabriella needed her. She had to get to her.

Nina threw on her clothes and returned to find Quentin wearing his coat and boots and arguing with Colin.

"It's snowing, the roads aren't great, and you're not thinking straight. Quentin, I can smell liquor on your breath. Let me take you."

"Get out of my way." Quentin shoved the detective aside. "Nina, get your coat. I'll warm up the car."

"Listen to me," Colin begged but her husband was gone.

Nina struggled to pull on her winter boots and do up the buttons on her coat. Where was the car seat? Had she left it upstairs? No. She'd left it in the car with the stroller after shopping the day before.

"Nina, Quentin shouldn't be driving," Colin said.

She was at the door, Isabella squirming in her arms, when she realized she didn't have her purse. She didn't have her pills. She thrust Isabella into Colin's arms and ran upstairs. He was calling after her, but Nina couldn't hear him and didn't care. She grabbed her purse, tossed her pill bottles in, and raced back.

She scooped Isabella from Colin and lurched out the door. As she stumbled down the snow-covered walkway to the car, three words kept screaming in her mind.

Gabriella is alive.

CHAPTER SEVEN

Detroit, Michigan

Nina

"MR. AND MRS. LeBlanc, you should prepare yourselves before you see your daughter." The RCMP officer led them down the hall of the Children's Hospital of Michigan.

Because they were Canadian, the Royal Canadian Mounted Police was involved, along with the Michigan State Police who had found Gabriella and the FBI. The male US authorities acted happy to leave the female RCMP officer to deal with the parents.

"We were told Gabriella's okay." Nina was jogging a bit to keep up, while manoeuvring the stroller around patients, visitors, and staff.

The pretty, young woman stopped at the elevators and held the doors open for Nina and Quentin. "Well, there are things you need to know." She pressed the button for the seventh floor. The doors slid closed and the elevator jerked upward.

Nina plucked her six-month-old daughter from the stroller and held her tight. "I don't remember your name." It felt important to know the woman's name before hearing what she was dreading.

The elevator stopped and the officer ushered them out. They stood together in the hallway, and Nina bounced and soothed Isabella.

"It's Laura." Her eyes were warm. "Mr. and Mrs. LeBlanc, your daughter went to a bob-house. Do you know what that is?"

"Of course we do. It's a shack that's dragged onto the lake for ice fishing." Quentin's tone was rude. He was exhausted and, lately, always impatient. Worse, Nina suspected he was hungover again.

Laura ignored him, addressing Nina. "She was with a dog, and she's very attached to it."

Nina wasn't sure why this was important, and said so.

"Well, she can't be separated from the animal. The child psychiatrist will provide you with more details on her mental state."

"What are you talking about?" Quentin asked. "We're in a hospital. Obviously the dog isn't—"

"We can take the dog," Nina interrupted.

Laura nodded. "I hoped you'd agree and took the liberty of involving a vet to expedite transport into Canada. I'll provide you with formal documents for the border."

Quentin threw his hands up. "No one cares about the dog. Did you catch the asshole who took her? Did you do anything constructive since you found her five days ago?"

Laura started walking and gestured for them to follow. "Yes, Mr. LeBlanc, we know who took her."

"Where is the motherfucker?" Quentin clenched his hands into fists, making the muscles in his arms bulge.

Laura stopped outside an office door and faced them. "Mr. LeBlanc, calm down."

"I will not calm down. You're going to take me to the fucker who stole my daughter."

"Quentin, I need to hear what Laura has to say," Nina said.

"Well, I don't. All I want to know is if you arrested the son of a bitch."

"An arrest wasn't possible," Laura said, entering the office and closing the door behind them. "The man is dead."

Quentin leaned against the wall. "That's the best news you've given us since we arrived."

"How?" Nina asked, even though she didn't want to hear the answer.

"We found him in a cabin in the woods where he lived with your daughter and the dog."

Quentin was in Laura's face in an instant. "He did not *live* with her. He kidnapped her. He was holding her prisoner. They weren't *living* together."

"Mr. LeBlanc, step back. Both of you please sit."

"Quentin," Nina tugged his arm and pushed him into a chair, "don't you want to know what happened?" She took the chair beside him, shifted Isabella to her knee, and held her husband's hand.

He glared at her. When she refused to drop her eyes, he reached for the baby. She handed over the warm, solid bundle and her arms ached with loss. Quentin leaned down and fumbled in the diaper bag by her feet. Two fat tears splashed onto the vinyl of the bag when he pulled out a bottle of milk.

"There was a pink cage in the corner of the cabin with a snow white bed inside." Laura's voice was gentle and kind. "The man was on the bed. His skull was fractured."

Nina held her breath.

"He may have fallen, or..." Laura swallowed. "We think he opened the cage door and lay on the bed where he subsequently died from his injuries. After she..." Laura licked her lips. "After he died, Gabriella left the cage and the cabin. Until the post-mortem is in or your daughter talks to us, we don't know anything else."

Did they think Gabriella killed him? What would the authorities do when they had the autopsy results? The monster abducted her. It didn't matter how she escaped. Nina took a calming breath, but her heartbeat stayed rapid and her stomach fluttered in panic.

During the drive to Detroit, she'd tried to visualize the future. Would Gabriella be the same child they'd lost? She had so many questions, and her desperate fear that she wasn't strong enough to cope felt crippling.

The office door opened, and the child psychiatrist they had met when they arrived marched to his desk. Nina had instantly disliked him and couldn't remember his name. She ignored him and directed her most important question to Laura. "Did he sexually assault my daughter?"

Laura glanced at the doctor, who nodded and waved his hand, indicating she could proceed.

Nina didn't need to hear the answer. Tears flooded her eyes.

Laura exhaled slowly. "I'm so sorry."

Nina could picture the pink cage and snow white bed. She could picture a monstrous, naked man looming over her tiny daughter. She shuddered and squeezed her eyes shut to block out the horrific vision.

Quentin was sobbing, and Isabella was crying along with him.

"Listen, I know there is no bright side to this." Laura took her hands. "But Gabriella won't have to suffer through a trial. She's alive. She's a beautiful, physically healthy child."

Physically healthy. The implication made her head spin. She couldn't do this. She didn't possess the skills to deal. Panic crawled across her stomach, and she gagged on the bile rising in her throat.

"Injuries?" she managed to whisper.

The doctor cleared his throat. "There are sections of flesh missing from Gabriella's inner thighs, buttocks, and lower back. She will have scars."

Nina swayed on the chair. She couldn't breathe and black dots bounced in front of her eyes. Laura gripped her hand until the pressure was painful. The black dots dispersed.

"Mrs. LeBlanc," the doctor said, "the wounds healed without infection. Plastic surgery will help."

"*Wendigo*," Nina hissed. "I told you, Quentin, it was *An Da Shealladh*. I saw him eating flesh. Now do you believe?"

Quentin's face paled. He tightened his grip on the baby, and Isabella squirmed and whimpered in his arms.

"What does that mean?" Laura asked.

"It's Gaelic and it's nonsense," Quentin said. "After Isabella was born, my wife went through a difficult time."

"My grandmother was a Scot Highlander," she told Laura. "*An Da Shealladh* means the 'two sights'. It's hereditary, passed from mother to daughter. I knew my daughter was alive because I saw her in my dreams. No one believed me."

"Nina, don't dredge this up again," Quentin said sternly.

She ignored him and spoke to Laura. "Cannibalism is believed by the Ojibway to cause possession by a powerful evil spirit, *Wendigo*. I know there's no such thing as a *Wendigo* but there are sick people who believe if they eat flesh, they'll attract this demon."

Laura looked skeptical. "I'm sorry. I don't know anything about Aboriginal or Gaelic folklore. I don't understand what makes you think cannibalism was involved."

Nina leaned forward in her chair. "The Ojibway believe you can see *Wendigo* in dreams. *An Da Shealladh* warns you in dreams. Don't you see? That's how they're connected." She turned to her husband. "Quentin, why else would I associate *Wendigo* with Gabriella?"

"Please, this isn't the time," Quentin said with a sigh. "You were sick. You had bad dreams. You read too many books on legends. Leave it alone."

She turned back to Laura. "The man, he was Native, wasn't he?"

Laura dropped her hands. "No, Nina, he wasn't. We've identified him."

"What about the cabin? Did you find anything relating to the culture?"

Laura shook her head. "No. The dog's name, I suppose. But I understand it's a popular name for dogs."

"What is the dog's name?" Nina asked.

"According to your daughter, it's Ganawenim. She calls him Gana. It means protector."

"I know what it means." Nina spun toward Quentin. "Explain how I knew that word when you found me in the cabin?"

Quentin refused to look at her.

"Nina," Laura said, "I understand how difficult this must be." She cleared her throat and stood. "The doctor would like to speak with you, so I'll wait outside." She left the office and gently latched the door.

Nina took Isabella from Quentin and hugged the baby against her shoulder. She hadn't seen that word at the Ojibway store on the way to the cabin. She didn't read it in a book until *after* her daughter disappeared. How would she know the word *ganawenim*? It wasn't a coincidence. It was *An Da Sheal-*

ladh. She was not crazy. Why would no one believe her? Her eyes filled with tears, and she dug in her pocket for a tissue.

"My first recommendation," the doctor spoke to Quentin, "is for the dog to stay with Gabriella."

"Where is the dog?" Nina asked.

"With your daughter," he replied.

Quentin frowned. "In the hospital?"

"Under the circumstances, it was necessary to make an exception."

Nina studied her husband. "There are shots."

He pounced on her comment. "Exactly my point. Obviously, a child-stealing maniac wasn't concerned about inoculating the animal against disease. It's preposterous that the dirty dog is in the company of my traumatized daughter."

"For you," Nina said. "You can take allergy shots."

Quentin's mouth gaped. "You've got to be kidding. We are not keeping a lunatic's dog."

"Haven't you been listening? We have to keep it for Gabriella's sake."

"I'm afraid I have to side with your wife," the doctor said. "Professionally," the word rolled off his self-important tongue like honey, "it's for the best to facilitate healing." He took a piece of paper from his desk. "I'm prepared to discharge your daughter this afternoon. You may take her home."

Nina's joy at discovering her daughter was alive morphed into terror over how she was going to take care of a child who had suffered such trauma. Things were moving too fast. "Isn't there anything you need to discuss with us regarding her care?"

He continued to scribble on the paper. "I've apprised a London child psychiatrist of the intricacies of her recovery. You have an appointment next week." He stood, handed Quentin the piece of paper and shook their hands. Nina could tell he was mentally checking them off his to-do list.

When they exited the office, a nurse was waiting outside the door with Gabriella. She was sleeping in a wheelchair. A large white Samoyed dog stood passively by her side.

Nina fell on her knees and embraced her child. She leaned back and scrutinized her daughter's face. Her hair still curled into natural ringlets but it was longer. Her face was pale. It looked a little gaunt. Nina gently squeezed Gabriella's upper leg. Yes, she was thin. There was a tiny, tape-covered cotton ball in the crook of her arm and a small bruise on the back of her hand from an IV needle. Her poor baby. She must be so scared.

"We gave her a strong sedative," the nurse said. "She'll sleep for several hours. When she wakes, don't be alarmed if she doesn't speak."

"We understand," Quentin said.

"Good. It'll take time, but having Gana will help." The nurse patted the dog's head. "He's a lovely, well-behaved animal and attached to your daughter." She knelt and gave Gabriella a hug. "Have a safe trip home. You can take the wheelchair out to the car."

"No, I'll carry her."

Nina moved aside so Quentin could pick up their daughter. He stood motionless, clutching Gabriella to his chest.

"I'll help you to the car." Laura took Nina's arm, leading her to the elevator.

Once the children and their new dog were loaded into the backseat, Laura shook Quentin's hand and turned to Nina. "Here is my card," she said. "I'll be in touch in a couple of weeks when Gabriella is settled. If you have any other questions, please call." With that, she made her way back to the hospital.

They stood beside the car and Quentin put his arm around her waist, smiling for the first time. "Do you want to find a hotel and drive back tomorrow?"

She wanted to ask him if he was afraid. She needed him to reassure her they would figure everything out and take care of their daughter together. Instead, she shook her head. "I can drive. You can nap in the back seat between the girls."

The girls. The words sailed across her tongue. Finally, it was plural and would never again be singular. Nothing else mattered. They'd figure things out along the way. It didn't matter how long it took or how hard it was.

Gabriella was her daughter. Nina swore she would sacrifice anything to keep her safe.

She rose on her tiptoes and lifted her face to kiss her husband. "Let's take our girls home."

CHAPTER EIGHT

Ten years later: London, Ontario

Isabella

"WHATCHA WANNA DO?" Isabella asked.

"We could play skully," Gabriella suggested.

Isabella rolled her eyes. "That's all you ever want to play." She tumbled onto her back and pulled Gana into her arms.

Her older sister flopped down on the grass beside her and studied the clouds. "That cloud," she pointed at the sky, "looks like a man hanging from the gallows."

More like a giraffe, Isabella thought. "Wanna hang out at the mall?" she asked, hoping to distract her sister from being her usual creepy self.

Gabriella snorted. "Right, like Mama would let us go to the mall alone."

"All my friends went on vacation this summer." Isabella sighed. "Not us, we have to stay home and camp in the stupid backyard."

It was Gabriella's fault. Something had happened when her sister was five, but Isabella didn't know what. Every time she asked, her parents wouldn't answer. She'd tried talking to her sister, but Gabriella claimed she didn't remember.

She rolled over and studied her sister. Before she could stop herself, she blurted out, "What happened when you were little, Gabby?"

"I had an adventure." Widening her eyes, she sucked in her cheeks and pulled her lips away from her teeth, a face that had terrified Isabella when she was little.

"It creeps me out when you do that." Isabella tugged a blade of grass from the yard and put it between her fingers to make a whistle. Gabriella wasn't going to tell her, so she may as well drop it. "When am I going to get boobs?"

Her sister sat up and ran her hands across her own full breasts. "You won't like breasts. You're a tomboy." She brushed her long, dark ringlets over her shoulder and flicked a piece of grass off her yellow blouse.

As usual, Gabriella was wearing a blouse with puffy sleeves and a blue skirt. Outdated and prudish. The red hair band with a bow was super-gross.

"Boys like beautiful princesses, like Snow White," Gabriella said.

Isabella doubted a boy would think the gross outfit was hot, but she'd been on the receiving end of her sister's bad temper plenty of times. She kept her opinion to herself, tossing the blade of grass aside. "Let's put plastic on the yard and make a water slide with the hose," she said. "I'm gonna get Joyce."

She tried to stand, but Gabriella clamped her hand on her shoulder and held her down. "Why don't you want to be with me?"

Isabella pushed against the weight of her sister and then lay still, hoping she'd let go. "You can play, if you want. Let go."

Lightning fast, Gabriella grabbed her forearm with both hands and gave her an Indian burn. "You don't need Joyce. You have me."

"Let go. That hurts!"

Gabriella dropped her arm, rolled over, and pinned her to the ground, sitting on her stomach. "Do you love me?"

Isabella looked up at Gabriella straddling her and nodded. "Sure, you're my sister."

Strong thighs dug into her waist. Fingers wrapped around her neck and squeezed.

"Am I your best friend forever, no matter what?"

Isabella couldn't breathe. Grabbing her sister's wrists, she tried to dislodge the long fingers from her neck. "Stop it," she gasped, clawing at her with her nails.

Gabriella released the pressure and Isabella swallowed hard. "Get off me."

"Answer the question, Isabella."

"S-sure," she sputtered, "we're BFFs."

Gabriella rolled off. "Remember our tea parties? Just you and me with our special friends? That was so much fun. I wish it could always be like that."

God, again with the stupid make-believe friend. "Gabby, they weren't friends. We made them up. I stopped doing it when I was six. I don't need an imaginary friend." Isabella rubbed her sore neck and shuffled her butt across the grass. If she could scoot far enough away, she'd be able to stand before Gabriella pounced on her again.

She wasn't fast enough. Gabriella grasped her hand, holding tight. "That's because you have me. You don't need anyone else."

Isabella jerked away and stood, brushing grass off her shorts and sleeveless blouse. She desperately wanted to talk about something — anything — else.

Her sister had spent her allowance on an ugly Disney princess figurine, but she could lend Gabby money. "Let's go to the convenience store. I'll treat."

Finally, an idea Gabriella seemed into. "That's okay, I don't need money," she said. "If we go fast, Mama won't know." She skipped to the gate, spun the combination lock, and disappeared.

Isabella threw a frustrated look after her sister and glanced at the house. Gabriella was right. They'd be back before Mama knew. With a twinge of guilt, she took off through the open gate and passed her sister before they were ten houses down.

At the door of the corner store, Gabriella peeked through the window. "Good, there are lots of kids in there."

Isabella wondered why that mattered but she skipped into the store and walked to the back. From the freezer, she selected a banana Popsicle, grabbed a Coke from the fridge, and took her items to the cash register. The boy behind the counter was cute and singing along with Madonna's "Like a Virgin" playing from a radio behind him.

He gave her a wink. "Bet you know how that feels."

She felt her cheeks flush, probably bright red. He rang up her purchases, handed her a plastic bag, and waved his hand for her money.

Outside the store, kids were coming and going but Gana was gone, which meant Gabriella had left. She always ditched her. This time, Isabella was glad. She'd rather hang out with her own friends.

She was about to cross the street to Joyce's house when Gabriella popped out from behind a tree. Startled, Isabella jerked back and her sister shoved her hard, knocking her to the ground.

"Why'd you do that?" she yelled, rubbing her skinned elbow before trying to pick up the scattered change spilling from her pocket.

Gabriella laughed. "Stop being such a baby, and I'll give you some of my candy."

"You didn't get any. You spent all your allowance yesterday."

She smiled. "You don't need money to get what you want."

"You stole?" Isabella was horrified.

Gabriella held out her hand. "Come on, get up."

Isabella ignored her outstretched hand and stood on her own. "Leave me alone, I hate you. I'm going to hang out with Joyce." She stuffed the handful of change into her plastic bag.

Beside her sister, Gana whimpered. Gabriella hung her head and muttered something Isabella didn't hear. Gana barked once and tugged on Gabriella's skirt with his teeth.

Gabriella glanced at her skirt with a snort of disgust and pulled the hair band off her hair. "Let's play skully." She undid the top two buttons of her blouse with a frown. "This colour is gross."

Isabella rolled her eyes. "Why do you wear it all the time?"

Instead of answering, Gabriella said, "Come on, just one game of skully. We'll get the tarp out of the shed and set up the sprinkler so you and Joyce can play on the water slide after the game."

Isabella hesitated. "I guess..." Joyce did enjoy playing skully and it was better with more players. "Fine, I'll run over to her house and we'll meet you at the driveway." Before her sister could insist on going with her, Isabella sprinted across the street.

At Joyce's house, she jogged through the back gate and into the yard. No one was outside. The back door was open, so she stepped into the kitchen. "Joyce?" she called.

Voices were coming from upstairs. Isabella walked to the staircase and was about to yell up when she heard her name.

"It's not Isabella," Mrs. McNamara said. "It's the other one." She sounded angry, and Isabella froze at the base of the stairs.

"Grace, that's not fair." It was Joyce's dad.

Isabella was scared of him because he was a police detective. He was nice to her, but he might not be if he caught her in his house without permission.

"You're going over to their house," Mrs. McNamara yelled, "and telling Quentin to keep his psycho kid away from our daughter."

Why was Mrs. McNamara calling her a psycho? She thought her friend's mother liked her. Tears welled up in her eyes and she held her breath, straining to hear.

"Is it any wonder she has issues?" Detective McNamara asked. "She was five, Grace. Five." His voice rose to a shout. "The pervert held her in a godforsaken cabin for six months. You said you didn't want to live near them, and I agreed to transfer to Toronto Police Services. We're moving at the end of the month. That's all you get."

There was a scuffling sound but the shock over discovering a pervert had taken her sister paralyzed Isabella.

"That's right, walk away, coward," Mrs. McNamara shouted. "Where are you going, Colin, or need I ask? Over to see Megan and that bastard child of hers. Funny how her husband killed himself a month after that baby was born. Why do you think he did that?"

The answering voice was cold and scary. "Why don't you tell me?"

"Oh, I don't know," replied Mrs. McNamara in a singsong voice. "Maybe it was the baby's thick head of strawberry blond hair."

"Meaning?"

"That baby boy is the spitting image of Sam when she was born. You remember Samantha, your legitimate child?"

A door slammed, jolting Isabella into action. Heavy footsteps headed for the stairs. She sprinted through the house and out the back door. Her fingers shook and she fumbled with the gate. It wouldn't open. He would catch her. It took forever to unlatch the bolt. Before she could escape, he called her name and she spun around to face her best friend's father.

"Are you looking for Joyce?"

She swallowed hard and nodded. Maybe he didn't know she'd been in the house. His eyes drilled into hers. Could he arrest her for eavesdropping?

"I gotta go," she mumbled and wrenched open the gate.

She sprinted across the street, not watching for cars, and ran home, stopping short at the end of her driveway. Joyce and her four-year-old sister, Sam, were talking with Gabriella.

"What took you so long?" Gabriella asked when she saw her.

Isabella couldn't breathe. Mrs. McNamara thought Gabriella was a psycho. Her best friend's mother hated her because of her sister. It was so unfair. How could she visit Joyce after they moved if Mrs. McNamara hated her family? She was so excited about spending a weekend in Toronto. Everything was ruined, and it was all Gabriella's fault, again.

Her sister was speaking to her but she couldn't focus. Suddenly, little Sam was howling. Gana was growling at Joyce. Before she could move, Gabriella hit Joyce. Isabella watched in horror while her sister hurled little Sam to the ground and attacked Joyce. For the first time in her life, Isabella felt true rage.

"I hate you, you ruin everything." Isabella tackled her sister.

CHAPTER NINE

Quentin

IGNORING THE 'KEEP out when closed' sign on the door, Quentin knocked and peeked inside Isabella's bedroom.

"Can we talk?" He picked his way through discarded clothing, crumpled papers, and books scattered across the shabby pink carpet.

"I guess." She buried her tear-streaked face in her pillow and then looked up at him with eyes ringed in red.

Quentin sat on the edge of the twin bed. "Bella, are you ready to tell me what happened?"

Her jaw tightened and she looked away. "I already told you. Gabriella and I had a fight."

"The McNamara girls say it was more than a disagreement. They claim Gabriella threw Sam and punched Joyce. They told their father you tried to defend them and your sister attacked you, beating you so badly your nose bled."

"Gabriella told you what happened. It was an accident," she mumbled.

"Where did you get that cut above your eye?"

"It was an accident."

Quentin sighed. "If your sister threatened you, Isabella, you need to tell me."

"Papa, I'm tired."

It exasperated him that she wouldn't talk to him. Something happened in the driveway but he couldn't get to the truth.

He decided to drop the subject of the fight and address the other issue. "Did you go inside Joyce's house this afternoon?"

"Why?" She refused to meet his eyes.

"Did you hear Detective and Mrs. McNamara talking?"

"No."

Quentin took her hand and poured some change into her palm. "You left it in the bag. They found it at the base of their stairs, Isabella."

Her eyes opened wide.

"Detective McNamara thinks you overheard an unpleasant conversation."

"They were arguing. I left right away," she said in a small voice. "Papa, am I in trouble for going into their house without permission?"

"No, honey. Detective McNamara is concerned you heard something you didn't understand."

"I didn't hear anything," she muttered.

She was lying. He could always tell with her, but he didn't know how to encourage her to open up to him. It was so frustrating. Leaning down, he kissed her forehead. "I love you more than the moon, the sun, and all the other stars. You can tell me anything."

"I want to go to sleep, Papa."

With a sigh, Quentin tucked the blankets around his precious girl and turned out the bedside lamp.

Standing alone in the dark hallway, Quentin felt irritated and helpless. After Gabriella's abduction, they'd worked closely with a therapist but it was pointless. She claimed she didn't remember anything about those six months, and no amount of therapy broke the barrier. But she *was* obsessed with Snow White. She even sewed her clothes to resemble Snow White costumes. Quentin thought about the hideous cabin where the man had imprisoned his daughter. He thought about the police photos of the tiny princess bed in the pink cage, and bile rose in his throat. How much did she remember?

He wandered down the hallway and stood outside his eldest daughter's bedroom door. From inside, he could hear her voice. Talking to herself again. For a reason he didn't want to think about too closely, he was afraid to enter. He dropped his hand from the knob and turned away.

Nina put down her book when he entered their bedroom. "Did you check on Isabella?"

He nodded and pulled off his T-shirt and shorts, tossing them on the wing chair by the window before climbing into bed in his underwear. "Gabriella attacked those girls this afternoon."

She removed her glasses. "Isabella told you that?"

He shook his head. "No, but she was lying."

"Quentin, sisters squabble," Nina said. "If Joyce and Sam were caught in the middle, it was an accident. Sam is too young to be playing with older kids." She snorted with disgust.

"This isn't the first disagreement that ended in violence. We have to do something before someone is seriously hurt."

Nina sighed. "You're overreacting, as usual. I don't know why you're so hard on Gabriella."

She was always like this when it came to Gabriella. It was infuriating. Why would his wife not see what was right in front of her face?

"Isabella lies to protect her sister, and she does it because she's afraid." He took a deep breath to try to squash his anger. "I want Gabriella to go back to the therapist."

Nina slapped her hands on the bed. "The doctor said there's no reason to refer her. There's nothing wrong with her. It's all in your head."

He sat up and punched his pillow. "The doctor doesn't see what we do. She manipulates him. You have to back me up and stop blocking my attempts to make him understand."

"Do you want your daughter to have the ugly stigma of mental health issues? Is that what you want?"

"We don't live in medieval times."

"Easy for you to say," she retorted bitterly.

Nina didn't have to explain what she meant. She hadn't brought up *An Da Shealladh* in years. He didn't know if she still believed she had 'two sights', or whatever she called it. They didn't talk about it. Considering the handful of pills she swallowed every night, it would be surprising if she dreamed at all. If he brought up the pills, she'd bring up his drinking and he had no desire to have that fight again.

"I respect your feelings," he said instead, "but I'm speaking with the doctor."

"If you spent more time with her, she wouldn't have a reason to be jealous of Isabella."

Here Nina was right — he did spend more time with Isabella. It was... easier. Gabriella, well, she was a liar. She would outright deny being somewhere, claiming she was in her room when he saw her leaving the house. Her lies were so outlandish it was insulting, yet she refused to back down. Worse, she showed no remorse. She acted contrite, if caught red-handed, but he felt it was disingenuous.

"I should spend time with Gabriella," he admitted, "but that's not the problem. When I was in the hall a minute ago, she was talking to herself again." He rearranged his pillows. His shoulders were tight and, like most nights, he couldn't get comfortable.

Nina reached for one of her bottles and shook two tablets into her palm. "She was probably talking to Gana."

He frowned. "No, she was having a full conversation. There were two voices."

"People make up voices for their pets all the time." Nina swallowed the pills and turned off the lamp. "She's fine. Go to sleep."

So long as Nina paddled up the river of denial, clubbing him with an oar every time he tried to help their daughter, there wasn't anything he could do. Feeling powerless and out of sorts, he lay awake in the dark and listened to his wife's breathing even out.

He was drifting off to sleep when something woke him. A shuffling sound, from the hallway. His eyes grew dry while he stared through the dark.

He climbed from the bed and skulked across the room to stand with his ear pressed against the door. Silence, then a soft clicking noise against the hardwood. A dog's toenails? Reaching out, he yanked open the door.

"Gana—"

The hallway was empty, but he was sure a door latched.

He grabbed his shorts from the chair, pulled them on, and tiptoed to Gabriella's bedroom. Quietly, he nudged open the door. The street light illuminated the room through the lacy curtains. Gana studied him from the foot of her bed but Gabriella appeared to be asleep. She could have made it back to her room and be faking. Did he believe she was lurking outside his bedroom door? Yes, he did and it made the hair rise on his arms.

Returning to his room, he quietly closed the door and listened. The house was quiet. He twisted the door lock, removed his shorts, and climbed into bed.

An hour or so later, he jerked awake, certain he'd heard the door jiggle. His heart pounded in his chest and his mouth was dry. Was *he* losing his mind, too? His lower face hurt from clenching his jaw. He opened his mouth wide and tried to relax the tense muscles.

He was being ridiculous. Why would his teenage daughter be creeping outside his bedroom door?

Because, a voice whispered in his ear, *there's something wrong with her.*

He kicked away the sheet and rolled over to stare at the locked bedroom door. In the humid darkness of the late summer night, Quentin wondered how it could be true that his sixteen-year-old daughter scared the shit out of him.

CHAPTER TEN

Gabriella

"IF YOU CRY, I won't let you out to play skully." He was whispering against her cheek. "If you fight me, you know what'll happen."

Pain, excruciating pain in her bum and back. Hands pushed her against the mattress, squishing her face and driving her agonized screams into the pillow. Everything faded away.

When she drifted back, there was the stench. A horrible smell of something sizzling in the pan he kept above the fire. The sound of lips smacking while he gobbled the meat.

"Where are you?" she whimpered.

"Here," said the voice of a girl she couldn't see. "Shh, go to sleep and forget."

She lifted her head from the bed and pink bars distorted the image of the man and the girl. Firelight flickered and she saw the man and the girl together as one person with two faces.

The images battled, each one taking turns in the foreground. They both disappeared and a skeleton demon emerged. Thin, stringy hair fell in gossamer strings across the monster's shoulders. The eyes were sunken cavities and skin hung from bone, falling in dripping clumps around its feet.

"Wake up." It loped across the room toward the cage, snarling and whipping its head from side to side.

The smell of decay filled the tiny cabin, and rotting hands reached through the bars of the cage. "Eat with me," it growled. Strings of saliva swung from torn lips. "Wake up NOW!"

GABRIELLA JERKED AWAKE and found she was standing in the hallway outside her parent's bedroom door. Confused, she scurried back to her room and sat on the bed, twisting her head to the right and the left, hunting for the familiar. There, against the wall, was her dresser. Under the window was her desk. Above her was the canopy of her bed.

"A dream, just a dream." Crying, she pulled Gana against her body and buried her face in his soft fur. He whined and licked her shoulder.

Instead of fading like lacy smoke, the image of the monster remained fixed in her mind. She sat still and waited, hoping she hadn't screamed aloud. If her parents woke, they'd ask her questions she couldn't answer.

Gabriella climbed from the bed and went to her dresser, touching each of her princess figurines. She grasped Snow White and held the china doll to her chest.

"Just a dream."

Gana jumped off the bed and whimpered, tugging on her nightgown with his teeth. Crying, she closed her eyes.

A moment later, she opened her eyes, glanced at the toy in her hand, and placed it back on the dresser. "Silly girl. It was just a nasty old dream."

She smiled at Gana, plucked her diary from between the bed mattresses, and began to write.

CHAPTER ELEVEN

Two Months Later: London, Ontario

Nina

NINA SAT ALONE at the kitchen table, absently turning the pages of a photo album. Her finger paused at the picture of them building the tree house the summer Isabella turned five. After Nina took the picture, Gabriella hit her sister with a hammer, breaking Isabella's index finger.

There they were, in every photo, a middle-class family doing ordinary things. What a lie. Behind each picture was the memory of an accident. Isabella was the victim of every mishap.

"Accidents," Nina whispered to the empty house.

The phone rang. She stiffened but made no move to answer it. It rang again and then a third time and a fourth. Finally, she picked up the receiver. "LeBlanc residence."

An authoritative male voice asked, "May I speak with Mr. or Mrs. LeBlanc?"

All the saliva in her mouth dried up. "This is Nina LeBlanc."

"Mrs. LeBlanc, this is Principal Harrington. I'd like to speak with you and your husband this afternoon." It was a command.

Nina closed her eyes. A new school year and they hadn't even made it to Thanksgiving. "I can come now." Her shoulders sagged.

"I require both you and your husband this time," he said. "How's six-thirty. Yes?"

"I suppose..."

"Good. I'll see you then." The line went dead.

This was her first summons from the principal. He left most disciplinary matters to his vice-principals. What had Gabriella done this time? Maybe the principal was unaware of the multiple times the vice-principal had ordered her to his office. That was stupid. He knew. She hadn't told Quentin about every school visit. She'd told him Gabriella was doing well, which she was academically. Socially, well that was different matter. Nina wiped away her tears with the back of her hand and replaced the phone receiver.

She went upstairs and stood outside her daughter's bedroom. The room was spotless. The bed, made with military precision, looked ready for inspection, and out-of-fashion clothes hung by colour in the closet. China princesses decorated the top of the dresser. The collection disturbed Nina. Once, she'd given Gabriella a Maid Marian figurine, but her daughter wouldn't add it to her collection. If it wasn't a Grimm fairy tale character, Gabriella didn't want it.

So different her two girls were. Going into Isabella's room, she bent to pick up dirty clothes littering the floor. The bookcase was messy, and papers cluttered the adjacent desk. A diary was open to a half-completed entry for yesterday's date. Nina closed the book without reading it.

If Gabriella had kept a diary, that might be a different story. She might be able to talk herself into forcing open the tiny lock to read the words hidden inside, in the hopes of understanding what her eldest daughter was feeling. But Gabriella was far too private — *secretive* — to write her most intimate thoughts.

She trudged downstairs to the family room off the kitchen and glanced at Gana, sitting stock-still by the patio door. The dog always sat in that guard stance from the moment Gabriella left for school until she returned in the afternoon. Nina had read that Samoyeds were sociable and playful. Gana was neither and she didn't like him.

"Gana, you want a treat?" She reached for the treat container and held out a dried chicken fillet. "Treat?"

The dog ignored her. He only accepted food from Gabriella. If she was late and Nina prepared his kibble, Gana would refuse to eat until her daughter emptied the bowl and refilled it.

Nina wished she had a relative or a friend to talk to, but there was no one. She sat alone in the family room, staring at the dark television screen. Quentin would be home soon and the fighting would begin, again.

AT SIX O'CLOCK, she heard the front door and watched Quentin scowl at Gana on his way through the kitchen to the family room. He sat beside her on their shabby brown sofa and tugged his tie loose. He studied her for minute and stroked her cheek. "Have you been crying?" he asked and took her hand.

"Don't bother changing. We have to meet the principal at six-thirty."

Colour sprang into his cheeks and he dropped her hand. "Christ, what did Gabriella do now?"

The genuine disgust in his voice when he spoke their daughter's name took her aback.

"Well," he snapped, "am I expected to guess?"

"He didn't say."

Quentin glanced at his watch. "I'm tired. I don't want to go to the damn school."

Nina glared at the brick fireplace across the room. "Well, this is part of parenting."

He abruptly stood, slapped the side of his leg, and stomped to the corner bar, tripping over the edge of the braided throw carpet. "Goddamn it, I'm so fucking sick of this."

When he grabbed a glass and a bottle of whisky from the bar, Nina quietly said, "Please don't have a drink. We have to go to the school."

He snorted laughter and poured a drink. "As if a high school principal doesn't keep a bottle in his desk to strengthen his constitution."

"Certainly not when I was teaching."

He sipped his drink and studied her over the rim. "You haven't been in a classroom in decades."

You'd be surprised, she thought.

"I'm sorry. I just..." He sighed. In a single gulp, he finished his drink and picked up his suit jacket. "Maybe it's good news. Gabriella's on the honour roll. Maybe it's about scholarships."

Without responding, she followed him out to the car and they drove the four blocks to the high school in silence.

They passed their neighbour's homes and Nina fought tears. Dads were mowing their lawns, instead of sitting in the house nursing a bottle of booze. Moms were tending gardens, rather than grieving in solitude over smashed dreams. Laughing children were playing basketball in driveways, without one sibling assaulting another. Why couldn't her family be normal?

By the time they reached the school parking lot, she was crying. She got out of the car and hurried ahead of Quentin to the entrance, wiping tears from her cheeks.

Inside, their footsteps echoed through the empty hallway. The principal, who was waiting in the administrative office, was a stout, bald man with kind eyes. His grey suit was crumpled and his tie was loose. He led them into his office and gestured to the two chairs across from his cluttered desk. They sat and Nina squirmed in the uncomfortable chair like a naughty child. She gazed at her feet and avoided the principal's eyes.

He cleared his throat. "I want to begin by acknowledging the terrible ordeal Gabriella suffered in her youth." Receiving no response, he added, "Over ten years ago, wasn't it?"

"Maybe you should get to the point," Quentin said.

"Yes, well, I wanted you to be aware we aren't unsympathetic to the adversity Gabriella has overcome."

"But?" Quentin exhaled in a puff. Nina smelled whisky on his breath.

"Mrs. LeBlanc, you've visited with Gabriella's vice-principal, well, to put it bluntly, regularly."

Quentin gave her a puzzled look.

"We're again experiencing challenges," the principal continued. "Gabriella is bright, and her marks are excellent, but—"

"What has she done?" Quentin cut in.

The principal shook his head slightly. "Gabriella pulled a knife on a student."

"She did what," Quentin roared.

Nina quickly asked, "Was she provoked?"

"The other student corrected her on a subject regarding his culture — a myth, I was told. A demonic spirit called *Wendigo*."

Now Quentin was glaring at her.

"I didn't say a word to her. She must have researched the legend on her own."

Looking as if he disbelieved her, he turned back to the principal. "What did Gabriella say?"

"She said she didn't do it, has never heard of *Wendigo,* and was in the library at the time of the incident. She was very convincing." He stared at them solemnly. "When two witnesses stepped forward, she refused to say anything at all."

"Are you expelling her this time?" Nina knew the answer.

This was not the first report of aggressive behaviour, but it was the worst. Each time, Gabriella adamantly denied everything, insisting she was elsewhere when the transgression occurred.

"Nina, did you know about this behaviour?" Quentin asked.

Not knowing what to say, she remained silent.

Quentin took her hand. "You should have told me."

"Mrs. LeBlanc, you were a high school teacher, is that correct?"

With perfect clarity, Nina knew where the conversation was leading.

"Have you considered homeschooling? Gabriella is extremely intelligent. With some help, she could receive early admission to university. Our social worker thinks she'll thrive in an independent learning environment."

"My daughter won't let me teach her."

Principal Harrington ignored her. "We'll act as academic liaison," he continued, "and work with the university's admissions office to facilitate junior matriculation acceptance."

"But I—"

He avoided her eyes and continued talking. "It's best for Gabriella. I'm afraid the students here are well aware of your daughter's past. Teenagers can be cruel."

"Is she being bullied?" Nina asked.

"Your daughter is a beautiful young woman. That, plus her past... well, it makes her a target. Many of the young men's comments are sexually inappropriate."

Nina lowered her head, fighting back tears.

"Why weren't we told?" Quentin asked.

"Well..." He sighed. "We gave her the space to learn conflict resolution. Evidently, we made a mistake. The social worker recommends that Gabriella return to therapy. That is a stipulation, if we're to help you."

Quentin nodded. "We'll have our doctor make a referral."

"About me teaching her," Nina began, only to have the men dismiss her by standing.

Principal Harrington extended his hand. "We'll help you so Gabriella can achieve her academic dreams."

When they left the school, Nina felt shell-shocked, troubled by the meeting's revelations, and overwhelmed at the idea of becoming Gabriella's only teacher.

Thunder rumbled in the distance and large droplets of rain splashed against her shoes. By the time they reached the car, they were drenched. When Nina looked up, Quentin's expression was as dark and unforgiving as the heavens.

CHAPTER TWELVE

Quentin

AS USUAL, THERE was no expression in Gabriella's large eyes. Gana sat rigid and alert by her side, while she perched primly on the edge of the chair with her hands folded in her lap.

She was a stunning young woman. Even in the shapeless blue skirt and outdated blouse buttoned to her throat, Quentin could see why she attracted male attention. He could also understand why kids would be nasty. It wasn't the clothes or stiff posture. It was her off-putting and narcissistic personality. Unlike normal teenagers who would be afraid of getting in trouble and act angry or defensive, Gabriella waited passively, same as she always did when they called her in for a chat.

Quentin grasped his wife's hand. He wanted to show a unified front, but he also needed the warmth of her body beside him. "We were called to the principal's office this afternoon. You won't be returning to school."

Not breaking eye contact, Gabriella replied, "I know."

"How do you feel about that?" Nina asked.

"It's fine."

Quentin frowned at her. "Won't you miss your friends?"

"I don't like the kids at school." Her lips pinched together imperceptibly.

"Do you try to get along?" he asked.

"They call me a slut, because I'm not a virgin." There was no embarrassment or regret in the statement.

Quentin had an overpowering urge to walk out of the room. Cowardly, he knew, but he couldn't talk about what had happened in that awful cabin. He couldn't think about what that monster had done to his daughter. He squeezed his eyes shut and clenched his hands into fists.

Nina put on the *therapist* voice that Quentin hated. "Rape isn't choosing to lose your virginity."

"Can we not talk about this now," he mumbled.

Nina looked at him as if he'd lost his mind.

"That's fine," his daughter turned and smiled at him in an artificial way, "I don't remember anyway."

Instead of letting it go and addressing the matter at hand, his wife said, "Gabriella, are you sure you don't remember anything?"

Over the years, she'd asked the same question hundreds of times. Quentin was tired of it. He wanted to focus on the crisis in front of them. The high school had expelled their daughter. How much worse did things have to get before Nina would open her eyes?

"I don't remember," Gabriella replied. "Who cares? He's dead."

Quentin ran the back of his hand across his dry lips and wished he'd poured a drink before they sat down. He didn't want to dredge up the past. He didn't want to think about it at all.

His daughter had killed her abductor while he slept, bashing in his skull with a pickaxe. Based on the post-mortem results, the blood spatter, and her bloody fingerprints on the murder weapon, the evidence was conclusive. Because she was a victim of kidnapping and unlawful restraint, the coroner had ruled the death justifiable homicide.

Over the years, Quentin hadn't been able to let it go. What haunted him was the amount of rage it would take for a child to swing a weapon with sufficient force to kill a man. He'd voiced his concern to her therapist, who told him that survival instinct under duress isn't an indicator of an inherent proclivity for violence. Intellectually, he agreed. Emotionally, he couldn't shake the feeling that there was something seriously wrong with his daughter.

"Sweetie, it's not your fault," Nina said. "Sometimes, good people have to do bad things to survive."

Gabriella's expression was blank. "It doesn't bother me at all," she said. "We don't like high school." She paused. "We do want to go to university."

Quentin rolled his eyes. He hated it when she spoke like the Queen, a bad habit she'd picked up years ago. No wonder classmates picked on her. Still, he pounced on the opportunity to change the subject. "Do you know what you want to study?"

"Biochemistry."

In a dark corner of his mind, Quentin imagined campus residence but he forced himself to refocus. "Your mother's background is in math, so it'll be an excellent partnership to prepare you for your exams."

"We don't need any help. We could pass the exams today. We'll go in January."

"I don't think *you* can," Nina said. "*You* need a certain number of high school credits to get *your* diploma."

Gabriella lowered her head and muttered something under her breath that Quentin didn't catch. Gana whined and butted the edge of her leg with his snout.

When she looked up, her eyes were angry. "No! We're going in January. Gabriella is an extraordinary case," she yelled.

Well, he'd wanted her to behave like a normal teenager and here she was being disrespectful, which he figured was typical for a girl turning seventeen.

"Gabriella, don't take that tone with us and please don't speak in the third person. People don't like it." Quentin took a deep breath. "Let's refocus. There are rules, you know."

Her eyes were hard purple marbles in her face. "Rules were made to be broken," she said. "Gabriella was bullied and left to defend herself."

"You brought a weapon to school." Quentin snorted in disgust. "You drew a knife on a fellow student. You're lucky the police aren't involved."

Her mouth twisted into an ugly sneer. "The boy was going to rape Gabriella. The school wouldn't help."

Nina's eyes widened. "Sweetie, come on, that's not true."

"He grabbed Gabriella's tit and said he was going to fuck her up the ass."

Looking as if Gabriella had slapped her, Nina exhaled in a gasp. Quentin had never heard his prudish daughter utter such vulgar words. Startled and unable to process what she'd said, a fight or flight sensation rolled over him. He stood and went to the bar in the family room.

He sloshed whisky into a tumbler with a trembling hand. Lies, always lies, with Gabriella. It was impossible to know what was true anymore. He snagged the bottle from the bar and took it with him to the living room.

"Why didn't you tell the principal, instead of claiming you weren't there?" Putting the bottle on the table, he sat on the sofa beside Nina. He downed his second drink and poured three fingers of whisky into the empty glass.

"They always take the boys' side. The male teachers laugh about it."

Quentin couldn't fucking believe it. "Gabriella, you're lying — again," he shouted, almost knocking over the bottle of whisky when he jumped up and stomped his foot.

Immediately, Gana stood and dropped his tail. The fur on his back bristled and his lips pulled away from his teeth. He growled low and deep.

Quentin held the dog's eyes, clenching his free hand into a fist. "You're making it up." He concentrated on keeping his tone calm. "You want to go to university in January and have decided to deflect blame so you can manipulate the school into giving you what you want. Do you think we're stupid? "

"Quentin, sit down." Nina pulled on his hand. "You weren't there. You don't know what happened."

Refusing to sit, he snatched his hand away and glared incredulously at his wife. "Are you kidding me? Are you going to let her lie to our faces? Can't you see she's doing this to get what she wants?"

Gabriella stood. "Like the Rolling Stones say, Papa, you can't always get what you want." She smiled coldly. "You know the rest." She brushed passed him with a satisfied smile, Gana following at her heels.

Quentin watched her go up the stairs. Nina was still on the couch, fighting back tears and shaking her head.

He picked up the whisky bottle from the coffee table and filled his empty glass, the Stones' lyrics running through his head. Staring out the front window, he muttered, "Practised at the art of deception."

CHAPTER THIRTEEN

Isabella

FROM THE BEDROOM doorway, her sister asked, "Why do you think they named you Isabella?" As usual, she hadn't bothered to knock before opening the door.

Refusing to look up from her desk, Isabella ignored her and continued to doodle on a piece of paper.

Papa was yelling, and she expected her sister to be upset. Instead, Gabby sounded fine. If Papa screamed at *her*, Isabella would be in tears.

After Gana trotted into the room, Gabriella stepped in and closed the door. Isabella didn't like her sister and the dog in her bedroom with the door closed.

"You replaced me," Gabriella remarked.

"What? That's not true."

"Then why did they give you such a similar name to mine when you were born the day I was taken?"

Isabella shrugged. "Parents are weird. Our names rhyme, that's probably why."

"You could be right."

Okay, something was up. Gabby *never* agreed with her.

"You're so lucky," Gabriella said. "It'll be easy for you in high school."

You're wrong there, Isabella thought. Kids were always after her to tell them all the gross details about Gabriella's abduction. Now she'd be the girl with the expelled older sister, and there would be no end to the rumours and gossip. High school would most definitely suck.

She kept doodling, hoping that ignoring Gabriella would make her go away.

"Everyone loves you," Gabriella went on. "You're perfect."

The conversation was making Isabella nervous. Horrible things happened when her sister was jealous.

"I'm not perfect," she said quickly, keeping her back to her sister. "You're beautiful and I'm not. Plus I suck at school compared to you."

Gabriella had snuck up behind her and was gazing down at her doodles. "Papa loves you," she whispered in her ear, "and he doesn't like me."

Isabella swallowed hard. "That's not true. Um... I should do my homework."

Ignoring her, Gabriella stroked her arm. "Sometimes, I wish you weren't here. Do you ever feel that way about me?"

All the time, Isabella thought. "I gotta do my homework now." She prayed to God to make Gabriella leave.

"Homework won't take you long," her sister said. "Things come easy to you, especially writing." She reached toward the desk and Isabella grabbed her journal.

She held the diary close to her body. "Gabby, lots of people write. It's not special."

Her sister shook her head. "I hate writing. Sometimes I have to read the same paragraph four times before it makes any sense."

Isabella rolled her eyes. "Whatever, I've seen you writing in that book you hide between your mattresses. Besides, your English grades are the bomb."

"There isn't a book between my mattresses, and I don't do the English assignments. My friend does."

Her sister didn't have any friends, but if she argued, Gabriella would go postal.

"I don't get why you keep a diary," Gabriella continued. "Aren't you worried people will read it?"

Well I am now, Isabella thought. She didn't say anything.

"Don't you write all the thoughts in your head in your diary?" Gabriella asked.

Isabella shrugged.

"What things wouldn't you write?"

Isabella desperately wished her parents would come upstairs. "I dunno. If I wanted to do something wrong, I guess."

"If you lied?"

Isabella nodded.

"What if you killed something?"

"I'd never kill anything," Isabella said.

"You might *think* about killing someone," Gabriella argued. "Thinking about something isn't the same as doing it."

"I'd never even think about killing anyone," Isabella insisted.

Gabriella smiled and headed for the bedroom door. With her hand resting on the doorknob, she said, "You'd kill someone if you had to."

"Never. I would never," Isabella said, her voice rising a little.

Gabriella shook her head. "That's why I could never keep a diary." She opened the door, and she and the dog disappeared down the hall.

CHAPTER FOURTEEN

New Year's Day, 1992: London, Ontario

Quentin

QUENTIN PAUSED WHILE shovelling the driveway to watch his daughters up in the tree house. Although he knew they used it as a private getaway when their three-bedroom home felt crowded, he was surprised to see them together now because he'd noticed Isabella was avoiding her sister. At times, it was like she was hiding from her. He didn't know what to make of it, but promised himself he'd keep a closer eye on them when they were together.

Chewing on the corner of his lip, he stood still and silent, watching their shadows move. The night before, Isabella had told him she needed to talk to him about something important. He'd had too much to drink during their New Year's Eve celebration to focus and could only remember telling her they'd talk later. Had she said it was about her sister? He'd hurry with the shovelling and call her in for that chat.

While he pushed snow into little banks along the side of the long driveway, he felt more optimistic than usual. In part, his cheerful mood was because of the morning shots to cure his hangover, but the real reason for his improved state of mind was that Gabriella had received junior matriculation acceptance to the University of Western Ontario for the winter term. Although his suggestion of moving her into residence appalled Nina, he was confident he could spin a case for it by September.

For a change, money wasn't an issue. Nina's grandmother had left Gabriella a generous trust fund that she'd inherit on her eighteenth birthday. For the rest of her life, his daughter would be financially independent and free to make her own decisions.

He put his weight behind the shovel and thought about his youngest daughter. He sensed Isabella was unhappy. Maybe it wasn't fair, but he blamed Gabriella. Moving her into the dorms was the perfect solution for everyone. She would learn to love the freedom.

Quentin was at the road, chipping at hard snow the plow had pushed against the base of the driveway during the night's storm, when he heard something. He stopped and listened. A few yards over, the two Shannon boys were in their front yard making a snowman. The head was too large, and they couldn't stack it on the body. It was almost to the top, when it slipped out of their mittens and plopped onto the ground.

Quentin dropped the shovel on the snow and walked over. "Having problems?"

Jeremy, the oldest, looked frustrated. "Can't get the head on."

"It might be too high. Let's see what we can do."

The ball was heavy with well-packed snow. By the time it was perched snugly on top of the chubby middle, Quentin was laughing hard and sweating.

Mrs. Shannon exited the front door with her two-year-old in her arms. "Cool snowman," she said.

"Mom, you're so lame." Jeremy giggled.

She laughed good-naturedly. "Am I too *lame* to make hot chocolate?" she asked. "Quentin, you want to come in? I could be coaxed into adding a bit of the Irish to our cocoa to celebrate the New Year." She stood aside, letting the kids rush up to the door.

"A bit of the old Irish would be welcome, me wee lass," he said.

"Colin McNamara is in town and dropped by." Quentin detected a slight blush creep into her cheeks.

Far be it for me to judge, he thought. He brushed snow off his jacket and joined Megan.

AN HOUR LATER, Quentin returned to his shovel. He was having trouble keeping his balance, and his gait was wobbly. He didn't want to finish shovelling. He had a bet riding on the Washington Huskies and wanted to watch the Rose Bowl game.

Once he'd cleared enough snow to move the car, he hustled to the top of the driveway and noticed Gabriella was still in the tree house with the late afternoon sun at her back. She was standing with her hands on the cedar railing, gazing at the snow drifting against the tree trunk. Without taking his eyes from her, Quentin stowed the shovel beside the house and opened the back gate. He followed his daughter's steady gaze down to the ground.

Something was lying in the snow. Gana? Quentin blinked and took a hesitant step through the gate. No, Gana was standing beside the ladder. He looked up at the tree house. Gabriella held his eyes. Where was Isabella?

Quentin's eyes shifted back to the object on the ground. "No," he moaned. "No, please, no."

The snow cushioned the fall. The snow cushioned the fall. The phrase screamed through his head when he charged toward the tree.

He became aware of screaming. From a place far away, in the functioning part of his brain, he recognized that the animal wails were rising from his own throat.

From behind him, the back door slammed. Nina. He couldn't understand her words.

Quentin burrowed his hands under the snow and pulled Isabella into his arms. Everything was foggy, moving in slow motion. He was aware of Nina kneeling in the snow beside him. Colin was at his other side. Quentin struggled to process what the man was saying.

"...911, Megan! Quentin, let me see... I'm a cop. I can help her."

Quentin reached for Nina, needing to hold her. His stomach convulsed and he vomited in the snow between them. The stench of whisky wafted into his face. He retched again, empting his stomach of the booze.

Nina was screaming and pawing at Colin's back, trying to get to Isabella. Her face was wild and contorted. "Don't touch her! Leave her alone."

"Quentin, help me." Colin covered Isabella with a blanket and tried to push Nina off his back.

Quentin crawled toward Nina, trying to grab her hands. Her arms flailed wildly. She struck him hard across the face.

Megan ran into the yard dragging a blanket. Tears streamed down her face. She threw the blanket around Nina, hugging her tight in an effort to trap her arms against her sides. "Please, Nina. Let Colin help her. The paramedics are coming. Quentin, I can't hold her. Help me."

A horn blared at the intersection and the warbling screech of sirens was deafening. Quentin grabbed Nina, dragging her off Colin's back. She was like a wild animal, bucking against his efforts to hold her.

Paramedics rushed into the backyard. From the corner of his eye, Quentin watched an EMT tear the paper from a syringe. He jammed the needle into the rubber stopper of a small vial and stuck the syringe into Nina's upper arm.

He let go and crawled toward his daughter. More paramedics were attending her. Colin took his arm, trying to help him to his feet.

"Come on," Colin said, "let them do their job."

Fire trucks and police cruisers were on the scene. People crowded around his daughter and his wife. He couldn't see Isabella. He couldn't reach Nina.

Kneeling helpless and paralyzed in the snow, he watched Colin shove Gana away from the ladder and climb up to the tree house. Quentin raised his eyes. Gabriella was still standing at the railing, staring at the pandemonium on the ground.

Gabriella...

The world started to blur. Quentin swayed and pitched forward, falling face first into the snow. Voices faded and black dots waltzed in front of his eyes. They merged until nothing remained but the cold, wet snow against his feverish face and then darkness.

PART 2: Till Death Do Us Part

CHAPTER FIFTEEN

June 2015: Toronto, Ontario

Sam

CARRYING GROCERY BAGS, Sam McNamara opened the door to her loft and turned off the alarm with a sigh of pleasure. She'd been home in Toronto for over a month, but every time she walked through the door, she still felt a little thrill of happiness.

Her last case had led her to a southern Ontario town where she'd exposed a commune as a cult and had met — then Ontario Provincial Police inspector, now boyfriend and business partner — Reece Hash. She and Reece had spent the past two months in Australia hunting for the escaped cult leader. Their prey had turned to predator, but authorities now *presumed* the psychopath was dead. No one in Canada or Australia — probably the world — grieved Mussani's death. Without a body, some people still speculated. Sam and Reece didn't. They'd witnessed the monster fall from the Bunda Cliffs during their final showdown.

Although Reece had made the decision to leave the OPP and temporarily turn to vigilante justice, he was now struggling to reconcile the cloudy ethics. Sam didn't get it. It wasn't as if you could change the past. The less you talked about nasty stuff, the easier it was to forget about it. Her miserable mother was a stellar example of what not to do if you didn't want to stay trapped in the past.

Beside her, Brandy whined and Sam reached into her pocket for a treat. Her dog gobbled it down with a tail wag of thanks and a big doggy grin, which made Sam smile.

"You're spoiled," she said. "This is what happens whenever you stay with Roger."

She set her groceries on the pristine countertop in her gourmet kitchen and unclipped Brandy's leash. The Golden Retriever went straight to her water dish. That sounded like a good idea. Well, not water. Being careful not to smudge the stainless steel, she opened the fridge and poured a glass of wine.

"What do you think, Brandy? Now he's joined our PI firm, Reece just needs to sink his teeth into a new case and he'll be fine."

Brandy wagged her tail in agreement.

Sam kicked off her canvas sneakers, took off her Blue Jays baseball cap, and ran her fingers through her short, strawberry blond hair. She winced. She'd spent the morning at the gym on the weights and her arms were burning, but she was proud of herself. She'd broken her weight limit, benching one hundred and twenty pounds, which was fifteen pounds over her body weight. At this rate, she was going to win the bet she and Reece had. It was all in fun, but competitive to the bone, Sam planned to exceed her lift goals, her running speed and her endurance level. She was going to whip Reece's ass.

Her thousand-square-foot loft was cool and quiet. The hemlock hardwood gleamed in the afternoon sun streaming from the floor-to-ceiling windows on the south wall. Frosted glass walls, framed with stainless steel, divided the bathroom that shared the north wall with the kitchen. Across the top of the kitchen and bath was the loft, which contained a master suite. A six-foot partial wall, constructed from the same glass and steel design, surrounded the upper loft. The rest of the open-concept main floor had an eighteen-foot ceiling and was wide open, with strategically placed modern furniture.

Revelling in her sleek, minimalistic oasis, Sam climbed the ladder staircase to her bedroom loft, stepped into the room and stared in horror.

"Oh boy, you've got to be kidding me."

Everywhere she looked, there were boxes with crap spilling out of them. Frowning, she dashed into the ensuite bathroom and shouted every profanity she knew. Plastic bags filled with junk littered the vanity's marble top, obscuring the double-trough sink. The glass-enclosed rain shower was the only clear floor space.

She collapsed onto the king-sized bed and groaned. This morning, Reece had told her he was picking up a *few* things from the storage locker he'd rented after selling his Uthisca house. This was not a few things. She was afraid to open the barn doors to the walk-in closet and laundry room. That nicely organized area would provide Reece with loads of space to squirrel away his treasures.

The front door opened. The hoarder was back. Sam marched down the stairs, ready to confront him.

Reece was shoving boxes and large plastic containers through the doorway. It was like a clown car. They just kept coming.

"What the fuck?"

He looked up. "What's wrong?"

She waved her hands around the room. "Reece, what is this?"

"I told you I was bringing over some of the important stuff."

"You've got to be kidding." She'd hate to see what he considered *unimportant*.

He scooped her up in a bear hug, and her feet dangled off the floor. "Geez, relax. I'll put it away."

She slapped at him until he dropped her. "Where are we going to put it all?" She eyed a large, ugly wooden thing he was shoving into a nook beside the door. "What the hell is that?"

"Cool, eh? It's perfect there. I rescued it from a demolition site in Uthisca last year. It's an antique church altar."

"And the Gods haven't accepted you as a sacrifice yet?"

He laughed. "It'll be great for keys and knick-knacks."

Sam loathed knick-knacks. "It doesn't match anything."

"Sure it does." He looked around. "The Aztec carpet."

"The living room carpet does not resemble something you'd wrap a virgin sacrifice in."

"Don't worry about it. Everything will work together, promise." He carried a gigantic box into the kitchen. "I meant to tell you this morning that a guy I went to university with back in the day invited us for dinner on Tuesday. I couldn't come up with an excuse."

She shrugged. "Sounds good, free food. Who is it?"

"A lawyer, Derek Martina."

Sam poured a second glass of wine and offered Reece a beer, which he accepted with a smile. "Married?" she asked.

"Yeah, her name is Gabriella. She attended Western University with us." He began to unpack the box, pulling out a horrifying number of gadgets.

"You've met her?" Sam frowned when weird kitchen stuff littered her gorgeous Carrara marble countertops. They were a decoration. She didn't *use* them.

In answer to her question about knowing the wife, Reece shook his head. "Not really. After he made junior partner in a law firm, Derek took a leave of absence to do an MBA. He'd be in his early fifties now, about fifteen years older than I am. Seems to me his wife is younger than I am."

"My age?" she asked.

He shook his head with a smile. "They have a son around nineteen, but she was pregnant when they married. I believe she was eighteen. I remember she dropped out of school." He went to the front door and lugged in another big box.

Enough. "There isn't space for any of that stuff." Sam put her hands on her hips.

"Lots of room, since you don't cook and never bought anything. Most of the appliances need to be on the prep counters."

"I didn't buy the stuff because I hate clutter," she argued.

Reece hoisted an enormous Kitchenaid mixer from a box. "It matches the stainless steel backsplash. Blends right in."

"But..."

Reece tucked a revolting bright orange Dutch oven onto the back burner of her precious Viking, six-burner gas stove. It was a piece of art to admire, not to touch.

When he unpacked a large, stainless steel contraption to hang pots, she felt like tackling him to the ground.

"Oh boy, I can't watch this." She needed to get out before she lost her shit. "I'm going to the office."

"Now my stuff is here, I'll make a fantastic dinner." The man was beaming.

"Everything will be put away, right?"

"You bet." He kissed her on the cheek. "Don't worry."

Oh, she worried. She looked around her once uncluttered, minimalistic home and sighed. Why didn't anyone tell her when a woman invited a man to live with her, he brought crap?

CHAPTER SIXTEEN

Gabriella

GABRIELLA DIDN'T WANT to have lunch with her boss. Jack Belinski was in the hallway guffawing over some joke, probably his own, while the head of HR fluttered around him like an egret devouring insects off a hippo's hide.

Arranging her face into proper expressions and acting engaged over lunch would be exhausting. *Get through the day,* she told herself. With a sigh, she rose from her seat and trudged to Jack's side.

"I was waiting," he said.

She resisted the urge to smack the sneer off his face. Instead, she forced her mouth into a submissive smile. She'd understood early on, if she wanted to keep her demeaning job, kowtowing to her idiotic boss was vital. Everyone acted like simpering peons around him. It took all her talent at subterfuge to hide the intensity of her dislike for this man.

"I'm assuming you've managed to sort out my dance card for this afternoon," he said.

A surge of annoyance engulfed her and it scared her. As far back as she could remember, she'd black out and lose portions of time when enraged. After the high school had expelled her, her father had insisted she return to therapy. In the doctor's opinion, the memory lapses weren't serious. He'd called them a 'unique defence mechanism', a psychological strategy created by her unconscious mind to protect her from unacceptable impulses and negative social sanctions. Gabriella would grow out of it, he'd said.

It troubled her that the blackouts still happened, but she was proficient at hiding the episodes. The therapist had taught her to say a phrase to help defuse her anger. She'd chosen, *breathe, it's just your life.* The problem was she often remembered saying it, but couldn't recall subsequent events. Still, the habit helped to centre her, which was better than attacking whomever or whatever had triggered her fury.

On their way to the building exit, they passed their twenty-five-year-old receptionist's desk. Jack cast an admiring glance and flashed a smile he probably considered sexy. Gabriella's stomach rolled.

Katrina looked up from her work and returned the smile in an awkward way. "Off to lunch, Mr. Belinski? Hi, Gabriella."

Jack leaned against the edge of her desk. "Yup, my executive assistant here has been with us for three months."

Actually, he'd hired her six months ago. It was a record for her. Her employment usually ended within a couple of months of hire. The complaint was always the same — she didn't fit in, and people didn't like her.

Jack asked Katrina, "How long have you been here?"

"Five months, sir."

"Ah, excellent. We'll celebrate with drinks." He winked at Katrina and spoke to Gabriella over his shoulder. "Set up drinks for next week."

Katrina didn't look pleased by his invitation. Since the receptionist was the only person in the office who was nice to her, Gabriella decided to return the favour by forgetting to book those drinks.

Her boss strutted to the elevator, and Gabriella trailed along behind, glaring daggers at the back of his balding head. When they reached the top floor, where he parked his Porsche Carrera GT, she suppressed the urge to shove him over the railing to the street below.

Getting into his car was a chore requiring gymnastic skills. Worse, she had to flick a grungy wad of tissue off the seat. Used paper cups, napkins, and gaudy brochures for ostentatious houses littered every available surface inside the car. Men were animals.

"After lunch, grab a garbage bag and clean out the car." Jack instructed, racing out of the garage and taking the tight corners at wheel-screeching speed.

Gabriella stared out the window, telling herself she could survive lunch. It was one hour. When you couldn't see the end of the day, you had to get through an hour at a time.

She relaxed when they pulled into the restaurant parking lot. It was a small Japanese restaurant with a reputation for cheap prices and quick service. Thank God, it may not even be a full hour of torture.

Inside, garish photos of sushi decorated the laminated placemats, and the table settings included paper napkins and disposable chopsticks. Dark drapes hid the windows and ugly track lighting hung precariously from the grimy acoustic tile ceiling, bathing the tables in dim light. How typical of Jack to treat her to lunch at the cheapest place he could find.

After the geisha-costumed server took their order, Jack leaned back and stared at her. "You've been with us for three months. What do you think?"

She wanted to reply that the women were toxic gossips, the men were pompous chauvinists, and it was sickening that every employee treated Jack as if he'd descended from heaven on an angel's back. It was a revolting feudal hierarchy, and she hated every second of the working day.

But she couldn't say any of that. "Your company is leading-edge." She smiled and took a dainty sip from her cup of green tea.

"Your role is to make my life easier," he said, "and we have problems."

Gabriella placed her teacup on the table. "Really? What kind of problems, sir?"

"Lack of stability." Jack frowned at her hands. "You're distracted."

She was arranging her chopsticks and placemat just so, a habit she'd adopted years ago. She folded her hands and did her best to look engaged.

Jack nodded. "Take my expense reports. Half are perfect, including the foreign currency. Our accountant couldn't do a better job. The other half are full of stupid mistakes. I also want to talk about document preparation. When you joined the firm, you edited a Request for Proposal and exhibited impressive writing skills. Last week, you proofed a RFP as if you suffered from dyslexia."

She did have dyslexia, which was why she hadn't wanted to proofread the proposal. He was lying. Last week was the first time he'd asked her to edit anything. Considering what a nightmare it was to struggle through the hideous task, she'd have remembered. Math was her strong suit, and his accusation about the expense reports wasn't true. "No one in Finance has brought any errors to my attention."

He snorted. "Let's face it, you don't accept criticism. That's another issue, Gabriella. You were refined and professional in your interview but your personality has changed, I suppose because you've grown comfortable. At times, you're immature and opinionated."

The arrival of their food saved her from having to respond. Wondering how well they'd washed the lettuce, she picked at the salad with her chopsticks.

Jack didn't touch his food. "People have told me you spend a lot of time with Mark."

"You've experienced computer problems." She placed a piece of cucumber into her mouth and chewed, trying to remain calm. Outside of computer-related questions, she never spoke with the IT manager.

Jack rolled his eyes and started eating his meal. "Look, you're married, right?"

"That's correct." Silently, she counted to ten.

"Your husband is a lawyer and has some lofty political aspirations. He's running for office, right?"

"Yes."

"And you have children?"

"Yes."

He looked up from gobbling his teriyaki salmon and waved a chopstick at her. "Your husband would be humiliated over his wife flirting in the workplace."

She wanted to shove one of her chopsticks into his eye. She put them down and straightened them so they lined up with the edge of her placemat.

She never flirted. She disliked men, and even tolerating her husband was a chore.

Jack studied her over the rim of his teacup. "If things are going to work out, you need to get a grip." He finished his salmon and put his elbows on the table. "You ever watch *Mad Men*?"

The sudden change of subject confused her. "You mean the TV show about advertising on Madison Avenue?"

He nodded. "That's the one. The secretaries were on the ball back then. They had it together." He raised his hand, as if expecting her to protest. "I don't mean the way women were objectified," he clarified. "All I'm saying is the CEO's secretary wouldn't embarrass her boss by flirting with male colleagues."

Black rage swirled around her, distorting her vision while a familiar feeling of detachment engulfed her.

Jack was still talking. "As my secretary, you're a reflection on me. Conduct yourself professionally." He keyed in the PIN for his credit card, handed the machine to the geisha, and passed Gabriella the receipt.

She stood and followed him to the door. Jack glared out the restaurant door. It was pouring rain. "Damn, my jacket is suede. The rain's going to ruin it."

Still struggling for control and desperate to ditch Jack for at least a minute, she held out her hand. "I'll get the car."

"Hey, good girl. That's what I mean about making my life easier." He tossed her the keys.

Water filled her shoes while she trudged through the downpour. "Breathe," she whispered to the rain, "it's just your life."

CHAPTER SEVENTEEN

Gabriella

"WHAT'S FOR DINNER?" her husband asked.

She always felt disappointed when Derek came home. It was hard to breathe when he was in the house. She had to watch every word she said and struggle to hide her simmering resentment.

Ignoring him, Gabriella spoke to the dog. "Want a treat?" She held out a slice of carrot.

"I hope it's not salad, I had that for lunch." Derek peered over her shoulder at the vegetables on the kitchen island.

"Hamburgers." She braced herself for the inevitable interrogation. Her husband was... particular.

"Homemade?"

"No, frozen Waygu burgers."

He sighed. "Come on, Gabby." He snatched the box to examine the ingredients.

Derek was a food Nazi, scrutinizing everything's nutritional value. Fighting to keep her tone neutral, Gabriella asked, "What do *you* want to eat?"

He slapped his hand against the countertop. "Stop making me out to be an asshole. It's reasonable for a man to expect his wife to make a homemade dinner. Are you going gourmet with hot dogs for Reece Hash tomorrow night?"

Ignoring the sarcasm in his tone, she replied with the name of the first dish that came to mind, "Beef Bourguignon."

She didn't recall her husband mentioning a dinner party. If she challenged him, he'd accuse her of selective memory again. It was a constant battle with them. Derek would make some claim and she'd argue it never happened.

"Let's hope they aren't preachy vegans. Reece was a carnivore in university, but you never know these days."

Gabriella hated dinner parties. Small talk was torture and being around people made her uncomfortable. One day without someone judging her and finding her wanting would be heaven.

Maybe it was some sort of business affair and she could hide in the kitchen, playing servant. "What does Reece do?"

"He was an OPP Inspector in some hick detachment in southern Ontario. His girlfriend, Sam McNamara, is a PI. Even *you* must have heard about her. You read newspapers, don't you?"

A woman was coming. Derek would expect her to entertain the girlfriend. "I know about her involvement with those deaths in Uthisca over the winter."

McNamara... why did that name sound familiar?

She recalled living near a family with that last name when she was a teenager. Her sister was friends with one of the girls, but they'd moved. Was Sam the name of the younger sister? The last thing Gabriella wanted was someone popping up from her past. She took a deep breath and tried to calm down. It wasn't an unusual name. She was overreacting, again.

But it was an intimate gathering with just one other couple. All dinner parties were torture, but hosting large events provided her with a legitimate reason to disappear into the kitchen without raising suspicion. This one promised to be a disaster. What was she going to talk to a PI about? She was on the verge of a panic attack, and the woman wasn't even in her house yet.

Derek took a carrot from the chopping board and nibbled on it. "Reece left the OPP and joined her PI practice after that cult mess. He was a real player in university, always had a herd of hot girls hanging around him. Smart guy, too." He shook his head. "I'll be interest to see why he threw it all away for this woman."

It sounded like Reece and Derek would have lots of catching up to do. If she was lucky, the girlfriend was one of those clinging women who were mesmerized by their partner's past. Gabriella again visualized herself hiding in the kitchen. "Were you good friends at university?"

"No, I'm fifteen years older. Ivey students stay together anyway. You know that."

It was too bad he hadn't respected that rule when she was seventeen and attending her second semester at Western over the summer. Her drunkard father had abandoned the family that April, and there was Derek. He was so good-looking, confident, and successful. Everything her father wasn't.

Derek had strolled over to her table at the quad, holding two coffees. "We're going to share an extraordinary experience," he'd said, handing her a coffee. "We're going to fall in love."

Within a year, she was pregnant and he asked her to marry him and follow him to Toronto. It was a chance for a fresh start, and she'd believed he was a man who would keep her safe. She'd been wrong.

She looked over at her husband, lounging against the kitchen counter. The grey in his hair made him distinguished, and the lines in his face gave him character instead of aging him. He was fit and handsome and a lying cheater.

"If you weren't friends, why invite him?" she asked.

Derek crossed his arms against his chest. "For Christ sake, I told you last night. His girlfriend's stepfather is one of Canada's richest men. We need support if I'm going to make it to Ottawa. Do you listen to anything I say?"

He hadn't told her anything about this last night. She understood he was preoccupied with the campaign, but this was gaslighting, a sick psychological game of twisting the truth so she'd doubt her sanity.

Instead of arguing, she continued to chop vegetables for the side salad, watching from the corner of her eye when he went to the dining room bar and poured a drink. He knew how she felt about alcohol, especially drinking through the week. It didn't matter to Derek. He never considered her feelings.

Twenty years of marriage and it was still all about Derek. She tried, but nothing was good enough for him. In some ways, their union made sense. If she'd married less of a narcissist, the man would have realized how odd she was and left years ago. It was a terrible feeling to know you have to settle because you aren't worth loving. Her father had taught her that awful truth. He hadn't left her mother. Gabriella knew in her heart that he'd left her.

She was a heartbeat away from a total meltdown. Weird dreams were interrupting her sleep, and exhaustion escalated her bitter anger over how miserable her life was.

After her father deserted them, Gabriella had tried to talk to her mother about the strange dreams. Mama claimed she'd inherited *An Da Shealladh*, warning her that the dreams were the 'two sights'. It was frustrating trying to explain the nightmares. She was in the dreams, acting in a way she wouldn't and doing things she'd never do. Mama was wrong because the dreams weren't *prophecies*. None came true. They were terrifying movie reels of her performing in someone else's life.

Thanks to her loser father abandoning them, her broken-hearted mother was insane when she died. The breast cancer she'd refused to treat was part of the issue, but Gabriella worried that mental illness had been Mama's real problem. She'd read it could be hereditary.

Again, thanks to her selfish, alcoholic dad, she'd looked after her mother alone while cancer rotted her body. The end had been awful. She couldn't remember her mother's final hours. Apparently, she'd called 911, but she didn't remember being home at the time.

The doctors were judgmental and suspicious. They had even accused her of overdosing her mother on morphine. She was eighteen and was the best caregiver she could be. It was so unfair. Was it any wonder she'd lost large chunks of her memory? All she could remember now was the anger and a deep-rooted fear of doctors, particularly mental health professionals.

Derek snapped his fingers in front of her face. "You're zoning out again. You have that absent stare." He flicked her jacket. "Why didn't you change out of your suit?"

"I just got home. Jack…" She paused while slicing the hamburger buns. "Ah… Jack wanted me to sort his divorce papers."

Was that the reason she was late? The Prima Donna had taken her for lunch. She'd walked through the rain to get his car in the restaurant parking lot, which was how she'd ruined her shoes. The rest of the afternoon was gone.

"I had lunch with Jack today," she told him. "I want to quit."

He studied her. "I know he's an asshole but I plan to ask him to donate to my campaign. You need to stick it out. Besides, your salary is pretty good, and we need the money right now."

"Jack told me he likes *Mad Men*, because the 'gals' get it."

Derek laughed. "No way."

She sighed. "Yes."

"Well, that gives you a point of reference, I guess. An insulting one, I give you that."

"I hate the job and loathe Jack."

"Don't be so intense," Derek said. "It's just a paycheque. Jack's a joke and his divorce is the talk of the courthouse. He's screwing the hell out of his wife financially."

He gulped his scotch, smacked his lips, and leaned across the large island. "I heard the hydro was turned off in the house because his wife couldn't pay the bill." He shrugged. "I get it since she never worked a day in her life."

"She did raise their two kids."

He shrugged again. "They don't live at home."

"So it's okay to leave your wife of thirty-five years destitute?"

"I didn't say that. You're twisting everything around. I'm the one who said he's an asshole." He marched to the bar and poured another drink. "You better be careful around those divorce papers," he cautioned with a sly look. "Opposing counsel has the right to subpoena you."

"I signed a non-disclosure and confidentiality agreement."

                                          L.E. Fraser

He laughed. "So? That's with the company, not with Jack personally. Come on, I'm curious. It's not easy to hide money, tell me how he's doing it."

Every night it was the same thing. All Derek wanted to talk about was Jack Belinski and his reputed net worth. Her husband didn't care how miserable she was. He didn't even bother to pretend any more. If she hadn't quit school, she wouldn't be in this mess. Gabriella turned to the sink, fighting back rage.

"I hear he's as rich as Bill Gates is," Derek said.

"Jack isn't even close to being in the same league as Bill Gates."

"You know," he said, "if you told me where the money was, I could extend a professional courtesy to his wife's lawyer by suggesting a few places to look." He put his arm around her shoulder and whispered in her ear. "Or I could speak to Jack about being fair. You know, scare him into doing the right thing."

Well, now she understood why Derek was pestering her about her boss's private life. Her husband wasn't above a bit of blackmail to secure funding for his political dreams. Jack was rich, stupid, and arrogant. An ideal target for Derek.

She squirmed under his touch. "That's unethical."

"I guess I shouldn't expect a secretary to understand anything about business."

Pure hate flowed over her, causing her to throw down the tea towel she was using to dry the knife. "I'm an executive assistant."

"Executive assistant, secretary, whatever."

She clenched her fingers around the handle of the butcher knife. "Fine, if you think my job is so unimportant, you won't care if I quit."

He pinched the bridge of his nose. "Why do you always have to be so dramatic?" He threw up his hands in exasperation. "I can't have a conversation with you. You're impossible."

He stomped out of the kitchen. A moment later, a door slammed. She waited a couple of minutes before creeping down the hallway to listen at the closed office door.

"I'm sick to death of trying to deal with her. She's going to ruin my chances of advancing in the party."

There was a long pause. When Derek spoke again, his voice was husky and slow. "Well, that does sound interesting, Counsellor. Are we talking about a small landing patch or are you smooth as a dolphin?"

Another pause, shorter this time, followed by her husband's voice. "Baby, I have no problem landing my plane in your hanger." His sickening giggle made Gabriella's skin crawl. "Yeah, give me an hour. I'll grab a shower and be right over."

A longer pause, followed by Derek's throaty laugh. "Yeah, I'll make it nice and clean for you. Get that red lipstick I like and meet me at the door in your stilettos, painted lips and nothing else."

Another whore. Gabriella wasn't surprised, but finding out for sure was infuriating. She'd moved him into the spare bedroom after the last affair. At least she possessed the self-respect to do that, but Derek took it as permission to pick up women whenever the notion moved him. Choking back angry tears, she returned to the kitchen.

How had her life become this sham? All she ever felt was fury. All she did was wait helplessly for something to change and hope things would improve. She closed her eyes, and a feeling of impending doom rose until she was suffocating. She stood still, whispering to herself.

A few moments passed before her eyes snapped open. "Cheating fucker." She tugged at the scarf around her neck and went to her room to change her clothes.

CHAPTER EIGHTEEN

Derek

DEREK PATTED A generous amount of Hugo Boss cologne on his shaved cheeks and neck, rubbing the remainder on the shaft of his penis. He carefully finished manscaping and stood at the mirror to admire how much bigger the trunk looked without the bush. Lacing his fingers behind his head, he thrust his hips and his penis waved at the mirror.

Naked, he left the bathroom and headed down the hall to his bedroom. Gabriella was talking in the kitchen. He paused. She must be using their new polycom because he could hear the person on the other end.

"I hate my job," Gabriella said.

"Then quit," came the reply.

"You know I can't do that."

A clear sigh. The audio quality was amazing. The state-of-the-art technology was living up to its reputation, so paying the extra had been the right decision.

"Life isn't all about money," the voice said. "You're a golden handcuff slave. Didn't you learn anything from me? You're not happy so stop being such a wimp and do something about it. At times like these, you have to be selfish. Enough is enough and I'm going to deal with it for you. If you don't get what you need, take it by force."

Lovely advice to give a wife and mother, Derek thought. Gabriella must have called her sister to whine about him again. Right, he was a jerk for expecting his wife to hold down a job. He made a good living but Gabriella loved to spend money. Who did her sister think was going to pay for the expensive house, cars, and redecorating? Derek went into his bedroom and slammed the door shut.

While slipping into jeans and a black Armani T-shirt, his stomach growled. The aroma of grilling meat seeped under the bedroom door. It was a dick move to complain about the burgers. His wife was a talented chef and a master on the grill. They might be frozen patties but she'd turn them gourmet. Was that bacon, too? His stomach rumbled again. He'd eaten a light lunch, which put him below his caloric intake for the day. Bacon was a treat. Maybe he'd apologize and grab a burger with her. Depending on how it went, he might cancel his date with Sonia.

With a final admiring glance in the mirror, he went downstairs.

In the kitchen, Gabriella was eating over the sink like an animal. Wearing a shabby blue Adidas sweat suit, with her hair in a messy ponytail, she was stuffing food in her mouth and barely chewing before jamming in more.

"Classy." He grabbed a burger from the plate beside her. "About earlier," he began.

He paused while reaching for the ketchup and scrutinized her. Blood was rolling down her hand and dribbling off her chin. He lifted the bun off his own burger and poked the patty. The meat was raw in the centre.

Again with the zoning out and not paying attention to a simple task. Why couldn't she focus? This was a perfect example of why he felt like a reluctant babysitter around his wife. "You didn't cook these. Stop eating it."

She continued shoving burger in her mouth.

"Did you hear me?" He struggled to keep his voice calm. "You didn't cook the meat. Stop eating it."

Still no reply or acknowledgement.

He tossed his burger in the trash. He couldn't deal with her. Let her get sick. She was a big girl and it was her decision. "I have to go back to work." He flinched at the lie.

No comment. Tomorrow, she'd claim he never told her. He scrubbed his fingers with a napkin, his stomach rolling at the sight of blood on the white linen. Knowing it was immature but not caring, he added, "Don't wait up." The idea of his frigid wife waiting up to have sex was comical.

Finally, she looked up from her meal and met his eyes. "The bolt on the shed isn't working. The door keeps blowing open in the wind. Gabriella wants you to fix it before you leave."

Placing his hands flat on the counter and taking a steadying breath, he forced himself to remain calm. "I've asked you hundreds of times not to talk about yourself using the third person."

She rolled her eyes. "What about the shed?"

"It's dark. I'll do it tomorrow."

"Well, it's up to you." She reached for a second burger. "You've got expensive stuff in there."

She never ate seconds, and why the fuck would she eat raw meat? Something was definitely off. Maybe she was PMS-ing.

He peered out the window to the back of the yard. It was dusk, but there was enough light to see the outline of the red shed. One door was open. She *was* right; he kept expensive tools inside. "I'll check the shed on my way to the car."

She smiled through a mouthful of bacon cheeseburger.

Derek paused in the process of putting on his leather jacket. She was always peculiar but this was extra weird, even for her. "What's the matter with you?"

"Nothing. What's the matter with you?" There was a carnivorous gleam in her eyes.

Did she know where he was going? Maybe not but she probably suspected. He grabbed his keys and left before she confronted him.

He crossed the dark backyard to the shed, grabbed half of the double door, and reached up to check the latch. A bit of fiddling and it clicked into place. His fingers felt wet, but it was too dark to see. Sighing, he pulled the other side closed, lifted the red door and jiggled it so he could get the sliding bolt to align with the latch and lock.

Worried about smearing whatever was on his hand on his clothes, Derek went to the porch light. Red paint covered the fingers on his right hand. He'd painted the shed on Sunday. Red pigments took over a week to cure properly, but it shouldn't still be wet to the touch. Maybe there was something wrong with the chemical compound. He lifted his hand and sniffed. The coppery odour made his skin crawl.

"Shit." He ran into the house and held his hand under the faucet. "Gabriella."

She wasn't in the kitchen.

"I cut myself on the fucking shed door." Water ran from his fingers in a pale pink stream, but he couldn't see a gash.

"How bad is the cut?"

Derek jumped. He hadn't heard her enter the room.

She looked at his hand. "I don't see anything."

"Well, did you see the blood?"

She arched her eyebrow. "No." She scanned the sink and examined his hand again. "There's nothing wrong with you."

He opened a drawer and rummaged around the contents.

"What are you doing?" she asked.

"Looking for a damn flashlight so I can check the shed."

"We don't have a flashlight up here. Nicholas took them downstairs to work on his computer."

Frustrated, he slammed the drawer shut. "Well, isn't that great. Why do you let the kids take whatever they want?"

"Maybe you clipped your finger," she said. "Isabella always says water makes it look as if there's more blood."

"I don't give a fuck what your sister says. Isabella this and Isabella that," he mocked. "I'm sick of it."

"There's a tiny cut on your index finger, right there." Gabriella twisted his finger to the side.

Derek saw a slice of broken skin. He remembered getting a paper cut at the office. It must have reopened. It was a lot of blood for a small laceration, but she was right. Mixing water with blood made it look worse. It wasn't bleeding now and didn't hurt.

He was opening the back door when her voice caused him to turn. "Off to the office?" She was shaking a bottle of nail polish.

Was that a smirk or was he paranoid? If she knew what he was up to, she should realize it was her fault. When she wasn't hiding in the kitchen avoiding him and the kids, she was fussing with her fingernails. She spent hours filing and polishing them and spent a fortune on hand cream. It wasn't as if she used her hands to pleasure him. Before they'd moved to separate rooms, she'd suffered through sex with stiff immobility, sucking in her breath with a cringe every time he touched her. It made him feel like an incompetent lover. Eventually it felt like rape and he gave up.

Without another word, he marched out the door. He might be better at dealing with her mood swings and weird behaviour if she was sexual. If they were intimate, maybe things would be different. Celibacy wasn't natural for men. Her rejection made him insecure, which was why he sought other women. Still, he felt guilty. Everything about his wife made him feel like shit.

Derek was pulling into Sonia's parking garage when something else hit him. When he'd returned to the house after checking the shed, his wife was wearing her usual prissy housecoat with her hair loose and held off her face by a hideous hair band that looked like a costume accessory.

Every day, her behaviour became more bizarre. He'd courted her because of her beauty and youth. Now she was ruining his life. He was going to have to do something about his ice queen.

CHAPTER NINETEEN

Gabriella

SHE WAS DRAWING a skully board on the driveway, taking extra time to ensure the box lines were straight and the numbers resembled calligraphy. In the middle, she drew a beautifully rendered skull.

From behind her, she heard a voice and turned to see Joyce McNamara and her four-year-old sister, Sam.

"Hi Gabby, is Isabella home?" Joyce asked, avoiding her eyes by shifting her backpack off her shoulder and holding it by the strap.

Her sister's friend didn't like her. The feeling was mutual. Joyce was always trying to take Isabella away from her. "We're going to play skully." She glared at Joyce, intending to make it clear she wasn't welcome to play.

"Ah... the buttons on your blouse are undone." Joyce's face flushed with colour and she tugged her bathing suit robe across her flat chest.

Gabriella glanced down to admire the way her breasts pushed against the top of her bra to display her cleavage.

"Jealous?" she asked smugly.

Joyce looked confused as well as embarrassed. "Ah, no, it's just... never mind. Is Isabella inside?"

With a shrug, Gabriella put the chalk on the driveway beside the skully board and brushed off her hands.

A moment later, Isabella charged down the sidewalk like a bat out of hell. She sprinted across the street, narrowly avoiding a car that leaned on the horn.

"Hey," Joyce said, waving. "We were walking home from the pool. Wanna come over to my house? We can make cookies."

She was doing it again, trying to steal Isabella. No one would ever take Isabella from her. Gabriella pushed Joyce aside and faced her sister. "What took you so long? I was waiting."

Isabella didn't answer. She was staring at her as if she'd never laid eyes on her before.

Gabriella was about to show off the great job she did on the skully board when she noticed Joyce's disgusting little sister sitting on it. Right in the middle, ruining the beautiful skull. The brat was scribbling all over the drawing she'd sketched with painstaking accuracy.

"Get off." She grabbed the fucker by the hair and dragged her onto the grass. "Don't touch, you little shit."

Joyce ran over to kneel beside Sam who was crying. "What's wrong with you?" she yelled. "She's little. Leave her alone, you psycho."

Gana growled low in his throat. Gabriella was lifting her hand to give the 'attack' command when she remembered she had to protect the dog. That was the promise she'd made. If Gana bit either of the McNamara bitches, their father would have her dog put down. More anger roared over her.

"She was just colouring on it." Joyce helped Sam to her feet and picked up both their backpacks. "Skully is a stupid game that no one even plays anymore." She crossed the driveway to stand beside Isabella. "I'm telling my dad."

Gabriella grabbed Joyce's shoulder, roughly spun her around, and punched her in the face. The backpacks dropped from Joyce's hand. Her eyes flew open wide and filled with tears.

Sam bit Gabriella's calf. With a bellow of pain, she picked the four-year-old up by her arm and hurled her. Sam hit the driveway hard and burst into tears.

"I hate you, you ruin everything!" Isabella tackled her to the ground.

Wrestling on the driveway, she twisted Isabella beneath her. "You have to love Gabriella." She punched Isabella in the face, satisfied to see the skin above her eye crack open and blood pour from her nose. She hit her again, swatting at Joyce who was hanging on her back, scratching her neck and pulling her hair.

Filled with blinding rage, Gabriella stumbled off her sister and advanced on Joyce.

"Fucking bitch," she snarled. "You'll never take Isabella away from Gabriella."

Joyce grabbed Sam's hand and the girls ran away.

"You aren't my sister," Isabella moaned.

Gabriella knelt and whispered into her ear, "If you tell, you know what'll happen."

Standing, she brushed off her skirt and went into the house, leaving Isabella crying and bleeding at the end of the driveway.

GABRIELLA WOKE WITH a gasp, expecting to be in her childhood bedroom. Her nightshirt was drenched in sweat, and her neck stung from Joyce's scratches.

"It never happened," she whispered. "I would never do that."

But it felt so real. It felt like a memory of something that happened yesterday. Her heart was pounding with adrenaline, and she was experiencing a fading sense of rage.

Sitting in her bed, she ran her fingers through her long hair and winced. She must have pulled her hair during the dream because the side of her head hurt. Leaning over, she switched on the bedside table lamp and took long, deep breaths.

It was just a dream. She'd researched dreams and had a fundamental understanding of the science. She needed to calm down and approach it on an intellectual level. Never having been creative, Gabriella knew she did better with the analytical side of a problem. That was why she'd chosen to study biochemistry. Black and white made sense to her. She hated reading fiction, finding the storylines nonsensical. She loathed movies. Some people might consider cooking creative, but it wasn't. Cooking was scientific. Perfect measurements of the right ingredients dictated the results. It was chemistry.

She scrambled out of bed and lurched to her desk. *Okay,* she thought, *that was the first inconsistency.* In real life, she'd never be able to draw a skull or create calligraphy-type numbers. Sitting at the desk, she opened her laptop and typed out what she recalled from the dream. She wasn't going to save the document and didn't care about the multiple mistakes she made. Typing was easier than writing, but organizing the letters was still a problem.

What did she know about the science of dreams? Speaking aloud, she murmured, "People only use a fraction of their brain's capacity when awake." She tapped her fingers against the desk. "When sleeping," she continued aloud, "the brain's untapped potential simultaneously creates and understands the dream world. It's your subconscious motivated by emotion."

Chewing on the corner of her lip, she realized she'd gone to sleep anxious over Tuesday's upcoming dinner party and worried Sam McNamara was from her past.

Dreaming of brutally attacking a four-year-old child was because of her fear over someone discovering what happened to her as a child. That and the fact she didn't want to have dinner with Derek's friend. She'd created this awful false memory out of fear and anxiety.

Someone finding out about the abduction terrified her, but even if it turned out the woman was her childhood neighbour, the family had moved when Sam was young. She wouldn't know what had happened. Gabriella relaxed. It was a stupid dream. As if she'd ever be out in public with her breasts hanging out like a gutter slut. Ridiculous. She closed the Word program, without saving her document, and put away the laptop.

Derek's Sam McNamara couldn't be the same little girl who lived down the street from her childhood home in London. Fate couldn't be that cruel.

When she climbed into bed, the only thing nagging at her was that she did forget things.

She was dozing off when she jerked awake, recalling the sensation of falling when Isabella tackled her to the ground. The sense of falling snaps you awake from a dream. Yet... that didn't happen.

The dream had continued. Like a memory.

CHAPTER TWENTY

Sam

"THEY LIVE IN Rosedale?" Sam asked.

"North in the Moore Park area." With a heavy sigh, Reece turned off Mt. Pleasant Road. "I wish I'd thought up an excuse. There's a documentary on the Discovery Channel I wanted to watch tonight."

"You can watch it on demand or download it," she said.

Reece was clean-shaven and wore a hint of aftershave. His sky-blue eyes shimmered in the twilight. From her position in the passenger seat, his dark eyelashes looked an inch long. Under his black T-shirt, his muscles bunched, and the one rogue tooth of his otherwise straight white teeth was showing. He was cringing.

"I don't like Derek Martina," he said. "He was an asshole in university, not to mention pushy and arrogant."

Reece was always worried about hurting people's feelings, and Sam wasn't surprised he'd agreed to have dinner with someone he disliked. "I heard he's being groomed by the Liberal caucus and plans to run for the Toronto Central riding," she said.

His lip curled into a sneer. "That's the rumour. McBride is stepping down from his seat. His wife has health issues, so Derek will try to take the Parliament seat in the by-election."

"Running for MP is expensive. Does Derek have independent wealth?"

He glanced at her. "Not that I'm aware."

Raising funds to run for office took guts. Derek needed well-connected friends and support in the caucus but also people to contribute campaign money. That explained the out-of-the-blue invitation. Derek was fundraising. Great. Wasting a perfectly good Tuesday night with a pontificating lawyer-slash-politician-slash-asshole wasn't a pleasant proposition.

Sam gazed out the window at the passing houses. "I hope his wife's nice. I bet I'll be stuck with her all night. What's her name again?"

"Gabriella."

"What does she do for a living?" She hoped it was something interesting.

"Executive assistant to an advertising CEO."

Oh boy, that sounded boring. "Any kids?"

"Yes," he said dolefully.

Reece wasn't a fan of other people's kids. Sam laughed. "Little kids who will be hanging around insisting we communicate with them, or big kids who will use the dinner party as an excuse to ignore curfew?"

"Teenagers." Reece grinned. "If we're lucky, they'll be off getting into mischief."

He slowed down to peer at the house numbers. "Why don't people make their house numbers bigger or better lit?"

"It's the one with the lights on, and the house numbers all shiny and reflective by the front door." She winked at him.

He grunted and pulled into the driveway of a large white two-and-a-half-storey Dutch colonial with dormer windows on the top floor.

They hadn't even made it up the slate path to the black front door before a dramatic voice exclaimed, "Reece, my man."

Snatching Reece's hand from Sam's grip, Derek gave it a vigorous pump. She noted that Derek placed his hand firmly on top, forcing Reece's into the submissive lower position.

Before Reece could introduce her, Derek pounced, draping a cashmere-encased arm around her shoulders. "And who have we here?" His condescension was as overpowering as his cologne.

Sam squirmed out of his grip and offered her hand. Entirely for her own amusement, she twisted her hand up to force his below and caught the flicker of surprise and annoyance on his face.

"Look at the grip on this one." He detached his hand. "Those are some scars. What did you do to yourself?"

She hoped he was too stupid to realize how rude his question was. "Happened when I dragged Incubus' last victim out of the fire."

"Ah yes, lone woman takes down serial killer. Two years ago, wasn't it?" He walloped Reece on the back. "It's good to see you, old friend. Let's get this party started."

Derek waved them into the living room. "Gabriella, come meet my good friend."

Sam sat beside Reece on a loveseat and gazed around the room. Nestled in a nook adjacent to the fireplace was a gorgeous black grand piano. Strategically placed family photos in sterling silver frames decorated the top. Beneath a stunning Persian area carpet, dark hardwood floors gleamed. Waterford crystal lamps dazzled on cherry wood tables, and beautiful modern art was displayed just so. There were birthday cards on the pink marble fireplace mantel and a carved book landscape sculpture that Sam was sure was an original Guy Laramée.

The decor was creative and original, but the room was giving her a strange vibe. It was cold, artificial, *too* perfect.

Derek was speaking again. "Sam, I suppose becoming a PI is a natural transition after dismissal from the police force. How do you like it?" His tone was conversational, his expression neutral.

Sam was stunned.

"Sam resigned from the force," Reece said. "She's writing her PhD thesis, in addition to being Toronto's top private eye."

That wasn't true. She fell into PI work after Incubus murdered her sister. She was an accidental PI, and Reece knew that. She wasn't sure she liked the job, which was why she was finishing her PhD.

Derek raised his eyebrows. "What are you doing your PhD in?" Before she could open her mouth, he waved his hand. "No, let me guess." He tapped his index finger against his lips. "Something gals like, I bet."

Sam didn't bother masking her dislike. "Psychology."

"Well, that might be useful in your line of work." Derek turned to Reece. "Do you remember that gal at Western who hung around the criminology students? Man, was she hot. She took psychology." Derek's gaze shifted to the doorway. "Ah, here's the lady of the house now."

Gabriella was beautiful. Her dark hair hung in shiny waves down her back. Beneath stunning eyebrows, her large eyes were a shade of blue that looked violet. She was tall and boasted a great figure. She resembled a fashion model posing for a photo shoot with her perfectly tailored white silk dress, flawless makeup, and neutral expression. Breathtaking women didn't intimidate Sam, but she was always curious why they put so much effort into their appearance. What a waste of time.

"The old ball and chain. She's not much to look at but she can cook." Derek winked at Reece and turned to his wife. "Speaking of food, where are the drinks and snacks?"

Before Gabriella could respond, a lanky young man sauntered into the room.

"I need some dollars," he told his mother. "Where's your purse?"

Sam expected his parents to correct the bad attitude and leaned back to watch the show.

"In the bedroom." Gabriella's words, spoken without inflection, matched her vague expression.

"So go get it maybe?"

Wearing skin-tight jeans and a long-sleeve T-shirt, the teenager was tall and thin with long, greasy black hair. He sported an eyebrow piercing, a snakebite on his lower lip, a septum nose ring that reminded Sam of a bull, and a black scaffold piercing in his right ear. His neck was tattooed. He probably thought it was hip. It resembled prison ink to Sam. Except for a complexion problem and puffy dark circles ringing his bloodshot eyes, he was good-looking in a musician/bad boy way. He looked stoned to Sam.

"This is our son, Nicholas. Nick, this is Reece, an old friend of mine from Western."

Nicholas tilted his head in their direction without acknowledging either of them verbally. One hand twitched at his side while his eyes roamed wild, never settling on one spot.

"Well," Nicholas's tone dripped with disdain, "do you see me standing here?" He snapped his fingers in front of his mother's face.

Gabriella didn't respond to her son's rudeness, but she also didn't back away from his aggressive stance.

"Going to pick up some babes with your buddies?" Derek grinned at Reece.

Sam doubted that. Nicholas looked as if he hadn't showered in a week. The more she studied him, the more she believed he had a drug problem.

"Not if I don't get some dollars." Nicholas leaned into his mother's face. "What's your deal, old lady?"

"Your mother is in her own world." Derek rolled his eyes at Sam and Reece, as if they agreed with him. He pulled his wallet from his pants' back pocket, removed some bills, and held the money out to his son.

Unbelievable, Sam thought.

"Don't do anything I wouldn't do." Derek chuckled.

Nicholas snatched the cash, nodded his chin at Sam and Reece, and left the house.

There was still no expression on Gabriella's face. "Please excuse me. I have something on the stove."

"Sure, you ladies go and gossip." Derek stared at Sam, his meaning clear.

Happy to ditch Derek, Sam stood. "Is that okay with you, Gabriella?"

"It's fine with her," Derek answered. "Let me get you that drink, Reece." He threw a dismissive glance Sam's way. "Gabby has wine in the other room."

"It's fine if you join me." Gabriella's posture suggested the opposite. The intensity of her stare, coupled with her creepy lack of expression, made Sam uncomfortable.

It felt as if Gabriella recognized her and wasn't pleased to see her. Sam didn't recall meeting the woman before. Considering Gabriella's stunning looks, she was sure she'd remember. Curious.

Once in the kitchen, Sam took in the impressive space. "Oh boy, you must be a serious chef."

"I enjoy cooking."

"Have we met?" Sam asked.

"Why would you ask that?"

Sam shrugged, confused by the alarm etched across the other woman's face. "I thought you recognized me."

"No."

A large white dog sat beside the kitchen island. He stood, walked over to Gabriella, and sat at her feet.

"Look at you. Aren't you gorgeous," Sam said and the animal allowed her to stroke its head. "I love dogs," she told Gabriella. "Samoyed, right? What's his name?"

"Ganawenim, I call him Gana. I've had him since childhood."

What? The woman had to be in her late thirties.

"Ganawenim is Ojibway," Gabriella muttered, adjusting the heat on the large commercial stove.

"Do you mean you've had the *breed* since childhood? Don't Samoyeds originate in Russia?"

"The name," Gabriella murmured, "means protector." A tiny muscle twitched at the edge of her eye.

The woman was agitated, and Sam couldn't figure out why. Maybe she was embarrassed over her son's awful behaviour. That made sense.

Silence stretched out. Reaching for a new topic of conversation, Sam turned to admire the fridge. "Wow, glass doors. I guess you have to keep your fridge clean." Her smile felt unnatural.

Gabriella stirred something on the stove. "Yes."

Sam gazed at the glass-fronted kitchen cupboards. The room felt staged for a magazine shoot. Everything about the house and the woman who lived in it was too perfect. It reminded her of *The Stepford Wives.*

If her son's crappy behaviour caused Gabriella's discomfort, it would be best to address the elephant in the room. "Reece tells me you have three children," Sam said. "Is Nicholas your eldest?"

"Yes."

Gabriella didn't apologize for her son's appalling behaviour or make any comment about her other two children.

"Did you attend Western with Reece and Derek?" Sam asked.

"I went to Western."

That was the end of that line of conversation, apparently.

"Reece tells me you work as an executive assistant in an ad agency."

Gabriella uncovered an elaborate multilayer cake and a bowl of icing. "I was fired."

"Oh." Sam felt embarrassed. "Um... when?"

Gabriella iced the cake in quick little strokes. "Security escorted me out this morning." She reached into the fridge and removed a pastry bag. "I was fired yesterday afternoon." Pink rosettes materialized around the base of the cake.

"They fired you without telling you? That's awful."

Gabriella moved the cake in a small circle so she could assess the sides. "It doesn't matter."

"You have a lovely home," Sam tried. "Dinner smells wonderful. Your husband is a lucky man."

Gabriella was in the process of removing dishes from the oven when she stopped short, closed her eyes and stood still, muttering under her breath. The dog barked once and stepped back.

When she looked at Sam again, she was furious. "Derek has a whore downtown." Disgust laced her voice, but she wore a frightening smile. "Gabriella is the lucky one."

Weird. Weird. Weird. Sam had no idea how to interact with this odd woman. Gabriella returned to her preparations, and Sam edged toward the door to the living room.

When she reached the doorway, her host looked up and removed her apron. "We're ready to eat," she said politely.

CHAPTER TWENTY-ONE

Reece

REECE BACKED DOWN the driveway too fast and slammed on the brakes to avoid smashing into a passing car. "Well... the food was amazing," he ventured.

Sam burst out laughing. "Who could eat? I've never been more uncomfortable. Gabriella told me her employer fired her today. Security walked her out without any explanation. Why in God's name would she host a dinner party?"

"Is that what that was? I thought it was a campaign fundraiser." He shook his head in disgust.

Sam was still laughing, but he could tell she was unsettled. "You okay?" He stopped at a light and studied her.

She rubbed her hands across her face. "Honestly, no. That was the worst night I've ever spent. What's wrong with that family? Did you notice how Gabriella talks in the third person? I hate it when people do that in jest, but she was doing it for real. Oh, and she told me Derek is having an affair but that's okay because it means 'Gabriella is lucky'. Seriously, there's something wrong with both of them."

At the next stop light, Reece reached over and did up her seatbelt. Ordinarily she was obsessive about wearing seatbelts. Her dad, a police detective,

 L.E. Fraser

had died in a car crash. The accident was why she'd left school and joined the Toronto Police Services. She'd hated being a cop, and he knew she wasn't fond of her current profession either. Part of the reason he'd agreed to join her firm was to offer her the option of leaving at some point. She'd make a better therapist. *A no-nonsense one*, he thought with a grin.

"Did you hear the way Derek talked to his wife?" Sam asked. "What a jackass. That's why I never got married."

Reece knew that wasn't true. Her parents hadn't enjoyed a happy union. Her mother was dead, apparently. Her only sibling, an older sister, was Incubus' second victim. That was the extent of his knowledge of her past. Reece didn't even know her parents' first names.

He wished she'd talk to him about her past, but Sam was a pragmatic *do it and be done with it* type of person who never wanted to discuss personal history. He was the polar opposite. Reece believed self-help required head-on analysis of things that hurt or disappointed you. That meant talking about it to process the pain. Pretending it never happened was emotionally stunting and robbed people of the opportunity to heal.

"Well," he said in discomfort, "it's unfair to judge marriage as a whole based on tonight."

At thirty-three, Reece wanted to get married. Five years ago, his fiancée had died of cancer. Recognizing he needed help to deal with Sarah's death, he'd found a therapist who taught him recovery tools. Slowly, his life became more than going through the motions, but he didn't believe he'd ever find anyone else to love. Then he met Sam. Sam's ambition was part of the barrier, but it was more than that. Something from her past haunted her. He wanted her to let him in so he could help her work through her feelings.

"What's up with that kid?" Sam asked. "Gabriella must be medicated to live in that house. Hey, that would explain her creepy zombie-like behaviour."

Reece turned into a Tim Hortons drive-through. After ordering coffee, he parked in the lot. "They were married when she was eighteen, so Derek's about fifteen years older. Maybe the age difference has something to do with their dynamics."

"You told me that, but it didn't register that Derek was over thirty and lusted after a teenager." Sam's eyes filled with disgust. "She wasn't old enough to make an informed decision. It must be a parent-child relationship. That would explain the patronizing tone he uses when he speaks to her."

He heard her mutter *pig* under her breath. "That doesn't explain why he treated you the same way," Reece said. "He's a chauvinist. Why would a woman allow her husband to speak to her like that?"

Sam shrugged. "No idea. She made some unflattering comments of her own."

"Really? I didn't hear her defend herself once."

"Well, she did. To me, at least. They're both weird. Birds of a feather, I guess."

"I can't picture her being a politician's wife. She's..." Reece couldn't come up with a suitable word to describe the woman. Gabriella's beauty took your breath away, but her personality was something else entirely.

"Weird is the word you're looking for." She laughed. "When I was helping her clear the table, I managed to get her to tell me she studied four semesters of biochemistry. God, talking to that woman was like pulling teeth. Maybe she's weird because she has a super high IQ." She took the lid off her coffee to blow on it. "Why is Tim Hortons coffee always too hot?"

Reece felt old. His lower back was throbbing and a tension headache tugged at his right temple. Derek had spent the evening trying to force him to agree to speak with Sam's stepfather about contributing to his campaign.

"He invited us because he wants Harvey to contribute to his campaign," he admitted. "He brought it up when you were in the kitchen with Gabriella. I told him flat out he had to talk to you because I've never met the man."

She was unperturbed and smiled. "He didn't ask outright, but he skirted the issue." She laughed. "Every time he tried to discuss campaign funds, I changed the subject. Your pal didn't like me much."

"Geez, we'll have to break up if Derek doesn't approve."

"Besides," Sam continued, "I'm used to people using me to try to get to my stepfather's money."

"You know, I'd like to meet the man someday."

"Maybe," she replied. "I don't know him well. My mother married him after I left home."

They sipped their coffee in silence and watched the lights of the passing cars.

"I didn't like the dog," Sam said.

Reece was surprised. "You love dogs."

She shrugged. "Not that one."

"Why not?"

"It acted like a service animal and never left her side once. Usually, dogs have personality. That one didn't. It was creepy."

Reece stared out the windshield. It was after midnight and traffic was still heavy. He missed Uthisca. He'd enjoyed running the OPP detachment because he hated cities. Correction, he disliked the people who lived in cities. He didn't understand why they were always running from place to place like rats in a maze. He didn't belong in Toronto, he knew, but he was in love with Sam, a downtown girl through and through.

It would help if he had some friends in the city. It wasn't that he didn't like Sam's friends, but he'd prefer to have a few of his own. He wasn't desperate enough to pick Derek Martina.

"Is Derek what Canadian politics has come to?" he muttered.

Sam shuddered. "Let's hope not. At least we don't have to see them again. In a few days this will be funny."

"I'll block it from my memory." He started the car.

"Let's go and hug our normal dog." Sam reached for his hand. "All that *Stepford Wives* bullshit makes me feel naughty." She wiggled her eyebrows at him. "Come be my sex slave, you subservient male."

Reece gunned the engine. "I wonder if my ex-OPP rank will garner any favours if we're stopped for speeding."

CHAPTER TWENTY-TWO

Derek

"MELISSA? MELISSA COULD you *please* come in here," Derek asked for the third time.

His assistant tapped on the door and entered his office. Timid as a mouse, she hovered by the door, wringing her hands together and avoiding his eyes. Derek sighed in irritation. His assistant's lack of initiative and cowering mannerisms annoyed the fuck out of him. What was the point of paying an assistant when she wouldn't do anything helpful?

Once he arrived at the office for a day packed with meetings, he realized he didn't have his phone. The day had started with Gabriella in one of her delightful moods, and, in his desperation to escape, he'd left his cell in the charger.

He asked Melissa to nip over to his house and grab it. Nick was heading out to Montreal with friends, was out of bed for a change, and would have handed over the phone. His house was a twenty-minute drive. But no, Melissa complained she was an 'administrative' assistant, not a 'personal' assistant. It wasn't her job. Bullshit! His firm paid her parking so her car was available in case he needed her to run over to the courthouse. According to Melissa, that was different. That was a professional task whereas helping out her boss by getting his cell wasn't.

　　　　　　　　　　　　　　　　　

He then asked Nick to swing by his office with the phone, but he refused. They were taking the 401 east to Montreal, and his son didn't want to ask his buddy to drive downtown. No amount of begging, bribing, or threats would make Nick change his mind. Was it too much to expect one person to show a bit of respect? He paid his assistant's salary, and he was paying for Nick's trip. His bad mood was one degree from boiling over.

"Melissa, where's your computer?" he snapped. "I want to dictate some notes."

"It's four-thirty, Mr. Martina," she mumbled.

He scowled at her. "Are we on government time? Do you have something more important to do?" He was satisfied to see her blush in embarrassment.

"You told me to remind you to pick up your sister-in-law at the airport."

"Damn it," he yelled. "The last thing I want to do is hee-haw to the bloody airport in rush hour traffic. Did you check to see if the flight was on time?"

"You didn't say which flight, sir."

"I told you it was Air Canada arriving at Pearson. Christ, take some initiative, you're supposed to be a legal assistant."

Her blush rose to her hairline. "I need the flight number or the city of origin."

"West Coast, Vancouver. I don't have the flight number."

She paused and Derek stared at her with what he hoped was an intimidating expression. If she told him checking a flight arrival also wasn't in her job description, he'd fire her on the spot.

"I'll see what I can find, sir."

She was probably going to call Human Resources to whine. He resisted the urge to march over and slam the door shut.

Why were all the women in his life so damn difficult? Derek sat at his desk brooding about Gabriella. He'd entertained the notion of divorce on more than one occasion, but the child and spousal support the judge would force him to pay would cripple him. He'd had to take a second mortgage on their house to fund his campaign, because he'd maxed out their line of credit for the down payment on his girlfriend's condo.

Nicholas was nineteen and their daughter was sixteen, but their youngest, Kevin, was thirteen. Unless Gabriella agreed to sell the house, which she wouldn't do when she found out how much he owed on the property, the court would allow her to reside in the matrimonial home with the three children. He'd be mortgage-poor without the benefit of living in the house.

The nasty truth was that he was broke and barely keeping the creditors at bay. There was only one option. Drastic, for sure, and it would take finesse and great acting skill, but Derek was confident he could pull it off. After all, politics was all about acting and misdirection.

His law partner, Marty, popped his head in the doorway. "Got a minute?"

"No, I have to drive to Pearson airport."

"You're in for a long drive, my friend. There's an accident on the Gardiner westbound. It'll be easier to go north to the 401. Who are you picking up?" he asked.

"My sister-in-law." He reached behind his chair for his suit jacket. "She's coming for a two-week visit."

Marty was frowning. "I don't recall Gabriella mentioning family. Don't they get along?"

"Not all families live in each other's back pockets like yours," Derek retorted.

"You should have asked her to use Toronto Island airport." Marty looked confused. "Doesn't Gabriella want to pick her up?"

Not that it was any of his business, but Derek replied, "My wife's car is in the shop." He took a small mirror from his pocket and checked his hair.

"I need to go over a few things. Why don't you have the corporate car service pick her up?"

Derek had spent all fucking day trapped in partner meetings. What else could Marty have to talk about? He took a deep breath and suppressed his frustration. "What did you need?"

"One thing is I want to know how it went with Pietre's stepdaughter last night," Marty said.

"Not as well as I hoped," Derek admitted. "Reece is pussy-whipped. He said if I wanted an introduction to Pietre, I'd have to ask McNamara."

"Well, did you speak with her about it?"

"Every time I tried to swing the conversation to politics, she interrupted and changed the subject. She's a real ball-buster."

Marty sat on one of the white suede chairs in front of Derek's monstrous glass desk. "She's a private eye, right?"

Derek nodded, wondering what was taking Melissa so damn long with the flight info.

"What if we throw some work her way and try to bridge a relationship?"

It wasn't a bad idea. He glanced at his watch and opened his office door. "Melissa? Any day now."

"There aren't any Vancouver Air Canada flights arriving at six o'clock," she said.

Fuck, how could this day get any worse? he thought.

"I checked international, and there's a six o'clock Air Canada flight arriving from LAX."

"That must be it." Derek leaned over and checked Melissa's screen. "Gabriella said West Coast. It never occurred to me she was talking about the US. I assumed it was Vancouver."

Marty had followed and was hovering beside him, crowding into Melissa's cubicle. "You don't know where your sister-in-law lives?"

His partner's nosiness always bugged the shit out of him. Years ago, Marty had appointed himself the patriarch of the firm, sticking his nose where it didn't belong.

"No, I've never met her." He hoped his tone was professional. "It's Air Canada from the West Coast at six o'clock so it must be that one."

Marty and Melissa exchanged a bemused look. "If you've never met her," Marty argued, "how are you going to recognize her? Do you have her cell number?"

He studied his partner. "Mary, I don't recall asking you to be my father. I'll see her outside arrivals. Stop worrying about it."

"Melissa," Marty said, "you better call Gabriella. It'll be a waste of time if he ends up going for nothing."

"I tried his wife already, but she didn't pick up her cell or the home phone."

"She's at work," Derek snapped. "There's no need to bother her."

Melissa lowered her eyes and wrung her hands together. "Oh, I tried her office. She doesn't work there any longer."

He felt the proverbial straw breaking his back. "That fucking bitch," he roared. "I'll kill her! All she had to do was keep it together for a few more days."

Marty put a hand on his shoulder. "Come on, Derek, calm down. You don't know what happened. Maybe they downsized. Talk to Gabriella before you jump to conclusions."

He imagined dollar bills with wings flying out of his grasp. "I planned to approach Jack Belinski about contributing to the campaign," he yelled. "The man isn't going to throw money my way after firing my fucking wife."

Everything was falling apart. Once his plan was in motion, Jack would have been sympathetic toward his plight, bending over backwards to help. The useless, fucking gash. He couldn't believe it. He should have done something about her sooner.

"Look," Marty said, "use the drive to the airport to gather your thoughts. We'll figure something out about the fundraising. Family, my friend, is all that matters. If they fired her, she's bound to be upset and will need your support. Now, about Pietre, do you want me to see what business we can swing to McNamara?"

"We're a corporate firm. What work do we have for a PI?"

"Well, I'm not sure but I'll talk to partners. It's going to be great exposure for our firm if you can snag a government seat."

Why was it he couldn't do anything for himself? Everything was about the fucking firm. Everything was a reflection on the firm or in the best interest of the firm. Derek was bloody sick of it.

Marty draped his arm around his shoulder. "Go get your sister-in-law. We'll talk tomorrow."

Derek shrugged off Marty's arm. He stormed out of the office, fuming at Gabriella. "Stupid bitch," he muttered under his breath.

　　　　　　　　　　　　　　　　　　　　L.E. Fraser

His wife was ruining him and any reservations he'd had over his plan evaporated. It was a case of survival of the fittest.

CHAPTER TWENTY-THREE

One Week Later: Toronto, Ontario

Sam

SAM AND REECE WERE lingering over a homemade — by Reece, of course — brunch. It was a gorgeous June day, and they'd decided to play hooky from work. They weren't going to open a newspaper or check email. A full day off with no distractions.

Reece stood and carried his plate into the kitchen, speaking over his shoulder. "What do you want to do today?"

"How about Luminato at David Pecaut Square? We can check out some of the artists, playwrights, and filmmakers." Sam popped the last bite of hollandaise-soaked English muffin in her mouth. The food Reece produced was almost worth the clutter that accompanied it.

"Dinner at Paese?" Reece asked.

"You got it. I'll make a reservation." Sam was picking up her cell when it rang. "McNamara."

"Hey Sam, Jim Stipelli."

Her heart skipped a beat. "What's wrong? Are Lisa and the kids okay?"

"They're fine," he replied. "Which you'd know if you'd swallow your pride and call Lisa."

She grunted. "It's complicated."

"So she tells me. Just give her a call, would you?"

Sam didn't say anything. Lisa Stipelli was, or had been, her best friend. They'd had a falling out a year ago when her friend met a smarmy self-realization guru. Sam suspected the asshole was interfering in Lisa's marriage and had loudly voiced her concern. The ensuing argument had damaged their friendship. Sam didn't know how to handle the conflict, so she did nothing, which was typical for her when faced with personal problems involving people's feelings.

"Fine, fine," Jim said. "I don't want to be in the middle, and I'm not calling about my wife. By the way, how's your mother?"

Sam turned her back to Reece, who was busy wiping down the countertops. "The same," she mumbled.

She'd told Reece her mother was dead because she didn't want him to meet her. Grace suffered early-onset Alzheimer's, but that wasn't the reason. Her mother was as mean-spirited as she'd been when she was healthy. If they met, Grace would tell Reece what happened with Liam, he'd leave their relationship, and she wouldn't blame him.

"Hello? Sam? I said I've got a job for you."

"Sorry," she said. "A murder case?"

Jim was Toronto's best criminal defence attorney and a pleasure to work with, but she was experiencing the usual feeling of dread when faced with a difficult case. It would be tough, whatever it was. Jim always took high-profile cases. He liked the media coverage and loved executing a legal miracle. Whatever Jim took on, most lawyers considered unwinnable.

"Yep, client is Derek Martina. He's a partner in a large corporate law practice, also dabbles in politics."

She cringed. "I'm afraid we've met."

"Oh? Well then, small world. His firm is advancing him the funds for his defence, which is where I come in. I went to law school with one of the senior partners. The cops charged Derek with first degree murder last night."

"Really? Who died?"

"His wife."

Sam was so startled she laughed. "Wait, what? Gabriella Martina is dead?"

Reece stopped loading the dishwasher and turned. She put the phone on speaker and snagged a legal pad and pen from the kitchen counter.

"You know the whole family?" Jim asked.

"We had dinner there last Tuesday. Reece went to university with Derek."

Reece wiped his hands on a dishtowel and walked over to stand beside her.

"Sam," Jim said, "are we dealing with a conflict of interest?"

"You're on speaker, Jim. No conflict of interest," Reece assured him. "What do the police have?" He dropped the tea towel on the counter and sat at the table.

"One piece of direct evidence and enough circumstantial to corroborate," Jim said. "They're still looking for her body."

"What's the direct evidence?" Reece pantomimed writing, and she slid over the pad and handed him the pen.

"A 911 call yesterday afternoon from Mrs. Martina on her home phone saying her husband had stabbed her."

"Oh boy," Sam said, "but without a body, why is she presumed dead?"

"When police arrived, the house was empty. There was blood in the kitchen and bloody fingerprints on a phone hidden in the kitchen closet. She put up a hell of a fight. There's a blood trail from the bedroom to the kitchen, and her bloody handprints are on the walls and doorframes. One of the large butcher knives is missing from the knife block. When they searched the house and grounds, they found Derek's prints in blood on the shed door."

Reece was scribbling notes while Jim talked. He looked at the list and raised an eyebrow.

"Enough blood to prove death?" Sam asked.

"No," Jim answered, "but there's more evidence, and, combined with the 911 call, there's enough to support the charge."

"Where did they pick him up?" she asked.

"He came home. The police believe he wasn't aware she called 911."

"They think he disposed of her body and went home to clean up," Sam concluded.

"That's the gist of it. There was a shovel in his trunk and a piece of blue tarp caught on the trunk frame. Forensics found her fingerprints on the release pull and strands of hair embedded in the carpet." Jim paused. "Guys, she wasn't dead when she was put in the trunk."

"If Gabriella was alive after he stabbed her, the trunk would be covered with blood," Sam pointed out.

"Forensic techs say no, not if she managed to free one of her arms, but her wounds were contained inside the tarp," Jim argued.

"Jesus," she muttered. "Where were the kids?"

"The oldest boy claims he was in Montreal with friends, but the cops are still trying to verify his alibi. The middle girl was at her boyfriend's place, and the youngest was hanging out with a friend."

"What other evidence have they got?" Reece was studying his notes.

"Derek's an inch from bankruptcy. Six months ago, he took out a life insurance policy on his wife for two million dollars. The police found Gabriella's diary, delineating Derek's affairs and psychological abuse. She thought he was trying to make her commit suicide."

"But that's her perspective," Sam said.

"He made death threats," Jim added. "In front of his partner and his assistant, Derek said he was going to, and I quote, 'kill the bitch'."

"Where does Derek say he was when it happened?" Reece asked.

"No corroborated alibi. His office verifies he left at four-forty-five. Derek claims Gabriella's car was in the shop, and he had to meet her sister's flight at Pearson."

"And where is Sis now?" Sam asked.

"No sign of her and no Isabella on any Air Canada flight manifest."

"Can't Derek reach her?" Sam finished her coffee, pushing the mug to the centre of the table.

"He doesn't have a phone number for her, doesn't know if she married and changed her last name, and isn't sure where she lives," Jim said.

She peered over Reece's shoulder and watched him put a question mark beside the word 'sister' in his notes and underline the word. She pulled out a chair, sitting beside him, and reviewed the rest of the notes.

"Did Derek stop for gas or coffee along the way?" she asked. "What about parking at the airport?"

"No stops and his partner tried texting him at a little after five-thirty to remind him of a six o'clock teleconference. He didn't respond and missed the call. Derek says he forgot his phone at home. He circled arrivals a few times and left around seven."

Sam slid over the pad and scribbled 'no phone', adding two question marks. "Derek's business requires him to be reached 24/7. If he forgot his phone, why wouldn't he go home and get it?"

"He had meetings all day and didn't have time."

She and Reece exchanged a bemused look. It was tough to swallow that a lawyer wouldn't have his cell phone.

"You can disable GPS tracking on your phone, but law enforcement can still track the history," Reece said. "The cops are going to be able to confirm the phone's location for the day of the alleged crime."

"And the fact his cell was at the house all day," Jim said, "doesn't help the prosecution or the defence."

"What about airport security?" Reece leaned back in the chair and linked his hands behind his head. "They must have noticed the car."

"It was crowded, there was a shift change, and a little girl lost her parents outside the taxi stand. No one can confirm or deny that Derek's car was there. I haven't seen them yet, but the cops have the airport surveillance tapes."

Sam took the pen and wrote *get copies of surveillance tapes* while Reece asked Jim, "How does Derek explain all the evidence?"

"No explanation for the stuff in his trunk. As far as the diary goes, he denied his wife would keep one, claiming Gabriella is dyslexic and hates writing."

Reece grabbed their mugs and got up to fetch the pot of coffee. He waved the pot at her.

She nodded and he poured her coffee. She considered the evidence. Did she want to take this case? "I hate to ask, Jim, but is there anything else?"

"Gabriella's car wasn't in the shop on Wednesday," Jim said. "It was parked at home in the garage. The service manager confirmed Derek made an appointment for regular servicing and told them to keep it overnight, stating he wouldn't have time to pick it up before they closed. Gabriella called in the morning and rescheduled, saying she needed the car."

Sam studied the pad of paper. The 911 call Gabriella made was a serious problem. No wonder the police had charged Derek. "Jim, if Derek did kill her and it was planned and deliberate," Sam said, "he did a bad job of it."

Reece nodded. "What about his bloody prints on the shed?"

"Derek alleges he cut his finger when he was trying to fix the shed door. That's the only explanation he has." Jim paused. "The blood isn't his. Derek is AB positive and the blood in the house and on the shed is O negative, Gabriella's blood type. Forensics is in the process of confirming the blood is hers, but the DNA matching will take time."

Sam uttered a short laugh. She wasn't sure if she wanted to take the risk of having her firm connected with something so open and closed. If she turned him down, he'd never use her again and his practice paid well. Would her firm survive if Jim pulled his business? If she earned a reputation of only taking *easy* cases, probably not.

"Do they have the weapon?" On top of everything else, if the cops had a murder weapon covered in Derek's fingerprints that would clinch the deal. She'd decline the case.

"No, not yet. I've emailed you copies of the police reports and the interviews with Derek, his assistant, and his partner."

Reece looked confused. "Why did you take this case, Jim? The evidence is overwhelming."

On the other end of the phone, Jim laughed. "Innocent until proven guilty and I love a challenge. Sam knows that. I didn't climb to my status by being cautious. If you want to be top dog, you have to win against insurmountable odds. Besides, with Derek's political standing, it's going to be high profile."

She again considered how to decline the case. Her firm would be in the news. The bad press over the Uthisca Bueton cult had been awful, and she didn't want to go through that again.

"Where is Derek now?" Reece asked.

"In lockdown," Jim answered. "I'm waiting to hear from the Crown."

Sam caught Reece's eye and frowned, pointing at the notepad.

"The police have the airport surveillance footage, is that right?" Reece asked Jim.

"Correct."

"If they charged him with murder," Reece said, "it means they didn't find his car on the tapes."

"That's my assumption, yes. I'll know more when I see the rest of the paperwork and speak with the Crown."

"Any idea what they'll do about bail?" Sam asked.

"He's an attorney and attached to the community so there's no reason to think he won't show up for court." Jim paused. "But I'm not sure."

"Because they don't have the body," Sam guessed.

"That's right. The Crown might argue he could destroy evidence related to their investigation."

"Then again," she said, "if they release him and he's guilty, there's a chance he'll lead them to the body."

"I'm confident I can argue for release pending trial, and his business partner," Jim paused and they heard papers rustling, "Marty Alderson, has offered to act as surety. If necessary, his firm will advance any deposit to the court that's ordered."

Silence stretched out. "Well?" Jim asked. "Are you signing up for the ride?"

Sam caught Reece's eye, and he nodded, mouthing *why not?* He looked excited.

"I guess." She hoped her lack of enthusiasm wasn't evident in her voice. "Usual retainer and hourly rate?"

"Plus expenses and a five-thousand-dollar bonus if you find anything I can use to acquit him," Jim said.

The bonus, along with her regular fee, would enable her to take a few months off to finish her PhD thesis. "Okay," she reluctantly agreed. "Since the cops are searching for Gabriella, where do you want us to start?"

"Find Isabella."

CHAPTER TWENTY-FOUR

One Week Later: Toronto, Ontario

Reece

DEREK'S CAR WASN'T on the airport surveillance tapes. He'd lied. Gabriella's body was still missing. Jim had worked his magic, and the court released Derek on a $100,000 consent bail, with a $50,000 deposit to the court. He was under house arrest, when he wasn't with his surety, Marty Alderson.

Derek's newest defence was that his wife had set him up to ruin him. Without a body, Reece was willing to entertain the idea. Since Gabriella was close to her sister, they needed to find Isabella.

Reece parked in the Martinas' driveway, and Derek opened the front door while they walked up to the house. His bravado and false charm had vanished. Dark circles shadowed his fatigue-lined eyes, and he was pale, which made the age spots on his face stand out. His formerly flawless hair was a mess, and a tuft stuck up at the back of his head.

Derek opened the door just wide enough for them to slip in sideways in single file. "Lots of reporters," he muttered.

That was an understatement. The press were having a great time. When Reece squeezed by him, he caught a whiff of ripe body odour, and, looking back, he saw Sam's eyes widen. She discreetly pushed at him to move faster.

Inside the house, Reece got straight to the point. "Jim wants us to find Isabella. Where can we start looking?"

"Did Jim tell you I think my wife did this?"

Much to Reece's dismay, Derek cried. He walked to the living room and collapsed onto the sofa, pulling a tattered tissue from the pocket of his fleece hoodie.

Sam appeared unmoved by the tears. "Where can we look for Isabella?"

"Do you think Gabriella's with her?"

"We don't know but we need to find the woman," Reece said.

"They grew up in London." Derek sniffled and blew his nose.

"We can't find birth records for Isabella LeBlanc born in London." Reece took a seat beside Sam. "It might help if we could speak with someone who knew the family. Do you know the address?"

"I never went over. Her father was a heavy drinker when I met Gabriella, and her mother was sick." He thought for a moment. "Reece, what's the name of that residential area east of Westmount Mall?"

Sam took out her phone. "It looks like Norton Estates."

"Yeah, that's it."

"We can pull the property archive records." Reece turned to Sam. "Rather than going door-to-door, it'll be easier to check ownership dates to find someone living there now who was there when the LeBlanc family owned their house."

Sam nodded. "What are her parent's names?"

"Her mother's name was Nina," Derek said. "She's dead. I don't remember Gabriella mentioning her dad's name. She hated him because he left her mother."

"Have you noticed anything missing from the house?" Reece asked.

Derek rubbed his hands over his face and slouched on the sofa. "My daughter went through Gabriella's closet. Nothing seems to be missing." He pulled something out of his pocket. "Her passport was in our safe deposit box. The police took her purse." He handed Reece the passport.

Renewed in July 2013, it was valid for ten years. "Did she take any trips outside Canada?"

"I don't remember," Derek said. "Maybe shopping in the US."

"We can notify Canadian Customs and see what they have on file against her passport number," Sam suggested.

"Was Gabriella older or younger than her sister?" Reece asked.

"I think older."

"You don't know? You married your child-bride two decades ago," Sam snapped, and Reece wasn't surprised she was reaching her limit with Derek quickly.

"I wanted to respect her privacy. She always got so upset if I brought up her family." Derek sucked on the inside of his cheek. "Besides," he added, "Gabriella was protective of her relationship with Isabella."

"Why?" Sam asked.

"She complained about me." He was staring at his slippers while he spoke. "Two nights before she disappeared, I heard them on the kitchen polycom and Isabella was furious."

Sensing another outburst from Sam, Reece gave her hand a warning squeeze. She shot him a scathing glare but nodded curtly and stood. "Where's your bedroom? I'd like to have a look around."

"Ah..." Derek's face flushed with embarrassment. "We have separate rooms. Hers is the last door on the right."

Reece caught Sam's eye. She looked curious that Derek didn't sleep with his wife but made no comment.

After she marched upstairs, Reece turned back to Derek. "Why was Isabella coming?"

"Gabriella didn't say."

"What did you *think*?"

Derek stuffed his hands into the pockets of his hoodie. "I thought she was leaving me," he whispered. "Gabby didn't have any friends. Isabella was her support, so I planned on telling her I loved her sister and asking for help. There wasn't any option except to admit I was an asshole and beg forgiveness. Then..." He chewed on his lower lip. "I... well... I was hoping my wife could stay with Isabella until after I ran for office. I needed to get her out of

                                        L.E. Fraser

Toronto. I was planning to tell her boss, Jack Belinski, she had a breakdown. I thought..." he mumbled something Reece didn't catch.

"Excuse me?"

"I thought Jack would be sympathetic and contribute to my campaign."

If it was true Gabriella was leaving the marriage, it went toward motive. Divorce was expensive when property and children were involved. "Did Gabriella imply she was leaving?" Reece asked.

"No, but after dinner with you, she asked me to pick up her sister the next day." Derek's expression was one of bewilderment. "It was out of the blue. We had an argument the night before, and... I don't know what I thought."

"What did you argue about?" Reece asked.

"Her job."

"Go on..."

"She wanted to quit. Jack Belinski is a chauvinistic jerk." Derek's lips tightened in anger. "I didn't like the way he treated her, but her job was to support him and that means doing personal shit beneath your pay grade. It bugged me that she took it so personally."

"I understand she was fired. Do you know why?"

Derek shook his head. "No, I found out when Melissa called her office. My wife was fired three or four times in the past couple of years, without warning or explanation."

"Why did she have such a difficult time keeping a job?"

Derek's lip curled. "Gabby didn't play well with others."

Didn't, Reece noted. "We'll need a list of her friends."

"What did I just say? She didn't have any. Except for her sister."

"Whom you never met," Reece replied incredulously, "and know nothing about, including her address."

Derek shuffled his feet against the carpet. "Last week, Nick received a birthday gift from his aunt, and Gabriella sent her gifts, but I've torn apart the house and can't find an address."

"Did a courier service deliver the gift?

Derek nodded. "Yeah, I guess. Gabriella took care of that sort of stuff. Why?"

"It might be a lead. I can see about tracing deliveries to the house." Reece tapped on his iPad to add that to his list. "Didn't your kids ask their aunt what city she lived in?"

Derek shook his head again. "I don't remember them ever talking to her on the phone."

That was tough to believe, but Reece kept his opinion to himself. "I need to speak with the kids."

"Nicholas is gone," Derek said. "You can speak with Anna and Kevin, I guess."

Sam had returned to the living room looking surly. "What do you mean he's gone?"

"He left when I was arrested. I haven't heard from him."

"Did the kids know they had an aunt?" Sam asked.

"Of course they did, what kind of question is that?"

"Let's see," Sam said. "No one ever talked to her or met her, she wasn't on any flights into Toronto, and the police can't find her."

"Are you saying I made her up?" Derek leaped to his feet. "That's absurd. Why would I do that?"

"I don't know." Sam sat down and crossed her arms in front of her chest. "You tell me."

"What would I gain from making up a sister-in-law?" The heat was gone from his voice. He looked scared.

"Picking up Isabella at the airport is your alibi," Reece said.

Sam was smiling at Derek. "Forgot about the massive number of security cameras at an international airport, eh?"

"I... ah..."

"Where were you?" Reece asked.

Derek licked his lips. "I... I was angry Gabriella lost her job. I did start to go to the airport."

"But you never made it. Where did you go?" Reece asked.

Derek mumbled something.

Leaning forward, Reece repeated, "Where did you go?"

"I went to Sonia's place."

Sam was on her feet in an instant. "Are you kidding me? Who the fuck is Sonia?"

"My girlfriend. If it comes out I'm having an affair, it'll ruin my political opportunities."

Reece couldn't believe it. Did he think a murder charge wasn't *ruining* his political career?

"Let me see if I've got this straight." Sam crossed her arms against her chest again. "Pissed off at your wife, you ditched your sister-in-law at the airport to get laid?"

With a sigh, Reece picked up his iPad. "Give me Sonia's full name, address and her contact details."

"Can't we leave her out of this?" Derek whined.

"No. Are you seriously this stupid, Derek?" Sam yelled. "Why hasn't she stepped forward?"

"Our relationship is casual. I'm sure she doesn't want to be involved in my mess."

Sam looked ready to smack Derek, so Reece jumped in. "If Sonia can confirm you were with her, they'll have to drop the charges. Have you talked to her?"

"No. She won't take my calls and I can't reach her."

"Are you suggesting she's not going to admit being with you?" Reece asked.

Derek shrugged. "Sonia passed the bar exam six months ago. She works for a firm that does legal aid. The pay is shit, the hours are terrible, and her clients are scum. She wants out. Being tied up in my mess will damage her reputation."

The shock on Sam's face mirrored Reece's disbelief. "Your girlfriend is going to allow you to stand trial for murder because she doesn't want to jeopardize her career?" he asked.

"She's twenty-five," Derek said. "Something like this could ruin her."

"Many women don't view sex as a recreational activity, Derek," Sam said in disgust.

Reece saw where she was going. "Maybe Sonia wanted your wife out of the picture."

Derek's eyes widened. "That's preposterous. Besides, I was with Sonia. She couldn't have done it."

"You said Sonia works with scum. She could have paid a client to do it," Reece said. "Did you tell her you were going to the airport?"

Derek nodded. "Sure, yeah."

"If Sonia wanted your wife out of the way and didn't want you implicated, you'd have an airtight alibi," Sam said. "You'd be on the airport's surveillance tapes, proving you weren't at your house at the time of the incident."

"But if Sonia was home alone," Reece said to Sam, "*she* wouldn't have an alibi. We're missing something." He turned to Derek. "When you arrived, was she planning on going out? Was she expecting a visitor?"

"No. She was alone."

Reece thought about it. "Does Sonia have a home landline?"

Derek nodded.

"Did she receive a phone call while you were there?"

Derek nodded again. "Yeah, her office called. Why?"

"Why didn't they call her work cell, do you know?" Reece asked.

"I do, actually. I was pissed off she was taking the call. I wanted her to let it go to voice mail. After she hung up, we argued. She told me she had to take it because she'd emailed her boss before she left to call her at home to review some case files. Her cell kept rebooting, and she gave it to IT. She left it with them because she wasn't feeling well and wanted to go home."

Sam was nodding. "She probably arranged the call. If she was ever under suspicion, she could prove she was home."

Derek laughed. "You don't know Sonia. She wouldn't kill my wife. She didn't care."

"We'll see," Sam said.

"I'm telling you, this is a set-up. The only person who could have helped Gabriella was her sister," Derek insisted. "All you have to do is find Isabella. She was in Toronto I know it. She must have arrived earlier in the week." He looked excited. "If I was driving to the airport by myself, I wouldn't have an

   L.E. Fraser

alibi. Gabriella specifically told me not to park because Isabella would meet me outside the arrival doors."

Reece considered that scenario. If Gabriella and Isabella had forgotten about the video cameras, they would assume Derek wouldn't be able to corroborate his whereabouts. But it was risky. He could have stopped for coffee or spoken to one of the security guards outside arrivals.

Before he could respond, Sam walked over to Derek's chair and leaned into his face. "Did you and Sonia get rid of your wife? Did you make up Isabella in case either of you came under suspicion?"

"Check the phone records," Derek yelled.

"The police did," Reece said. "Gabriella never made or received any calls that can be traced to Isabella. The polycom connects to your landline. You couldn't have heard Isabella on the speaker two nights ago because any dialled or received calls would have shown on the records."

"There were two voices," Derek insisted. "Gabriella must have had another phone."

"Derek," Sam said, "why would she hide her sister?"

"I don't know, but Isabella does exist. Wait, I can prove it." He scrambled over to the fireplace mantel to rifle through a stack of birthday cards. He waved a card at Reece. "This one, see? It has a note from Isabella."

Reece took the card. Unsigned, the note read: *Now you're legal, Nicholas, and can buy your own liquor. Happy birthday.* Odd sentiment for a card. He passed it to Sam, who looked puzzled.

"Can we see the other cards?" Reece asked.

Derek passed them to him. There was one from Nicholas's sister, one from his brother and one signed *Love Mom and Dad.*

"Is this one from Gabriella?" Reece asked.

"I wrote that card," Derek answered. "Gabriella was embarrassed about her handwriting. She bought the gifts but refused to write the cards."

Sam's eyes narrowed. "Derek, do you have something in the house Gabriella wrote — a note or grocery list?"

"I told you, she never wrote anything by hand. She put lists on her phone or printed them off the computer."

More lies. Jim's office had provided them with photocopies of Gabriella's handwritten diary. Was Derek's next claim going to be that his wife didn't write the diary?

Reece took a deep breath. "This handwriting," he waved the card at Sam, "isn't the same as the diary. The letters slant. It's backhand cursive. It looks to me as if it was written by a left-handed person."

Derek grabbed Reece's elbow. "You have to find Isabella. Why aren't the police looking for her?"

"The cops don't believe she exists." Reece was having a hard time trying to adjust from cop to private investigator. They'd already caught Derek in multiple lies, and Reece's cop-sense was screaming at him that Derek was guilty. It felt like they were trying to manufacture evidence to acquit him. It was a shitty feeling.

"The police are certain you killed your wife," he said. "They have hard evidence to support the charge. Right now, *we* have to find Isabella."

"The cops are supposed to be investigating. That's their job. I'm a taxpayer, and I pay their salaries," Derek said in a haughty tone.

Every taxpaying criminal's mantra. "Their job," Reece hoped he sounded supportive, "is to build an airtight case against you. It's up to us to give them reason to look at another suspect."

"Help me," Derek begged them. "I didn't kill my wife."

CHAPTER TWENTY-FIVE

Reece

THE NEXT MORNING, Reece strolled out of the bathroom and kissed the side of Sam's neck. "Off to London?"

"Afraid so."

He knew she wasn't excited about the five-hour round trip. After sorting through over twenty years of property records, he'd located an older woman who still lived down the street from Gabriella's childhood home. They'd decided Sam would do the interview.

"You're sure your family never lived there?" he asked again. "I saw the name McNamara in the property records. They sold in 1991."

"I told you that Joyce and I were born in Toronto."

"Maybe it's a relative you didn't know you had. Wanna take a look?"

"I don't have any relatives. Did Jack Belinski agree to talk to you?"

"I have a meeting with him this morning." Reece grabbed his travel mug from the kitchen counter. "By the way, Jim sent a text this morning. Sonia, Derek's girlfriend, denies she was with him the afternoon of the murder. He wants us to talk to her."

"I'll leak it to the press," she suggested. "If Sonia's lying because she doesn't want to be involved, let's involve her."

Reece nodded. "Good idea. We can speak with her face-to-face after a couple of stories are printed."

He held the door for her and waited for her to find her keys. "I'll walk you out," he said.

In the parking lot, he sat in his car and watched her drive away. Because of his past, he always felt uneasy when someone he loved got behind the wheel of a car for a long drive. With a sigh, he shoved his feeling of disquietude aside and started his car.

JACK BELINSKI KEPT Reece waiting for half an hour. The pretty receptionist peeked at him and picked up the phone. She whispered something and hung up, returning to her computer without looking his way.

The reception space was gaudy, to say the least. Confusing abstract art decorated garish red and blue walls that were better suited in a kindergarten room. The ugly, ultra-modern, uncomfortable furniture probably cost more than his car. To Reece, the decor represented city dwellers scrambling to be unique in a concrete box.

He turned when the hallway door opened and saw a middle-aged woman with 'lawyer' stamped all over her march up to the reception desk. "Katrina, where are Julie and Jack?"

"In Jack's office." The receptionist tilted her head toward Reece.

The overweight, stern looking woman walked over, and he dropped the magazine he was pretending to read and stood.

"Mr. Hash," she said, "I'm Gloria Thompson. They're waiting for us." She shook hands with him before turning on her heels and trotting away.

Reece followed her down the hall to a closed office door. She knocked once, didn't wait for a response, and opened the door, beckoning Reece inside.

Gloria handled the introductions. "Jack Belinski, CEO, and Julie Stewart, head of HR." She sat on the sofa. "This is Reece Hash," she added, and to Reece, it felt like an afterthought.

Jack was lounging in a purple leather armchair with his legs crossed and a bottle of designer water in his hand. Julie, a thin woman with sharp facial features, perched on the cushion edge of a matching chair. She appeared ready to bolt from the room at a moment's notice. Neither of them rose or offered their hand.

Off to a great start, Reece thought. He sat beside Gloria on a fluorescent orange sofa. Between the sofa and chairs was a lacquered glass table in a shocking shade of green. The one appealing feature in the room was the wall of windows to Reece's right, which had a wonderful view of east Toronto. To his annoyance, there were no curtains and he was sitting with the morning sun shining in his eyes.

Madam Lawyer spoke first. "On the phone, you said you have questions about Gabriella Martina's employment. As I told you, under privacy and labour laws, we don't need to speak with you."

This interview already wasn't going the way he'd planned. He thought they'd be upset about Gabriella's disappearance and cooperate. His hope was that Gabriella had talked to her boss or co-workers about her sister. She might have kept Isabella's address on her work computer. He was also hoping to see a sample of her handwriting. Just a technicality really, but he wanted outside confirmation that the handwriting in the diary was Gabriella's.

"I'm surprised the police haven't interviewed you," Reece said.

"Ah, but you're not with the police, now are you?" Jack said.

The sun was blinding him, and his temper got the better of him. "In which case I'm free to speak with the press about my investigation," Reece retorted. "Gabriella was murdered two days after you terminated her employment. I haven't read *that* in the paper yet."

"So what?" Jack countered. "Everyone knows her husband killed her."

Reece gave himself a mental kick. If they weren't on the defensive before, they sure would be now.

Gloria jumped in. "Mr. Hash, what do you want to know?"

Reece took a breath and started over. "Did Gabriella have a work cell phone?"

Julie shook her head. "No, she refused to take one. Since she didn't ask the company to pay her personal plan, we didn't care so long as Jack could reach her twenty-four-seven."

"How about her work computer? Any chance she kept personal contacts in her address book?"

"No, employees aren't permitted to keep personal data on our computers," Julie answered. "I can confirm she didn't breach the policy because I checked the laptop before turning it over to Jack's new EA."

That was disappointing. "Why did you fire her?"

Before Julie could open her mouth, Jack spat out, "She's a nutcase, not to mention insubordinate. Intolerable and—"

"We terminated her for a number of reasons," Julie interrupted, "one of which was unprofessional conduct." Julie was a low-talker, and Reece had to lean forward to hear her.

"You had cause?" Reece asked.

"Gabriella said—" Julie began, at the same time Jack declared, "She insulted me. What would you do if your secretary insulted you to your face?"

"I'm sure I don't know," Reece replied. "How did she insult you?"

"Called me an aging Spanish porn star."

Reece smothered a chuckle. Jack was an arrogant-looking man whose appearance suggested he was trying hard to pretend he wasn't over sixty. He was wearing skinny jeans and pointy-toed Italian shoes. He'd used gel to puff up his thinning hair, and his forehead was shiny and tight. Reece suspected Botox injections.

"Well," Reece forced his face to remain neutral, "that could be taken as an insult, yes."

"Could be?" Jack scoffed. "She's deranged."

"Why did she say it, do you know?"

Jack laughed. "How the hell should I know? I took her out for lunch to discuss ongoing problems. When we were driving back to the office, she drove like a maniac and hurled insults at me."

"Ongoing problems," Reece repeated. "You experienced performance management issues?"

"Yes," Julie said, a little too fast in Reece's opinion.

"What type of issues?"

"She was two cans short of a six-pack," Jack said.

The guy had a wealth of nasty ways to describe his assistant's mental health without giving concrete examples. Reece turned his attention to Julie, shading his eyes against the sun's glare. "What type of issues?"

"She had a difficult time managing Jack's calendar. Gabriella often double-booked him, removed meetings from his calendar, and forgot to send cancellations for the ones she rescheduled."

Finally, something of substance. Reece stood and moved to the wall of windows, leaning his back against the window so the sun wasn't in his eyes. He opened his iPad to make notes. "Anything else?"

Jack had to crane his neck to see him. "She talked to herself. Muttered under her breath." Jack spun his finger around his temple. "And not just *to* herself, but *about* herself. *Gabriella is feeling this* and *Gabriella thinks that*," he mimicked in a screechy, soprano voice.

"She did seem," Julie paused and appeared to be searching for the right word, "distracted at times."

Jack snorted. "Because she was chatting up male employees all the time."

That didn't sound like the woman he'd met. "She was a flirt?" Reece had difficulty keeping the disbelief from his voice.

"Well," Julie said softly, "sometimes, she was too social in the workplace."

"With the men." Jack grunted and looked disgusted. "I felt bad for her husband. Word on the street is he was a sure winner for McBride's Parliament seat. That poor son of a bitch. Can't say I blame him for losing his temper."

Gloria frowned. "What Jack means is—"

"I meant what I said." He glared at Gloria. "Derek Martina has great potential. Being shackled to a fruitcake would have destroyed his chance to make it to Ottawa."

Gloria stood. "I believe we're done here. Mr. Hash, we terminated Gabriella Martina without cause within six months of employment. We provided her with a generous severance package, which we didn't need to do under the *Employment Standards Act*. We had sufficient grounds to terminate her with cause. It was a bad fit, and Jack has made it clear they didn't share a trusting relationship."

Reece remained standing by the windows. "Did anyone witness her insulting Mr. Belinski?"

"What difference does that make?" Jack demanded. "I'm the CEO."

Reece couldn't shake the feeling that Jack was fabricating the allegations. Although he hadn't known Gabriella well, he had spent an evening in her company. If anything, the woman was reserved, too quiet. The idea of her hurling insults at her boss was tough to believe. He wasn't learning anything helpful and it was frustrating.

"I understand she showed up for work the morning after you fired her. Any idea why?" Reece asked for no other reason than curiosity.

"It was odd," Julie said in a voice shy of a whisper. "Jack told me what happened, and we drew up the termination papers. At five o'clock, we called her into HR and told her we were ending her employment effective immediately. The next morning, she was sitting at her desk as if nothing happened."

Definitely strange behaviour. "Was she upset when you told her you were firing her?"

Julie frowned. "No. She seemed... well..."

"She laughed." Jack stood and stretched. "Gloria and I have a meeting." He shook Reece's hand briskly. "Julie will see you out."

After they left, Reece turned to Julie. "Did you tell her why she was being fired?"

"No," she said. "I offered to provide feedback at a later date. Jack prefers it that way for terminations."

Firing an employee without telling her why was too similar to a dictatorship for Reece's taste. Not for the first time, he felt grateful he didn't work in this kind of corporate culture.

"Is it true she laughed when you fired her?" he asked.

Julie nodded and appeared puzzled. "Yes, it was strange," she said. "That was part of the problem, you see. Gabriella had an odd personality. It's difficult to manage a person when they lack consistency."

                                                L.E. Fraser

They were walking through reception to the exit when Reece asked, "Did she ever talk to you about her family or was there a co-worker she talked with?"

Julie frowned. "No. To be perfectly honest, I didn't care for her, and I suppose she sensed that. I can't think of anyone in the office who liked her."

Reece resisted her attempt to herd him out the door. "Do you have anything with Gabriella's handwriting on it, maybe her application form?"

She shook her head. "All our HR forms are PDF interactive. Our employees fill them out online. I'll take that visitor badge for you."

Reece couldn't believe there wasn't a sample of Gabriella's handwriting at the office. She was a secretary for God sake. "I need to see something with casual handwriting on it. Julie, it could be important to the case. Gabriella has children. They don't know what happened to their mother. You could help us find her."

As intended, his comments flustered the timid woman and she blushed. "If it's important, I'll see what I can find." She scurried down the hall. A few minutes later, she was back with a file folder.

The receptionist looked up. "Julie, if you need Gabriella's handwriting, Gabby wrote notes on Jack's expense report." She handed Julie the form.

"Katrina, expense reports are confidential." Julie glanced at the document. "That's not Gabriella's handwriting." She gave the receptionist back the paper.

Reece stepped forward, hoping to catch a glimpse of the writing.

"Yes, it is," insisted Katrina. "I recognize it from the other expense reports she submitted."

Julie turned over the document before Reece could see it. "Someone in Finance must have made those notes. This," she pulled a document from the file folder she was holding, "is Gabriella's handwriting."

Katrina looked at the paper in Julie's hand. She was clearly confused and about to say something, but Julie interrupted her and spoke to Reece. "Gabriella edited this document the week she started." She handed him the file.

The writing was neat cursive with letters that leaned to the right. It matched the handwriting in the diary. He thanked Julie and left.

Gabriella had written the diary — an angry tale of psychological abuse and emotional neglect perpetrated by her cheating husband. A man now accused of her murder.

CHAPTER TWENTY-SIX

Sam

LONDON'S NORTON ESTATE was a nice circa-1960s suburb, and Mrs. Shannon's house was a side-split, brick ranch with stunning flower gardens. The neighbourhood gave Sam an odd feeling of déjà vu.

Parking at the side of road near the Shannon home, she got out and walked toward a woman crouched in the grass beside a peony bush. "Mrs. Shannon?"

The woman stood and shaded her eyes. "That's right."

She looked to be in her early sixties. Her hair was short and the dark brown dye job was a home effort. She was wearing a short-sleeved blouse and a loose pair of blue cotton pants with bright pink rubber protectors strapped around her knees.

Sam handed her a business card and identification. "I'm a private investigator from Toronto, and I'd like to ask you some questions about the LeBlanc family, if you don't mind."

Mrs. Shannon pulled off one of her gardening gloves and took a pair of reading glasses from the pocket of her blouse. Her eyes darted from the card to Sam, her expression a mix of bewilderment and distress.

Puzzled, Sam asked, "Is everything okay?"

"I, ah, it's just I haven't heard that name in a while." Her demeanour went from polite to closed-off in a matter of seconds. "What's this all about?" She brushed dirt from the seat of her pants.

"Do you recall the family?"

"Of course." She wasn't meeting Sam's eyes.

"Did you know their eldest daughter?"

She nodded curtly. "I did."

Hoping to shock the woman into being more helpful, Sam said, "The Toronto police believe she was murdered."

The woman's eyebrows rose. "Murdered? That's awful." She didn't ask follow-up questions, but Sam sensed some of her resistance give way.

"I'm working for her husband's lawyer," she said, leaving out the tiny detail about Derek's arrest.

"Well," Mrs. Shannon bent to collect her gardening tools, "we can't be having a conversation about murder on the front lawn." Plopping the tools into a wicker basket, she headed for the house.

Taking that as her cue, Sam followed.

Inside the house, Mrs. Shannon scurried to a side table, snatched a photo, and stuffed it in a desk drawer. Her eyes roamed around the room and she moved two more photos.

Curiosity piqued, Sam took her shoes off in the doorway and noted where Mrs. Shannon put the pictures, in case she should have a moment alone to see what all the fuss was about.

Mrs. Shannon beckoned her into the kitchen. "I can offer you iced tea."

Sam hated iced tea, but accepted to be polite. "How well did you know the LeBlanc family?"

Mrs. Shannon took a pitcher from the fridge, poured two glasses, and handed one to Sam. "Not well," she said. "My boys are younger."

"How old are your boys?" Sam swallowed a mouthful of cold tea and tried to hide her grimace.

"Jeremy and Ralph are Irish twins, as they say, so there's a year between them. They're twenty-nine and twenty-eight." She sat at the table across from Sam. "Ryan's twenty-five."

"How old is Isabella?"

Mrs. Shannon looked at her as if she was crazy. "How old is Isabella?"

"Yes, Isabella LeBlanc. Is she younger or older than Gabriella?"

"Well... She was younger."

Derek wasn't lying. Isabella did exist. "Wait, sorry," she said. "She *was* younger?"

"Yes," Mrs. Shannon said slowly. "Isabella LeBlanc is dead."

Sam slammed down her glass. "Dead? When? How?"

"The winter of 1992. It was New Year's Day. She was eleven or twelve. She fell out of their tree house," Mrs. Shannon said. "Hit a branch on the way down and broke her neck. I always thought it was too high. Quentin built a railing around it, but..." her voice trailed off.

Sam's mind was reeling with all the new questions this discovery brought up. "Can you tell me what happened?"

Mrs. Shannon got up and opened a cupboard, extracting a bottle of whisky and pouring a lot into her tea. She offered the bottle and Sam declined.

After half an hour and a lot of whisky, Mrs. Shannon finished her story about the afternoon Isabella LeBlanc died.

Sam's head was spinning. She thought about her own sister's death. From what Mrs. Shannon had told her, Gabriella and Isabella had been very close. "Poor Gabriella," she said.

Mrs. Shannon played with the teaspoon on the table. "Have you seen the *Village of the Damned*?"

She nodded. "Sure."

"After Isabella died, well that's what Gabriella was like," she said. "The strange way those alien children walked and the lack of expression in their faces."

Mrs. Shannon stood and cleared the glasses from the table. She stumbled and fell against the counter. "I'm due at the church in twenty minutes."

Sam followed her to the front door, wondering if she should offer to drive her since the woman had consumed so much booze. It wasn't any of her business, so she kept her mouth shut and leaned down to pull on her sneakers.

"You don't remember me, do you? I... I remember you so well from the neighbourhood, you know? Scarcely out of nappies and full of spit and vinegar but always such a sweet little thing."

Sam stood and smiled. "You've confused me with someone else. I'm a born and raised Torontonian."

"No," she insisted. "Grace went home to her mother to deliver. Colin was heartbroken he missed his daughters' births." She took a small step toward Sam. "You were his favourite. Colin always said Joyce favoured your mother, but you were his, just like your brother would have been if he hadn't—" she hesitated, "if Malcolm hadn't died as a baby."

The entryway closed in on Sam. "I... I never had a brother," she stuttered.

Mrs. Shannon leaned against the doorframe. "Oh dear, I shouldn't be saying all this. I'm sorry. It was such a shock to see you. You look so much like your dad."

Sam needed air. She grabbed her purse, mumbled something she hoped passed for goodbye, and bolted out the door.

In the car, she struggled to calm down and think clearly. Reece had seen the name 'McNamara' in the property records, and Megan Shannon knew the names of her parents and sister. It was possible... But why would her parents lie and tell her they had always lived in Toronto? Why would they hide the tragedy of a deceased infant?

If they had lived in London, her dad would have been with London Police Services. She could find out.

Sam started the car and drove back to the 401. She spent the whole drive worrying about her family instead of the case. Did it matter if they had spent a few years in London without telling her? Maybe not, but it did matter that she didn't know about her brother. She'd thought she and her father had shared a close relationship. His dishonesty stung.

She was almost home before she was able to force herself to put her own problems aside and focus her attention on the case. There were more questions now than answers, and she needed to bring Reece up to speed. Isabella did exist, but she was dead.

Had Gabriella believed her sister was alive, or had Derek created a 'phantom Isabella' to drive his wife insane?

CHAPTER TWENTY-SEVEN

Sam

DESPITE HER EFFORTS to focus on the case, Sam couldn't stop replaying the end of her conversation with Mrs. Shannon. Instead of going home, she drove to the office. Reece had left the Norton Estate property records on his side of the partner desk. Her parents' names were there. They had owned a house in Norton Estates from 1978 to 1991, meaning she was four when they returned to Toronto.

Megan Shannon hadn't lied about that, so Sam dug deeper. What she found turned her world upside down, and the shock was debilitating. She didn't deal well with emotion and was fluctuating between rage and confusion over her father's lies.

Living in London wasn't his only lie. He'd had bigger secrets.

Being a suspicious person at heart, she wondered why Mrs. Shannon had hidden household pictures. What was it she hadn't wanted her to see?

In *The London Free Press* newspaper archives, she found an article from 1989 about Hugh Shannon's suicide. He'd stepped in front of a freight train at a downtown railway crossing, leaving behind a wife and three boys. The youngest boy had been a month old.

It took minimum effort to find photos of the three boys on Facebook. The two older ones weren't too interesting but the youngest, Ryan, was a different story. He was completing a medical degree at Dalhousie University in Halifax. He was the spitting image of her father. Ryan could be her twin.

What she didn't find in the London or Toronto newspaper archives was an obituary for a *Malcolm McNamara*. She dug back as far as 1977, the year her parents married, but found nothing. Moving on to Canadian Vital Statistics, she searched birth certificates but there were no births registered to Colin and Grace McNamara in London.

Recalling that Mrs. Shannon had said Grace went home to Toronto to give birth to her and Joyce, Sam changed her search parameters and found a birth certificate for a baby boy born in Toronto to Colin and Grace McNamara on February 10, 1979. She cross-referenced the date and found his death certificate. He'd died in London on March 20, 1979. The cause of death was sudden infant death syndrome.

She had a deceased older brother that her family had never acknowledged. They hadn't even honoured him with an obituary. He was born twenty months before her sister, Joyce, so eight years before Sam.

It wasn't too much of a stretch for Sam to understand why her mother pretended Malcolm never existed. Grace refused to discuss anything unpleasant, even if it was important. Born into an upper-class family in Bath, England, her mother had attended private boarding school from the age of eight. Raised to repress feelings, Grace believed expressing emotion was vulgar. As a child, if Sam cried out of disappointment or frustration, her mother sent her to her room. Negative thoughts were to be stifled behind a smile that was a lie.

Around his wife, her father had been reserved but he'd been different in private. Sam believed he'd always been open and honest with her. Why would he have kept this a secret? How could Dad pretend his own son had never existed?

Because he had a replacement son outside his marriage, Sam thought bitterly. Her father was a liar and a cheater. The shock made her knees weak.

She'd contacted the London police for a copy of Isabella's accident investigation, and Colin's name was all over the incident report. Instead of being home with his family on New Year's Day, he'd been in London with Megan Shannon and her baby. His baby.

Anger was easier for her than sadness, and she punched the top of her desk. "You lying piece of shit!" She threw his picture from her desk. It smashed against the wall and the glass shattered. She retrieved it and hurled it in the wastebasket.

Running her fingers through her short hair, she paced the office. She worshipped her father. He was the reason she'd entered Toronto Police Services. Worse, he was the reason she'd pursued a career as a private detective when she left the force. She slumped onto the chair, taking deep gulps of air. Everything she'd assumed about her father's character was a lie.

How did he even get away with it? Grace was a control freak who had kept her husband on a short leash. It made no sense. A tiny voice inside Sam's head spoke up. *Maybe Grace knew about his second family.* Her stomach rolled.

Steadying herself, she decided she needed to know for sure. There was one person who would know the truth. The whole truth. Sam swallowed hard and opened her laptop. In order for Dad to sneak out of Toronto on a regular basis, his ex-partner would have had to cover for him.

Her fingers trembled when she opened her contacts, wondering if she'd kept the email address, and, if she had, if it was still active. After everything that happened, if Liam received an email from her, would he even answer? Wouldn't he delete it and avoid the pain?

Branded into her memory was the disappointment on her father's face when everything had fallen apart so many years ago. Sitting in the chair across from him, she'd promised never to screw up again if he would forgive her and help her to make things right.

He'd died in a car accident three years later, when she was twenty-one. The drunk driver of the other vehicle had insisted Colin had driven into the guardrail on purpose. Grace enjoyed reminding Sam at every opportunity that her father had chosen to commit suicide rather than live with the shame of what his daughter had forced him to do.

She sat staring at the blank email body and the populated address field. The cursor flashed in the subject line, waiting for her to type out *I need to ask a question.* Then she could add her cell number to the body and press send.

Did she have to tell Reece what she'd discovered about her dad? She needed to think about that. Professionally, it wasn't pertinent to their case. He'd want to know as her boyfriend, but there was no way she could tell him this without opening up about her family. She couldn't do that. He wouldn't want to be with her if he knew the truth.

For now, I'll take a page from Mother's book, she thought sourly. She'd go home to Reece and hide how upset she was. Her mother had taught her well how to repress feelings and pop on a fake smile.

Under no circumstances could Reece find out about Liam. Reece, a cop through and through, would never understand what she'd forced her father to do.

Sam wrote the email and pressed send.

CHAPTER TWENTY-EIGHT

Sam

WHEN SHE ARRIVED home depressed and exhausted, it was a relief to find the loft empty. Reece wasn't there and she didn't care where he was because she wanted to be alone. She carried Brandy upstairs, settling the dog under the covers before she lay down for a nap. When she woke, she felt ashamed of how emotional she'd been at the office.

Emailing Liam was stupid. She always made horrible decisions when she acted impulsively and didn't take time to analyse the risks unemotionally. Thank God, he was too far away to come to Toronto and confront her. No need to panic and overreact. After so many years, he'd most likely ignore an email from her.

There wasn't any reason to tell Reece what she'd discovered about her dad. She didn't share Reece's sentiment that you should talk about all your shitty personal history. She loved Reece, but the life they were building had nothing to do with the past. It was best to leave skeletons hidden in the closet.

Her past was more complicated and shameful than most, but Reece didn't need to find out. It wasn't any of his business. She could update him on their case without mentioning her father. It didn't matter if Colin was at the scene of Isabella's accident over two decades ago. The point was that Isabella was dead. Gabriella wasn't with her.

It was time to put away her family drama and focus on her job.

"You're awake," Reece remarked when she and Brandy strolled into the kitchen. He was at the stove, stirring something that smelled deliciously garlicky.

"And starved. That smells amazing." She sat at the table, which was already set.

"You okay? It's unlike you to nap."

She pasted a smile on her face. "Long drive. The air wasn't working in the car," she lied. "I've got a lot to tell you."

He laid dishes on the table. "Awesome, give me a sec to grab the rice and let her rip."

While they ate, Sam debriefed him. "Isabella LeBlanc died on January 1, 1992. She was born in Sault Ste. Marie, Ontario, on July 20, 1980." Sam filled him in on everything Mrs. Shannon said, minus the part about her father being there and her family living in London.

"Geez, Derek's a better liar than I thought." Reece reached for the bowl of rice.

She shrugged and sipped her wine. "I guess there's a chance Gabriella was pretending her sister was still alive."

"I spoke to Derek's business partner after my meeting with Belinski. Marty and his wife met Gabriella numerous times, and neither recalls her saying anything about a sister."

They ate in silence for a few minutes, enjoying the shrimp scampi and rice pilaf while a City and Colour CD played in the background.

"Any word from Canadian Customs?" She eyed the five shrimp sitting on his plate.

He sighed, stabbed two, and put them on her plate. "Gabriella visited the US in April. She crossed from Sarnia, Ontario, over the Blue Water Bridge into Michigan." Reece frowned. "Derek thinks she went shopping."

She put down her fork. "Why would she shop in Michigan? That's twice as far as New York."

"Don't know, but she spent two nights in a motel in Copper Harbor," he said.

"Where's that?"

"It's on Lake Superior in northern Michigan at the top of the Keweenaw Peninsula." He shook his head. "It doesn't make any sense. It's over twelve hundred kilometres from Toronto, so it would have taken her about twelve hours to get there."

She raised her eyebrows. "Is the shopping extra special?"

"No. It's an outdoorsman's dream come true. Great fishing, wildlife and hiking."

"Gabriella didn't strike me as a tree hugger," she said. "Were you able to talk to anyone at the motel? I don't suppose they remembered her three months later."

"Oh, the manager remembered her, told me she was 'hot'." Reece winked. "Besides, she was travelling by herself off-season. They're open year-round but don't have much traffic on weekdays in April."

"What did he say?"

"She didn't make a reservation and arrived after ten p.m. on April 4th. The manager said she went straight to her room. The following morning, she went out around nine and didn't come back until the evening. He tried to talk to her, said she was polite but not engaging. He figured she was there on business."

"Was she alone?"

He nodded.

She grabbed her phone and opened websites for Copper Harbor and the motel. "I don't get it. What do you think she was doing there?"

"No idea. Derek said Gabriella hated hiking and camping."

"The average temperature in April in that part of Michigan is a couple of degrees above freezing. Why would she drive over twelve hours to spend two nights in a remote nature resort on Lake Superior?"

"I don't know, but she took her dog," Reece said. "She had to present the vaccine report at the border to get him across, which is why they had the motel's address." He got up and took their plates to the dishwasher.

"The dog," Sam shouted. "I can't believe I forgot about the dog." She kicked herself for losing focus. "Where is he?"

"I was wondering the same thing. I figured at home, but Derek said no."

"That dog never left Gabriella's side when we were at dinner. Derek made some nasty comments about him." She pushed back her chair and patted her stomach. "I'm going to end up big as a house if you keep cooking like this."

"That's my plan, making you fat and lazy so I'll win our fitness bet." He grinned at her. "You should prepare yourself. I'm confident you'll be buying me dinner."

She laughed. "Dream on. Your ass is going down."

He sat at the table and leaned back in his chair. "Anyway, about the dog. Derek figured the police took it."

"That's stupid. The cops wouldn't take the dog."

"Well, we've found Isabella. Did you call Jim and tell him?"

"Yeah. He says it opens up new questions about Gabriella. He wants us to keep digging into her life."

Reece nodded. "Okay, so we're still on this. I left a message for the Copper Harbor Sheriff. Curious, I guess. But, now we know Isabella is dead, we should at least entertain Derek's theory. Maybe Gabriella took the dog and framed her husband."

"Or," Sam said with a sigh, "Derek killed the dog when he killed his wife."

"Yeah, I don't think that's what Jim has in mind for us to focus our investigation on."

"I know. But, between us, unless we find someone who corroborates his story about Gabriella talking to her dead sister, I'm inclined to believe he might have."

Reece reached for his wine. "I'm curious to see discovery from the Crown. Her medical records should be in there, since Derek says she asked for the insurance policy because she found a breast lump. Maybe she saw a mental health professional after her sister died."

"Have you finished reading all the diary transcripts Jim's assistant emailed?"

He nodded. "Grisly stuff. What a miserable life, but that's her interpretation of events. There are always two sides." He polished off his wine, stood, and walked into the kitchen, standing with his back to her while he ran water into the large trough sink. "I followed up with the other companies Gabriella worked for over the past few years."

Sam got up and opened the dishwasher to load the rest of the dishes. "Anything of interest?"

"She wasn't popular. All the terminations cited personal conflicts." He put a clean pot on the counter. "I can see how it would be tough to be around her a lot. She was an odd woman." He grimaced.

"I doubt all the problems were because of her personality. Gabriella was gorgeous." She reached up and hung the dried pot on the hanger over the island. Convenient. She'd been horrified when he'd unpacked it a few weeks ago, but it was growing on her.

"What do looks have to do with being disliked?" he asked.

"I bet Jack made a pass that crashed and burned."

Reece chuckled. "I suppose, but we're missing something. You know I feel sorry for her, stuck with Jack Belinski at the office and Derek at home."

She topped up her wine glass. Reece never drank more than one glass so she corked the bottle and stowed it in the wine fridge, which she noticed he'd restocked. Not bad at all, this cohabitation thing. She took her wine to the sofa.

"She picked both her husband and her job," Sam said. "Often people choose to be unhappy." She thought about her father and the choices he'd made. "If she was unhappy, she didn't need to stay in the marriage." She felt her face flush with anger and took a deep breath. She needed to concentrate on the case, not on her father's lies.

Reece sat beside her and rubbed the back of his neck. "By the way, the handwriting expert analyzed the card Derek claimed Isabella wrote. The handwriting doesn't match the diary or the sample from Derek. The handwriting analysis does suggest a woman wrote the card. I also saw a sample of Gabriella's handwriting from her job. I'm not an expert, but the writing looked the same as the diary. It didn't look anything like the writing in the card."

"If Derek created Isabella to play mind games with his wife, would he go so far as to have someone pretend to be her? Maybe get a woman to call and write the cards?"

"I suppose, but you're forgetting about the phone records," Reece reminded her. "There aren't any rogue calls."

"Okay, maybe Derek stuck to written correspondence to psych out his wife and lied about Gabriella chatting on the phone," she speculated.

He studied her. "We're working for Jim, Derek's *defence* attorney. We're not going to get that bonus if we don't find something Jim can use toward acquittal."

"I know," she agreed with a sigh. "Did you read that story in the paper yesterday?"

He rolled his eyes and nodded. "Another reason we have to find something, *anything.*"

The article was about Sam and nasty, suggesting her new partner distracted her. It hinted that the OPP had asked Reece to resign after the Uthisca events, going on to recap the deaths from her last case and suggesting she should turn in her licence. She'd be damned if she changed careers on anyone's terms but her own. Besides, the five-thousand-dollar bonus would provide enough padding for her to finish her PhD. Then she'd have options. Reputation and money were riding on them finding something Jim could use.

They sat in silence for a few minutes, each lost in thought.

"That diary bothers me, but I can't figure out why."

On his own train of thought, Reece sighed and said, "I can't find Nicholas."

She sat up. "Any chance he had anything to do with this?"

Reece shrugged. "The police confirmed his alibi. He was in Montreal, and his buddies corroborated."

"Why the weird look on your face?"

"They're not credible, in my opinion. Two of them have rap sheets for dealing, and one did time for aggravated assault."

"From what we witnessed in June, Nick didn't hold her in high esteem but what's his motive?" she asked.

"If Nick framed his dad and Derek was convicted, the insurance money would go to Gabriella's estate, which would be divided between her children," Reece said. "I'm going to keep looking for him. I did speak with the other two kids. The daughter, Anna, is a genuine horror. Looks like a sixteen-year-old hooker." He sighed. "Anna and Kevin didn't strike me as being too upset over their mother's disappearance. How horrible is that?"

She nodded, unsurprised. There were numerous entries in Gabriella's diary about how out of control the kids were. She grabbed the transcripts from her bag. "They could be torn because of their father's presumed involvement, and parent-child relationships are complicated, especially with teenagers and young adults. Truth is that some of Gabriella's diary entries about the kids were also apathetic. Listen to this:

Anna's a stupid bitch. At times like these, Papa would say that children have to respect their parents, even when they don't agree with them. Spare the rod and spoil the child. You have to be tough in every aspect of life. Do it to your neighbour before she does it to you."

Reece picked up a few sheets and flipped through them. "That's at least the tenth time I've heard that."

She looked up from the sheets. "It's the only time I've read her calling her kids names."

He shook his head. "No, not that, the phrase: *at times like these.*" He dropped the sheets he was holding and leaned against the back of the sofa, lacing his fingers behind his head. "Do you want to have kids someday?"

Her stomach rolled. She didn't want to talk about feelings. She sure didn't want to talk about kids or think about babies. "No."

"Why not?" he asked.

"I don't know." She reached for her glass of wine and drank it down.

"I never wanted kids," he admitted. "They're okay to visit, but I don't want my own. I can't figure out if it's because I'm too selfish or too generous."

Interesting. She knew he wasn't fond of other people's kids but didn't know he didn't want his own. It was probably something she should ask him about, but she didn't want to talk about babies.

As if on cue, her furry baby trotted over and licked her hand. Brandy's back legs shook when she attempted to climb on the sofa, and Sam leaned down to pull her up. It hurt to see how frail her Golden Retriever was becoming. She didn't want to think about the decisions she'd have to make down the road. Brandy curled into the corner and put her nose between her paws.

Sam was surprised when Reece pulled her close and rubbed her back.

"She's not doing too badly for an old girl. No need to worry yet," he said.

She pulled away and looked at him.

Reece smiled. "I saw your face when she was climbing onto the sofa. She's doing okay and still thinks she's a puppy. In fact, she needs a walk."

Sam got up and went to Reece's antique church altar, where she'd tucked the leash and doggy bags. She paused and ran her fingertip against a water ring left behind by a preacher who was long dead. The altar gave her the creeps, and she'd like to figure out a way to get rid of it.

Reece and Brandy joined her. "The expression on your face is priceless." He stroked the top of his altar. "It'll grow on you," he said with a grin and opened the front door. "Come on, I want to work off the few shrimp I ate."

Sam attached the leash and studied Brandy. She liked her dog more than she liked most people. She would die for her dog. More importantly, Brandy would die trying to protect her, which begged the question: what had happened to Gabriella's dog?

CHAPTER TWENTY-NINE

Sam

THE MEDIA WAS having fun. Derek's case was news, and everyone wanted a piece. Over the past three days, the papers had capitalized on the Sonia angle, writing about Derek's lover and his claim that he was with her. There was lots of speculation over whether Derek's girlfriend had something to do with Gabriella's alleged murder.

Sam figured Sonia was sufficiently spooked. It was time to confront the woman, apply some pressure, and see if she caved. Assuming, of course, Sonia was lying about not being with her lover at the time of the incident.

But before she spoke with Sonia, Sam wanted to search her condo and see what secrets she had. She'd picked a weekday afternoon for her first visit. Sonia should be at work. Assuming the hallway wasn't busy, picking the condo lock wouldn't be a problem. Reece had given her a professional set of lock picks for her last birthday, and she'd spent hours practising, much to the dismay of her friends who believed their homes were impregnable.

This would be her first time 'officially' using the picks. That left the problem of the building door. The sidewalk entrance was clear glass that displayed a vestibule with a call-up box for guests and a locked door that led into the lobby. She counted three outdoor surveillance cameras. There would be more in the vestibule. If the building employed security guards, an officer would be monitoring the cameras, most likely from a lobby desk. She couldn't see through the mirrored, one-way glass that divided the vestibule from the lobby interior and had no idea if a guard would be incredulously watching as she busily picked the lock. Her best approach would be to enter with a resident.

The Bloor Street sidewalk was bustling outside the condo building, so she grabbed a coffee from the adjacent Starbucks and picked an outdoor table so she could watch the door. When an older woman approached the building, Sam fell in behind her. The woman was juggling numerous plastic grocery bags, while trying to balance keys she had hooked around her index finger.

Sam intentionally bumped into her. "Sorry, I wasn't paying attention. I live here. Want some help getting to the elevator?"

The woman turned and smiled, gratitude lighting her face. She handed Sam three bags. "Thank you. It seems I got a bit carried away with my shopping today."

They entered the vestibule together. "Here, I'll dig out my keys and open the front door for you." Sam attempted to reach into her pocket.

"Oh no, that's okay, mine are right here. If you take this," she handed her another bag, "and grab the door when it buzzes, we'll be all set."

Inside, Sam carried the groceries to the elevator, while the woman chatted about prime rib that Loblaws supermarket had on sale. With a wave of thanks, the woman got off on the seventh floor, and Sam rode alone to the fifteenth. She was reaching for her lock picks when the neighbour's door opened. The skunky aroma of pot wafted into the hallway.

"Oh, you scared me!" The woman giggled. "You're earlier than Sonia expected. I don't think she's home." She was wearing a T-shirt with the words *Lana loves Charlie* written above a photo of her with a guy who looked a bit like Axl Rose in his younger days.

"Yeah, I made good time. You must be Lana, Sonia's talked about you," Sam said with a smile. She took a chance. "We're all getting together while I'm here, right?"

Lana smiled. "Sonia didn't say anything but I'd love to."

"Can you let me in? You have her key, right?"

Lana frowned. "Well, yeah, I do. I knew you were coming, but she didn't say anything about giving you the key. How did you get through the front door, did she tell Jeremiah to let you in?"

Jeremiah must be the body builder in the tight blue security shirt who had been sitting at the lobby desk when she came in. He'd glanced at the woman she'd entered with and returned to his magazine.

"Yeah," Sam said, "I guess she must have talked to him when she left."

That made no sense. If Sonia had wanted her guest to wait in her condo, she'd have asked security to escort her upstairs.

Quickly, Sam added, "Boy, he's a bulldog. I had to show two pieces of id. You're lucky to have such great security. Anyway, he had to do something for a resident so I was hanging around waiting for him to take me upstairs to open the door. Then I thought I'd take a chance and see if you were home."

Lana relaxed. "Well, you're lucky I was here. I was on my way out. I'll grab the key." A few seconds later, she returned. "I can't believe how fucked up everything is. I never liked her boyfriend," she shuddered, "but, wow, murder? That blows my mind."

"You know he was married, right?"

Lana shrugged. "Sure. It's less complicated, let the wife deal with all the shit that goes along with a husband." She grinned. "As a girlfriend, he treats you like gold and takes his bad moods home to his old lady."

"Did you see him here the night his wife was killed?"

She shook her head. "I don't remember. Why?"

"No reason. Hey, I left my car in a lot down the street. How do I get into your parking garage?"

Derek had told them he'd parked in the underground and went up to the condo via the garage elevator. Lobby security wouldn't be able to confirm he'd been there, since he didn't access the front lobby doors or the main elevator. If parking access cards linked back to specific residents, they'd be able to verify entrance and exit time stamps. Most security companies kept access records because they weren't large data files. It wouldn't prove Derek

　　　　　　　　　　　　　　　　　　　L.E. Fraser

had been Sonia's visitor on the night of the incident, but it would prove she was lying about being home alone.

"You need a card to use the garage," Lana said. "Sonia can get you one."

Sam felt a flutter of excitement. "Are the cards allocated to your unit number?"

"No, they're registered to the building. If you're having multiple guests, you can get extra from security."

That was disappointing, but not too surprising.

"Are there camera's in the parking garage?"

She knew it was a long shot. Private security rarely kept surveillance footage for over a month because it took up too much bandwidth. It was worth checking out, and she made a mental note to ask Reece to follow up.

"Yes." A flicker of suspicion crossed Lana's face. "You seem awfully interested in our security. Why?"

"Jealous, I guess. My building security sucks." Sam accepted the key and stuck it into the lock. "I've gotta use the facilities, so I'll see you later. Thanks for not making me wait in the hall." She went inside and closed the door, which latched with a whisper.

Inside, a short hallway led into the living space. "Wow," Sam muttered. "Having a sugar daddy has definite advantages."

The windows faced north and the view was spectacular. The units on the other side would face south toward the lake. Those would have a higher price tag. Derek had saved himself a few bucks.

Dark hardwood floors highlighted modern furniture designed from white leather and steel. The side tables were stunning, crafted from heavy glass that perched on metal-sculpted bases. Abstract art hung on the walls and softened the otherwise sterile ambiance created by the minimalistic decor. The room was spotless and resembled an expensive art gallery.

"A bit of OCD, Sonia?"

Sam opened a decorative silver box and found a chunk of hash, a vial of thick golden liquid and a small bag of white powder. She snooped through the modular wall unit, looking behind the pieces of art and flipping through books.

Sonia owned a ton of books, but no fiction. All the titles were self-help, and she hadn't hidden anything between the pages. With the exception of the books, there wasn't anything of a personal nature in the room.

Sam sauntered into the kitchen and opened the fridge. Some fruit and veg, a tub of non-fat yogurt, two bottles of Mumm's champagne and a jar of Beluga caviar, the expensive white stuff. The freezer held six trays of ice-cubes and a bottle of Grey Goose vodka. The cupboards were bare. Either Sonia ate out or she suffered from an eating disorder.

There were four doors off the hallway. The door to the left was a laundry room with a stacked washer and dryer, a folding counter, and a drying rack with silk lingerie hanging from the metal rails. The next was a guest bathroom that was sterile and felt unused. The master bedroom was to the left. She went into the ensuite bathroom. Sonia had dedicated one vanity drawer to men's toiletries. Sam sniffed the cologne. Derek wore the same overpowering scent.

She searched the bedroom next and found nothing of interest. The nightstand drawer housed a pair of fuzzy pink handcuffs, a tube of Kama Sutra prolonging gel, a bottle of Viagra prescribed to *Derek Martina*, six boxes of condoms, and a vibrator. The closet contained more clothes than one person could wear in a lifetime. All designer labels. Sam wrinkled her nose at the number of shoes.

"Who needs thirty pairs of shoes?" she muttered.

There were no pictures, love notes, or memorabilia concerning Derek. Maybe he was right. Maybe Sonia was using him to pay for her luxury lifestyle, and he was using her for sex. She left the room and stood outside the final door. Locked. Why would someone lock a door in their home when they lived alone?

She took out her pick case and studied the five-pin tumbler lock. Strange selection for an inside door. Selecting a tension wrench and a Bogota rake pick, Sam held the wrench in place with her left thumb and index finger while jiggling the rake with her right hand. The lock clicked and she nudged open the door before tucking her tools into the leather case and putting it into her pocket.

Inside was a messy, disorganized office where Sonia appeared to spend most of her time. She was a pig at heart. No wonder she didn't want anyone to see the room.

From the desk, Sam picked up a picture frame with eight photos. All of Derek. More than half of them were candid shots — sneaky, voyeuristic photographs that Sam was ninety percent sure Derek didn't know about. Scrapbooking paraphernalia littered the top of the desk with an album open to a blank page about halfway through. Sam flipped back to the beginning. Concert ticket stubs, restaurant receipts, newspaper articles and transcripts of recordings.

Derek: I'm sick to death of trying to deal with her. She's going to ruin my chances of advancing in the party.

Sonia: I don't want to talk about the bitch again. I have a surprise for you. Do you still want to play Catholic schoolgirl, sugar? I picked up the perfect outfit and went to the spa. The sweet spot is waiting for you, just the way you like.

Derek: Well, that does sound interesting, Counsellor. Are we talking about a small landing patch or are you smooth as a dolphin?

Sonia liked to tape phone calls with her boyfriend and type out the transcripts to put in a memory book. Creepy.

She took a picture of the page, flipped back and took a few more. Sonia wasn't in love with Derek. She was obsessed.

She was closing the book when it fell and a piece of paper fluttered to the ground. It was a clipped newspaper article about a Liberal fundraising dinner. There was a photo of Derek and Gabriella. Sonia had scratched out Gabriella's face, and the weight of the scribble had torn the paper.

"Shit," Sam whispered, "a lot of rage went into that."

"Who are you? What are you doing in my apartment?"

Sam spun around. She'd been preoccupied with taking pictures but Sonia must have known someone was inside. She'd entered as quietly as possible.

The stun gun she held was probably responsible for her false sense of security. Sam laughed at her. A skinny woman wearing five-inch stilettos wasn't going to be too hard to handle. The stun gun was a complication. It was similar to the ones the police carried, which meant Sonia could fire it from a distance.

"What the fuck are you doing in my house?" she screamed.

"I'm the PI working with Derek's lawyer. I wanted to talk to you." She took a step forward.

"Don't fucking move, bitch." Sonia pointed the stun gun at her. "What gives you the right to snoop around my shit?"

She took a calming breath and held Sonia's eyes. "Your neighbour let me in, which I suspect you already know. She texted or called you, right? Interesting that you didn't just call the cops or ask the gorilla downstairs to come up with you. Could it be you don't want anyone to see what you keep in here?" She gestured behind her, and Sonia's eyes darted to the desk and the scrapbook.

Sam rushed forward, grabbed her wrist, and twisted her arm behind her back, pushing Sonia's thumb toward the inside of her wrist. Sonia squealed in pain and stomped on Sam's foot. The stiletto heel did some damage. Furious, she threw her weight against Sonia's back and smashed her into the door. The stun gun dropped to the floor. Sam kicked it into the hall. With her free hand, she grabbed Sonia's neck, pinching the pressure points under the woman's jawbone and pushing upwards.

Sonia gasped and stopped struggling, sliding down the wall to her knees.

Sam dragged her into the hall and picked up the stun gun. "Get up." She released Sonia's arm. "We're going to the living room."

Sonia rubbed her neck and wiped her tears with heel of her hand. For a minute, she didn't move. Then she used the wall for support, struggled to her feet, and limped toward the living room. At the entry hallway, she darted for the front door.

"Shit." Sam grabbed her by the hair and threw her back into the living room. "Running? Really? Where are you going? Sit the fuck down." She picked her up by the armpits and tossed her into a chair.

Sam looked at her sneaker and frowned. A dime-sized hole had punctured the canvas and blood leaked through. It hurt, but wasn't too bad.

"Goddamn it, look what you did to my shoe. The only thing I hate more than shopping is wrestling anorexic women to the ground." She turned the stun gun over in her hand. "Naughty girl, Sonia, these aren't legal. Did Derek buy it for you?"

"What do you want?"

Sam sat on the sofa. "Let's start with why you're lying about being with Derek the night Gabriella disappeared."

"He wasn't here."

Sam laughed. "Okay, you were all by your lonesome. Your little scrapbook in there strongly implies you have something to do with Gabriella's disappearance. Let's give the cops a call." She reached for her cell phone.

"That's my personal stuff. You can't give it to the cops. I'm not a suspect, I was here and can prove it," she said.

Sam rolled her eyes. "I know. Your office called your landline. I suspect you also spoke with a neighbour or popped out to the convenience store." She shrugged. "Something to ensure you had a great alibi and couldn't be at the Martinas' house at the time of the incident. You don't need to be at the scene of a crime to be involved."

"What? No way. Is that what you think?"

"You work with disreputable people. You strike me as a girl who knows how to finagle what she wants. You're in love with Derek Martina and you hated Gabriella. Solid motive for conspiring to murder."

The colour drained from the woman's face. "I wanted him to divorce her. I never wanted her dead."

Sam smiled. "But Derek wasn't going to divorce his wife, was he?"

Sonia licked her lips and lowered her eyes.

"Did you pay someone to kill Gabriella?"

She shook her head. "No," she whispered. "That's not what I wanted. I didn't want the kids. I wanted Derek to leave her and give her sole custody."

"That's not how it looks," Sam said. "Defacing Gabriella's picture tells a different story."

Sonia was quiet for a minute and then she said, "Fine, Derek was here that night. He didn't go to the airport. He came over all pissed off about his wife being fired. Are you happy?"

"Why would you lie?" Sam asked.

"He's an asshole, and he's getting what he deserves." Sonia started to cry, her face twisting with hate.

"What did he do that made you want to destroy him?"

"He was selling the condo and putting me out on my ass. Have you any idea how hard it is to find affordable space downtown?"

Derek's girlfriend was tall with huge breast implants that were out of proportion to her physical frame. Expensively styled, short blond hair framed a round face with large blue eyes and full lips. She was pretty and spent time and money accentuating her natural assets, but she didn't hold a candle to Gabriella's ethereal beauty.

"What else does he pay for?" Sam asked, eyeing Sonia's black and gold sandals with the iconic Walter Steiger's curvy heel design signature. Her sister, Joyce, had been a label chaser and had owned a pair.

"The condo fees," she glanced down at her shoes, "and he gave me a credit card for clothes and stuff." Her cheeks flushed with embarrassment when she added, "My student loans are killing me. Derek promised to refer me to a decent firm after the election. He said it was a conflict of interest while he was practising law full-time." She laughed and wrapped her arms around her thin waist. "How stupid am I to believe that making a recommendation to another lawyer was a fucking conflict of interest?"

"The night Gabriella disappeared did Derek say why he wanted to sell the condo?"

"He said he couldn't afford it. Said he was broke. He told me it was fun but it was over. I was a luxury he couldn't afford. The prick said he didn't want any dirt coming up while he ran for office and that included me." She cried harder. "Like I was a fucking prostitute."

Dumped by her sugar daddy, it was starting to make sense. Sam sighed. "That's why you lied. It was payback."

She wiped the back of her hand across her nose and nodded.

"Derek could go to jail," she pointed out. "Do you hate him that much?"

"Does it matter anymore?" Sonia asked. "Everything's over. I lied at the examination for discovery under oath. I'll be disbarred." She stood and walked to the kitchen, speaking to Sam over her shoulder. "That's gotta be a record. I only completed the call to the bar in January."

Sam followed her and leaned against the counter, shaking her head when Sonia offered the frozen bottle of vodka.

"That fucking prick ruined me," Sonia said. "He wasn't even any good in bed."

"You have to recant and tell the truth," Sam told her.

Sonia nodded. "When I got home from signing the statement, I knew I was fucked. I don't know why I did it. I was just so pissed off. I didn't consider the consequences." Tears streamed down her cheeks and dripped off her chin. "I'll lose my job and have to move back to Winnipeg. My dad's going to love that. He always said I was a whore." She walked into the living room, drinking from the bottle of Grey Goose.

"Do you want me to take you to Derek's lawyer? You can recant to him. He'll help you."

Sonia laughed. "Right. Like the famous Jim Stipelli is going to cut me any slack."

"He's a good guy. Don't sell him short."

Sonia stood staring out the window. "I can't believe I was so stupid. What's wrong with women? Why do we fall in love with selfish assholes?" She sighed. "I met him at a bar. I was with a date when Derek sauntered over to the table with two martinis. He leaned down and said to me, 'We're going to share an extraordinary experience. We're going to fall in love.' He handed me one of the martinis and walked away." She took a long drink from the bottle of vodka. "I went to that bar every night for two weeks, hoping to see him again. He suckered me with a line he's probably used a hundred times."

Sam took the bottle from her hand. "Every woman can tell a similar story. It's happened to us all at least once."

Sonia looked her up and down. "I doubt you ever chased after a jerk with simpering submissiveness, ruining your life in the process."

Sam smiled. "You'd be surprised. We need to go now."

Sonia picked up her purse and looked around the living room. "I fucking hate white furniture, and my seven-year-old niece could have painted a better picture. Everything Derek picks is shit."

CHAPTER THIRTY

Sam

JULY STARTED BADLY for Sam, and the past two days had been outright awful. First, the Crown refused to believe Sonia's claim that Derek had been with her when Gabriella made the 911 call. Instead, the evidence the cops had collected from Sonia's condominium implicated her in the alleged murder. The condo building only stored video surveillance data for fourteen days, and Reece was unable to find any evidence to prove that Derek had been at the building. He had gone door-to-door, trying to find a resident who saw Derek in the garage, the elevator, or the hallway on the night of the incident. Typical for this investigation, he netted nothing.

Second, yesterday had been her father's birthday. Sam didn't agree with reminiscing about a loved one on the date of his death. It was morbid. She enjoyed celebrating her dad's life and remembering his accomplishments on his birthday. This year, the only achievement that jumped to mind was his talent at lying and living a double life with a second family. It sucked.

She was coming out of the kitchen when Reece walked through the front door with Brandy.

"You were up early." She screwed the lid onto her enormous coffee mug.

"Sam, are you alright?" he asked in a tone that matched the suspicious expression on his face.

"Sure, why?"

"You were roaming around in the middle of the night, and I heard you crying."

"Well, yes, I did get up. I had tummy trouble, but I wasn't crying." The lie effortlessly slid from her lips. She'd inherited her father's talent for deceit, apparently.

In an effort to change the subject, she asked, "What are you up to today?"

His stare was so intense that she dropped her eyes and pretended to hunt for her keys.

"I have a meeting with Jim," he said. "He had the pre-trial meeting with the Crown, and they've set a date for the preliminary hearing in the provincial court for July 21."

"Oh boy, that's a couple of weeks away. Does the Crown have enough for the judge to indict?" she asked.

"It seems so. What are you doing today?" Again, a cop's suspicious gaze and a cold tone.

"I'm meeting with one of Gabriella and Derek's neighbours. Her kids attended school with the Martina kids. I figured I may as well talk to her since she knew Gabriella." She tugged on her running shoes.

"Meet me at the office when you're done. We need to talk." He gave her a quick kiss and walked out without waiting for her.

'We need to talk' was never a good thing to hear from your boyfriend. Great, third shitty day in a row.

SHE DROVE DOWN Inglewood and stopped in front of a large three-storey brick house, parked behind a black Honda Accord, and walked to the front door.

She rang the bell and waited. No one answered. She peered through the bay window to the right of the candy-apple red door. The glass patio doors at the back of the open-concept space were open, and sheer drapes billowed in the morning breeze.

She went around the house to the wooden gate that led into the back-yard, knocked, and hollered, "Hello."

A barrage of barking was her initial greeting, before a cheerful woman's voice yelled, "Hi. Let me corral the dogs."

There was a scuffling of toenails and more barking before the gate opened. The woman held a fawn Pug under one arm, a black Pug under the other, and a second fawn stood at her feet.

"Sorry," she said, "getting in and out is an exercise in dexterity and de-termination."

Sam slipped in and closed the gate. "I love dogs. I have a Golden Retriever."

The woman placed the two Pugs on the ground. "I know this sounds strange, but I need you to sit on the steps to the deck."

The second her butt touched the wooden step, the three dogs assaulted her legs. She patted them, and they wagged their corkscrew tails while pink tongues panted from squished faces lined with wrinkles.

"Pearl, Porsche, and Cole." The woman pointed at each in turn. "If a visi-tor sits on the welcome step, they usually behave. Sam McNamara, I as-sume?"

Remaining on the step, Sam held out her hand. "You assume correctly, Mrs. Sousa."

The woman was in her mid-forties and was tall and thin with shoulder-length blond hair. She was standing with her feet in ballet's fourth position. Women with perfect posture intrigued Sam because of the level of self-discipline it took. Then again, she may have been a dancer at one time, which would explain the woman's natural grace and confident stance.

Mrs. Sousa walked to a teak patio set beside a large kidney-shaped pool, leaving her on the 'welcome steps'. Unsure how long she was required to sit while the dogs welcomed her, Sam stayed put.

Over her shoulder, the woman said, "Call me Cataleya." She sat at the table and laughed when she looked over at Sam. "Oh, sorry, you can get up. Pop a squat on a chair. There's coffee."

Sam removed Porsche from her lap and joined Cataleya. The three puggies waddled behind her.

"What a pretty name," she said.

Her host laughed. "My parents were hippies. Help yourself to coffee."

"Thanks for agreeing to talk with me." Sam reached for the decanter of coffee. "Derek told me your kids go to school with his children."

Her smile faltered and there was a strange intensity in her face. "My youngest attends North Secondary with Anna, yes."

"Are they friends?"

"No." Cataleya's lips pressed together tight.

Sam didn't care about the Martinas' kids, so she dropped it. "How well do you know Derek Martina?"

"He was over with Gabriella a couple of times for parties, but I haven't seen either of them for at least two years." Cataleya took a sip of her coffee. "Gabriella and I used to be friends." She gazed across the backyard at the garden. "Look, maybe this was a mistake." She glanced back at Sam. "I don't know anything about them. I don't like Derek anyway. Not that I want him to go to prison if he's innocent, but nothing I can tell you will help him."

"Do you believe he murdered his wife?" Sam asked.

"No." She snorted. "That would take passion. Derek's too full of himself to kill anyone."

Sam got straight to the point. "Did he have a girlfriend?"

"Want the list alphabetically or by year?" Cataleya looked disgusted.

"Was she aware of her husband's affairs?" Gabriella had told her Derek had a mistress, but Sam was curious to see if she'd told anyone else.

"She was a smart woman so I assume she knew."

"If she was unhappy, why didn't she leave?"

"I didn't say she was unhappy."

Sam frowned. "I don't see how you could be happy when your spouse is cheating on you."

"You aren't married with children, are you?"

She shook her head.

"Many women ignore a lot to maintain a certain lifestyle. Add kids and things become complicated." Cataleya sighed. "As far as the cheating goes, Gabriella didn't act as if she cared."

"What about her, did she have affairs?"

Cataleya laughed so hard, coffee spilled from the mug she was holding. "Oh gosh, sorry!"

"Here." Sam grabbed a napkin and passed it over. "I'm assuming the answer is no."

"Not a chance. Gabriella loathed men and hated sex."

"She told you that?"

Cataleya nodded. "As I said, we were friends at one time."

Interesting. Hating to engage in sex with your husband could be for a number of reasons, but hating sex in general typically pointed to past trauma.

Sam decided to start at the beginning. "When did you meet her?"

Cataleya reached for a pack of cigarettes. "Do you mind? I picked this seat because the smoke will blow away from you."

"No problem," she lied. She hated cigarette smoke.

"They moved in ten years ago, and we met the first day of school. I invited her for coffee, and, over time, it became a habit." There was something off about her voice.

"Did you like her?" Sam asked.

Smoke hung in the air like floating lace. "I did. Then I didn't."

"Why not?"

"She changed, but when I say that aloud, I know it's not true. There were always two sides to her. At times, she was refined. Other times, she was, I don't know, intense. She could change right before your eyes."

"Was she a drinker?" The dinner party had been so uncomfortable Sam couldn't recall.

"There wasn't any correlation between alcohol and her mood swings, if that's what you mean." Cataleya fidgeted. "She... well... she *changed*."

They sat in silence for a moment, and then Cataleya spoke. "It was two years ago when her peculiar personality hit home. Starting high school was stressing out Elijah, my son. Gabriella told him that high school was two tours of duty in a vicious war. It was hell and there were casualties. Her advice was to keep his back to the wall, do his time, get out alive, and never look back at the horror. Elijah was hysterical by dinner."

Harsh advice for a scared kid. "Did you talk to her about it?"

"Sure, the next day." Her eyes were angry. "She denied saying it. When I called her out, she muttered something under her breath and then started shouting and insulting me." She studied her earnestly. "She morphed into a different person."

"Sounds like she had an anger control problem and couldn't deal with confrontation," Sam said. "Did Gabriella ever talk about her sister, Isabella? Or did Derek?"

"Not really. I mean, I knew she had a sister. They talked on the phone at the kids' basketball games." Cataleya sipped her coffee. "Gabriella would excuse herself, and I wouldn't see her again until it was time to leave."

Sam was confused. "Why do you think it was her sister?"

"She told me it was."

"Her sister called her cell?"

Cataleya shrugged. "I guess so, why?"

"Did the phone ring?"

"I suppose so."

"Did you hear it?"

"No, she had a Bluetooth headset. What's going on?"

Sam licked her lips. "Nothing, just curious."

"She doesn't have a sister, does she?"

Perceptive woman. "She did," Sam said, "but she died when they were kids."

"Aha," Cataleya murmured. "You know, every time she was yakking on her phone, I felt she was faking the call."

"Why would she do that?"

"I figured the telephone call was an excuse to avoid social situations." She peeked at her watch. "Shoot, it's almost ten. I need to drag the kids out of bed."

Sam stood and remembered the dog. "Do you have any idea where her dog is?"

"Isn't he home?"

She shook her head.

"Well, Derek must be relieved. He doesn't like dogs, including mine."

She was walking toward the gate when something else occurred to her. If Gabriella had faked the telephone calls, maybe she had written the birthday card. "Do you have anything with Gabriella's handwriting on it?"

"Not that I recall. She used the computer for invitations and cards, said she was embarrassed by her handwriting."

Everyone kept telling them that but it didn't make sense. The handwriting in the diary was neat, and there was no reason why Gabriella would be embarrassed.

They shook hands and Sam noticed the perfectly painted white tips on Cataleya's nails. "Completely off-topic, but I've always been curious. How do you apply the white polish so straight on the tips of your nails?"

"Most people go to a salon. I do it myself. Ambidexterity." Cataleya winked.

Ambidexterity. Sam rolled the word over in her mind. She must have murmured it aloud because Cataleya said, "It means I can use both my right and left hands."

Hopeful, Sam asked, "Can you write with both hands?"

"Only one-percent of the population can. I happen to be one of them."

Taking a pad from her back pocket, she opened it to a blank page, took a pen from her other pocket, and handed them to Cataleya. "Can you write something with each hand for me?"

"Sure." When she finished, she handed back the pen and pad.

Sam studied the words: *It was the best of times, it was the worst of times.* Cataleya had formed the words well, but the handwriting wasn't the same. The angle of the letters was different. The weight of the ink was lighter and darker in different places. Sam felt a puzzle piece falling into place.

"Cataleya, thanks for talking to me." She returned the pad to her back pocket.

"No problem. Give me a minute to corral the dogs." She called the Pugs, and they trotted after her to the patio doors.

SAM DROVE DOWN the tree-lined street and parked outside the Martinas' house to call Reece.

"You remember that handwriting expert you talked to?" she asked when he picked up.

"Sure."

"Can you contact him and ask if science can match ambidextrous samples?"

"Interesting. When will you be at the office?"

"An hour or so. I'm stopping at the University to speak with my PhD adviser."

"Alright, see you then."

She hung up and gazed at the attic windows in the Martina house. They looked like eyes. The Dutch colonial reminded her of the home in *The Amityville Horror.*

A knock made her jump, and she turned to find an old man tapping on the passenger window with the end of a cane. She opened the car door and hopped out.

"I live there." He gestured to the house beside them. "Why are you loitering around the neighbourhood?"

She dug out a business card and handed it to him. "I'm a PI looking into the disappearance of Mrs. Martina."

He eyed her with skepticism. "Private dick, eh? Little thing like you, wonders never cease."

"Did you know Gabriella Martina?"

"Yup, she's a weirdo."

"How so?"

"Used to see her in her backyard from my porch. Got a covered one, had it put in..." His eyes fogged over and then he nodded. "About two years ago now."

"That's nice. Why do you say Gabriella was strange?"

"Didn't say strange, said she was a weirdo. Caught her red-handed burying a dog on the property line last summer." His nose crinkled with disgust. "Thing would rot and attract wild animals. Told her so, too. Lots of other options. We cremated our German Sheppard, and Mary planted a rose bush and put the ashes in the earth. No reason to bury a dog on residential property."

"Well, I suppose that's true." It was sad, but Sam wasn't about to argue with the old man. She reached for the car door.

"Identical one at her side."

She turned. "Say what?"

"You heard me. Burying one with a clone in its place. Tell me that isn't weird."

"Did you ask her about it?"

He bobbed his head. "Right I did. She said the kids would be upset. The dog — can't recall its name — was sick so she bought a new one before the vet put down the other."

Gabriella probably hadn't wanted her children to witness the dog's burial. People often bought a new animal when a pet died, especially when young children were involved. Usually, the dogs weren't identical, but to each her own.

"Speaking of the dog," she said, "have you seen it?"

"Nope. Good riddance, too. Nasty thing. Always growling at me." He looked at his watch. "My story's on the TV."

She followed him to his front door. "Did you hear anything the night she disappeared?"

He tapped his ear. "Don't hear so good. Leave the TV loud. Told the police I didn't hear a peep."

"Thanks," Sam said before he disappeared inside the house.

She thought about Gabriella all alone in the backyard digging a grave for her dog. It was beyond sad. She understood replacing your dog. If Brandy died, she'd get another dog right away, and it would be a Golden Retriever.

She didn't understand pretending a loved one never died. A voice whispered in her head, *Isn't that what your parents did when your brother died?*

CHAPTER THIRTY-ONE

Reece

THE OLD WINDOW air conditioner wheezed death rattles, and the office was an oven. Reece stripped off his shirt and gulped water while he waited for Sam.

That morning, he'd made the decision to discuss the office space with her. It represented both of them and was a humiliation.

It was over an Italian bakery in the Palmerston district at College and Bathurst, and he couldn't deny the smell of fresh bread and cannoli was mouth-watering. His issue was he liked to have his car, and there wasn't any parking. Worse, the office was a complete contrast to Sam's sparse, modern home. It was three hundred square feet of disaster.

Sporting a circa-1970s decor, the office boasted hideous wood panelling and a big emphasis on ugly orange. The carpet was a shabby burnt orange that might have been shag back in the day. There were stains on the carpet around the door and scattered beside the desk. Orange plastic blinds hung on the window, which had a piece of plywood wedged in the side to accommodate the air conditioner.

The furniture looked as if she'd rescued it from the side of the road. A crooked wicker table held a scarred white enamel bar fridge and a coffee maker that reminded him of the one his mother used when he was a kid.

Rusted metal legs precariously held up two orange plastic chairs perched in front of the splintered partners' desk. The filing cabinet was so dented it listed to one side.

The space was gross, plain and simple, and Reece wanted to move to new digs. But change didn't sit well with Sam. She was already upset, and it had something to do with her trip to London. He'd definitely heard her crying last night and couldn't understand why she'd lied.

He'd suffered too much loss to deal with lies. His parents and twin brother, a PI, had died in a car crash, and his fiancée, Sarah, had lost her fight with cancer a month before their wedding. A friend had talked him into seeing a therapist, and although the progress was slow, Reece was able to learn self-help tools to recover. Self-help required one-hundred-percent honesty from himself and the people around him. His cop instinct was screaming at him that Sam was lying to him about something big, and he didn't know what to do about it.

He loved Sam and wanted a transparent relationship, but he understood she needed to feel safe before she'd let down her walls and share. Something devastating must have happened to make her so cynical and self-protective.

One explanation for her silence was that she didn't trust him. That hurt and it was driving him nuts imagining what was causing her so much shame that she felt she had to hide the truth, regardless of the damage it would do to their relationship. She knew how he felt about lies, and withholding the truth was the same as lying. There wasn't a damn thing he could do about it, and it was making him suspicious and resentful.

Sitting in the gross office boiling to death wasn't improving his mood. Reece wiped sweat from his eye and reached for his cell to call and suggest meeting at the air-conditioned loft when she threw open the door.

"Oh boy," she gasped. "It's oppressive out there with the humidity." She laughed at him lounging in the chair bare-chested. "I'm surprised you're still wearing pants."

"I'd offer to take them off, but it's too hot," he grumbled.

She collapsed onto a chair. "We have to fix the air conditioner."

                                    L.E. Fraser

Or we could move to a professional space where we could meet clients, he thought.

Sam's short strawberry-blond hair was stuck to her cheeks and forehead in limp curls, and, when she stripped off her T-shirt, her abdomen muscles rippled under her tank top before settling into an impressive six-pack. She was taking their fitness bet seriously and working out regularly. He wasn't confident he'd win. Having trained with an ex–US SEAL, his girlfriend was proficient in hand-to-hand combat, and Reece understood her sister's murder was Sam's motivation to rely on herself to stay safe.

At five-foot-three and one hundred and five pounds, Sam sometimes looked deceptively fragile. She did not resemble a delicate flower now. The veneer of sweat made the muscles in her arms look like they belonged on a MMA fighter. Reece was proud of her.

"Geez, you expect me to focus now?" He grinned. "How did your interview go?"

Chuckling, she took the pad from her back pocket and opened it. "What do you think of this?"

He glanced at the words. "I'm guessing whoever wrote it is ambidextrous."

"You can tell?"

"No, you called and asked about ambidexterity."

She laughed, but it sounded disingenuous. "Sorry, the heat is killing my brain cells. Hey, let's have some cold wine to help the massacre along."

Sam never drank before dinner. Still, he pulled out a bottle of lukewarm wine and a beer from their decrepit bar fridge.

He handed her a glass of wine and cracked open his beer. "I bribed the handwriting expert with lunch, and he claims there are many variables to consider when matching samples to an ambidextrous person."

Slumped in the chair, she rolled her eyes with an exaggerated sigh. "Why are experts so reluctant to offer an opinion?"

"Samples frequently lack sufficient matches to reach a definitive conclusion," he said. "I had to suffer a boring dissertation about the JonBenét

Ramsey case and the ransom note that numerous handwriting experts reviewed when Patsy Ramsey was a suspect."

She raised her eyebrows. "Bet that was enlightening."

He swallowed a mouthful of warm beer and shrugged. "At least his air conditioning worked."

She laughed and filled him in on her interview with Cataleya Sousa.

"I suppose I can buy that Gabriella would pretend to receive a call as an excuse to get away from socializing," he said.

Sam laughed. "A date once did that to ditch me. While he was talking on his cell about a work emergency, his phone rang. He was too stupid to turn it off before faking his getaway call."

"I'm not sure why you'd pretend the call was from your dead sister," he replied. "That's odd. Do you think Gabriella wrote out the cards with her less dominant hand and pretended they were from Isabella? That's beyond strange."

"Maybe it was a peculiar way to keep her sister's memory alive." She sounded unconvinced.

"I did some digging on the Internet while I was waiting for you. People can learn to use their less dominant hand — athletes do it all the time — but to write well is rare," he said. "The writing in the card wasn't neat, but you could read it. I don't think Gabriella wrote it."

"Maybe she asked someone to write the card," she suggested.

"Who? She didn't have any friends." He tossed his empty beer can, bouncing it off the wall and into the recycling bin. "Why did you want to talk with your PhD adviser?"

"Mrs. Shannon told me that Gabriella was close to her sister. Isabella's death would have been catastrophic, especially if they were together at the time of the accident and she couldn't save her," she explained.

"Are you suggesting she thought her sister was still alive?"

"No." Sam twirled the stem of her wine glass between her fingers. "She didn't talk about Isabella to enough people. I think it was survivor guilt and post-traumatic stress. Dr. Raczynski specializes in PTSD, which is why I wanted his advice. People use defence mechanisms to deal with horrible

  L.E. Fraser

events they can't process, like the sudden death of a loved one. It starts in the denial stage of grief."

"There was a woman in Uthisca who fell asleep at the wheel, killing her children. A month later, she was still setting places for the kids at the dinner table," Reece said. "If that's what you're talking about, it is delusional."

While he was talking, her cell pinged. A text message. She picked the phone up from the desk but didn't look at it.

"I don't think Gabriella believed Isabella was alive." She looked thoughtful. "Have you ever talked to yourself?"

"Not with an imaginary friend." The cell pinged again. He frowned. "Are you going to check that?"

She waved her hand. "It's not important."

"How do you know? You haven't even looked at it."

"Forget about it. I'm not talking about imaginary friends. People visit cemeteries and chat with the dead person. What do they do if the cemetery isn't local?"

Reece understood what she was driving at. "Okay, let's say Gabriella understood Isabella was dead, but she kept her..." he paused to search for a word, "*essence* alive. You're suggesting Derek misunderstood. There weren't any calls. What Derek heard was Gabriella speaking aloud to work out a problem."

"Yup, pretty much. Derek never saw her on the phone. He heard her in the kitchen. He assumed she was on the polycom."

Standing, he paced the small office. "But Derek claims there were two different voices. Did she make up a voice when she talked to herself? Sam, that's crazy."

Her cell rang and she glanced at the ID, swiped the call to voicemail, and turned off the phone. Sam never turned off her cell.

"No, Derek lied about hearing two voices," she said.

"What about the gifts and cards? Her kids confirmed they received stuff from their aunt."

Sam sighed. "Well, that's why I think Gabriella wrote the card. She must have bought the gifts. I haven't had any luck tracing package deliveries to the Martinas' house."

Reece opened a second warm beer. "If Derek knew Isabella was dead and wanted to push his wife over the edge, maybe he bought the gifts."

"If he could make everyone believe Gabriella was delusional, it would lend credibility to his allegation that she asked him to pick up Isabella at the airport," she said. "We're back to believing Derek is a monster who psychologically tortured and murdered his wife." She sighed. "Did you see Jim today? What was in discovery?"

"They have a witness who saw a silver four-door sedan pull into the Martinas' driveway shortly after five on the night of the murder. Just before the cops arrived, he saw the car leave."

"Derek drives a silver four-door sedan. Was it a BMW?"

"The witness can't confirm. He assumed it belonged to Derek." Reece handed her a file. "Take a look at this. A man abducted Gabriella during a family vacation in Batchawana Bay when she was five. Six months later, a fisherman and his son found her on the US side of Lake Superior. She was walking on the ice, dressed in an animal skin."

Her eyes had widened while he spoke. "My God, why didn't Derek tell us?" She bent to the file and read the sheets.

"He claims he never knew."

She scanned the papers, and her expression was grim. "Jesus," she said, "Cataleya told me Gabriella loathed men and hated sex. No wonder."

"Read the medical intake."

"There were scars on her body. It says flesh was removed." She sounded shocked.

"Did you see where they found her?"

"Copper Harbor," Sam said. "Three months ago, Gabriella returned to where she was rescued. What has this got to do with the murder trial?"

"It goes to motive," Reece replied.

"How?"

"A frigid wife with mental health issues, a cheating husband with lofty political dreams and a large insurance policy. Sex, money, and ambition are convincing motives. The Crown is claiming that leaving the marriage would be a cataclysmic nightmare that would cost Derek a fortune and ruin his political aspirations. The easiest route was to murder his wife and be the grieving husband campaigning for harsher criminal punishments."

Reece reached for his shirt. "Cataleya Sousa's statement does more to hurt Derek's defence than help it." The shirt stuck to the sweat on his back and chest. "Regardless of our guesses at Gabriella's motivations for faking calls with her dead sister, it lends credibility to the suggestion of mental illness."

"We're missing a big piece of the puzzle." She flipped through the file, stopping at a sheet. "If Derek claims that he didn't know Gabriella was a victim, why did he think his wife's body was mutilated?"

"She told him she had skin cancer when she was a child."

"And he believed that?" Sam went back to reading. "Reece, did you see the part about the dog?"

He nodded. "Yeah, she was with a white Samoyed when they found her."

Sam's frown deepened. "The dog's name was Ganawenim. I know that name." She paused and her eyes widened. "That's also the name of the Martinas' dog, but Gabriella called him 'Gana'. She told me the name is Ojibway for 'protector' and she'd had him since childhood."

Reece snorted. "The animal would be over thirty."

She told him about her impromptu meeting with the old man after she left Cataleya.

He thought of Brandy. "My God, Sam, replacing your dead dog with the same breed is one thing, but giving it the same name?"

"Where is the dog, did Jim know?" she asked.

"No. The first officers said there wasn't a dog on the scene. Forensics confirmed there wasn't any canine blood. No white Samoyed turned into the Humane Society or Animal Care and Control. The dog's disappeared."

"Whoever killed Gabriella must have killed the dog." She sounded dubious.

"The Crown's alleging Derek poisoned the dog so it wouldn't defend its mistress, murdered his wife, and disposed of both."

"Or Derek's right and Gabriella took her dog when she left." Sam sighed.

Reece understood her frustration. They kept circling back to the same theory, and nothing they investigated netted any answers. All they had were more questions.

"What about her medical records?" she asked. "If Derek's telling the truth and Gabriella asked him to buy the insurance because she found a breast lump, can we prove that?"

He shook his head. "She had a physical two weeks before Derek took out the policy. She never mentioned a breast lump to her doctor."

"Derek lied again."

"Or Gabriella lied so Derek would buy the policy," Reece speculated.

"It bothers me she didn't reference a cancer scare in her diary. Isn't that the sort of thing you'd write about?"

"Good point. The other thing that bugs me is Derek claims she wanted the insurance to protect the kids," he said. "If so, why list Derek as the beneficiary and not the kids?"

"I'm assuming she must have seen a mental health expert after her abduction, was there anything in her health records?"

"No juvenile records," Reece answered.

"Didn't her Toronto physician request them?"

"Gabriella refused to list previous physicians, and Ontario health records weren't combined into a single system, so he couldn't obtain records without her cooperation," he said.

"Since there was a court order for the records, didn't anyone contact OHIP for her juvenile file?" she asked.

"Under the *Personal Health Information Protection Act*, juvenile records are kept for ten years after the patient turns eighteen. After that, they can be destroyed," he explained. "Gabriella filed to have them destroyed."

"Why?"

"Since she changed doctors after receiving confirmation that the records were gone, my guess is she wanted to hide being victimized." He stood and stretched out his back.

"If Gabriella disappeared on her own, she'd take her dog, Reece."

He nodded. "Yup."

"We need to find Quentin LeBlanc. Maybe she's with him or contacted him." Sam grabbed her T-shirt and went to the door. "I have a quick errand, so I'll see you back at the loft where there's air conditioning and cold booze."

Reece followed her and locked the office door, not that he cared if someone broke in and stole everything. "Any chance you'll be near a drug store? I need shaving cream."

"Sure."

They were at the stairs when he said, "I meant to ask, what happened to your father?"

She stopped in her tracks, and he almost knocked her down the stairs.

"Be careful." He laughed. "Geez, recovering from broken legs together doesn't sound too romantic."

No funny remark or snide rebuttal. Strange.

"M-my father?" She sounded cautious and alarmed.

Confused, he asked, "How did the photo break?" He pointed in the direction of the office.

"Oh, right, the picture. Yeah, it fell. I mean, I knocked it by accident and it broke."

Before he could ask how it broke on the thick carpet, she turned on her heels and ran down the stairs.

CHAPTER THIRTY-TWO

Sam

SAM SMILED AWKWARDLY at her stepfather's assistant. For some reason, she regressed to eight years old when she visited Harvey's office.

"Dear, how lovely to see you. It's been a long time," Marsha Ratcliff said.

Sam shuffled her feet. "Ah... It has been a while. Um... How's your family?"

Pushing seventy, Marsha had worked alongside Harvey for over fifty years. Sam couldn't figure out why she wouldn't retire. Her husband was a retired Ford worker, Sam knew. Harvey offered a generous pension plan, and along with the Ford pension, Marsha and her husband could enjoy a nice retirement. Yet, here she was outside Harvey's office guarding his schedule with an iron fist.

"Jessica had another baby. That makes four grandbabies, and we couldn't be happier," Marsha said with pride. "Thank you for asking. Is your stepfather expecting you?"

She shook her head. "Can I sneak in for a quick visit?"

"I can arrange that for you," Marsha said. "Go on in, dear, he'll be so pleased to see you." She reached for the phone with one hand and looked up a card on an archaic Rolodex with the other, presumably to cancel Harvey's

next meeting. Sam knew that in Marsha's world, family always took prece-
dence.

Sam knocked and eased open the office door. "Hey there, got a minute?"

Her stepfather smiled with delight, stood, and met her at the door. "What
a pleasant surprise." He gave her a hug.

"You look great for an old guy," she said.

He laughed, waving her to the sofa at the end of his corner office where
his sitting area took advantage of stunning views of Lake Ontario to the
South and Queen's Park to the west.

Her stepfather wasn't an attractive man. He was short and stout, what
some people refer to as a 'fireplug'. He was bald on top with a wispy grey
fringe circling his pink head. He wore thick glasses with heavy black frames
he'd owned forever. His grey summer suit stretched tight across his sloping
shoulders, and the pants were an inch too short.

Sam found that rich men who ascended from debilitating poverty were
often frugal to a fault. Harvey might fit that profile when it came to himself,
but he was generous with other people. In addition to running a global land
development enterprise that rivalled Donald Trump's, Harvey spearheaded a
charitable organization that generated millions of dollars every year. His
largest contributions went to Alzheimer's research because of her mother.

Grace had met Harvey twenty years ago when Sam was eight and her
mother had volunteered at a charity event his organization had held. Her
parents had befriended him, and Harvey had been a huge support after her
dad had died. Grace had married him within a year, two years before the
Alzheimer's diagnosis.

Sam wasn't surprised when Harvey, who was always one to speak his
mind, said, "You should visit your mother."

She nodded but didn't reply.

"I read in the papers that you're working with Jim Stipelli on Derek
Martina's murder trial."

She cringed. *Everyone* was reading about her involvement. "It's not going
well."

"Do you know what the difference is between a successful person and a failure?" he asked.

Although she could think of numerous differences, Sam shook her head.

"A successful person fails until they don't. Is the case what brought you here?"

"No, I have another problem and need help." She paused before adding, "And some advice."

She considered asking him about what she'd discovered in London but didn't. If it turned out Harvey knew she'd had a brother who died, she wouldn't be able to forgive him for not telling her. Never ask a question when you can't handle the answer. It was safer to avoid it.

She was positive Harvey didn't know anything about her father's affair with Megan Shannon or their son, Ryan. Her father wouldn't have shared something so personal. If her mother knew, Grace would view her husband's weakness as a humiliation and would studiously ignore it.

Besides, Sam had a much bigger problem.

She chewed on her lower lip. "I emailed Liam. Worse, I sent him my cell number."

Harvey's eyes widened.

"I have questions about my dad," she said. "Liam can answer them because he was Dad's partner on the job.

Harvey never pried, and she knew he wouldn't ask about the nature of the questions. That wasn't the point.

"Contacting Liam was a mistake," he said bluntly.

Mistake was an understatement. Emailing Liam was idiotic. She hadn't weighed the risks and had let her need to ferret out the truth overshadow her common sense. Now she was in a dangerous position because she'd acted with rash impulsiveness. Worse, her stupidity was forcing her to ask her stepfather for help, and she hated asking anyone for help.

Feeling miserable, she said, "Harvey, you paid him off when he surfaced after Dad died. I was... well, I was hoping you could negotiate something again."

"That was a long time ago. He'd just found out what you did. Liam hadn't processed his grief or rage." He looked concerned. "My offer could make things worse."

She nodded. "I know, but please try."

"Have you told Reece what happened?

She shook her head.

"Oh, Sam," his eyes were heavy with disappointment, "you can't lock your past in Pandora's box."

She didn't reply. A student of Greek mythology, Harvey's advice always used a reference.

Looking worried, he asked, "Is Liam still in Australia?"

"As far as I know. He texted a few times." She handed him a piece of paper. "This is the number the messages are coming from. Considering his profession, it's probably a throwaway."

Harvey took the paper and glanced at it. "Did you reply?"

She shook her head. "I've received a couple of calls from a blocked number. I didn't pick up."

"What did you say in the email?"

"I asked him to call me."

Harvey raised his eyebrow. "Yet you didn't pick up when he tried, and you ignored his text messages." He sighed. "You need to explain the reason you contacted him or you run the risk of him misunderstanding your intentions."

"I can't. I can't hear his voice." She felt a wave of shame.

"If I contact him, he'll think I'm influencing you again. He blamed the adults in your life for what he lost. Time and distance doesn't always make the heart grow fonder. Liam may hate you."

She thought about her father's funeral. "He always blamed me, and he was right. I deserve his contempt. Please see what you can do."

"Liam is not one to back down from a fight. He'll come to you," he predicted.

She disagreed. "No, he didn't try to contact me when Reece and I were in Australia in the spring. He must have read in the papers we were involved with Mussani's death."

"That was different. *You* hadn't reached out to him. Now you have. Liam will come."

"That can't happen, Harvey," she whispered. "What would Reece think?"

Harvey leaned forward and grasped her hands. "Tell Reece the truth, Sam."

"He was a cop, he'll never understand."

"Do you love Reece?"

She nodded.

"Then grow up."

She pulled free her hands, stunned by the heat in his voice.

"Emotionally mature people don't lie to the ones they love. Lies of this magnitude end in disaster every time."

"I'm not lying, Harvey." She felt her face flush with indignation. "It happened years before I met Reece. It's in the past and isn't relevant to our relationship."

"If that's true," Harvey countered, "why would he care? You are lying because you're withholding information you believe will influence Reece's decision to be with you."

"I'm not the same person I was back then," she retorted. "Why do I have to share ancient history with everyone I meet?" She stood and paced the large office in quick, angry strides. "I'd rather be alone than have to sacrifice my right to privacy."

"Be careful what you wish for." He stood with a sigh and walked behind his desk.

"Will you contact Liam?" she asked.

"Quid pro quo, Sam. You're here for my help so do me the honour of listening to my advice or we'll find ourselves here again."

"I'm sorry. It's not that I don't value your opinion. I'm just..." She let the thought drift away. What was she? Stressed was too shallow a way to describe her feelings since Liam contacted her. Terror came closer, but there was no way she'd admit to a living soul she was scared. She felt the same level of self-disgust over fear as she would if she were caught crying.

"Let's cut to the chase," Harvey said. "If you want a healthy relationship with Reece, tell him before he finds out. Your back's against the wall, and that's the only option you have. Remember what Liam is and what you took from him. It doesn't matter how far away he is. Liam will come back to Canada."

When she didn't reply, he asked, "Are you familiar with Cassandra in Greek mythology?"

"A little."

"Apollo gave her the gift of knowing the future while condemning her to be rejected and disbelieved." He leaned back in his chair and studied her.

"I know," she said, seeing where he was going. "She predicted the destruction of Troy."

"And could do nothing to stop the tragedy because no one took her seriously," he finished.

"You're wrong. Liam won't cross the globe to see me," Sam argued. "It's too far."

"Do you know why Apollo turned Cassandra's gift into a curse?" he asked.

"Because she denied him." Sam's fear swirled inside her like a living parasite.

"To men like Liam, distance is immaterial."

She swallowed hard and walked to the door. "I should go," she mumbled.

His voice called her back. "Sam, a question."

She turned.

"What have you told Reece about your mother?"

"Nothing much. Why?"

"You've told me a great deal about him. In fact, I feel like I've known the man for years. Why haven't you brought him to meet us?" Harvey demanded.

She lowered her eyes, again chewing on her lower lip. "I... ah... well. We were out of the country and..."

When she looked up, the disappointment in Harvey's eyes was more than she could stand.

"Trying to run from your past ends in tragedy every time," he said.

"I should go." She walked briskly to the door.

How in God's name had she ended up in such a mess?

TWO WEEKS LATER, Harvey sent her a text. *Life's true tragedy is that the young disregard the opinion of their elders.*

She didn't need to call her stepfather. She understood perfectly. His offer to Liam hadn't landed well. Her past was catching up to her.

Liam was coming to Canada.

CHAPTER THIRTY-THREE

One Month Later: Toronto, Ontario

Sam

IT WAS THE end of August, and they hadn't found Quentin LeBlanc. The man had vanished. Jim was riding her ass, the press were being dicks, and she wished she'd never taken the case. She had to find something — anything — that would help Jim to establish reasonable doubt.

To make matters worse, Reece's mood these days was either withdrawn or cantankerous. Confronting him wasn't an option because he'd twist the discussion into another inquisition over her secrecy. She was surprised he wasn't shining a bright light in her face while grilling her.

Since she was lying to him, the prudent course was to avoid it until she figured out how to deal with Liam. Then she'd find a way to tell Reece at least part of the truth.

The First Canadian Place elevator arrived, and a herd of people crowded out, but it was after seven and they had the ascending car to themselves. They rode to the fifty-seventh floor in strained silence.

Jim was waiting in reception looking impatient. "Did you find Quentin LeBlanc?"

"No." Sam followed him to his office.

Jim's office had always perplexed her because it was a mix of contradic-
tory styles. An intimidating collection of Tolstoy and Dostoevsky first
editions filled a heavy, wooden bookcase framed by whimsical watercolour
art. The desk was an Italian antique but the lamp belonged on a space station.
Modern red leather chairs circled a Queen Anne mahogany dining table that
faced an interactive whiteboard. Today, the board displayed a child's drawing
of a big yellow Pikachu with rosy cheeks. The kids must have visited over the
weekend.

Jim waved them to seats. "Tell me what you found."

Reece stood by the door looking sour. "Quentin worked for London Life
and transferred from London to Victoria in June of 1992, six months after
Isabella's death. He disappeared in March of 1993."

"Can you elaborate?" Jim asked.

"One day he didn't show up for work," Reece explained. "Great-West
Life bought London Life in 1997. I talked with the director of human resources in Winnipeg, and Quentin's HR file includes a Victoria Police
Department incident report. It states that the VicPD checked his apartment
and Quentin was gone. No signs of a struggle and no reason to suspect foul
play."

Jim frowned. "Did he take his belongings?"

"It was a furnished apartment."

"What about a car?"

"Didn't own one," Reece answered.

"How about his bank?"

"Quentin deposited his pay weekly but took the money out in cash,"
Reece said. "He closed the account the day he disappeared. I'll let Sam
debrief you on what she found." Reece closed his iPad case and folded his
arms over his chest.

"No arrests or civil claims. He had dual citizenship — born in Canada to
American parents," Sam said. "After his birth, they returned to the States and
came back to Ontario when Quentin was thirteen. His parents are dead, and
he was an only child of only children."

Jim sighed. "He could be in the US."

                                              L.E. Fraser

"It's possible. He didn't renew his driver's licence or provincial health card," she said, "and no T4 tax slips were issued to him after 1992. Nothing shows up on a credit check — including credit cards — and there's no death certificate registered in Canada."

Reece walked to the windows and stood gazing out. Sam noticed how tired he looked. He wasn't sleeping, and she knew it was because he was worried about her. When you loved someone, it was a shitty feeling to be responsible for his unhappiness.

When he spoke, he sounded dejected. "Quentin LeBlanc dropped off the face of the earth the year Nina LeBlanc died and Gabriella married. Jim, if you want to search the US, it means collaborating with someone across the border. We don't have access to information."

"If he's stateside," Jim said, "he left Canada before Homeland Security was founded. Governments weren't as suspicious in the early 1990s. You didn't need a passport to cross the border from Canada into the US."

Sam nodded. "He could have walked onto the Coho ferry from Victoria to Port Angeles, Washington, with nothing but a driver's licence."

"Are you working any other angles to find him?" Jim asked.

"I took a copy of his last driver's licence picture," Sam said, "and put it through an aging app to try to get an online hit. Nothing turned up but I posted ads with the picture online and in Canadian and US papers."

She stood and paced the office. "Quentin won't be happy about us publicly searching for a name he tried to kill." Infusing confidence in her tone, she added, "Someone might recognize the picture and contact us. *If you see something, say something* is a campaign people in both countries take seriously."

"The Internet is a powerful tool, and he's bound to stumble across those ads," Jim agreed. "If I were him, I'd call and try to get you off my back without giving up my location."

"Based on what Derek told us," Reece argued, "Quentin was a drunk. If he lived with substance abuse, the aged picture won't be an accurate depiction of how he looks today."

"The question is why he disappeared in the first place." Jim was a result man and didn't deal well with negativity.

Sam jumped in before pessimistic Reece could open his mouth and do more damage. "Fear." She sat down at the table. "He owed scary people money, he saw something he didn't want to tell anyone about, or he was threatened."

"I might be able to use Quentin's disappearance as a possible explanation for Gabriella disappearing and create reasonable doubt of her death." Jim sighed.

"Are you worried?" she asked.

He erased Pikachu from the whiteboard. "Here's what we have." He wrote down the evidence against Derek.

When he was done, Sam leaned back in the chair and reviewed his list. She was aware of most of the evidence, but the tarp was new information. "I didn't know about the blood inside the shed on the remaining tarp or the credit card receipt from the purchase."

"Derek says he didn't buy them," Jim explained, "but there's a charge from Home Depot on his Visa statement for a two-pack of industrial tarps a week before the murder."

"If Gabriella had Derek's credit card PIN, she could have used it," Sam said. "No signature makes it impossible to prove irrevocably who made the purchase."

"I'm making that argument."

"Did they test the age of the blood in the house and the shed?" Reece asked.

"I don't know," Jim said. "Why?"

"In university," Reece said, "we were given a case study on insurance fraud. The perpetrator tried to fake his death by cutting himself over a period of weeks and freezing the blood. Forensics was able to tell based on the blood's chemistry."

Jim looked skeptical. "Why didn't Gabriella leave sufficient blood to prove death?"

"Reece, didn't she study biochemistry?" Sam asked and he nodded. "Then she'd know a chemical was needed to prevent coagulation, same as blood banks use. I'm assuming it would show in testing."

"You're probably right." Reece swivelled his chair to face Jim. "If she drained her blood at the time of the incident, she could have staged the crime scene with enough to prove violence before she called 911."

"Agreed, but we can't prove it." Jim studied his list and continued, "If we assume Gabriella's dead, there's Sonia. She was obsessed with Derek and had a ton of evidence in her condo implying she hated Gabriella and wanted her out of the picture. She also has known ties to criminals."

Sam didn't argue but didn't believe it. She'd interviewed her numerous times. Sonia didn't know Derek was dumping her until the night Gabriella disappeared. She didn't have a reason to frame Derek or to kill Gabriella. It didn't make sense.

Her phone rang and she powered it off.

"Not answering, Sam?" Reece's tone was all innocence. "Maybe you'd prefer privacy. Want to step out and return the clandestine call?" With an ugly smirk on his face, he turned to address Jim. "That's been her modus operandi lately."

It wasn't surprising that Reece had taken note of the many times over the past few weeks she was either texting or whispering into her phone before retreating to the bathroom to finish the call.

"Reece, I–"

He interrupted. "Forget it. Excuse me, I'm grabbing coffee."

"The kitchen is down the hall to the right," Jim told him.

Reece nodded his thanks, glared at Sam, and stormed out.

After he left the office, Jim asked, "Problems in paradise?"

Sam pinched the bridge of her nose. "No, Reece is..." She hesitated. What *was* he? "Tired and cranky," she mumbled.

Jim waved off her explanation. "Reece is a good guy. Be patient. Cops have a difficult time switching sides by transitioning into the private sector to work for the defence. Let's get back to this."

Happy to let it drop, Sam looked at the massive amount of evidence on the whiteboard.

"The *pièce de résistance,*" Jim said, "is that Derek mentioned to people — all on the Crown's witness list — that Gabriella wouldn't be around to interfere with his campaign."

Still looking grumpy, Reece returned with his coffee. "We need to prove she's alive."

"We've missed something about the diary," Sam said. It didn't feel as if Gabriella contrived the diary to put Derek in a bad light, because the anger and hate portrayed her as aggressive. "Jim, can I see your copy?"

He rifled through a box and handed her a transcript. "The other problem," he said, "for me I mean, is that Derek Martina is an asshole. A jury is going to hate him." He laced his hands behind his head and studied the whiteboard.

"Are you putting him on the stand?" Reece asked.

"Haven't decided. I can't let him perjure himself, and he has low impulse control. Opposing counsel will rip him to shreds."

Sam put her hands on the diary transcription. Finally, it hit her. "It isn't written in personal, first-person format." She separated the sheets and handed Reece and Jim a pile. "Look for references to 'my kids' or 'my husband.'"

They sorted through their piles. Reece separated several sheets. "There are first-person references." He read aloud, "*In my opinion, the world would be better off if Derek wasn't in it. I hate him.*"

Jim quoted from his pile. "*It sucks that a man would call his wife a cunt. I hope he eats shit and dies.*"

Frustrated, Sam shook her head. "It never says, 'Derek called me.' The writer never refers to Gabriella's kids, husband, or job in the personal form. Listen to this: *At times like these, I wish the man would drop dead. Playing racket ball at a hoity-toity club doesn't make him an athlete. He's such a fraud. What a miserable life. There has to be a way I can help.*" She dropped the sheets to the table. "See what I mean?"

Reece frowned. "No."

"Who is she planning on helping? She's talking about her own miserable life. It doesn't make sense," Sam insisted.

"Are you suggesting she didn't write it?" Jim asked. "Her daughter told the police she saw her mother writing in the book, and the only fingerprints were Gabriella's."

Sam tapped her knuckle against her lips. Something danced around the misty edges of her memory.

"Many people told us Gabriella spoke in the third person," Reece reminded her. "She wrote the way she spoke, that's all."

"If it was third-person, it would say 'Gabriella thinks' and it doesn't," Sam argued. "It says 'in my opinion' but not 'my kids'."

Reece shrugged. "So what? She felt like an outsider looking in at her own life."

Sam silently read the entry for Mother's Day.

Derek took the kids out to play golf. They didn't invite their own mother. I remember Mother's and Father's Day in London and the funny barbeque hats and aprons. Every year Papa drew a skully board on the driveway. She always loved skully. That didn't change. I think it was because he let her play skully as a reward if she didn't cry. She always obeyed, but I fought. She was the fairy princess. He loved her, but hated me.

Jim took the sheets from Reece and put them in the file box along with his own. "I hadn't anticipated a cancellation coming up on the court's calendar, but we're on record requesting a speedy trial. We're stuck with the October trial date." He frowned. "I don't need to remind you my reputation isn't the only one on the line here."

He didn't. Sam knew how badly hit her investigation firm would be if the court found Derek guilty of murder. Discovering Isabella was dead, finding Sonia's obsessive memorabilia and establishing that Gabriella chatted with her dead sister all went to motive. If she were investigating for the Crown, she'd be doing a bang-up job.

They were in the elevator when Reece said, "I'm sorry about what happened in Jim's office. It was immature. Sam, we need to talk."

"I know," she agreed. "I... ah... there's something I have to do but I won't be long."

His expression was stony. "It's after eight."

"It won't take long, Reece. I'll meet you back at the loft."

"I'll come with you and we'll go out for dinner and talk."

"I'm meeting someone."

He put his hand on her arm. "Please cancel your plans."

She avoided his eyes. "It won't take long."

"Sam, what the hell is going on with you? Why are you so secretive? Who are you meeting? Is there a reason you have to do this tonight?"

"Is there a reason you're interrogating me?"

"I wasn't aware I was doing that." He ran his fingers through his hair with an exasperated expression. "Maybe that's what it'll take for you to be truthful."

"I can't go out alone without your permission, is that it?"

His expression darkened. "What? That's ridiculous. Why are you getting so defensive? Ever since you went to London, you've been acting sneaky. Who keeps texting and phoning you?"

"Reece, I'm not interested in a relationship with a jealous and paranoid man," she retorted.

That hit home. Instantly, his eyes changed from angry to hurt. She reached out to him. "Reece—"

"Forget it." He stuffed his hands in his pockets and walked away with his shoulders hunched and his head low.

CHAPTER THIRTY-FOUR

Sam

WHEN SHE PULLED into the parking lot at Scarborough Bluff Park, a black Harley motorcycle was in the lot, meaning he'd also chosen to arrive early. She took the gun from the glove box and put it in her jacket pocket. Keeping her right hand in her pocket, she crept through the woods, easily remembering the route to the secluded beach where they'd met in secret when she was young.

He was facing the lake, watching the setting sun wash the water's surface with bands of colour, but he heard her approach. She saw his shoulders stiffen. She stood a metre away, waiting for him to turn. When he did, her throat closed, the assault of memories catching her off guard.

Blond hair hung to his shoulders in sun-kissed waves, and his face was clean-shaven with only tiny lines hinting at his true age. Faded jeans rested low on his hips with a studded black belt and a silver Hells Angels *Totenkopf* buckle. A plain white T-shirt accentuated the lean muscles in his torso, and tattoos covered the visible skin on his arms. Simple red letters stood out on his left bicep, AFFA. The letters meant, *Angels Forever; Forever Angels.* Beneath the red letters was a black diamond with *1%* inscribed in the centre. Her father had told her that the tat signified 'outlaw intent'.

Liam was a study in contradictions, the heavy black ink and biker attire not quite believable against the elegance of his long, tapered fingers with neatly clipped nails. His grey eyes were hard and suspicious, but his expression was neutral. Sam sensed no immediate threat.

"Warm night for a coat," Liam remarked.

She let go of the Glock, removed her empty hands from her pockets, and clasped them at her waist. "You shouldn't have come."

"Then you shouldn't have contacted me." His voice was cold. "Tell me why you did, Samantha."

She avoided his eyes, staring across the lake and breathing in air stained by a sour odour from the rotting vegetation that floated on the water's surface. More concerned about someone seeing her with Liam than with her safety, she'd chosen the spot for privacy. She hadn't anticipated the force of the memories nor had she considered how isolated the stretch of beach was. She wasn't safe, physically or emotionally, and she cursed her own stupidity.

"I—" She stopped and took a breath. "I have questions about my father."

He dropped his cigarette to the sand and crushed it beneath his boot. "Doesn't that sound dumb to you?"

She shuffled her feet against the sand but didn't drop her eyes from his. "Did he ever talk about a woman named Megan Shannon in London? Did he have a child with her?"

Liam crossed the sand to stand at the water's edge with the toes of his boots in the lapping waves. He looked west and Sam followed his eyes. The sun was a huge ball of orange between dark purple clouds, and thick brush strokes of red and yellow streaked the horizon, tinting the edge of the still water with splashes of pink. She remembered all the nights they'd spent together watching the sunset, and her heart ached over how naïve and trusting she'd once been.

How many times had she wished for the memories to die so she could experience a reprieve from the shame and regret? She'd never imagined she would be here with him again, forced to confront what she'd spent her life trying to forget.

"You were his partner on the job." Sam took a step and stood behind him. "Dad trusted you." The hypocrisy made the words catch in her throat.

He stiffened but didn't turn. "There a second meaning beneath that statement?"

"That's not what this is about."

The breeze pushed away the strands of sun-kissed hair, and she spied the tiny diamond stud in his earlobe. Eleven years ago, she'd saved money from her after-school job to buy him the earring. It broke her heart he still wore it.

"Liam, did he have a child with Megan Shannon? Is that why he transferred to Toronto from London?"

"You want to talk about a stranger's child? That's the reason you contacted me?" His eyes were angry, but she could see the pain and disappointment. "We're done here." Liam turned to walk away.

She laid her hand on his upper arm. The physical contact created an electric sensation that ran from her fingertips to her heart. "Please, wait."

He stopped and turned to study her. "I thought..." He reached up and caressed the side of her cheek.

She pulled away and took a step back. Her emotions were spinning. "He was my father," she whispered. "I need to know the truth."

The speed his expression turned to anger frightened her. "The Queen of Deception *needs* to know the truth?" He spat the words at her.

Feeling vulnerable, she took another step back and reached for the comfort of the gun. When she moved her hand toward her pocket, Liam grabbed her wrist, spinning her around. He pushed her back against his chest and roughly crossed her arms over her breasts. He drove her hands into her throat. The air rushed from her lungs, leaving her breathless and wheezing.

She threw back her head, trying to hit his chin or unbalance his stance. He squeezed her wrists harder, crushing the bones and numbing her hands.

"She'd be ten," he hissed into her ear. "I think about her every fucking day."

She couldn't breathe. She couldn't move against his death grip.

He shoved her away from him. She stumbled and fell to her knees. In a single motion, she grabbed the gun from her pocket, shifted into a crouch and spun around to face him. She pointed the gun at his chest.

"Go ahead, Samantha." Liam held his arms out. "Kill me like you killed our daughter."

The pain in her wrists made her grip waver. He laughed at the gun shaking in her hand. Without a word, he turned and left her crouching in the sand.

Slowly, she thumbed on the safety and lowered the Glock. She stood and watched Liam climb the escarpment to the trails leading back to the parking lot. She turned away to watch the dying sun embrace the purple horizon.

She remembered her innocence when she lay beside her father on the dock of their summer cottage. She remembered the sweet apple wood and vanilla fragrance of his cigar and the laughter of children tubing on Lake Muskoka. She had loved him unconditionally, and she had destroyed him.

Liam had worked undercover with the Toronto Guns and Gang Task Force prior to moving to homicide. He was twenty-nine, and her dad hadn't been pleased about partnering with a young man he considered burned out by undercover work. Their relationship was cautious and distant until it evolved into one of mentor and protegé.

She was sixteen when Liam and some other cops spent a weekend at their Muskoka cottage. Skulking in the shadows, she'd watched from the side of the cottage while the men set up a stage in the backyard, running extension cords that snaked from the cottage to power the amps.

When Liam had stripped his T-shirt over his head, the ink on his back was exotic and tantalizing. She'd asked her dad what the profile of the skull with feathered wings on the helmet meant, and he'd explained the type of work Liam had done.

That night, with the music reverberating across the black lake, Sam had stood quietly on the party's outskirts, watching the golden god with the bass guitar slung against his naked midriff while his fingers flew across the strings. She remembered thinking he'd been born to hold a guitar.

Liam was her first, and she'd loved him with an intensity you allow yourself just once in a lifetime, when you are too young to understand that infatuation is precious but fleeting. It lasted a year in secret.

She'd found out she was pregnant simultaneous to discovering Liam had maintained allegiance to the Angels. Her father had been right. The undercover work had messed with Liam's head until he could no longer differentiate the person he was from the person he'd pretended to be.

Liam had promised to leave the club for her and their baby. When the ultrasound confirmed they were having a girl, Liam's joy had convinced her he would keep his promise.

And then came the night from hell. He'd stopped at the east Toronto clubhouse and instructed her to wait in the car. Five minutes later, he returned and threw her the car keys, yelling at her to go without him.

She'd scrambled from the passenger seat, sliding across the gearshift to the driver's side. Men had poured from the clubhouse, and motorcycles had roared into the yard from every direction. On the arriving men's jackets, she'd recognized the rival gang's Outlaws insignias. With shaking hands, she'd sped into the night, leaving Liam behind to fight the war.

Two Outlaws died that night. Whether Liam was one of the shooters, she didn't know. She never saw him again.

Scared and hopeless, she'd confessed everything to her dad. He'd sat beside her at the kitchen table with his face drawn and pale, the butt of a wet cigar resting in the ugly ceramic ashtray she'd made him in grade two for Father's Day. She'd watched him age before her eyes and when he stood and walked away from her, his shuffling gait had broken her heart.

Within a week, Liam had resigned from the force under the guise that his mother was ill in Australia. Her father never spoke of him again, but she knew he'd covered Liam's deception and tampered with evidence to conceal his partner's involvement with the motorcycle club. He hadn't done it to protect Liam. He'd done it to save his daughter. If the Outlaws had discovered a cop's daughter was pregnant by a rival gang member, her life would have been in danger.

She had an abortion, erasing her final connection to Liam, but her father changed. It was as if the secrets she'd made him carry had slowly eroded his pride and self-worth until he lost himself amongst the lies.

He died two years later in a car accident. She'd wept by his grave, knowing she'd never be able to forgive herself for the compromises she'd forced her father to make.

Liam's true character surfaced when he returned for the funeral, expecting to meet his daughter. When she told him she'd had an abortion, it took four cops to pull him off her. Grace had stood in the cemetery screaming obscenities at her while her sobbing sister clung to their mother. Harvey was the only one who had understood her shame, guilt, and regret.

She had to let go of the past. If she didn't, she'd destroy everything she was working so hard to build — her company, her relationship with Reece, everything. Her father was dead. It was time for his daughter to move on.

WHEN SHE ARRIVED home after midnight, she closed the front door and savoured the solitude of the darkness, blinking when a lamp switched on by the window. Her throat closed when she saw Reece on the chair beside the sofa.

Before he could speak, she said, "We need to talk."

"Where were you?"

"I've been keeping secrets. I'd like to try to explain, if you'll let me." She took a tentative step into the centre of the large, open space.

Reece shook his head. "I know what you've been hiding. You had a visitor." The lighting was too dim for Sam to see his face clearly.

"A visitor?" She felt a rush of panic. "Who?"

"He didn't tell me his name."

"What did he want?"

"To tell you that Ryan Shannon is your father's son. He said he's done bleeding for you. He's broken the only promise that ever mattered to him."

She walked to the sofa, sat on the edge, and twisted in her seat so she could see Reece's face. His expression was blank, but he gripped the arms of the chair so hard his knuckles were white.

"Liam was my dad's partner on the job," she said.

Reece's expression was unyielding. "He was wearing his cut — his club jacket — with his patches. You're telling me your father was partnered with the Vice President of the Hells Angels Australian chapter?" He laughed an ugly sound that frightened her.

"Let me explain. It's..." She stopped, not knowing where to start.

"You had an intimate relationship with your father's partner, a man close to twice your age. He made a point of taking off his jacket. I'm assuming you're the 'Samantha' he has tattooed on the inside of his left forearm."

She took a deep breath. "Listen, you were right. My family lived in London. I didn't know. They moved the summer before Isabella died." She spoke fast, hoping he wouldn't interrupt. "My father was at the scene of Isabella's accident. He was visiting Megan Shannon. They had a child together. His name is Ryan Shannon. He's doing graduate work at Dalhousie. Reece, my father lived a double life. He—" her voice wavered, but she held it together, "he had a second family and lied to me my whole life."

Reece refused to look at her. "I don't care about any of that. I care that Liam flew across the world to see you. Tell me the fucking truth. Did you want to see Liam? Is that why you contacted him and lied to me?"

"I wanted to know about my father," she said.

"Unbelievable. Know what that looks like to me, *Samantha*?" he shouted. "It looks fucking suspicious."

"I didn't want him to come here. I asked him to call me so I could ask about my dad."

He ignored her. "Liam had lots to say to me," he said with an ugly laugh. "I suppose it's the old bro code." He stood and paced the room in angry strides.

"What did he say?" she asked.

Reece spun around and faced her. She had never seen him so angry.

"Did your father compromise the murder investigation of two Outlaws so the authorities wouldn't discover Liam's connection with the Angels? Did Liam kill those men?" His voice was even now and that scared her more than his shouting.

"Answer the question," Reece demanded. "Was your father a dirty cop? Did he protect a murderer?"

This was why she hadn't wanted to open up to him. He'd never be able to understand.

"Answer me. Did Colin McNamara tamper with evidence in a homicide investigation?" he yelled.

"Yes. Are you satisfied? Yes, he tampered with evidence," she yelled back.

"Your dad was a detective sergeant and a good cop. Why would he compromise everything he believed in and risk destroying his career?"

She stood and faced him. "Because, Reece," she yelled, fighting tears, "I was at the clubhouse that night. My father didn't want anyone to know Liam was involved with me. I was seventeen and pregnant with his child."

He looked as if she'd slapped him. For a few minutes, he said nothing.

"If Liam was charged with murder," he finally said, "there was a chance the Outlaws would kill you in retaliation."

She nodded.

"He didn't protect his corrupt partner. He protected his daughter."

"And it ruined him. I ruined my own father." Sam put her face in her hands and sobbed, wrenching cries that tore from her throat.

Reece gathered her in his arms. "I'm sorry. I've known for months you've been lying and keeping secrets. I didn't know what to think when Liam showed up. I'm so sorry, please don't cry."

"My mother told me I was a whore and Dad drove into the guardrail on purpose because he couldn't live with what I made him do."

Rubbing her back, Reece hugged her tighter. "No, baby, it was a horrible accident."

"I don't know any more. He wasn't the man I thought he was at all. My father was a liar and a cheater. My parents even lied about having a son. Why wouldn't they have talked about my brother, Malcolm?"

"Who's Malcolm? I thought you said your half-brother's name is Ryan?"

"I mean my parents' baby. He was born two years before my sister, Joyce," she said. "I found his death certificate. Malcolm died when he was six weeks old."

"Wait a minute." He pulled away and looked into her eyes. "Are you saying you found out about all this months ago when you were in London?"

She nodded miserably.

"No wonder you've been so upset." He pulled her close. "Can you talk to your stepfather?" he suggested. "Would your mother have told him about Malcolm before she died?"

She shook her head. "I have to talk to you about Harvey, too."

Reece seemed confused. "What about him?"

She was downloading too much information too fast. She took a deep breath and shrugged off her jacket, pulling the sleeves of her shirt down to hide the bruises on her wrists. Something else she'd have to lie about. If Reece discovered Liam had physically hurt her, he'd hunt him down and go alpha male on his ass. Liam had nothing to lose, and Sam visualized Reece shot and bleeding to death on the side of the road. She shuddered.

He took her hands and held her eyes. "It's okay," he said. "You can tell me. What about Harvey?"

All she said was, "He wants to meet you." Before he could ask anything else about Harvey, she turned the conversation back to her family. "Why would my parents lie about living in London?"

Reece pulled her onto the sofa and his eyes filled with sympathy. "I don't know. On top of losing a child in London, if your father had an affair that produced a son, maybe they wanted to close that chapter. Don't you remember anything about living in London? What about your sister, wouldn't she have been in school?"

Sam wiped her eyes and shook her head. "My mother home-schooled Joyce until grade seven when I went to kindergarten. I would have just turned four when they sold the house in London. Joyce and my mother were close. They loved secrets. Besides, my sister and I didn't get along."

"Does it matter that you lived in London?"

Sam shook her head again. "No, all that matters is I ruined my father. My mother's right, I'm poison. I destroy everyone who loves me."

"You aren't a bad person, Sam. You were young and caught up in something you didn't understand." Holding her hand, he said, "I don't judge your father for what happened. If it were my daughter, I probably would have done the same thing."

In her mind's eye, she saw her father sitting across from her at the kitchen table the night she told him she and Liam had betrayed him. "People are a product of the choices they make," he'd said. "The joy of life is that every new day offers the opportunity to make better choices. Happiness is a choice. All it takes is the strength to leave the past behind and forgive."

She clung to Reece for several minutes, basking in the relief washing over her after so many years of guilt and secrecy.

"Aw, baby, please don't cry." Reece hugged her against his chest. "Your father did what he thought was best for his family." He pulled away and titled her chin up with the end of his index finger. "Don't you see? He kept you safe, Sam. That's what mattered to him. So what if he travelled back and forth during the years Ryan Shannon was growing up? He didn't leave your mother, and I guess we'll never know why, but he didn't abandon Megan Shannon's son, his child."

Seeing so much love in Reece's eyes, she realized forgiveness wasn't reliant on understanding why people did what they did. She was wrong to think that ferreting out the truth would bring her closure.

She finally saw her father honestly: as a man, not a hero or a god. Her dad was a lonely man who found love in his life but couldn't find the strength to make the choice to be happy.

She leaned forward and kissed Reece. "Thank you," she murmured against his neck.

"This means one of us has family," he said. "Do you want to contact Ryan? We could take a trip out to Halifax and meet him."

"Maybe," she said, grateful she'd have Reece with her if she decided to go. She wasn't any good at bridging relationships, but Reece was. "It's all so overwhelming right now."

"I understand but give it some thought. Let's go to bed. We can figure everything out in the morning." He stood and held out his hand. "When can I meet Harvey?"

When she stood, the stress flowed out of her body and left her weak and exhausted. She'd had enough confession for one night but made a silent promise to tell Reece about her mother in the morning.

"I was thinking over Christmas."

"I can't wait." He turned her shoulders so she faced him and wrapped his arms around her waist, pulling her close to his body. "I love you," he said, "and I can help you work out some of this shit. You can't go through life pretending painful things never happened. You have to face it head on and deal."

"I'm going to get better at it," she promised.

"That's all I ask," he said and kissed her.

PART 3: Closure is an Overused Word

CHAPTER THIRTY-FIVE

October 2015: Toronto, Ontario

Derek

MARTY WAS WAITING in the driveway at seven-thirty in the morning, as usual. Over the past four months, Derek had tried to convince himself it was fun having a car service. Bullshit. The alternative to sitting in Marty's car was sitting in a jail cell. Pending the trial, a condition of his release was that the court wouldn't *allow* him to leave his property without his surety, Marty. House arrest was bad but having his business partner driving him back and forth to work was humiliating. He felt like a grounded sixteen-year-old who had failed his driving test.

"Good morning to you," Marty declared cheerfully the second Derek opened the car door.

"Good morning," he mumbled.

It wasn't just the driving. It was the talking. From the moment he settled dutifully on the passenger seat, Marty never shut his mouth.

"I grabbed you a Java, my friend, a nice hot double-double, just the way you like."

"Thanks." Derek reached for the brain juice. He hated morning people who felt obliged to share their jolliness with everyone in sight.

"How are you feeling?" Marty asked.

"Fine."

Marty's eyes drilled into the side of his head while they waited at a stop light. "You're not nervous?"

"No."

They pulled into traffic, and Derek enjoyed two minutes of blissful silence before the chatter resumed.

"You can talk to me. I'm here for you, my friend."

He gulped his coffee, burning the top of his mouth. "I'm fine."

"I'd be a wreck." Marty laughed half-heartedly. "Has Melissa cleared your schedule for the trial?"

"Of course," Derek snapped.

"Does Jim Stipelli have any idea how long the trial will take?"

"No."

Marty slammed on the brakes. Derek sloshed coffee across his hand and onto the crotch of his pants. "Damn it," he yelled, clenching the cup, and spilling more scalding liquid on the front of his shirt before he wrestled the wet, mangled cardboard into the cup holder.

"Sorry," Marty said. "The guy in front doesn't have any brake lights. There are napkins in the glove compartment." He pulled forward, keeping his distance from the beat-up car. "It was lucky there was a cancellation in the court calendar. Four months is great due process for a judge and jury trial."

What kind of an asshole considered it lucky to be standing trial for murder? An earlier trial date could mean incarceration in a maximum-security prison before Christmas.

Marty was still chattering away, but Derek closed his eyes and did his best to ignore him.

Sitting beside Jim at the preliminary hearing in the Ontario Court of Justice, listening to the Crown's overwhelming evidence, was awful. The September jury selection was equally as horrific. Jim had used all twenty of his peremptory challenges, and they were still stuck with a jury made up of people Derek didn't consider his peers.

He couldn't figure out how things had unravelled the way they had. The Crown didn't believe Sonia was *now* telling the truth about being with him.

This was all her fault. The stupid bitch had discredited herself by first swearing she wasn't with him and then changing her tune. Worse, she was too stupid to destroy her disturbing, obsessive memorabilia before the cops issued a search warrant for her home. Why did he always pick fucked-up women? The pictures she took were sickening. She'd been creeping around stalking him for months, and he hadn't even suspected. Sonia and Gabriella had probably planned this thing together to ruin him. Bitches, both of them.

"Derek?" Marty said. "I asked how you felt about things."

"Since I did not kill the woman, I'm confident our legal system will triumph." What a lie. He wasn't at all confident, but he'd be damned if he let Marty know how scared he was. Derek was confident the court would screw him over. His temper turned from sour to toxic.

"Have your investigators found anything to help?" Marty asked.

He snorted laughter. "If they were working for the Crown, they'd be doing fantastic." He took a breath and tried to settle his raw nerves. "We have a witness who can testify the loony-tune claimed to be speaking with her dead sister on her cell phone. I don't understand why no one believes me. She told me to go to the airport and pick up her make-believe sister. The fact someone can testify that the crazy bitch was chatting up a ghost proves that."

Marty sighed. "Well, it might provide some doubt, if you'd gone to the airport."

If he'd gone to the fucking airport, he wouldn't be in this mess. He didn't need *Father* pointing out the obvious. "She did this to me, the stupid bitch. She set this up to ruin me."

"Derek," Marty began, "your wife is dead and—"

"She is not dead. She's out there laughing her ass off," Derek shouted.

"Maybe we should change the subject." To Derek, the way Marty said it implied he was irrational.

"You're the one who brought it up," Derek retort in aggravation. "I didn't kill the bitch. No one stole anything and no one cared enough about Gabriella to kill her. This is a set-up. Sonia was probably in on it. That would explain why she lied and said I wasn't at the condo." He pounded his fist into the dashboard.

"That's enough! Calm down," Marty said sternly, scrunching his face in disapproval.

Derek wanted to whack him upside the head. He sipped his coffee and ignored his partner.

"I'm not a criminal attorney," Marty continued in a condescending way, "so if that's the way Stipelli is spinning your defence and he's confident he can pull it off, I'll go along."

"Go along? You'll go along?" Derek shouted. "I did not kill my fucking wife. Sonia probably did. She works with scumbags. Easy enough to get one of them to do her a fucking favour. A couple of bucks and a quick blowjob. Badda bing badda boom, Derek pays the price for not being sensitive enough."

Marty parked in his reserved space in the parking garage and got out of the car. When he stomped to the elevators, not bothering to wait for Derek, it was obvious he was angry.

Derek took his time following him. He didn't give a shit if Marty's nose was out of joint. He joined him at the elevator and took out his phone, studiously ignoring his business partner.

Marty jabbed the button for the elevator. "Derek, contain your shit. I'm sick of your attitude."

He ignored him and fiddled with his phone. He wasn't in the mood for a lecture from *Father*.

"First you say Sonia and Gabriella planned a frame," Marty said, "and then you say Sonia arranged to have Gabriella killed. Enough already."

"Okay, *Dad*," Derek scoffed.

"I've had complaints from the staff, and two of your clients called last week to say they'd pull their business if we didn't reassign their cases."

"Who complained about me?" Derek demanded, shoving his phone into his pocket.

"It doesn't matter. The point is that people are losing trust in your abilities. The press is killing us, and people don't want to be around you."

"Who complained about me?" Derek crossed his arms against his chest and glared at Marty.

Marty threw up his hands in exasperation. "I'm trying to help you, Derek, and your sole focus is on who ratted you out. Use today to wrap up and start your leave of absence this afternoon."

The elevator doors opened. "I'm fine." Derek punched the button for their floor.

"It's not a request." Marty stared straight ahead at the door.

"What are you saying?"

"As managing partner, I'm telling you today will be your last day." Marty's tone was unyielding. "The partners have agreed to stand by you, until after your trial, but we're holding a vote to determine whether we buy you out."

"You can't do this," Derek said.

"It's already done, my friend." Marty got off the elevator and marched through reception to his office.

Marty had the authority to ban him from the business. If the other three partners supported the decision, Derek's shares were insufficient to give him leverage. They couldn't fire him, but there was a clause in their partnership agreement that gave them the right to buy him out on a unanimous vote.

Gabriella was still ruining his life. "That fucking gash," Derek mumbled under his breath.

"Pardon me?" Melissa asked with a wary look.

"Nothing." He stomped into his office.

A few seconds later, she was hovering inside the door. "Can I get you a coffee?"

He waved the soggy paper cup at her. "I'm drinking a coffee. Look at it, right here in my hand, Melissa."

She cleared her throat and pursed her lips. "Mr. McBride wants to speak with you. Your calendar is clear, so I confirmed him for nine o'clock."

"Oh." Derek took off his suit jacket and draped it over the back of his chair. "Did he say what it's about?"

Melissa shook her head.

"Well, that's fine." Derek felt cheered. "Maybe he's ready to confirm the date he's resigning his MP seat."

"He wants Marty to attend."

"Marty is not the one putting everything on the line to run for office. I don't want him there, so don't bother him."

Melissa's face was blank. "I asked his assistant to move his nine o'clock so he could attend."

"I don't care. Call her back and tell her you made a mistake." Derek opened his email. Little activity, which was the norm these days.

Melissa was still standing in the doorway. "I didn't make a mistake. Marty asked to be present for any meetings you have today. Mr. McBride is bringing members of the Liberal caucus, and it didn't strike me as good news." Her smile was tight, a smirk.

Surprised by her insubordination, Derek watched her stroll out of his office. She didn't bother to close the door or to review the rest of his schedule.

McBride bringing a delegation with him to the meeting wasn't a good sign. There were rumours he wasn't stepping down, that the leader of the Liberal party, Justin Trudeau, had asked McBride to remain in the Parliament seat.

Goddamn Gabriella, he thought with venom. If the caucus pulled support, it was because of her and this defamatory allegation he was a murderer. Why hadn't he recognized the potential she had to ruin him sooner?

CHAPTER THIRTY-SIX

Three Weeks Later: Toronto, Ontario

Sam

TELLING REECE HER mother was alive was harder than Sam thought, and procrastinating had complicated the situation. After Liam's visit, she'd tried a number of times to tell the truth but couldn't find the words. She had to figure it out before they visited Harvey over Christmas. Short of locking Grace in a closet — tempting, but Harvey would object — Reece would meet her mother.

Since discovering the truth about her father, Reece was encouraging her to open up about her past. She'd shared with him the crappy relationship she'd had with her sister, how devastated she was over Joyce's murder, and the horrible things her mother had said to her. They'd even discussed how her mother had broken down at her sister's visitation, clinging to the minister and begging him to tell her why God had taken Joyce instead of Sam.

But she couldn't bring herself to admit that Grace was alive. She didn't want a relationship with her mother. The woman made her feel like shit.

The problem was that Reece put value on family and believed 'talk-therapy' could salvage any relationship. Sam disagreed. No good came from rehashing the past. When a relationship made you hate yourself, it was best to end it and never look back.

Grace had raised her with cold-hearted insistence that one always ignored conflict and negative feelings, so it wasn't fair for Reece to expect her to change a lifetime of conditioning in a few months. Regardless, he would insist an honest discussion between all parties would fix everything. Sam shuddered to think how that would go over.

"You okay?" He turned from the stove and studied her earnestly. "You're quiet."

"Just imagining what restaurant-quality dinner you're treating me to," she said. "I'm hoping for steak or a pork chop."

"Hum... prepare for disappointment." He put the plate in front of her.

No meat. She wasn't in the mood for a vegetarian delight. The plating was pretty, but the sauce was brown and chunky. "What is it?"

"Pumpkin ravioli with walnut apple butter, mademoiselle." With a triumphant smile, Reece bowed at her. "I roasted the pumpkin and made the pasta."

"Pumpkin." The word rolled across her tongue.

"Don't you like pumpkin?"

"Sure, when it's carved into a jack-o-lantern." She shoved ravioli through a sea of greasy brown butter sauce. Immature, she knew, but she hated pumpkin and squash. With a flick of her fork, a walnut tumbled off a square of mush-filled dough.

He burst out laughing. "I didn't know you hated pumpkin. I detest applesauce so I get it. It's a texture thing." He slid her plate over to his side of the table. "I'll have it for lunch tomorrow. What are you going to eat?"

She gave him a brilliant smile. "What I lived on before shacking up with a gourmet."

Reece chuckled. "Let me guess, pizza."

She got up to rummage through the freezer. "You can eat pumpkin, and I'll have a meat lover's pizza."

Reece popped ravioli in his mouth. "What happened in court today? Was it any better than my experience yesterday?"

For the past two weeks, she and Reece had taken turns attending Derek's trial, hoping to hear something worth investigating.

"No." She puckered her lips and rolled her eyes. "If we don't find something to help Jim win, he probably won't hire us again. There isn't a shortage of PIs in Toronto." She sighed. "I was counting on the bonus. I was hoping to take some time off to focus on my PhD thesis. This sucks."

"There's still time. Don't give up yet. Has the Crown wrapped up?"

She put the pizza in the oven and nodded. "Gabriella looks like a poor waif out of a Charles de Lint novel. When they talked about the missing dog, a woman on the jury wept." She dropped the pizza box into the recycling bin. "Derek looks like a monster. God, if this was the US and there were cameras in the courtroom, the whole country would be out with pitchforks. The artist's drawings in the paper are bad enough."

Reece scraped pasta sauce onto his fork. "McBride and the Liberal party pulling their support a week before the trial didn't help. Garnered a lot of press for Derek, all bad."

She crinkled her nose in disgust. "And for us — did you read the statement the Crown Attorney made, thanking us for the great work we've done in providing *him* with additional evidence?"

She squatted and peered through the glass in the oven door.

"A watched pizza never cooks," warned Reece.

"Derek's attitude in court is also hurting him," she said. "He's... cavalier, I guess is the word."

"We have to find Gabriella," Reece said. "We have to work on the assumption she's not dead."

If they were going to salvage their firm's reputation, he was right. "Without identification, she must be in Canada," Sam said. "But without friends or money, where? What's she doing, living in a box under a railway bridge?"

"If this was planned, she has false documents. She could be anywhere in the world."

He was right. The question was how Gabriella did it. "We've gone back twenty years in the Martinas' finances. There aren't any discrepancies, and buying forged documents is expensive. I still say the key is finding Quentin LeBlanc."

Reece drank his wine in silence for a few minutes. "Well, if she framed her husband, it took careful planning. It's not as if she's experienced in murder. There was nothing on her computer search history except for Amazon downloads of books and movies and online decorating tips." He paused in thought and then added, "You know, I'm surprised about all the books she bought. When we were at dinner in June, she told me she wasn't a fiction reader."

She'd also tried to engage Gabriella by discussing books and movies. Gabriella had offered monosyllabic answers before shutting down the topic by stating she didn't like fiction entertainment. What an odd thing to lie about. Sam opened the oven door to peek at the pizza.

"If you keep opening the oven, it won't cook. You're letting out all the heat."

"I'll turn it up a bit." She adjusted the dial, and he ran over to check.

"You can't cook frozen pizza at five hundred degrees." He adjusted the heat to four-twenty-five. "Gabriella could have researched how to stage a crime scene on a different computer, but it didn't belong to the family." He leaned his back against the sink. "The police checked the kids' and Derek's."

"Maybe she used an Internet cafe or the library." Sam grinned. "Or watched *Dexter*."

Reece laughed.

She crossed her arms with another sigh. "We need a money trail or a witness who saw her. Anything to prove she was alive after the alleged murder." She took a plate from the cupboard. "It's ready."

He knelt to check. "It's not ready. Give it five more minutes." Reece took his plate from the table and put it in the dishwasher.

"Still like being a PI?" she asked sarcastically.

"It's hard," he admitted, and it surprised her that he'd taken the question seriously. "You have the same questions but none of the authority to get the answers." He picked up his wine glass and swirled the contents.

"Well," she said, "it's nice having you around to brainstorm, not to mention all your provincial and federal police contacts. Gold mine."

Reece lowered his eyes and circled the edge of his wine glass with the tip of his index finger. "Right, I've spent five months begging for favours."

"Ah, the catfish feeling."

He looked quizzical.

"You feel like a bottom-feeder." That never bothered her, but she could understand why it upset Reece.

He went back to rubbing the lip of the glass with his finger. "The frustrating thing is I don't think Derek is guilty," he said. "There was no blood spatter on Derek's clothes when he was arrested, and he was wearing the same thing he'd been wearing at the office."

"But the police believe he changed before the fight," she said. "He killed her and grabbed his original clothing before he dumped the body and the blood-spattered clothes he wore during the murder."

"Yes but Derek's a lawyer. It doesn't make sense. Even though he doesn't practice criminal law, I can't believe he'd be stupid enough to leave so much incriminating evidence."

Putting on her psychologist hat, she said, "Under severe stress, people don't act logically. Anger is a base emotion that erases common sense, turning people stupid."

"Another thing, what if the kids had come home?" Reece said. "The youngest son, Kevin, was at a friend's house and the girl, Anna, was out with her boyfriend. Teenagers are unpredictable. There was blood all over the walls and floors. Why would Derek leave the house in that condition?"

She turned off the oven and left the door open to cool the pizza. "Good point. Why not wrap her in the tarp, pop her in the trunk and go back and clean the scene before disposing of the body?"

Reece poured a second glass of wine, which was out of character for him.

"If we're right and she's alive, why did she bother doing this?" Sam asked. "It's risky, she'll never be able to see her children again, and it's difficult to plan a frame of this magnitude and disappear."

"She was smart. Her GPA for the three semesters she studied biochemistry was over ninety percent. We're talking off the charts analytical deductive reasoning."

"I'm not denying that she *could* do this, I'm confused over *why* she would do it. Gabriella had grounds to divorce Derek, keep the house, and have custody of the kids. Even Derek admits—"

Reece held up his hand to interrupt. "Yeah, but divorcing him wouldn't ruin him. If the court convicts him, the Law Society will revoke his licence. Then there are Derek's political aspirations. Canadian politics may be lacking decent candidates, but we don't elect criminals convicted of murder. It's doubtful his children will forgive him for murdering their mother, and the cost of his defence is bankrupting him."

She nodded. "I suppose she had good reason. Watching your husband cheat right under your nose would be tough to swallow." She thought about how distant and angry her own mother was when she was growing up. "Lots of fathers abandon their kids when they want out of a relationship. Maybe Gabriella didn't care about ditching her kids."

She took the pizza out of the oven, cut it into quarters, and grabbed a paper towel. Sitting at the kitchen table it occurred to her there was a flaw in her theory. "The thing that doesn't add up is Cataleya Sousa told me Gabriella wasn't unhappy in the marriage. It sounded like she was okay with Derek satisfying his carnal needs elsewhere, because she didn't want to have sex with him."

"I don't know. The diary didn't sound like she was okay with things," Reece argued. "In fact, the entries completely contradict the woman we met. They're full of rage and hate."

"If Gabriella planned the frame, she planned her disappearance equally as well," Sam said. "If she obtained another identity, we can't find her without a lead. Money is the logical place to start. Even if she has credit cards under the assumed identity, she needs cash. Any suggestions?"

"No, I'll keep thinking about it." Reece looked troubled. "I need to talk to you about something." His face was serious, and she hoped he wasn't about to talk marriage.

In the past two months, Reece had asked her to marry him twice. He'd even bought a gorgeous ring. It was sitting on his bedside table beside the pile of ratty paperbacks, cooking magazines, and treasures he loved to hoard.

It wasn't that she didn't love him, but she didn't believe in the institution of marriage. If you wanted to be with someone, you didn't need a piece of paper proclaiming your commitment.

He surprised her by saying, "I've been talking with Toronto Police Services. I'm considering returning to law enforcement."

It didn't come as a shock to her that he was reviewing his options. Reece wasn't enjoying the private sector, she knew. The Toronto police would be lucky to have him. If that were his decision, she'd support him.

Truth was if she couldn't figure out a way to help Jim win the case, she'd be looking for a new career herself.

CHAPTER THIRTY-SEVEN

One Week Later: Toronto, Ontario

Sam

THEY WERE GOING to meet Jim at his office and, miraculously, Reece agreed to leave his car at the loft and take public transportation to First Canadian Place. He wasn't pleased about it and wasn't bothering to be a good sport either.

Sam couldn't understand it. With the price of gas and parking, it was illogical to insist on driving everywhere. A streetcar constantly ran east and west on Queen Street. Jumping on and off was convenient, and she'd even bought him his own transit pass. Nevertheless, he was all suspicious and twitchy whenever she forced him to use it.

They entered the car, and Reece peered around the interior as if felons on their way to a maximum-security facility populated the streetcar.

"So," Sam adjusted her hand on the handle strap when the car jerked to a stop, "about—"

"Shh," Reece interrupted. "Not here."

"Reece—"

"Wait until we're off," he insisted sotto voce.

All she was going to ask him was what he wanted to do over the holidays. Annoyed, she rolled her eyes and gazed out the window until they reached Bay Street.

They exited the streetcar and walked south to King. Reece linked their fingers and trotted along happily, pacing his strides so she wasn't jogging to keep up. The sidewalk was crowded with pedestrians, some of whom definitely looked sketchy, but Reece was unperturbed. Apparently, criminals weren't interested in street muggings, preferring to attack hapless passengers trapped on the streetcar.

"I was trying to ask you about Christmas," Sam said.

"Well…"

"Uthisca," she guessed. "Betty Welsh invited us."

"I know you don't want to go." His voice was heavy with disappointment.

It wasn't that she didn't like the Welsh family, but they lived down the street from what had been Bueton Sanctuary, the cult she'd exposed a year ago. After a case ended, she never looked back. It was how she kept her sanity intact. The problem was Reece had roots in Uthisca, and he was close to the people involved in her last case. He wanted to go home for Christmas.

"We can do something else," he said, but the cheerful tone sounded a bit forced to her. "I still get to meet Harvey, right?"

She swallowed hard. "Yeah, and we need to talk before we go. It's important."

"That sounds ominous."

"Not really. I'll tell you tonight at dinner."

While they walked along, Sam thought about the best approach to break the news about her mother and decided to tell him in a restaurant. Reece wasn't the type to cause a public scene. "You owe me dinner out, remember?"

"Ah, the fitness bet you won." He winked at her.

She suspected he'd let her win, but that wasn't the point. They walked in comfortable silence, moving several times to allow rude pedestrians to pass. Sam stuffed her wallet into her coat pocket and kept a firm grip on it.

"Let's go somewhere fancy for dinner," Reece suggested. "I like that black dress you bought in Australia and those high-heeled shoes, too."

She laughed. "Oh, I see how it is. Forcing me to put on a girly frock as a bit of revenge for losing the bet, eh?"

This man had done everything in his power to love her without limitation or judgment, accepting everything about her, including her complicated and unpleasant past. Now, she was going to confess another lie. The least she could do was agree to spend Christmas in Uthisca. Without compromise, relationships were doomed to fail.

"Visiting the Welsh family for Christmas sounds good," she said.

Reece stopped walking, turned her shoulders so she faced him and scooped her up in a hug. People moved around them in a parting wave. "Thanks," he said. "You don't have to wear heels tonight," he added with mock solemnity.

She burst out laughing. "The dress will look ridiculous with sneakers. You can have the shoes." She linked her arm through his, and they continued to stroll south through the financial district.

AT JIM'S OFFICE, the receptionist escorted them to a boardroom and left them to help themselves to coffee. Jim walked in while Sam was deliberating over a cheese bagel or a strawberry Danish.

"A moment on the lips, a lifetime on the hips," he said with a sigh, eyeing the pastry in her hand. "It must be nice to have the metabolism of a hummingbird."

Taking a big bite of the Danish, she grinned. "Yup."

"Before we get started," Jim said, "Lisa wanted me to invite you guys for Christmas."

Choking on the bite of pastry, Sam sputtered, "What?"

He chuckled and reached into his briefcase. "Here, an invitation and everything."

"Oh, you're having a party?" For a minute, she'd thought her best friend was reaching out to salvage their friendship. Exasperation mingled with her disappointment.

Jim waved the card at her. She took it and slipped it into her pocket.

He winked at Reece. "Read it out loud."

Reluctantly, she tore open the envelope and extracted the card, which had a Golden Retriever puppy on the cover. Opening the card, she read, "*I may not be as loyal but I couldn't love you more. I miss you and I need your friendship. Please come home for Christmas. Love Lisa.*"

Embarrassed, she blinked back tears and took a gulp of coffee.

"Well," Jim said, "is the answer yes?"

"A thousand times yes," Reece agreed with enthusiasm. "I can't wait to finally meet her, and I'm hoping to see horrid pictures of when they were girls."

"Don't say anything to Lisa," she said. "I'll tell her myself." One gesture deserved another. Her friend was trying, and Sam wanted to get better at recognizing people's efforts.

"Great, that's settled," Jim said. "Sit down and I'll debrief you on the trial."

"What's your prediction?" Reece asked.

Without missing a beat, Jim replied, "Conviction. He'll be at Millhaven before Christmas."

Millhaven Institution was a maximum-security federal penitentiary in Bath, Ontario, outside the city of Kingston. Since the closure of Kingston Penitentiary in 2013, the segregated unit at Millhaven was now home to the notorious serial rapist and murderer, Paul Bernardo. Derek's pomposity and arrogance would be short-lived in that place.

"What'll happen to the children?" Sam asked.

"Since you couldn't find Quentin LeBlanc, there are no living relatives," he said. "Regardless of Derek's faults, he loves his kids. He's scrambling to set up Marty Alderson as guardian for Kevin and Anna to keep them out of the foster system."

"What about Nicholas?" Reece asked. "He's over nineteen and could be guardian to his siblings."

Jim shrugged. "He left home before his father's trial. Besides, before you tracked down the motel owner in Montreal to confirm Nick's alibi, he was on the suspect list."

"He was at Covenant House youth shelter on Gerrard last month," Sam said. "I put out some feelers and a contact let me know. We'd already cleared him but I went to see him anyway." She shook her head. "The kid's a mess. He was too high to hold a conversation, but I can try again and ask him to reach out to his father." She'd done her best to coax Nick into a treatment program, but he didn't want help. It was sad, but it was his choice.

"I'll mention it to Derek. Nicholas isn't his major concern right now," Jim said.

"If Derek's convicted, what happens to Gabriella's life insurance?" Reece asked.

"The kids weren't contingent beneficiaries, and there's no will, so the money will be paid to her estate," Jim said. "Marty applied for appointment as estate trustee, but Nicholas also applied. The court will most likely name her son."

The policy was for two million dollars. Sam was aghast. "He's an addict. There's no guarantee he'll share the money with his siblings."

"Marty's aware. He's prepared to challenge the application, but it's up to a judge," Jim said.

"Are there any thoughts about the dog, Gana?" she asked.

"Derek's insisting Gabriella is alive and took the dog she loved. If he killed her, he killed the dog. Poison is the best guess."

"Where did Derek acquire poison?" Reece asked. "You can't go to your local hardware store and buy pesticides with a strychnine poison base. The Canadian government regulates anything containing active poison. There were issues in Uthisca because registering requests to buy potent rodent poison outraged farmers."

Putting her elbows on the table, Sam cupped her jaw between her hands and chewed on her baby fingernail. "We checked and Derek didn't travel outside Canada in the past year. Even if he did, he'd have to smuggle the pesticide, which isn't easy."

Gana was muscular and strong. If Derek attacked Gabriella, her dog would attack him. Yet there were no marks on Derek when the police arrested him and no canine blood at the crime scene.

"Gana was like a service animal," she said. "They're trained not to eat anything that isn't given to them by their master."

Jim frowned. "So? Derek was one of his alphas."

She shook her head. "No he wasn't. Gana was Gabriella's dog."

Picking up her train of thought, Reece said, "If Derek poisoned meat, Gana wouldn't eat it."

"Would a dog in the K-9 unit eat something that wasn't offered by his handler?" she asked.

Reece shrugged. "I don't know. I never worked with them around food."

Her cell rang and she glanced at the caller ID. Cataleya Sousa. She stood and moved toward the wall of windows to take the call. "McNamara."

"Hi Sam," Cataleya said. "I hope this isn't a bad time."

"No, it's fine. What's up?"

"Back in June, you asked for a sample of Gabriella's handwriting. My daughter and I were chatting about the trial, and I told her about our conversation. She has a graduation card from Gabriella she kept because it has a Pug on it."

In the background, Jim and Reece were continuing their conversation. "The dog was a domestic pet, not a service animal," Jim was saying, "and I've argued Derek didn't procure poison. The Crown's rebuttal is that he concocted something from plants."

She missed what Cataleya said. "Excuse me, say again?"

"Maybe she was left-handed but taught to write with her right."

"Gabriella was right-handed." There was a ton of barking on Cataleya's end of the line and it was hard to hear her.

"Sorry," she yelled. "My kids are trying to harness the dogs for a walk. I was referring to the sloppy backhand cursive. My son's grade one teacher made Elijah use his right hand and that was the result. Turns out he's left-handed."

"Backhand cursive?" Sam repeated. What was she talking about?

"The letters slant to the left, not the right. I understand why she was embarrassed. Gabriella was dyslexic. In two places, the letters are backwards."

"Cataleya, we need to see that card right now. Can you send me a pic?"

　　　　　　　　　　　　　　　　　　　L.E. Fraser

"Sure, will do as soon as I we hang up."

After disconnecting, she waited for the picture to arrive and opened it. She held her phone out to Reece. He frowned and passed it to Jim.

"That's the same handwriting as the card Derek told us was from Isabella," Reece said.

"It doesn't look like the diary." Jim pulled a few photocopied sheets from a file on the conference table, perusing them with an expression of bewilderment. "I don't get it, why did Gabriella write one way in the diary and another way on the cards?"

Reece looked perplexed. "If she sent the cards and gifts she claimed were from her dead sister, why would she use that writing style on a card to a neighbour's kid?"

"Because Derek only *thought* the card was from Isabella," Sam said, exasperated at their oversight. "It wasn't. Gabriella gave it to her son. We never asked Nicholas. He was gone when you talked with the younger kids."

"Okay, why two handwriting styles and why aren't there any examples of dyslexia in the diary?" Reece asked.

"Dyslexia is worse if you're stressed. Maybe Gabriella wasn't concerned about anyone reading her diary, so she was able to produce the words." That explanation felt wrong but she couldn't figure out what was tickling the back of her mind.

Jim shrugged. "It's curious but not relevant. Gabriella wrote the diary. Her daughter saw her, and Gabriella's fingerprints were on every page."

"When are you presenting closing arguments?" Reece asked.

"Monday," Jim answered. "I need you guys to find something. You have seventy-two hours before the jury deliberates."

"Looks like you'll have to take a rain cheque for dinner tonight," Reece told her and grabbed his jacket.

She wasn't too disappointed to postpone her confession about her mother.

CHAPTER THIRTY-EIGHT

Sam

CONSIDERING IT WAS the beginning of December, the weekend was beautiful, with clear blue skies and a high above freezing. Sam, Reece, and Brandy were strolling on the boardwalk by Woodbine Beach, south of Lakeshore, enjoying the Sunday afternoon weather. Trotting along with a swagger radiating happiness and a large doggy grin on her face, Brandy was in good spirits.

"That raw food diet is making a difference," Sam said.

"Except there's no room in the freezer," Reece grumbled. "We need to buy a deep freeze."

Where was he planning to put a big, ugly freezer? They'd figured out how to make the hideous church alter work but she wasn't having a freezer in the middle of her living room.

Her cell rang and she stopped walking to grab it from her pocket. "McNamara."

Reece waved at an empty bench and they sat.

"Why are you looking for me?" a male voice barked from the phone.

Sam frowned. "What?"

"I'm on a throwaway cell so don't bother trying to trace this," he growled.

She had the Google Voice app on her phone and pressed four to record the call in progress. The ambient noise level was high in the park, so she didn't put it on speaker for Reece. The caller would notice.

"Quentin LeBlanc?" she guessed.

"Why have you posted shit all over the Internet?" he demanded in a gravelly tone.

Finally, something she tried was netting results. Excited to talk with Gabriella's father she began by saying, "The police think your daughter was murdered in June."

"Evil doesn't die," he hissed.

Strange reaction. Forging ahead, she asked, "Mr. LeBlanc, have you been in contact with her since June? If she's alive, do you know where she might be?"

"My wife, Nina, had *An Da Shealladh*, the Highlander's 'two sights'. I didn't believe her. It was *Wendigo*. That's what came back to us. A demon." His voice rose to shrieking hysteria, and Sam moved the phone away from her ear. "It destroyed everything I loved. It took everything away from me. It was evil reincarnated."

She covered the phone and whispered to Reece, "The guy's nuts." Reece leaned his head toward the phone, and Sam held it so they could both hear.

"It's going to find me. What will it take for you to remove those pictures?" Quentin demanded.

It's going to find him? Sam took a deep breath. What she wanted to know from Quentin was how Gabriella processed her sister's death. The gifts for the kids that Gabriella claimed originated from Isabella were bothering Sam. They were missing something important. "I need you to answer a few quick questions."

Reece poked her shoulder hard and vigorously shook his head. "Sam, the man is unhinged," he whispered.

She ignored him. "Can you tell me about Gabriella's relationship with her sister, Isabella?"

The pause was so long, Sam thought he'd hung up. When he finally spoke, his tone was flat. "Gabriella killed Isabella."

"Isabella fell out of your tree house," she said.

"Gabriella pushed her."

"Did you see her do it?" Sam asked incredulously.

"When I found my daughter, Gabriella was standing in the tree house smiling down at me. The railing was too high for someone to fall by accident." He was yelling again. "She murdered her sister and tortured her mother."

Sam felt goosebumps scurry down her arms and legs.

"My beautiful Isabella," Quentin said with a sob. "So trusting and forgiving. Gabriella, she was a monster." His voice hardened. "She lied without shame. She was manipulative and cold." Fear laced his words and his voice trembled. "She was cruel to everyone except that damn dog she brought back from hell."

For the rest of her life, Gabriella had owned a male Samoyed she called Ganawenim. Sam had always thought Gana was an important part of the puzzle but couldn't figure out why.

On the other end of the phone, Quentin's breathing was loud. "The day we buried Isabella, Gabriella traipsed into the living room with her hair in a ponytail, just like Isabella wore hers. She was wearing one of Isabella's tracksuits. This thing sat on the sofa and rambled, mimicking Isabella's voice but it was malicious. It was the worst of Gabriella unhidden." He choked on tears. "Isabella had recognized it. My sweet girl, she'd tried to talk to it, she'd tried to save her sister. It killed her before she could tell us the truth."

Sam felt the gears turn in her mind. She could hear tiny clicks when the pieces fell into place.

Quentin's voice was ragged and torn. "It said it was in that godforsaken cabin. For months," he said, "it tortured us, threatened us, told us it could take over when it wanted. It said—" He gasped and coughed, struggling to catch his breath. "It could control Gabriella because she'd think it was her sister. No matter what we did, Gabriella didn't accept Isabella was dead. She believed she talked to her every day. She believed she could see her."

Finally, Sam understood why the writing style in the diary troubled her so much. Gabriella didn't write it. "Dissociative identity disorder," she whispered.

"Don't lay that shit on me," Quentin screamed. "Years of working with useless doctors after that pervert took her. They never saw what that thing was. My daughter never came back from that cabin. *Wendigo* came back."

"Was Gabriella's personality inconsistent before her abduction?" Sam asked.

"I'm telling you that thing wasn't my daughter. The only emotion it had was rage." He was crying in earnest.

It made sense now. The alter personality emerged during her abduction, developing in that pink cage. It wasn't uncommon for alter personalities to grow to overpower their host.

"After Isabella died, when you first recognized the other..." she hunted for a word that wouldn't set him off, "side of Gabriella, what did you do?"

"My wife blamed herself for Gabriella's abduction, and Nina's guilt grew until it took over everything. She refused to speak of Isabella's death or Gabriella's behaviour. Gabriella was the only child she had left, and she couldn't accept the idea of institutionalizing her."

"That's why you left," Sam said.

"I left the woman I loved alone and sick with that thing. I'm a despicable coward and a drunk. Take down the postings or it will find me," Quentin said. "*An Da Shealladh* passes from mother to daughter. It hunts for me in her dreams. I feel it crawling over my skin. I'm trapped on a skully board, and all that's left is to run from the killer."

'Unhinged' was an understatement. The man was insane. "What will find you?" Sam asked.

"I've read the newspaper stories. That man did not kill Gabriella. She's gone but it's not dead. It did this." His voice broke while he spoke.

Sam forced herself to keep her voice calm and detached. "Where would she go, Mr. LeBlanc? Gabriella doesn't have money or friends."

He laughed again, a hard, cold sound. "She has dollars. Nina's grandmother left her a trust fund. After my wife died, Gabriella was able to access the money."

"No," Sam said, "we've looked. Gabriella didn't have any money."

"If you think it would be in her name, you're a fool. If you think she told her family about it, you're an idiot." Quentin laughed. "But you'll never find her. That thing will never let you have Gabriella."

"Mr. LeBlanc, where would she go?" Sam asked.

"To hunt and to eat the flesh of human children," he yelled. "To become what her abductor created. To be *Wendigo*."

He hung up and she put the phone in her pocket.

"I caught most of that," Reece said. "What the hell is *Wendigo*?"

"It's a native myth about an evil spirit. All bands that believe in the myth think humans turn into a *Wendigo* if they're cannibals. They also believe a person can see *Wendigo* in dreams and can even become possessed by the demon in the dream," she said.

"That's ridiculous," he scoffed, "subject matter for horror fiction."

She shook her head. "No, the reason I know about the myth is that, in psychological terms, *Wendigo psychosis* is a condition describing a cultural disorder where the afflicted wants to eat flesh."

"What the hell is *An Da Shealladh*?"

"No idea, he referenced Highlanders so it must be Gaelic."

Reece's frown deepened. "You said dissociative identity disorder. Isn't that so rare it's considered malingering?"

She nodded. "I studied it at Queen's and again here in the PhD program. Doctors have confirmed less than three percent as legitimate cases. Reece, they're often females. People diagnosed with it suffered terrible childhood trauma."

"Quentin said they took her to doctors. Why didn't someone understand?" he asked.

"DID is seldom diagnosed in young children," she told him. "I doubt it was suggested about Gabriella in the 1980s. As an adult, I bet she refused to see a psychiatrist."

He nodded. "That's right. A referral was in her medical records but she never followed up."

"People with DID rarely seek medical help." Sam shrugged. "They believe they suffer strange dreams and blackouts when stressed. Many times, they're accused of things they don't recall doing, but they ignore it because it's too confusing and frightening."

"Wouldn't Derek or the kids notice?" Reece asked.

"They did. Derek heard her talking in two voices in the kitchen. He assumed she was on the polycom with Isabella."

Reece swallowed hard. "People at work also noticed. That's why Jack Belinski kept saying she was nuts."

"They didn't know what they were seeing. I think Cataleya Sousa suspected, but she didn't outright say so."

Cataleya had come close, Sam realized. She'd cited examples of Gabriella appearing to be two people, but Sam hadn't made the connection. She recalled the intense way Cataleya had looked at her during the interview. She hadn't had the courage to make such an outlandish suggestion.

Reece folded his hands between his knees. "Both Jack and Julie told me Gabriella would mumble something under her breath and act crazy."

"Breathe, it's just your life," Sam whispered.

"What?"

"That's what she said in the kitchen at dinner in June. Then, her alter — it must be — told me about Derek's affair. The phrase must be a mantra Gabriella says when she's uncomfortable or upset."

They sat in silence, and Sam thought about the events in the kitchen. She'd met Gabriella's second personality. Something occurred to her. Just before the switch, Gana had whined and pulled at Gabriella's skirt. "Shit," Sam whispered.

Reece looked up. "What?"

"That's why I kept saying the dog was like a service animal," she said. "People who suffer from epilepsy often have service animals because dogs can sense a seizure coming. The dog warns its owner, so the person can find a safe place."

"I don't get it."

"Dogs sense a great deal. Domestic dogs can smell cancer. There's plenty of documented evidence of it. I believe Gana 'knew' about his mistress's dual personalities. He tried to warn Gabriella before the alter personality emerged."

Reece looked across the lake. "This is unbelievable but it makes sense. When I interviewed Jack and Julie," Reece said, "Julie told me at times the math side of Gabriella's duties was well executed and the English was a train wreck. Other times, the opposite was true."

"Gabriella studied biochemistry. I bet the other personality was creative. That also explains why Gabriella showed up for work the morning after her termination," she said.

"They didn't fire Gabriella. They fired her alter. Sam, can we prove this? You taped the call just now, right? Will the tape be sufficient if we call witnesses who saw the second personality? Quentin said the family did deal with doctors. We might be able to track down a doctor in London who treated her."

Standing, she took Brandy's leash from Reece. "We need to talk to Jim. Producing the tape at this point in the trial might be worse. It's hard to believe Derek didn't suspect something. He's self-involved, but he's not stupid."

"It provides a strong motive." Reece frowned. "Can you imagine Gabriella switching in the middle of a political gathering with press in attendance?"

"The money Quentin told us about is the key to proving she's alive. Now we know it originated with Nina's grandmother, we can trace it. Gabriella wouldn't be able to set up anything to remove her name from the money until after her mother's death in 1993."

"I have a friend with the OPP, a forensic financial analyst. I can call him for advice," Reece suggested.

"Good, do that. We need to get Jim up to speed. I'll call and have him meet us at his office."

After calling Jim at home and asking him to meet them in an hour, they hurried back to the loft to drop off Brandy.

"If we can find the money," Reece said when they turned onto Queen Street, "it may be enough to prove Gabriella's still alive."

"If not," Sam said, "Derek is going to prison for a crime that didn't happen."

CHAPTER THIRTY-NINE

One Week Later: Toronto, Ontario

Sam

"GABRIELLA'S ALTERNATE PERSONALITY planned the frame and took months to weave the web." Sam flopped onto one of the red chairs in Jim's office.

Pacing the large space, Jim countered, "Let's agree that Gabriella has dissociative identity disorder — a condition we can't medically validate, let's not forget. It doesn't prove Derek didn't kill her."

"What I don't understand is that Gabriella's sister was a nice person. Gabriella's alter isn't nice," Reece said.

"It isn't her sister," Sam explained. "The second personality assumed her sister's identity after Isabella's death, but it was around long before she died. It's a mixture of whoever took over when Gabriella lived in that cage and something dark that developed under the influence of her abductor. From the diary, we know it's a very angry personality. It could be sociopathic, and I think we need to assume it's now stronger than Gabriella is."

Jim sighed. "Fascinating but pointless. Tick tock, people, the clock is running out and I've never lost a case. I'm not about to start when the defendant is innocent."

Sam ignored him. "When Gabriella was in that pink cage, she'd enter a fugue state when the personality took over, most likely when her abductor tortured or sexually abused her. I doubt Gabriella remembered — remembers — anything about those six months. The alter personality did. Does." Sam shook her head.

"Is Quentin right, did Gabriella kill her sister because she confronted the alternate personality?" Reece asked.

"It's possible, especially if it's sociopathic. Gabriella wouldn't have killed her sister," Sam said. "Her alter would if it viewed Isabella as a threat. Or Quentin twisted a senseless accident into something far uglier because of his own issues."

"Did Gabriella know about the second personality?" Reece asked.

She shrugged. "I don't think she lied when she denied doing the things she was accused of when she was in the altered state. Remember the night we were there?"

"What about it?"

"Gabriella was flustered when we were talking. I was sure she recognized me but she denied it. Now, I realize she did recognize me. My sister, Joyce, would have been the same age as Gabriella's sister." Sam paused. "I bet Joyce and Isabella knew each other, maybe they were friends. Since I didn't know we lived in London, I didn't understand why Gabriella was acting so weird around me. The last thing Gabriella — or her alter — would want is someone popping up from her childhood."

Reece nodded. "Considering she went to so much effort to have her juvenile medical records destroyed, that makes sense. She tried to eradicate her past."

"The more I tried to get her to engage in small talk, the more stressed she got," Sam said. "Then she... well, changed. Whenever Gabriella couldn't handle a situation, it gave her alter personality the power to take over. That's what happened with the dog."

Jim looked bewildered. "What has the dog got to do with anything?"

"When Gana was ill, the other personality emerged," she explained. "Gabriella never faced the grief of her dog's death. She wasn't aware it happened. On some level, she knew something was wrong, but the mind is a funny thing. When Gabriella was weak, the alter personality was able to take over and Gabriella would lose large chunks of time. Can you imagine how terrifying that would be? Her marriage was bad, she didn't have any friends, and her social isolation forced her to find ways to self-justify the episodes."

"I talked to Derek about the dog," Jim said. "He said his wife — or her alter, I suppose — told him every time she replaced the animal. It bothered him she gave the dog the same name, but he didn't want to contradict her and have to explain to the kids why their mother was pretending it never happened."

Reece frowned. "How did he react to the DID theory?"

"Believes it," Jim answered. "He mentioned a couple of incidents, including two nights before she disappeared when she asked him to go to the shed to fix the door. Gabriella was always strange. Over the years, he ignored it."

"I don't like Derek and he's the most selfish person I've ever met, but I'm not surprised he didn't jump to the conclusion of DID. It's rare," Sam said.

"What else have you got?" Jim asked. "I can't request a postponement based on the voice recording of a deranged man. A man, I'll remind you, we can't call as a witness because we don't know where he is." He exhaled in frustration.

"The afternoon she disappeared," Reece said, "a witness thought he saw Derek's car. Gabriella must have rented a vehicle that looked like Derek's, which means she dropped it off after the alleged murder. We checked car rentals in the Greater Toronto Area and no one recognized her picture, so she could have rented it outside the city. Sam is running Gabriella's photo through rental agencies across Ontario."

"The problem is," Sam continued, "you can drop off the rental after hours. Most agencies have a drop box. It's possible no one saw her."

"Well," Jim mused, "it would help if I could prove she rented a car. Gabriella's the one who called the service station and said she couldn't take her car in because she needed it. There would be no reason for her to have the rental."

"If someone recognizes her photo," Sam knew it was a long shot, "we'll discover the name she used to rent the car. I can confirm there's no evidence she's using the name, *Isabella LeBlanc,* but since Gabriella's purse was in the house, we can bet her alter personality has identification. Assuming it's still using it, we'll have a solid lead."

"Gabriella or the alter personality visited Copper Harbor, Michigan, two months before she disappeared," Reece said. "That must factor into this somehow."

Jim twirled a pen between his fingers. "Any chance she's there?"

"I sent the sheriff a picture, and he didn't recognize her," Reece told Jim. "But there's a lot of country and wilderness out there. Truth is she could be in the vicinity. The sheriff said he'd have no way of knowing if she didn't interact with anyone or go into town. He's talking with state police and distributing the picture."

"How are you doing with tracing the money?" Jim asked.

"The executor of her mother's estate was a lawyer who was in practice alone and died over fifteen years ago," Sam said. "Reece can explain the angle he's working."

"My OPP contact referred us to a private sector forensic financial consultant. Quentin isn't lying. There was money left in trust to Gabriella and a lot of it. He traced it from the grandmother to Nina. He's following it from there." Reece sighed. "Because of the time constraint, I'm calling in some major favours. The price tag is high."

Jim was unperturbed. "How long will it take?"

"Depends," Reece said. "The financial investigator *will* find it, but her mother died over twenty years ago. What we do know is Nina broke the trust when Gabriella was seventeen, which she was empowered to do. We found a holding company, but Nina dissolved it a few months before she died. She did a good job burying the money, and we have to assume she taught her daughter to do the same."

"Jim, if we provide you with evidence of the money's existence, is that enough to show reasonable doubt?" Sam asked.

"No, you'll need to prove she accessed it after her assumed death." Jim sighed. "If she is alive, is there any chance she'll find out your guy is digging into her accounts?"

Reece shrugged. "We're not being discreet. We're making noise in the hope it spooks her."

Jim stood, signalling the end of the meeting. Sam collected her stuff from the table and put on her jacket.

"I'll speak with the Crown and the judge," Jim said. "I'll present what we have and file to postpone closing arguments. I might be able to buy you three more days to find something." He walked them out. "Sam, Lisa's asking about Christmas."

Caught up in the investigation, she hadn't contacted Lisa. "Oh boy, I forgot all about it. Is she mad I didn't call?"

Jim rolled his hand. "Are you two joining us?"

"Christmas Eve, right?"

Jim nodded. "Italian feast, same as always, but you're welcome to stay for Christmas Day."

"No thanks, we're going to Uthisca. I'll visit Lisa this afternoon. I can see in your face she's pissed I didn't acknowledge her invitation."

"Finally, the Rock of Gibraltar moves. Thank God for small miracles. Remember, Gerbera daisies are her favourite." Jim winked.

"In vivid colours," Sam confirmed. "Thanks for negotiating a truce, Jim."

He waved her off. "You're sure you don't want to be with Grace and Harvey? Lisa would understand if you wanted to spend Christmas with your mother."

Sam felt her eyes widen. In her peripheral vision, she saw Reece, who was in the process of putting on his jacket, freeze and drop it to the floor.

Unaware of the problem, Jim continued, "We ran into Harvey last week Christmas shopping. He told us your mom is having luck with a new medication. Grace's good days are improving."

Reece pick up his jacket. He brushed by her without a word. When she raced into the hallway, the elevator doors were sliding closed.

Reece was gone.

CHAPTER FORTY

One Week Later: Toronto, Ontario

Sam

"JIM CALLED," REECE said over the phone. "We're to meet him at his office. Gabriella's confessed."

He disconnected before Sam could say anything, and he didn't offer to wait for her to reach their office so they could go together. She grabbed her keys and raced out of the loft, leaping into a cab before it shot through the lights at Parliament Street.

Did this mean Gabriella had turned herself in? They'd found the money and could prove she'd accessed it after her disappearance, but they hadn't found her.

On Friday afternoon, the forensic financial investigator unravelled the twenty-year-old web of holding companies to discover that Gabriella had signed transfer documents two days after her alleged death. She'd had no option but to sign the transfer *Gabriella LeBlanc*. Although her mother had moved the money numerous times between different holding companies, she'd neglected to change the Articles of Incorporation on the parent company. After Nina's death and the death of her lawyer, Gabriella LeBlanc was the sole director.

Gabriella had moved the money to a numbered account in the Cayman Islands back in June. Last week, she must have realized they were closing in on the money because she moved it again. They didn't know where she put it, and the trail was cold. The Cayman bank would only disclose they had opened an account for Gabriella LeBlanc in June, and she'd transferred the funds and closed the account last week.

Forgetting to move the money before she disappeared in June was a stupid mistake. But Sam wondered if Gabriella had maintained enough control that her alter personality didn't understand the complicated financial side. Gabriella's talents were financial whereas her other personality's skills were not.

It didn't matter because the money could be anywhere, and Gabriella — or her alter, whichever the case may be — didn't need to be in the same country as the money. Jim was presenting the new evidence on Monday morning and was confident it proved Gabriella was alive. Sam had no idea why she'd step forward.

At First Canadian Place, in her haste to reach the elevator, Sam slipped on the cleaning crew's freshly waxed lobby floor. She arrived at Jim's office sweaty, out of breath, and limping.

"What's going on?" she asked. Reece was already there but he turned his back when she entered, refusing to look at her.

"Gabriella sent me a DVD," Jim said.

Sam was stunned. "I don't understand."

He brought up the video and they watched the short, single frame. Gabriella was sitting against a white wall with a copy of *The Globe and Mail* from a week ago.

My name is Gabriella LeBlanc Martina. I called 911 shortly after five-thirty p.m. on June 11, 2015, and told the operator that my husband, Derek Martina, had stabbed me. I faked my death and framed my husband for my murder by planting evidence in Derek's car, staging a crime scene at our home, and disappearing. I'm very sorry and deeply regret my actions.

Jim clicked off the monitor.

"Why would she do this?" Sam asked.

"Maybe this will tell us." Jim passed her a sealed envelope with her name on the front. "It was in my mailbox at home this morning along with the

DVD." He put up his hand to ward off her interruption. "Before you ask, the police did canvass the neighbourhood, and no one saw anything. There were no fingerprints or DNA on the envelope or the contents. We have no way to trace where it originated from or who delivered it."

Sam tore open the envelope. The letter was typed. She read the words silently and then read it aloud to Jim and Reece.

Dear Samantha,

I remember you because you're the only person I ever met with green eyes, and you look just like your father. My sister, Isabella, was your sister's friend. You'd be too young to remember me.

I knew you would eventually find out the truth, so I'm giving you what you want in the hope it ends your investigation. I didn't know the process of moving the money out of the account or I would have done it before I disappeared. It was stupid, but at times like these, one must look at the positive. You can't find it now, and I have no reason to think you'll ever find me, should you even bother to try once they drop the charges against Derek.

Yes, I broke the law and the authorities will issue a warrant for my arrest, but I doubt they'll spend money and resources on an international manhunt. I will tell you I'm not in Canada, and you can assure Derek I'll never bother him or the children again.

I know my sister is dead. I didn't for a long time. I know about my other personality. We've been seeing a therapist and are working hard to fix the things that went wrong.

By now, you know what happened to me when I was a child. You know Quentin is a drunk. You've met Derek and have seen the kind of man he is. Samantha, all I'm asking for is a chance to take back my life.

You had a sister who died, just like me. Please try to understand how much I've suffered. Please leave me in peace to heal.

Sincerely yours,
Gabriella

No one said anything. Sam stared at the letter and dropped it on top of the table.

"What do you make of that?" Jim asked.

Reece picked it up. "I'm surprised Gabriella bothered writing it. I suppose it doesn't matter why she did." He dropped it back to the table and turned away to look out the window.

Sam ran her finger across the typed words. "There's that phrase from the diary again — *at times like these*. Repetitive phrasing in speaking and writing is an unconscious personal habit, like a tick. It doesn't make sense because we know Gabriella didn't write the diary."

Jim frowned. "What's your point?"

She tapped her finger against the letter. "The letter says she didn't know the process of moving the money or she'd have done it before she staged her death. Gabriella *did* know the process. She's the one who set it up."

She was quiet for a moment, thinking about the ramifications. "I don't think Gabriella wrote this letter," she said slowly. "Her alter personality did."

Jim stood. "Well, it doesn't matter which personality wrote it or recorded the video. I've spoke to the Crown, and we're meeting with the judge tomorrow morning. They'll drop the charges against Derek."

Sam stood and put on her jacket. "Jim, do you want us to look for her?"

He shook his head. "My job was to defend Derek and find evidence to acquit. Personally, I don't care where his wife is or why she did this."

"It's the cops' job to find her," Reece said. "She's committed fraud and obstruction of justice, at the least. If she isn't in Canada, the RCMP will be lead."

The letter bothered her. To Sam, it meant Gabriella had relinquished control to her alter personality, but maybe Gabriella had suspected she was losing control. Maybe she'd ensured that *Gabriella LeBlanc* had to sign the transfer documents. At the end, she may have tried to save Derek and expose her other personality. What if she was hoping someone would help her?

Jim was telling Reece, "Accounting will settle up, including the bonus. Good job on tracing the money and the rest of the work you did. Appreciate it." He ushered them to the door. "Are we still on for Christmas Eve?"

  L.E. Fraser

Without answering, Reece said, "I have to run. See you later, Jim." He shook Jim's hand and left.

Sam watched him go. He hadn't spoken a word to her. Same as usual over the past week since discovering she'd lied about her mother. Reece made sure he was out of the loft before she woke and didn't come home until after she was asleep. He hadn't debriefed her on the forensic financial investigator's report. He'd sent it to Jim and left a copy on her desk at the office. It broke her heart.

"Sam? Christmas Eve?" Jim repeated.

"Sure, we'll see you there."

While she waited for the elevator alone, she wondered if she'd be spending Christmas with Reece at all.

CHAPTER FORTY-ONE

Sam

WHEN SHE RETURNED from Jim's office, Reece wasn't there. He didn't come home until after two a.m. She spent the morning waiting for him to get up and worrying about how to talk to him. A few minutes ago, she'd heard the shower. She was pacing the living room in short, nervous strides waiting for him to come downstairs.

She was determined to talk to him and wouldn't take 'no' for an answer. He'd had enough time to work through the shock of discovering her deception about her mother. Jim had accidentally dropped the bomb eight days ago.

The case had taken most of their focus, but Sam knew Reece well enough to understand he never acted spontaneously. He took private time to process what hurt him and to sort out his feelings to ensure he was able to apply reason before reacting. Over the past week, she had respected that process, but their relationship was in serious trouble. If she didn't take the initiative to open communications by acknowledging she'd hurt him, there was a good chance Reece would leave.

This whole mess was entirely her fault. She had to own what she'd done and try to explain her reasons, without sounding as if she was justifying or mitigating her lies. She loved him and had to get him to talk to her before it was too late.

He was coming downstairs when her phone rang. She planned to send the call to voicemail but saw it was Jim and answered, "Hi, how'd it go?"

Watching Reece from the corner of her eye, she listened to Jim. After he finished speaking, she said, "That's great news. What's Derek going to do now?"

She tried to get Reece's attention to offer to put the call on speaker, but he turned his back and picked up a *Gourmet Magazine*.

With a sigh, she ended the call, walked over to Reece and stood in front of him, hoping he'd look at her.

"The charges were dropped." She tried a smile that felt a little desperate.

He didn't return her smile. "Obviously, since the woman's not dead." He sat on the sofa beside Brandy.

She ignored his belligerent tone. "Derek's buying a law practice in Winnipeg. He wants to raise the kids out of the limelight. He also told Jim he should have seen how sick Gabriella was and tried to help her. He's not going to look for her, says she deserves to be left alone. It sounds as if Derek blames himself." She sat beside him on the sofa. "The thing that bothers me is I'm sure the alter personality wrote that letter and taped the video. Call it a hunch, I guess."

He didn't lift his eyes from the article in the magazine. "You've said a thousand times, PIs are paid to do a job, not to worry about justice. What difference does it make who or what she is?"

Sam patted Brandy's head. "I never said I don't care about justice," she said. "I don't know. Those diary entries are so full of rage."

"What's your point?" he asked.

She shrugged. "The alter personality wrote the diary. What if the alter did kill Gabriella's sister? What if it's dangerous?"

"There's no proof that Isabella LeBlanc's death was anything but an accident. Your father was on the scene. If your dad was suspicious, wouldn't he investigate?"

"An investigation would disclose he was with Megan and his son," she pointed out. "But, you're right. If he'd suspected foul play, Dad would have done something. I feel... well, concerned, I guess."

"It's over and you have the money to finish your PhD." He dropped the magazine on the table and walked to the kitchen.

Sam followed, leaning against the kitchen island and blocking his exit. "Reece, we need to talk about my mother."

He shook his head. "There's nothing to talk about."

"Yes, there is. My mother's not a nice person, but I shouldn't have lied to you. I was trying to avoid the whole thing because that's what I do when I can't handle something. It's the way my mother raised me. Never talk about anything unpleasant, don't share your feelings, and always pretend everything's fine when it's not. Deniability and avoidance are the tools I was taught."

That sounded like justification. She didn't blame him for not responding.

Trying again, she said, "I told you she was dead when we started dating because it was less complicated. I didn't think it was a big deal. I don't have a relationship with Grace, and I didn't want you to try to force one on me."

Great, that sounded like mitigation and blaming. Frustrated, she gathered her thoughts, realizing the best approach was the simplest: apologize. "I handled everything badly. I'm so sorry. You have every right to be upset and disappointed. Can we please talk about it?"

"I'm leaving tonight. I'm going to Uthisca. It's best if you spend Christmas with Jim and Lisa. We can talk after the holidays," he replied.

She exhaled in a gasp. "I don't want you to go."

"Why?" He held her eyes with no expression on his face.

"I love you, Reece."

He didn't move from the sink. "Yet you lie. You keep secrets. That's not love." His voice was ragged and he turned away. "I don't know what we're playing at here. You won't marry me, and we don't have the kind of future I want. I need commitment and honesty. I need to be able to share my life with someone."

"That's what I want, too. I know I've done a shitty job showing you. I know you deserve better but please don't go. I do love you, Reece."

When he turned, a glimmer of hope flashed across his face. She knew it wasn't too late. Reece had a forgiving nature, and he still loved her. She could fix this. All it required was for her to move outside her comfort zone and be dead honest.

She took a deep breath. "I haven't lied about anything else. I want to change and it's because of you. You make me a better person." She lowered her eyes. "You make me like myself."

He took a step toward her, and she looked up and smiled at him. She loved Reece's faith — his ability to forgive, process disappointment, and give the people he loved a second chance.

"Please stay. Please give me another chance. I promise you we do have a future," she said.

"There can't be any more lies, Sam."

She crossed her heart. "I promise. Please forgive me?"

He paused but his answer was in his eyes. He stepped forward and wrapped his arms around her. "I forgive you," he murmured against her hair.

She pulled away and held his eyes. "I have one more request."

He looked puzzled. "What's that?"

"Marry me." Sam felt a wave of peace roll over her. She'd never been so sure of a choice in her life.

He stood motionless in front of her, his eyes searching hers. "What?"

"Please marry me."

"You're sure this is what you want?"

"Positive." She laughed at his goofy grin. "On one condition," she added quickly.

The happiness on his face faded. "What's that?"

"You ask my stepfather, Harvey, for his blessing."

Reece laughed. "At our age? You're kidding."

"No, he'll get a kick out of that. In fact, he'll love it. He's old-school." She wrapped her arms around his waist. "Besides, you have to meet your future mother-in-law. Strap on your seatbelt and amp up your courage, fiancé, you're in for one hell of a wild ride."

He lifted her feet from the ground and swung her around. "She can't be that bad."

"Oh boy," Sam said with a laugh, "are you in for a surprise."

EPILOGUE

February 2016: Northern Michigan

"EVERYTHING IS TAKEN care of," Declan O'Reilly said to the woman in front of him. "Here is a copy of the deed and the rest of the legal documents." He handed her the bulky manila envelope.

"You said when we met in April you were going back to Ireland," she said.

He nodded. "Yours was the last real estate deal of my career. I'm going home to the Wee County. That's Louth," he clarified. "Just in case you know the geography."

The woman gazed through her wraparound sunglasses at the cabin. The brim of her baseball cap shadowed her face and hid most of her hair. He'd never had a good look at her, even when they'd met in April to discuss her desire to find remote property near the Keweenaw Peninsula. Her clothes were too bulky to determine her figure, but she was tall. She never took off the large dark glasses. She'd told him in April she had an eye condition.

Declan studied the cabin sitting in the middle of nowhere. After leaving the main road, it had taken over two hours to reach it. If it weren't for the unseasonably warm temperatures, even with the powerful plow attached to his four-wheel-drive truck, they wouldn't have reached the cabin at all.

"They're forecasting a storm over the next few days," he warned her. "There's a snowmobile in the shed, and you can access town along the lake, but you gotta be careful. Lake Superior doesn't freeze over."

"I know. I lived here when I was a child," she said.

Declan scratched his beard. To the best of his knowledge, no one had ever lived in the cabin. The Michigan Treasury Department had owned the unclaimed property for over thirty years. If she'd lived in the area, Declan supposed that was why she was so specific over what she was looking for when she contacted him in the spring. It wasn't any of his business.

"There's a new generator in the shed and lots of propane to run her. The structure is sound and I did basic repairs but—"

"You didn't tell anyone about our transaction?" she interrupted.

He shook his head. "You said it was to be anonymous, and I respected your wishes."

It was getting dark, and he wanted to be on the road. There was something strange about her that unnerved him. Declan was anxious to end their affiliation. Truth was he felt a bit afraid of the mysterious stranger.

He backed toward his truck one small step at a time. "I had the septic system and the water well checked for you, too." Regardless of how foolish his feeling was, his feet were itching to get to the safety of the truck.

She didn't move. She stood straight and still, staring at the cabin with her large white dog sitting like a statue by her feet.

"Stocked some groceries," Declan added. "The deep freeze in the shed is full and you have enough dry goods for months, but you'll need to make a run into town in a few weeks," he said.

"We'll hunt," she said, turning to him and smiling.

There was something frightening about the smile. Declan couldn't figure out why, but he had the sudden, overpowering urge to run. He turned to leave and stumbled on the snow, scrambling to his feet while feeling vulnerable with his back to her.

When he reached the truck, he spun around to face her. He blindly groped at the door handle with a rising sense of panic. He took a calming breath before managing to yank open the door. Once inside the truck, he felt safe and a little foolish.

Before closing his door, he raised his hand in a final wave and shouted back to her, "Welcome home, Isabella."

The End

  L.E. Fraser

ACKNOWLEDGEMENTS

I OWE A huge debt of gratitude to my fantastic editor, Sadie Scapillato, and my copy proofreader, Elizabeth West. Let's hope I followed all their great advice.

Writing takes a team of talented people so I'd like to thank my 2015 web developer, Mike Doyle, for redesigning the website and turning it into an efficient marketing tool.

US Author Joseph Hirsch generously provided critical notes on the final draft. His work is amazing, if you're looking for a good read. Paula Henderson shared her wealth of knowledge on addiction and recovery, in addition to beta-reading three drafts. It takes a true friend to read the same thing multiple times. Ottawa fantasy author Krista Walsh — another gifted storyteller worth checking out — spent hours sharing her expertise on indie versus traditional publishing. The Batchawana First Nation of Ojibways was patient in answering questions and correcting facts.

I want to thank the readers who asked me to keep writing about Sam McNamara's adventures after reading *Simon Says, Perdition Games*. As Blanche DuBois says in *A Streetcar Named Desire:* "I have always relied on the kindness of strangers." In my case, it's not because I've lost all contact with reality... at least I hope not. You see, writing is the art of speaking to strangers, and when those strangers are kind enough to share their opinions, the stories grow stronger.

Most of all, thank you for reading *Skully, Perdition Games*. Sam and Reece are returning protagonists, but each novel has a new plotline.

Authors appreciate the time readers take to give their novel a whirl. I'm requesting a bit more kindness by asking you to write a review on Amazon and Goodreads to offer your feedback. My goal is to provide you with a few hours of well-deserved entertainment. Good or bad, your opinion is priceless.

Haven't read *Simon Says, Perdition Games* yet? Turn the page to read the first two chapters. Enjoy!

Thank you,
L.E. Fraser

www.perditiongames.com

Twitter: **@perditiongames**
Facebook: **perditiongamesseries**

SIMONSAYS
PERDITION GAMES

By L.E. Fraser

Amazon reviewers are saying...

5 The prefect thriller, with a number of ups and downs.*

5 This is a must read!*

5 ...forward moving, fast paced plot...*

5 This is not a novel you can predict throughout.*

5 Incredible writing and editing.*

PROLOGUE

SYLVIA SHOVED THE hem of her sackcloth robe into the twine around her waist. Her heart was racing, and, every time she tried to breathe, there was a stabbing pain in her chest. She ran.

Thorns sliced open the vulnerable skin of her arms, and she swiped her right hand against the sharp twigs to try to protect her face. Blood dripped from the end of the middle finger on her left hand where the detached nail hung to the bed by a string of bloody tissue. Still, she ran.

Without warning, a piercing pain shot through her chest. Her stomach convulsed and bloody vomit spewed from between her cracked lips. She stumbled and choked on the blood that ran down her throat. She stopped running.

From directly behind her, she heard a pitiful whimper and a soft swishing sound, like air escaping from a balloon. The noise of breaking branches was intrusive in the dark forest. She froze and waited in fear, expecting to hear the gleeful shouts of their pursuers.

After a moment of absolute silence, she whispered through the darkness, "Get up, Mandy, we have to keep moving."

"I can't."

She leaned down and felt around the rough ground until she hit flesh. She ran her fingers along the girl's forearm, grasped Mandy's thin wrist and pulled hard. The body barely shifted. "We can't stay here."

"I can't run any further."

Mandy was making little meowing sounds that broke Sylvia's heart. If they rested, he'd catch them. They couldn't give up. They were too close to freedom. She took a deep breath. "The road is at the top of the escarpment, we can make it."

"I can't," Mandy repeated through her tears.

Sylvia sat down hard, and her knee smashed against a boulder. Agony shot across her kneecap, and a spasm seized her calf muscle, forcing her to bite on her tongue to keep from crying out in pain. Shuddering tremors ran down her legs. She curled into a fetal position on the ground beside Mandy and wept in pain and frustration.

She was twenty-eight and had volunteered to be Mandy's mentor when the sixteen-year-old had arrived at the sanctuary six months earlier. When she made the decision to try to escape, she took her protegé with her. Now, the responsibility weighed heavily on her shoulders.

They'd left just before ten o'clock at night, and she'd struck the sentry with a plank stolen from the lumberyard. Fear had weakened her grip and coated her hands in sweat. The club slipped at the point of impact, and her blow had barely slowed the man's attack. He'd thrown her to the ground, hurled aside her weapon, and savagely kicked her. He would have killed her, but Mandy had grabbed the makeshift club and bludgeoned the man. To-gether, the women had dragged him to the side of the shed, but Sylvia couldn't commit murder. That was her first mistake. They would discover him. Mussani would know what she'd done, and there would be no mercy if he caught them.

"Go on without me," Mandy whispered.

She dug deep to find the strength to go on and slowly sat up, groaning in pain. "We stay together. It's our only chance. Get up." The desperate words echoed loudly through the forest, and she pressed together her split lips. She could see Mandy's eyes shining with fear.

They waited in tense silence and then Sylvia whispered, "He's coming. He's close now. I feel him. We can't stay here."

"I'm so scared." Mandy grasped her hand. "Why did we do this? We shouldn't have done this." Hysteria laced her voice and she was gasping for breath.

"We're going to be okay," Sylvia promised. "The road is at the top of the escarpment." She wiped the back of her hand across her mouth, and it was sticky with bloody mucus. She was thankful that the darkness camouflaged her injuries. She was not okay and knew she didn't have much time left.

She removed the tie to her robe and shivered when cold air rippled against her naked flesh. She made a slipknot at each end of the rope, gliding one circle over her injured hand. The rough hemp caught the torn nail and ripped it free from her finger. The intensity of the pain made her cry out.

"Sylvia?" Mandy whimpered, with a pitiful hitch in her young voice.

Fumbling to find Mandy's hand, Sylvia secured the other slipknot around her wrist and squeezed the girl's hand. Now the rope connected them for better or for worse. As the clouds parted and the half moon looked down on them, they ran.

JB WATCHED MUSSANI light a cigarette, and the misshapen flame from the lighter bobbed in the wind. The moonlight turned his dark eyes into mirrors that reflected the cigarette ember. A reddish orange dot glowed in the middle of the pools of darkness in his face. JB turned away, alarmed by what he glimpsed in the disembodied eyes.

"Whatcha wanna do?"

Mussani took a deep drag from the cigarette, and the red ember shone again in his eyes. JB shuddered and dropped his gaze to the ground.

Father Mussani nonchalantly leaned against the front grill of the Jeep. His tone was calm and melodic when he said, "We wait."

Toeing the gravel at the side of the road, JB tried to emulate his companion's casual stance but his brow broke out in perspiration, and the pits of his chambray work shirt were sticky with sweat. Unable to endure the darkness and silence, he asked, "What if th-th-they don't c-c-come this way?"

Mussani flicked the burning cigarette into the woods. "They'll come."

"Could head s-s-south," JB suggested.

"To the lake?"

He felt his cheeks flush with embarrassment. "C-c-could have a b-b-boat," he stuttered, ashamed of the difficulty he had in spitting out the four miserable words.

Father Mussani ignored the stuttering, and gratitude washed over JB. Father never commented on the speech impediment or suggested the stutter meant he was stupid.

Mussani pulled a flask from the inside pocket of his ceremonial robe, unscrewed the top, and put the bottle to his lips. The smell of whisky tainted the wind. He didn't offer the flask, and JB didn't expect him to.

The road was north, the lake was south, the valley was east, and the woods were west. The sanctuary farmland ran between, with its buildings along the east border beside the valley. As usual, Mussani was right. The sisters would walk north to civilization, but they'd have to travel through the acres of woods that hugged the road. There were no paths through the thick brush and mature trees, and they'd need to climb a steep escarpment to reach the road. JB didn't think they could negotiate the trek without light. It had been raining for a week, and the forest ground was slick and treacherous. At least one of the sisters had a serious injury. A shiver of shame scurried along JB's spine.

"W-w-what should we do when they g-g-get here?" he asked.

"She has lost the vision. If possible, she will transcend. That's the only way to achieve self-realization."

"She's my friend." JB pulled at the crotch of his pants, a nervous habit his father had beat him for when he was a kid. He'd tried to stop but he couldn't.

One of the reasons he'd joined Bueton Sanctuary was because people didn't laugh at him over his bad habit, his stutter, or the birthmark that scarred his right temple.

"She's a sister and has broken the oath. Are you questioning the Creed?" Mussani asked.

The clouds broke apart, and the silver crest of the half moon winked. For just a moment, the moonlight illuminated Mussani's face. What JB saw in those dark eyes made him look to the ground and exhale a single puff of fear.

With his head lowered submissively and his hands clasped tightly against his chest, he said, "I'd never disobey the Creed." Although shamed by his quivering voice, he was proud that his passion had empowered him to speak the words without stumbling over the first syllable. Feeling doubt and confusion, JB gazed up at the heavens to hunt for a star to wish upon, but there were none.

SYLVIA HAD MANAGED to lead Mandy north along the irrigation tracks, so crossing the acres of fields was easy. The orchard had been tricky. When they hit the woods that crested the land, they were both confused about what direction they were going. If they fell off course, and Mussani sent out the dogs, the animals would tear them apart. The road was their only hope.

Mandy had stopped crying, a small mercy for which Sylvia was grateful. The trouble she was having breathing, the unsecured robe, and the freezing temperature had forced her to slow to a shuffling trudge, but the gentle tug on the rope indicated that Mandy was still moving behind her.

As she towed the terrified adolescent, Sylvia accepted she'd made a terrible mistake. What she was putting the girl through was worse than the initiation ceremony would have been. Her decision to take Mandy and run, without a plan to ensure they escaped, was stupid. If he caught them, he'd kill her and, although he probably wouldn't kill his pet, Mandy would pay a high price. There was no turning back. She had to get the girl to safety.

The half moon's light in the cloudy sky was now stingy, and the frigid wind was merciless. Their feet were bare, and the escarpment was becoming harder to climb. In places, they had to crawl in single file. At a spot where they could walk upright, she shoved aside jagged branches and held her arms behind her to try to keep the sharp twigs from slapping Mandy's face. Each time she stumbled, Mandy grasped the loose fabric of her open robe and pushed on her back to steady her. Under the indifferent eye of the moon, they slowly ascended the steep hill.

She turned to glance over her shoulder, slipped in a puddle of mud, and lost her balance. She grasped at the trees in an effort not to fall back down the hill. With a startled cry, Mandy's hands pawed and pushed at her back to try to balance her. Sylvia swayed for a moment and then pitched backwards, rolling over Mandy and sliding downhill. Dragged by the tethering rope, Mandy tumbled after her and crushed Sylvia's face into the moist, decaying leaves.

A rainbow of light exploded in front of Sylvia's closed eyes. She could feel the warmth of her blood streaming down her chin, and her mouth filled with the coppery taste. Every time she tried to breathe, there was a crackling sound in her chest. She felt like she was drowning, and the night air tasted metallic. She was certain one of her broken ribs had punctured her lung. If she died in the woods, Mandy wouldn't make it out. They had to get to the road. She fought against the pain and focused on Mandy's hysterical yelps.

"Get off," she whispered, forcing the two words from her bruised lips.

The girl pathetically whimpered, and her breath was hot and wet against Sylvia's neck.

"Get off," she grunted.

Mandy rolled over and the tethering rope stretched taut across Sylvia's back. They lay together on the cold ground. Above them, the moon slithered beneath a cloud. The darkness was a black velvet blindfold. In that moment, Sylvia knew God had finally turned His back. He was showing them their destiny, and it was hell.

JB TRIED TO keep track of time by the number of cigarettes Father Mussani smoked. Ten minutes was the average time to smoke one, and Father had

L.E. Fraser

puffed on five. He figured there were about thirty minutes between butts, so that meant they had waited at the side of the road for nearly three hours.

JB wished he had the sense to leave. He had nowhere to go. He wished he had the courage to save Sylvia. He knew he did not. He sensed Mussani coming into his space and took a small, involuntary step back.

"Problem, JB?" The voice came from his immediate right.

"I was wondering b-b-bout the ceremony."

"Why?"

He struggled to stay immobile, hoping Mussani couldn't smell his fear. "H-h-how can she be initiated?"

"She'll be initiated here."

"What about the w-w-witnesses?"

"Two, Brother, we only need two," remarked Mussani.

JB asked the question that had nagged at him ever since Mussani's second cigarette. "Who will g-g-guide Sylvia?"

Father didn't answer. His silence spoke volumes to JB.

"I c-c-can't. Sh-sh-she's my friend."

Several moments elapsed before Mussani spoke in a slow, even pitch. "You've been initiated, Brother, and cleansed to guide the metamorphosing of the worthy. Sister Sylvia is a traitor."

JB remained still and silent at the side of his Messiah.

"Are you questioning the Creed and the ordinances, which you swore had saved your miserable soul? Don't you believe that the doctrines of our existence are absolute loyalty, confidentiality, and—"

"And obedience," JB interrupted, anxious to redeem himself in the eyes of his mentor. He felt sweat trickle to the loose waist of his sackcloth pants.

"And obedience," Mussani agreed. His voice filled with enthusiasm, "Look, Brother, a shooting star!"

"SYLVIA, LOOK A shooting star!" Mandy's voice sounded so young and innocent. "Wishes come true on shooting stars. Make a wish, quick before the tail fades."

Sylvia tried to focus on the star blurring and flashing before her eyes. She wished for Mandy to make it to safety. Her eyes rolled, and she opened her mouth to let the bloody saliva run from the corner of her swollen lips. She placed her palms on the ground and pushed her broken body to its knees. Agony exploded in her chest, forcing her to bite hard on her lip to keep from screaming. She tucked one foot underneath her and stood.

"Come on, Mandy. Road, over the hill."

"Did you make a wish?" Mandy asked as she stood up and followed along behind.

"I made a wish," Sylvia agreed and closed her eyes against the tears.

FROM THE DARKNESS, JB heard them. He knew they were very close, but he couldn't see them. Sister Sylvia was advising Mandy to stay in the ditch, and her voice was thick and wet sounding. He heard her pain, and it made the hair rise on his neck.

Mussani ignored them and continued to lean against the front bumper of the Jeep. He was merely waiting, like a lion carefully stalking its prey. After several motionless moments, he reached into the Jeep and switched on the headlights.

In response, JB heard Mandy cry out, "Sylvia, I see a car!"

They watched in silence as she crawled up the ditch, standing at the top to wave her arms. A frayed piece of braided hemp circled her right wrist.

Mussani slid through the darkness to the girl. "Find the other one."

JB reluctantly jumped into the ditch, walking ten metres before his boot hit something solid. He carefully slung Sylvia across his shoulder and trudged up the steep slope to the road where Mussani waited.

"Move her by the tree and wake her."

JB lowered his friend to the ground, and, from the corner of his eye, he saw Mussani take Mandy's hand. She blinked and shaded her eyes from the glare of the car's lights but stood silent and still. Her eyes widened with horror when she looked from Mussani to Sylvia, who was now visible in the harsh light.

JB propped Sylvia against the thick trunk of an elm tree and groped for her hand. She tensed at his touch but didn't open her eyes. He pinched her arm and wept.

His pinch drew her back to consciousness, and she struggled to stand before giving up and slumping weakly against the tree trunk.

He studied her in the harsh light from the Jeep. Her lower teeth and gums were visible through a gaping tear in her lip. Pink foam coated her lips and dark blood stained her chin. It had flowed down her neck to pool in the hollows of her collarbones. Her left eye was black and swollen closed. Blood covered the hand he held, and one of her fingernails was missing.

Her head slowly turned toward him, and recognition flickered in her eyes. They'd been friends and lovers, and he could tell she believed he'd betrayed her.

JB grasped her hand hard and tears dripped down his cheeks. "I d-d-didn't t-t-tell. He knew."

"It wasn't her fault," she whispered. "Swear you'll protect her." She gasped for breath. "Swear you'll get her home to her sister."

He turned away from her and stared at the dismal scene in front of the Jeep. Mandy was sprawled on her back against the gravel, with her robe around her neck in concertina folds. Her young, lustrous skin was translucent in the cruel white light from the Jeep. Mussani knelt before the girl, anointing her trembling flesh with the initiation oil, pinching her nipples and forcing her legs apart. He grabbed her hips, thrusting himself inside her. Mandy's screams cut JB's heart. He covered his ears to block out the terrifying cries. After a few minutes, Mussani violently turned her to her stomach, grabbed her around the waist and pushed himself inside her from behind, pressing her naked body against the sharp stones on the road. She was no longer screaming, and JB prayed she was unconscious. He dropped his hands from his ears and held tightly to Sylvia's hand, averting his eyes from the brutality he'd vowed to witness.

Sylvia raised her head to the heavens. "Lord, we are still your children. Why have you abandoned us?" The light faded from her eyes. Her broken body drooped to the ground.

A bolt of lightning lit the sky, and a single star, lonely in solitude, twinkled in the darkness. JB watched the star blink once and twice, and then it vanished like an angel's tear.

When Mussani completed the initiation ceremony, JB stood and went to the Jeep. He felt sick to his stomach, and his skin was crawling with goosebumps. Mussani tightened the gold, braided rope around his thick waist, lit a cigarette, and smiled.

"What about h-h-h-her?" JB nodded toward the dead woman sprawled at the base of the giant elm. He swallowed the sour saliva gathering in his mouth and wiped the back of his hand against the clammy sweat on his forehead.

Mussani unscrewed his flask of whisky. He took a long drink and shrugged.

JB swallowed hard and let grief wash over him. Sylvia had never teased or rejected him. For the first time since joining the life at Bueton, he felt doubt.

As if aware of his disloyal thoughts, Mussani laid his arm across his shoulders. They stood together in the artificial light from the Jeep's headlights.

"It's sad," Mussani said, and his expression showed deep sympathy. "Her death was an accident, Brother. The woods are dangerous and off limits."

"There w-w-was blood on her l-l-lips."

"Sylvia was a traitor. Brother, hold tight to your faith and remember that not everyone is worthy of rising to the next level."

Mussani flicked the cigarette toward the Jeep, and the smoldering filter fell on Mandy's grubby robe. She crawled across the road toward her Messiah, guttural whimpers tearing from her throat. She reached for him.

He grasped her hand and pulled her to her feet. "My poor child, look at how betrayed you were by Sister Sylvia. Come, it's time for you to go home." He was smiling, but JB saw no kindness in the expression.

JB turned his back and went around the front of the Jeep to the passenger door. "I swear," he whispered to the wind.

With a final glance at his lover's dead body slouching against the giant elm tree, JB climbed into the Jeep and closed his eyes.

CHAPTER ONE

Estelle

ESTELLE GAZED OUT the large kitchen window over the sink. She didn't care about the maple, oak and birch trees dressed in their fall finery. The sun skipped across the smooth surface of the pond, and the frost painted the grass in the fields with shimmering patterns of light, but it didn't move her. She wasn't grateful for nature's seasonal gifts. She'd grown up poor, with an abusive father who took pleasure in controlling his family. What Estelle cared about now was ownership. She knew money was power, and power meant obedience. That was exactly what she wanted, and she didn't care how reluctantly people offered the obedience.

She stood beside the dishwasher and, with a twitch of irritation, realized it was still making a weird noise. She'd asked Duncan to fix it, and he'd mumbled that their ranch hand could take care of it. The machine continued to clank and groan, like an old man shuffling to the washroom. She suspected Duncan broke it when he steamed trout in the dishwasher. Her foodie husband had arrived home from the city excited by the bizarre recipe he'd negotiated from the chef of a five-star restaurant, and now the bloody dishwasher wasn't working. The trout hadn't even tasted good. There had been a hint of detergent in every bite.

The dogs started barking, and she peered out the library window to see who was coming up the lane. Maybe it was Dean, and maybe he was planning to fix the dishwasher. She disliked Dean Crats because he made these peculiar remarks blanketed with subtext, which he'd drawl with a snide smirk.

Instead of Dean's truck, it was a delivery van, although the directive on the gate clearly stated that the stable office received all deliveries. Angry, Estelle stomped to the mudroom, snagged a jacket from the cedar closet, and stepped out the French doors.

The weather was unseasonably cool. Summer had arrived early, but the warm weather had departed fast. Winter was now nipping at October's tail, and the Farmer's Almanac warned that it would be a long season permeated with blizzards. The inclement weather made her unhappy because it was wreaking havoc with her renovation plans. She didn't care that the cold weather had destroyed most of the local crops. Her neighbours' financial worries weren't her concern. Estelle didn't believe in counting other people's money.

A cheerful male voice was drifting across the crisp air. Her uninvited guest was chatting to the dogs and addressing them by name, which meant he was someone local. She walked down the path that ran through the meticulous gardens and met the man at the wide driveway. Estelle rubbed the chill from her hands and waited for him to state his business.

"Hello there, Mrs. Reid, fine bright day today. How have you been? How's your family?" He strolled around his van to the back doors and extracted a wrapped box of flowers.

She didn't reply. She didn't like visitors, especially chatty visitors.

"It's a bit cool for the month. These are for you. The order came in from Italy."

He looked vaguely familiar, but she couldn't place him. His hands were calloused, and his fingernails were dirty. His face was weathered, and grey stubble decorated his jaw line. He had an accent that might be Scottish, but it was difficult to tell. The short, thin man was dressed in a grubby pair of denim overalls and a plaid shirt with the sleeves rolled up. She thought it was an unprofessional outfit for a deliveryman.

He passed her a large bouquet wrapped in festive paper and tied with maroon twine. "I think you're the first person around here who has ever received flowers from overseas."

She took the box. The wrapping was creative, and the bulk of the packaging and weight of the vase implied that it was an expensive arrangement. Her husband always bought her flowers from the city. She doubted that a florist working in Uthisca had any design skills, but she could smell roses on the cool wind so perhaps it wouldn't be too bad. If the order came from overseas, it was probably a birthday gift.

"I suspect it's from my daughter, Veronica. She and her family frequently travel in Italy," she said.

"How's your other daughter doing?"

Estelle looked up at the man. The box with the towering vase started to slip through her fingers. How could a simple question be so complicated? She wrapped the palm of her left hand more securely around the bottom of the box and glared at him.

He shuffled his feet against the pebbles. There was no judgment or malice in his face, only simple curiosity. The intensity of her stare, coupled with her refusal to answer his question, seemed to embarrass him. He dropped his eyes and turned away to shut the van doors.

"Okay then, you have yourself a good day," he mumbled.

It occurred to her that she should tip him. "Wait here," she said. "I'll be right back."

She turned around and marched back to the house. Once inside, she placed the vase on the quartz countertop of the shelving unit in the mudroom, closed her eyes, and focused on slowing her racing heart.

After they'd bought the ranch in the town of Uthisca, their youngest daughter had lived with them for nearly six months. It wasn't surprising that someone from town would remember her, which was why Estelle drove an hour to an adjacent town to shop. She hadn't been in a Uthisca store in over two years.

Her chest felt tight, and she was having trouble catching her breath. The smell of scorched coffee made her stomach roll. She tried to concentrate on the sweet strains of an aria from Puccini's *Madame Butterfly* playing from the wireless speakers. How's your other daughter doing? The question kept bouncing around in her head, drowning out the opera like a ridiculous jingle you can't stop humming.

With a steadying breath, she grabbed a few coins from the dish on the table and went back to the driver, who was leaning against the bright Gerbera daisy logo on the side panel of the van.

He stepped forward to meet her and seemed about to say something. Then he glanced at the coins in her outreached hand, frowned, and looked back at her face.

"Thank you for delivering the flowers." She waved her hand at him, annoyed that he didn't just take the money and go.

Instead, he looked as if she'd slapped him across the face. "Neighbours don't take money 'round here for a simple kindness, Mrs. Reid." He glared at her.

Why would a tip offend the stupid man? He seemed angry when he climbed behind the wheel of the van and recklessly raced down the gravel lane to the main road. She watched the van disappear around a clump of trees. Etiquette dictated tipping for deliveries this far out in the country. She'd done nothing wrong.

Her hand shook when she tucked the coins into the pocket of her jacket, and the weakness infuriated her. She would call the store and complain. Clearly, they'd made the right decision by purchasing their flowers from the city. Nevertheless, she may as well open the arrangement and see what it looked like.

Back at the house, she stopped in the mudroom to pick up the box. She placed it on the marble countertop of the kitchen island and opened the wrapping to caress the pink roses, white tulips, and Cymbidium orchids. Orchids were her favourite, especially exotic orchids. Much to her surprise, it was a lovely arrangement. Veronica had excellent taste, and the flowers would look spectacular in the living room on the side table.

She selected a Waterford crystal vase that would highlight the delicate orchids. After arranging the flowers, she tossed the florist's vase into the recycling bin and eagerly plucked the card from the forked stick. She read the card once, blinked and read it again. She eyed the flowers with suspicion. The card read, *Happy Birthday, Mother. Jasmine.*

Estelle retrieved the original vase from the recycling bin and shoved the flowers into it, jamming the forked stick into the arrangement, and crushing an orchid. She picked up the large vase, carried it into the sunroom, and plunked it onto the cluttered table. Water sloshed out and soaked the morning paper.

"So, we're expected to believe Jasmine is in Italy," she said to the dogs trotting at her heels.

More than likely, her daughter had contrived an elaborate plot to make it look like she was in Italy. Chewing on her lower lip, Estelle eyed the arrangement. She picked up the vase and went outside to the deck, depositing the delicate flowers on the outdoor table. She rubbed the chill from her arms and scurried back to the kitchen. She could still see the flowers. She closed the mahogany blinds to the deck and went into the living room.

She hadn't spoken to her daughter in years and tried very hard never to think about her. Was Zach in Italy, too? She ran her fingers through her short hair, wandered back to the kitchen and sat on a barstool. Estelle made a point of never sending presents to Jasmine and wished her daughter would return the favour. She and Duncan had opened a trust fund for their grandson, Zach, and made a generous deposit for each occasion, but that was it. She cursed her daughter's obstinate nature. Why couldn't she leave well enough alone?

Duncan would ask if she'd phoned to thank Jasmine. If she said no, he would scamper to the damn computer and email her, regardless of the fact that he had no interest in a relationship. Every time a gift arrived, Estelle lost control and lectured him about his hypocrisy, but he still ran to the computer.

Her morning was ruined, and she felt anxious and irritable. She pulled on a jacket and tugged on a pair of heavy-soled walking boots, a morning ritual that preceded the dogs' daily run through the fields. As always, the two bullmastiffs gathered around her with unconditional love and sharp barks of excitement. She tugged on their floppy brown ears, gave them each a generous pat, and ushered them outside. At the steps leading from the deck, she watched them take off in a gallop to the fields.

She turned and studied the flowers. There they sat in all their glory, mocking her. Carefully selecting her favourite flowers wasn't a thoughtful gesture. It was Jasmine's passive aggressive way of reminding her mother that she didn't care enough to send meaningful gifts herself. Oh yes, there was lots of subtext woven around those seemingly innocent blossoms.

Estelle tilted her head and studied the crooked table. She nudged the teak table leg with the toe of her boot. The heavy table didn't move. She grasped it and shoved. The arrangement tumbled off, and the glass vase smashed against the deck. She smiled slightly, collected a garbage bag from the mudroom, and returned to stuff the squished blossoms and shards of broken glass into the sack.

Whenever her mind drifted to Jasmine, Estelle thought of Amanda, and she didn't like thinking about her either. She looked across the rolling green fields and spied the dogs in the far south paddock. They were chasing something. Probably a rabbit. If she went to the mailbox, they wouldn't notice. She never took them to the mailbox because she worried they'd be hit by a car. North Road rarely had traffic, but she worried just the same. If they decided to have an adventure and took off down the road, she wouldn't be able to control them.

She hurried down the lane to the mailbox with the jaunty red flag pointing up at the bright blue sky. There were several greeting cards, but there was nothing from her youngest daughter.

"Well, isn't that nice. Not even a card for her mother on her birthday," Estelle muttered.

Amanda had left home two years earlier. At first, Estelle and Duncan had assumed it was adolescent defiance, and they'd waited for her to come home. Five weeks after her disappearance — two weeks after her sixteenth birthday — Duncan involved the police. During her interview, Estelle told the Inspector that Amanda was with her sister. It was important to her that no one gossiped about her daughter running away because that would imply there was something negative in her home.

The truth was that a month before she disappeared, Amanda had grown obsessed with non-traditional religious doctrines. The fanatic sermonizing hinted at a mental health issue, and it bewildered and scared them. They did their best to ignore the behaviour, assuming Amanda's extremist attitude was because of their recent move to Uthisca from Toronto. They figured she'd return to her quiet personality once she settled into their new home and made friends at school.

Instead, Amanda had refused to decorate her new room, claiming every stick of furniture was wasteful and excessive. She systematically drove away anyone who tried to connect with her, claiming they were materialistic sinners. Not a single teenager graced the doors of their new home, which left her unhappy parents the sole audience for her to regale with unorthodox views on communal love and peculiar ideologies of collective consciousness.

Duncan found a boarding school that would accept Amanda mid-semester, but she disappeared the night before she was to leave. They believed she was with her sister, and Jasmine was lying to them. They'd agreed that the best plan was to move on with a stiff upper lip, until Amanda came to her senses. That was two years ago. They were still waiting.

Estelle dug into the deep pocket of her jacket and extracted a small white business card for a Toronto private investigator. When Inspector Hash had told her they were closing Amanda's case, he'd offered Sam McNamara's card.

She gnawed on the corner of her thumb and wondered if she really wanted to find Amanda. In a very dark place, she'd felt relieved when her religiously obsessed daughter had left home.

Picking at the white card, she walked around the house to the fields that lay beyond. In the south paddock, she could see the herd of wild horses. They seemed skittish, and she shaded her eyes against the sun's glare and hunted for her dogs. They were lying on the deck, waiting for her return. The dogs had killed the rabbit, or it had won the game and escaped. Estelle whistled for them and spun the small card. Fine, she decided, she would hire Sam McNamara to locate her wayward daughter.

It occurred to her that Amanda might not want to come home, but it didn't matter. Estelle would get what she wanted. After all, money was power, and power meant obedience.

CHAPTER TWO

Betty

"AND SHE OFFERED me a tip, a handful of bloody coins! She stood there waving her manicured paw at me as if I were a pimple-faced teenager!" Harry repeated for the twentieth time since the family had started dinner. "She didn't even recognize me, and I've been over talking to her husband a dozen times over the past two years. We're the only neighbours that stupid woman has!"

Margaret, their eighteen-year-old daughter, giggled and reached over to hug her father's slouching shoulders. "Oh, Daddy, forget about it, she probably doesn't know Mom owns the shop."

"It's called Welsh Florist, Margaret! Our name is plastered all over the van," he argued. "She's a snot. You can see her snobbish attitude in the way she carries herself." He got to his feet and began prancing across the kitchen floor. "See what I mean, like she's the Queen of England."

The kids laughed and Betty smiled at her husband.

"And," he said, while sitting back at the table, "her voice is peppered with contempt, like it's a real nuisance to have to speak with the peasants. She's too skinny for a woman her age. She has to be pushing sixty. Everything about that," he stopped and looked at the kids, "old witch suggests she's never done an honest day's labour in her life."

"Alright, Harry, that's enough," Betty said. She'd have liked to get through one family dinner without someone complaining about something.

"I hate that woman. I don't like a single thing about her," Harry complained.

"You don't even know her," Betty calmly replied and stood up to clear the table.

"Doesn't matter."

"You can't hate someone you barely know," she argued. She could easily imagine the look on her proud husband's face when a neighbour handed him a couple of toonies. She stifled a giggle. He was right – the woman was a bitch with more money than common sense.

"You don't need to know someone well to hate her guts," he grumbled.

"Don't be so immature," Betty gently scolded.

Harry scowled at her, and she kissed the top of his head and picked up his plate and utensils.

Their sixteen-year-old son, Bart, grabbed the last roll, just before she removed the basket from the table. "Did you see the horses, Dad?" he asked, stuffing the bread into his mouth.

Before Harry could answer, twelve-year-old Hope jumped in. "I never get to see them from the road." From behind her grubby glasses, her eyes shone with innocent excitement.

"The stable is nicer than our house. I'm surprised *Lifestyles of the Rich and Famous* hasn't been around to do a segment," Harry grumbled.

Betty gave him a hard stare, poured him a cup of coffee, and placed a thick slab of chocolate layer cake on his plate.

He glared at her. "Betty, you don't like that woman either, so don't be so judgmental." He suddenly grinned. "Hey, why don't you tell the kids why you never went over to ask for your precious pie plate? Little bit of pride there?"

Two years ago, she'd taken a homemade apple pie over to welcome the Reid family to Uthisca. She'd dropped it off without Estelle offering a word of thanks or an invitation for a cup of tea. Mrs. Reid hadn't even bothered to return the pie plate. It was hand-painted ceramic. Her mother had given it to her when she got married. For twenty years, it had perched in a place of honour in their old china cabinet. It wasn't expensive, but she shouldn't have to go over and ask for it back.

Harry chuckled at her and winked. She frowned and handed her youngest son, Willy, his dessert. Before she let go of the plate, the fourteen-year-old had his fork up and was digging into the layer cake.

Hope delicately picked at her dessert, but didn't eat it. She also hadn't eaten any of her dinner. Betty was very aware of her daughter's skill at moving food around on the plate to make it appear that she'd eaten. Her youngest child was painfully thin, and Betty constantly worried about her health.

"Think they'd let me ride the horses?" Hope asked.

Bart and Will both laughed and sprayed a rain shower of chocolate crumbs from their mouths.

"That's disgusting!" Margaret squawked. "You're pigs. Cover your mouths."

The boys oinked at their sister and shoved their faces into their cake.

Margaret crinkled her nose in disgust. "I doubt Mrs. Reid will let you ride her horses," she told her sister. "But hey, the Wilder family has a mare, and Richard told me I could bring you over to ride any time you'd like."

Hope didn't look impressed. "You just want to go 'cause you think Richard's dreamy. That mare is a hundred years old."

Margaret giggled. "Well, Richard is pretty good-looking."

"I heard the Reids are going to breed and show Arabian horses," Willy said. "Dean told me they were bringing in more this spring." He glanced wistfully at his empty plate and then stared at the rest of the cake on the kitchen countertop.

Betty ignored him. He'd already had two plates of chicken, six rolls, four glasses of milk, and a huge piece of cake.

"Why in God's name do they want Arabians in this climate?" Harry muttered.

Margaret opened her mouth to reply, but Harry kept talking. "Margaret, don't bother trying to educate me again on what's trendy. It's not vogue to have useless horses you don't know how to take care of."

Margaret smiled. "Wow, Dad used the word vogue in a sentence. I must be getting somewhere. Now, if I can just get him into designer overalls."

"Harry," Betty said, "you don't know if they can take care of the horses, and they have Dean Crats."

"With the way that uppity woman has him acting like her personal contractor, I'm surprised he has any time for the horses," Harry retorted.

"Well, they can't do construction in the winter." Margaret got up and began to clear the table. "She'll probably hire someone to do the stable work and leave Dean to train the horses. They have an arena attached to the stable."

Betty figured she was right. Mrs. Reid would pay someone to help with the animals. The seed of an idea took root.

"Saw Dean Crats at the Co-op yesterday," Bart said.

Betty stopped pondering her idea and looked up. "What were you doing at the Co-op?" Her son liked to skip school. You had to listen carefully because it was always a possibility that the adventure had taken place when he should have been in math class.

He rolled his eyes. "It was after school, Mom. Dean says they're building a meditation room in the building they attached to the main house."

His family stared at him. A meditation room in Uthisca?

"Honest!" Bart exclaimed after a few seconds of silence.

"Who knows, maybe if she takes up yoga she'll be nicer. I agree with Dad. I think she's a—"

"Margaret! Don't you finish that sentence," Betty warned.

Margaret swept her long chestnut hair behind her ears and examined her purple fingernails.

Betty thought her daughter's polish colour made her nails look like she'd slammed all ten fingertips in a car door. She didn't criticize because motherhood was all about picking your battles. However, she was sick of talking about the Reids. It was time to nudge the conversation in a different direction.

She picked up a thick book from the table beside her eldest daughter. "Is this for school?"

"Yeah, in Advanced English Lit. It's the fiction novel that won the Governor General's Literary Award."

Her daughter sat back at the table, and Betty read the back cover. "I've heard about it. Is it any good?"

"I guess. It's not really my style," she answered.

"What's it about?" Harry eyed the book suspiciously.

Betty knew he was hoping it wasn't a deranged piece of pornography camouflaged as literature to confuse gullible parents. He constantly complained there were no moral boundaries in society any longer. Yesterday, he'd arrived home from town ranting about how two teenagers were practically having sex on the bench outside the Co-op.

"Harry, stop worrying, it's not erotic literature."

He nodded but didn't look convinced. "What's it about?" he asked his daughter again.

"We're discussing how the sandbar is the metaphor because it illustrates Jessica's life. She's the main character, and it's her life story," Margaret explained.

Bart, Willy, and Hope clamoured to their feet. "Can we be excused?" they asked in unison.

"Go ahead," Harry said. "Chores, Bart and Will, and homework, Hope," he recited.

"Willy-boy, I'll give you five bucks if you take out the garbage and feed the hogs," Bart offered.

Betty was immediately suspicious.

Will's eyes narrowed. "Why? Watcha gonna do?"

"None of your business, I don't have to answer to you," Bart retorted.

"You do have to answer to me," Harry said sternly. "Where are you going? Who are you going with and what are you going to be doing?"

"Gary got a new video game. Thought I'd go check it out."

"Do your own chores, and curfew is ten o'clock. Ask Gary's dad to drive you home or call. I don't want you walking along the road at night," Harry said.

"Thought maybe I could take the truck," Bart mumbled.

Betty glanced at Harry and shrugged. Three months earlier, Bart had earned his licence. She didn't know how to deal with the scary situation of her teenage son driving, especially at night.

She wasn't surprised when Harry dug the keys from the pocket of his work pants and threw them to Bart.

"Thanks, Dad, I promise I'll go straight there and come straight home."

Harry nodded. "You change your plans, give us a call."

"And, Bart, remember it only—"

"I know, Mom! It only takes a second to make a decision you'll regret the rest of your life, and there isn't a do-over," he quoted sarcastically.

"Fine," she said. "There's to be no music while you're driving and keep your eyes on the road. If you break our trust, we'll remove you from our insurance and you can dig your bike out of the shed."

"Yes, ma'am, I know the rules." He gave his father a hug. "Thanks for the truck, Dad."

After Bart ran out to do chores with Willy on his heels and Hope had reluctantly dragged her backpack up to her room, Margaret continued where she'd left off. "In Jazz Belrose's book, the sandbar represents Jessica's life because it's only seen at times."

"So, she doesn't feel that people see her?" Betty asked.

"Well, she thinks they see her some of the time — like, you don't always see a sandbar, but it's still there," Margaret explained.

"Don't know much about sandbars," Harry admitted. "I've never even seen one." He picked up the book and studied it while Betty poured them all fresh coffee. "Why did she call it *Dear Mary Magdalene?*"

"My teacher says the book has to do with the Gnostic Gospels and Mary Magdalene's relationship with Christ."

"It sounds boring," Harry muttered.

Betty sat at the kitchen table and shoved the rest of the dishes to the side. "What are you doing the essay on?" She used to love essay writing in university. Although she'd majored in biological science, she'd taken as many elective literature classes as she could.

"My essay thesis is on Jessica Cross's belief that Mary Magdalene created the Order of the Divine Feminine, a secret society."

Harry continued to look bewildered and peeked at his watch.

Margaret read from her notes. "The book discusses the hypocrisy of religion. It's about how bad people use religion as an excuse to do what they want and how people follow a leader."

"If you believe in God, you're stupid?" There was a twang of annoyance in Harry's voice.

"Well, sort of, I guess. It's just a book. Do you want to read it, Daddy?"

He flipped through the pages. "Sure." He didn't sound too excited.

"I have homework, and I'll give Hope a hand with hers."

After Margaret left, Betty kissed her husband. "You're a very nice man, Harry."

"Well, I got chores."

"It's Thursday," Betty said with a seductive smile.

"So it is, Betty-girl. Got any of them sexy, smelly candles I've been hearing 'bout, or should I drive over and ask Mrs. Reid to borrow a few? Never know, maybe she'll offer me a tip."

Hope

HOPE sat at the low stool in front of their white dressing table. She'd positioned the three narrow mirrors so she could see the front of her face and the sides of her head. She studied her reflection with a sigh. It was as depressing as always.

"You have homework." Margaret came into the bedroom, took the hairbrush from Hope's hand, and started brushing her hair for her.

Hope just sat there, hating her limp brown strands and the fresh crop of blackheads on her forehead, which was too wide. The ones on her jaw — too square — had turned to whiteheads. Mom had scrimped on groceries to buy the facial wash and astringent the pharmacist recommended, but he'd warned them that things would get worse before they improved. At least he'd been honest.

"Why am I so ugly?" She held her sister's eyes in the mirror, daring her to contradict her.

"I don't know," Margaret said slowly, "but I think it'll change when you get older."

Hope sighed. That's what they always said. Her mom said she was beautiful, which was just plain stupid. Margaret told her it was a stage. Her brothers told her boys liked nice girls better than hotties. That one was so dumb it made her laugh.

"Oh, I just remembered. I bought something for you today." Margaret rummaged through her backpack and handed her a small white bag.

Hope peered inside. The bag contained six silver butterfly barrettes. "They're so pretty." She pulled them out and examined one. "Look, their eyes are little blue jewels."

Margaret smiled. "Here, I'll help you put them in."

Her sister grasped a ribbon of hair, twisted the lock, and attached the clip. She tucked in the end, secured the barrette, and moved on with determination.

They looked terrible, but Hope made a huge effort to smile. "They look very pretty. They'd look nice with your blue dress. You're wearing it to the New Year's Eve dance, right?"

Margaret blushed. "Well, yeah. I'll borrow them, if that's okay."

She knew Margaret had been saving her babysitting money for something. Probably the hair clips because they went with her dress. Hope sighed and considered giving them back. They were probably a pity gift her sister hadn't intended to give. Mom always said that giving a gift was a better feeling than buying yourself something, so she hugged her sister. "Thanks, I love them and you can borrow them any time you want. You don't have to ask or anything."

"Isn't your book report on *Little Women* due next week?" Margaret asked.

"I haven't finished." She rolled her eyes. "I guess I didn't read it right 'cause I can't answer the questions."

"It's a hard book. I can explain it to you." Margaret picked up the novel and lay on her single bed. Hope climbed onto the bed beside her.

"There were four sisters. Meg, she was the eldest, Jo, she was a bit of a character, Beth, she was very delicate, and Amy. Amy is twelve when the book starts, just like you."

The one part of the book Hope did remember was the line that described Amy as a regular snow-maiden — pretty Amy with her curly golden hair and blue eyes. "She was pretty. She wasn't anything like me," Hope said.

Margaret hugged her. "Well, of course she wasn't like you. Amy is vain and likes to throw temper tantrums."

Betty

BETTY ADJUSTED THE pillow and rolled over. A minute later she rolled to the other side, removed the pillow, and rolled onto her back.

"What's wrong?"

She sighed deeply. "Nothing, guess I'm not tired. Maybe I'll go down and have a nice cuppa."

Harry paused for a heartbeat. "Was the... ah... the love okay? If not, well maybe I could..."

She laughed and hugged her husband. "The loving was just fine. It always is!" She kissed him and slid out of bed and into her housecoat.

Harry sat up. "Bart's home. I heard him come in a while ago."

She stuffed her arms into the old housecoat and sighed. "I know, go back to sleep. All I need is a bit of quiet and a cup of tea."

Betty tiptoed down the hall and opened the girls' bedroom door. Hope had climbed into Margaret's bed, and the girls were spooning. She adjusted the covers, kissed her precious baby girls, and went to the boys' room.

Bart was snoring. She stood over the bed and sniffed his hair. She could detect a faint whiff of cigarette smoke, but it wasn't strong enough to suggest Bart had been the one smoking. It also wasn't skunky enough to hint at something other than tobacco smoke. She crossed the room and tried to find Will under the cocoon of blankets. He was clutching a stuffed bear. It embarrassed him that he still slept with the toy, but Betty thought it was sweet and gave the bear's nose a pat.

In the kitchen, she plugged in the kettle, took a mug from the cupboard and a tea bag from the jar, and looked out the window over the kitchen sink. From the angle of the window, she could see lights from the Reid stable. When the Reids had first moved in, Betty had been concerned when she spied lights late at night. Now, she understood that Mrs. Reid left the lights on timers.

The stable she had ridden at as a child had an Arabian. If Hope could learn to ride a magnificent horse like that, it would do wonders for her self-esteem. If it had been anyone other than Mrs. Reid, Betty would have been willing to swallow her pride to ask if her daughter could exercise the horses.

But it wasn't anyone else, and she didn't want to ask snobbish Estelle for a favour. Then again, maybe Hope could do chores in exchange for the privilege of riding the horses.

Maybe, Betty thought, *I could take over fresh baking and make the offer.* She had a dish she was planning to give to the church bazaar, so she could use that.

"Make a pot, Betty-girl." Her husband wrapped his rough hands around her waist, held her back against his chest, and kissed the side of her neck. She patted his hand and cried.

"There, there, nothing can be that bad," he soothed.

He held her for several minutes, and then he led her to the table, pulled out a chair, and eased her into the seat. He made the tea, brought out the milk and sugar and sat beside her.

Stirring his tea, he simply said, "Talk to me."

She smiled weakly and wrapped her cold hands around the cup. "It's Hope, that's all. Her teacher called yesterday to say she might not pass the semester, which means she'll fail the year."

Harry winced. "If she's held back a year, her problems at school are going to get a lot worse."

Betty looked down at her tea. "She doesn't have any friends."

"I know."

"Why are kids so cruel?" she sobbed. "Willy told me they call her 'Hideous Hope'. He says they pick on her all the time and I've read some of the things they say on Facebook. Do you think she's experiencing hard-core bullying?"

"I don't think they're physically beating on her, if that's what you mean," he said.

She laughed bitterly. "Verbal abuse and teasing is what damages kids deep down and forever, especially for a girl!"

Harry sighed. "I know. If you want my two cents, boys are easier because we can teach them how to box, and they can learn sports. There are ways to increase a boy's self-confidence through puberty. It's harder for girls because it seems to me it's all about looks. I don't get it."

Betty didn't agree that boys had an easier time during puberty and adolescence. When it came to self-confidence, all children agonized over their appearance.

"What about contact lenses?" she suggested.

Harry shook his head. "Dr. Kowalski said she can't wear them, remember?"

"Well, there's laser surgery, he said that was a choice." As soon as she uttered the words, she wished she hadn't. She knew how expensive it was. The words hung in the air like a veil of smoke.

"We have to think about Margaret's education."

"She's at the top of her class and valedictorian. Maybe she'll get a scholarship," she said.

"You know there aren't enough scholarships to go around."

"We could take out another loan," she suggested.

"And then a second to send Bart to university and a third when Willy's ready? Come on, Betty."

Feeling like she was grasping at straws, she said, "Naja, at the beauty parlour, thinks highlights could help to control the oil and add colour." When she saw her husband's face, she quickly added, "She said she'd do it herself, as a gift."

"Sounds like unnecessary charity."

"There's a dermatologist. Maybe the doctor could refer us to one in the city."

Harry was silent.

"It would be covered by OHIP, and it wouldn't cost us anything," she said.

"The trip into the city would cost us money, and we don't have medical insurance for prescriptions."

Betty felt a surge of anger wash over her. "For crying out loud, are you willing to neglect your daughter's health because of the dollars?"

Harry looked up with pain in his eyes. "I'm doing the best I can."

She lowered her head. The anger disappeared as fast as it came. She felt an overwhelming sense of emptiness. She loved Harry, but she hated the farm and the life it forced them to live.

Harry finished his tea and sighed. "Go ahead and take Naja up on her offer. If she wants to give Hope a gift, it isn't my place to say no." He paused before adding, "And... ask the doc for a referral in the city. We'll go as a family and visit the universities. Maybe the trip will make Bart try harder to get better grades."

Harry looked exhausted. Betty took the cups to the sink and stretched.

"Come on, let's go to bed." She wrapped an arm around his waist, and they walked through their dark home.

As they left the kitchen, Betty glanced behind her at the lights in the Reid stable. When the Reids moved in, they had a daughter Margaret's age living with them. A teacher had complained to Betty that the Reids had sent the child to private school, implying Uthisca Secondary wasn't good enough. To the best of Betty's knowledge, the girl had never returned.

Maybe the Reids didn't have everything after all. Betty couldn't imagine life without her precious children or fathom the loneliness of sleeping alone every night. Whatever her husband's faults, she wouldn't trade her life for a huge house without family to fill the rooms with love and laughter and the occasional tears. From the front window, Betty spied a single star brightly blink before a cloud hid it from sight. Goosebumps scampered down her arms and legs.

"You cold, Betty?"

"No, I just got a minute of the willies. Guess someone walked over my grave."

Harry scooped Margaret's book from the hall table. "That's an old wives' tale," he grumbled, studying the book.

"I'm an old wife." She plucked the book from his fingers. "I'm still not tired. Will it bug you if I leave the light on for a bit? I thought I'd start Margaret's book, if it's okay with you if I read it before you do." She knew he didn't have the time or the desire to read the long book. She would read it and explain the story to him so he could chat with Margaret about her essay.

He grinned sheepishly. "Sure, if you'd like to have yourself a little read that'll be just fine."

She tucked *Dear Mary Magdalene* under her arm and followed Harry upstairs to the bedroom. No, she decided with sudden certainty, money wasn't everything.

Amazon *– Simon Says, Perdition Games*
Kobo *– Simon Says, Perdition Games*
Barnes and Noble *– Simon Says, Perdition Games*
iBooks *– Simon Says, Perdition Games*